THE
CANDIDATE

THE CANDIDATE

A NOVEL OF
SUSPENSE

PAUL HARRIS

Vantage Point Books and the Vantage Point Books colophon
are registered trademarks of Vantage Press, Inc.
FIRST EDITION: July, 2012

Published by Vantage Point Books
Vantage Press, Inc.
419 Park Avenue South
New York, NY 10016
www.vantagepointbooks.com

Manufactured in the United States of America
ISBN: 978-1-936467-38-9

Library of Congress Cataloging-in-Publication data are on file.

9   8   7   6   5   4   3   2   1

As always, for Moira

"Some rise by sin,
And some, by virtue, fall."

Measure for Measure, William Shakespeare

PROLOGUE

MOUNT PLEASANT, IOWA, 5 WEEKS BEFORE THE IOWA CAUCUSES

IT HAD BEEN twenty years since she last loaded a gun with the intention of killing a man. Now she stared at the rifle lying in front of her in the half-light and was afraid she had forgotten how to use it. The weapon's lines and curves appeared unfamiliar and alien. With hesitation, she reached out a hand to befriend this strange creature and forced herself to touch it. It felt cold, hard and heavy in her hands. A feeling of relief coursed through her. She closed her eyes and held the weapon close, cradling it like a child. Her lost child. She sighed softly.

She remembered.

The muscle memory locked inside her flesh for two decades forgot nothing. Only her mind had been distracted by her recent second life; an existence that now evaporated away in the face of this old sensation. Her fingers, alive with sudden electricity, grasped the solid, dull metal of the barrel. She made herself calm, breathing softly to find the quiet, still, inner place that would allow her to complete her task. A single bead of sweat traced a path down her forehead. She pressed her face against the barrel and wrestled her feelings under control.

For a long minute she crouched there, high in the dark rafters of the school gymnasium, hugging the rifle to her breast. Soon her pulse calmed and her mind became focused and alert, aware only of the physical sensations around her, numb to doubt or conscience. She thought only of why she was here and her task ahead.

It was before dawn when the woman broke into the school and climbed up into a gantry hidden in the maze of beams and rafters of the sports hall. Now she had been lurking up in the dark of the roof like some ghostly spirit for almost eighteen hours. She had lain there, watching cleaners come and go, until finally volunteers arrived to set up the chairs for the meeting. She expected security too, but instead she just saw a couple of policemen glance around idly and then sit themselves in a corner, hands tucked into gun belts over which middle-aged paunches spread. Then the crowd trickled in, people murmuring softly to their friends or gathering in small groups to chat and catch up on gossip. She sat above them, not listening to the words drift up to her in a language she had once gleefully learned but now sounded grating and alien to her ears.

She expected to feel something when he at last entered the room below. He walked in to the sounds of an echoing pop song, wildly out of place in a room full of elderly people. Her eyes ran over his figure; a man she had not seen for so long, drinking him in. She had wondered what it would feel like. But she felt nothing. She was too far in to the killing zone to let anything disturb her. Her mind was a place of absolute quiet and purpose. Like a Zen garden, her thoughts were a series of abstract lines and sharp corners leading to one place: the target she imagined on his heart. After he began to speak; that was when she would fire.

She balanced the rifle in her hands, testing its weight, and then put it to her shoulder where its stock nuzzled like the nose of a faithful hunting dog finding its master. She loaded the weapon carefully, slipping a golden bullet into its dark chamber. Then she squinted down the barrel, one eye closing while the other widened in anticipation. She looked down the length of the rifle and into the light below, sweeping over the stage where he stood. She aimed the gun directly at him, the notch of the sight firmly planted in the middle of his chest, forming a tiny dark cross at the center of her vision.

She readied herself for the moment, but a sudden flash of gold behind him distracted her. She looked up over the barrel of the gun and saw a familiar head of striking blond hair.

His wife.

Her gaze lingered on the woman, and the sight of the gun drifted to one side. Old memories disturbed the placid calm of her mind. She thought of places far away and long ago. Of her own flesh and blood, now lost to her. She shook her head to dispel the visions and quickly bent down to the gun again. Her finger slowly tightened on the trigger, ready to squeeze the reluctant metal into life and unleash her judgment.

CHAPTER 1

SENATOR JACK HODGES stood in front of the crowd and smiled, his handsome craggy face cracking open like a cave in a granite cliff. The high school gymnasium was only half full, perhaps 50 or so people sitting on a motley collection of chairs. Hodges had no doubt the school's basketball team got a bigger crowd to watch their games than his faltering run for his party's presidential nomination ever could. The gathering was mostly Iowa farmers, coming into the town on a bitterly cold November night from their frozen fields and isolated homes in this south-eastern corner of the state. They stared at him with hard eyes, almost daring him to convince them that they should vote for him. But he expected no less. Iowa audiences were always tough. They were long immune to the constant parade of candidates trooping through the vital state that voted first in the nomination contest. Each audience knew it had the power to make or break any candidate, but to Hodges this crowd looked especially hard. His staff had told him that Mount Pleasant was a college town. They said a smattering of students and teachers would show up: a key demographic that he desperately needed to boost his anemic poll numbers. But, as he surveyed the room, he knew the biting chill had kept them huddled in their cozy dorm rooms. Only the farmers never seemed to notice the cold. They always showed up.

Hodges waited patiently for the school's principal to finish introducing him. He was a rotund, jolly man, whom Hodges met briefly just 15 minutes before. They had talked amiably enough, but Hodges sensed that even this man, whom his staff assured him was a locked-down supporter, was skeptical of his chances of ever winning the state. Or even that he could finish in the top five. Hodges listened to the man's patter, skimming over the familiar details of his life, sketching out the warrior-politician meme on which his campaign pinned their fading hopes.

"Senator Hodges is now the junior Senator from Indiana, but he has a record of serving his country at home and abroad. He was a three-star General who helped win the Cold War. He later risked his life in Iraq and served in Afghanistan," the principal said.

But Hodges paid little attention. He glanced backwards, just briefly, at his wife Christine, who sat on a plastic chair off to one side, looking dazzling in a white suit. He winked quickly at her and she smiled back. Hodges laughed inwardly, feeling a surge of fortune, as he became aware his cue was about to arrive. The principal was finishing up with a phrase that had become familiar but which Hodges increasingly doubted had any basis in reality. "I give you the next President of the

United States! Senator Jack Hodges!" the man said, his loud enthusiasm far outweighing the smattering of polite claps from the crowd. Hodges strode forward and grasped the man's hand firmly.

"Thank you, sir," Hodges said. "Good job." Then he turned to face the crowd. He paused, regarding them with a clear expression that quieted the room. He let the silence last just a second or so longer than was comfortable, building an expectation. Then he began, exactly as he had started a hundred speeches already, all across Iowa and New Hampshire and a dozen other states. He spoke simply, and directly, his passion never wavering one iota, always opening with the same words.

"Let me tell you how we're going to save this country…" he began.

But then he stopped.

Perhaps it was the tiny but quick movement of the assassin's head that caught his eye. Or else it was that strange instinct, shared by all animals, of an awareness of being watched, of being something else's prey. He had felt it in Baghdad and Kabul countless times. But here in Iowa? Almost disbelievingly, Hodges, his skin crawling and with the hair on his arms standing on end, squinted up into the rafters of the gymnasium.

His eyes took a second to focus and then his mind took two seconds more to understand what he was seeing: up in the eaves a shadowed figure crouched, holding a rifle. The barrel was pointed directly at him. Even at this distance he thought he could see the assassin's finger starting to squeeze the trigger.

He felt frozen still, as if held in place by some invisible hand. Behind him he sensed Christine frown and follow her husband's gaze up into the roof. Then she saw the figure too. But Christine did not freeze. She screamed.

"There's a gun!" she yelled.

It was a sound that seemed to break a spell. The world around Hodges exploded into chaotic movement. Christine leapt to her feet, her chair clattering to the floor. He took a step toward her, glancing backwards to see the rifle tracking his movement. But now the stage was a frantic mess of running and shouting people. Hodges grabbed Christine and stepped in front of her, shoving her behind him, and he put up one arm, seeking to ward off whatever fire might come their way.

An explosion suddenly echoed around the gymnasium with an unearthly ear-splitting crack. Hodges felt the hot, scalding breath of something kiss his cheek as it sped by and he felt a spray of angry concrete chips from the wall behind him strike his back. Then he hit the floor, taking Christine with him, covering her with his own body. He waited for another bullet; his breath roaring like an enraged bull, his heart thumping so loud that he felt it would burst through his chest. But a second shot never came.

Up above, the assassin had dropped her rifle. She collapsed into a ball, curling up in fetal position, hugging her knees to her chest and muttering to herself something that sounded like a prayer in the rasping language she had learned at her mother's breast. She repeated the words again and again and then thirty seconds later two overweight cops, screaming and sweating, guns drawn and ready to fire, clattered up the steel steps to her hideaway. They grabbed her and twisted her arms fiercely behind her back. One of them aimed a kick at the small of her back, crunching the toe of his boot into her spine. She fell silent now, not even grunting in pain at the blow. The two men shouted questions at her, pushing their faces into hers. But she looked away, twisting her neck in their grasp and closing her eyes as if in meditation. She did not speak again.

CHAPTER 2

THE WINTER NIGHT fell swiftly as the car swept along the stretch of interstate highway between Iowa City and Des Moines, hiding the gray, frozen landscape in darkness. The furrowed fields, with their deep, black earthen grooves flecked with snow, disappeared into the gloom.

But Mike Sweeney barely noticed the change. He steered the car with one hand, while his other gesticulated in the air as he talked to the two college students in the backseat. He spoke quickly and passionately, his free hand sweeping out or thumping the dashboard. He was so caught up in his subject – Senator Jack Hodges – that he mistook the wide-eyed interest of his audience for enraptured attention, when instead much of it was fear that the car might swerve off the road.

"He's the real thing," Mike said, using the pitch that he always found effective when hitting Iowa's campuses for the campaign. "He's not like other politicians. When Senator Hodges tells you something, it's because he believes it. Not because some focus group has told him it's popular."

The two students, a boy and a girl, nodded their heads in agreement. Mike had picked them up at Iowa State University, after addressing a small crowd too bored to go to their lectures. Mike cut a dramatic figure on the stage with his six foot tall frame and shock of close-cut red hair that made his green eyes stand out like rock pools in his pale face. He spoke for 30 minutes, without notes, stalking the stage like a lion, trying somehow to infect his audience with his own passion. Yet it didn't really work. These two were the only ones to put down their names to volunteer and so, on the spur of the moment, he offered to give them a tour of the campaign's Des Moines headquarters. Now they were getting the full scale "Sweeney treatment."

There was no doubt Mike believed what he said. He was no shallow campaign staffer, in it for the money, hopping from one campaign to another. In fact, at 29 years old, this was his first political campaign; he had abandoned his job in Florida, working with unskilled immigrants in the state's agricultural industries, to join Hodges' cause.

"I'd never seen anyone like him," Mike explained to his audience in the backseat. "He made me believe. For the first time in my life, I found a politician who actually meant what he said. So I left Florida. I figured, why help a few people struggling to get by, when I can help change the whole system?"

He meant it too. Mike first saw Hodges speak at a fundraiser in Orlando, just a few miles from the orange plantations in which thousands of laborers existed in almost slave-like conditions. Mike only went because he thought he might make some useful contacts in his latest effort to improve worker conditions. It was the end of a long day and he was lounging exhaustedly at the back of the room when Hodges began to speak. It was electrifying.

Hodges shocked the audience of local bigwig party donors, speaking off-the-cuff and lambasting them for standing by while their country split apart at the seams, with the rich growing richer and the poorer sinking into the mire. Mike doubted whether Hodges raised much money that night, but the candidate gained one fervent new convert. He signed up the next morning. A week later he left Florida for Iowa.

"But can he really win Iowa, Mr. Sweeney?" one of the students asked.

Mike turned back to look at the kid. He flashed him his most confident grin. "Not only can he win, but he will win," he said.

The two students looked at each other and smiled. Mike turned back to face the road, feeling mildly guilty for lying. The fact was, Hodges' campaign was always an outside bet. The General-turned-Senator had a loyal following, but he was new to politics; he hadn't even served a full term in the Senate yet. Established party leaders, including seven others also running for president, turned their back on him as soon as he announced his candidacy. Now, after three months of hard slog, Hodges had barely made a blip in the polls. The vastly experienced frontrunner, Virginia Governor Harriet Stanton, was still far ahead and even her nearest rivals did not include Hodges. As press coverage of the race heated up, the Hodges campaign was an afterthought to the bigger, richer campaigns, a footnote and not much more. But Mike still believed. He would never give up.

Mike glanced at his watch. It was 7:00 pm. Maybe the latest batch of polls would show some good news.

"Let's switch on the radio, see if we can catch the headlines. Senator Hodges was out in Mount Pleasant today. That should have made a story," he said to the students trapped in the backseat.

Mike reached over to turn on the car radio, and what he heard next nearly sent the car spinning into a ditch.

"Senator Jack Hodges survived an apparent assassination attempt today..." the radio announcer said.

Mike slammed on the brakes. The car jolted and swerved violently and one of the students yelled out. Mike struggled with the wheel, turning it into the skid, preventing the car from veering out of control. It juddered to a halt on the cold shoulder, just as an enormous 18-wheeler swept by, its horns blaring. The wind from its back draft shook the car like a leaf. Mike ignored it and turned up the radio.

"...Hodges was unharmed in the incident in which a shot was fired at the presidential candidate. His assailant has been arrested but not identified. Police sources say the would-be assassin was a woman and possibly homeless or mentally ill."

Mike looked back at the two students. They were pale-faced and scared. Whether from the news or the near crash, he could not tell.

"Jesus Christ," he said to himself. Then, without another

word, he slammed his foot down on the accelerator, flinging the car down the highway again. Behind him, in the backseat, the students held each other's hands.

———

DENISE "DEE" Babineaux stood in the dingy, dirty surroundings of Hodges' Des Moines campaign headquarters and surveyed the mess around her. The room was a pigsty at the best of times and these were far from the best of times. Piles of pizza boxes teetered like ailing skyscrapers encrusted with rust-like sauce stains. Posters and pamphlets were strewn across desks and half-full coffee cups lay everywhere. People buffeted around the room like ships caught helpless in a storm, shouting and running around in chaos. Above them all a large flat-screen TV was tuned to a cable news channel. The news anchors repeated the few known facts about the attempted assassination on Senator Hodges. Dee shook her head. The people in this room just did not get it, she thought as she listened to the volunteers talk about their shock and anger over the botched assassination. They did not understand what she did. This was fantastic. For the first time ever, the faltering Hodges campaign was big news.

"All right, everyone!" she shouted as the top of the hour approached and the cable news shows prepared to reboot themselves. "Let's cut the crap, stop running around like headless chickens and do some goddamn work."

Dee's accent was pure Louisiana Cajun, lilting and

twanging, carrying a feeling of warmth and sunshine even when it conveyed the harshest of words. The room quieted instantly because everyone was in awe of Denise Babineaux. Not only was she Hodges' campaign manager, she was a political legend. Hard-drinking, hard-talking and with a line of insults that could cut like a razor, she was that rarest of creatures at the top of the political food chain: a woman. Not only that, but she was gay. Openly out and proud to anyone who asked. Though few cared to. She was simply "Dee"; a force of nature that defied anyone's label but her own.

She had been in the campaign game for more than 30 years now, fighting twice as hard as any man she ever met and never once giving ground. She was terrifying, inspiring and seen as a rogue operator. Too much so, it was rumored, to get the top job on Harriet Stanton's campaign. So instead of settling for a junior position with Stanton, she picked out Hodges and became his campaign manager, placing an outside bet that he could upset the race. Or, as she often admitted after a few drinks: "It is better to rule in Hell than serve in Heaven."

Dee dug out the remote control for the TV from under a pile of discarded napkins that were coated with some unknown fast food condiment. She dangled the remote between two fingers, keeping the sticky plastic away from her body, and winced theatrically.

"Ya'll are disgusting," she said. "Your mamas should be ashamed to have raised you."

Then she pointed the remote at the TV and turned up the sound. The assassination attempt was the top story, as it had been for the last two hours. But now the news anchor promised fresh footage of the incident. Dee was eager to see it. She sensed, deep down, that this could change everything. That this one single moment would give them new life.

The TV showed the new video clip; shot blurrily from someone's cell phone camera. The footage was chaotic, confused, and it veered from side to side. For a moment Hodges could be seen, standing and speaking on the stage, then Christine was screaming, then the film collapsed into a mess of frames and shots of people's feet as a loud bang rang out and chairs were pushed over. Then the TV switched to a series of new still photographs, taken by the lone wire photographer assigned the usually dull task of following Hodges around. That was when she saw it.

It was a single frame freezing a moment in time. But it was a work of art. Hodges stood dead center and behind him, his wife Christine crouched down as the Senator held her back with one arm. His other hand was thrust out ahead of him, and he stared back in the direction where the shot came from. His face looked set in stone, determined and unafraid. Dee realized what he was doing: protecting his wife, putting his own body in between the shooter and Christine. Using TIVO, Dee paused the TV and rewound. She froze the shot and stared at it, feeling alone in the crowded room, suddenly full of the knowledge of where this could go. She savored the feeling like a prayer, thankful beyond measure. Then she went to work.

"This is it!" she yelled. "I want this picture everywhere. I want you to blog it. I want it on Facebook and Twitter. I want

you to email it to your friends, your families, even your goddamn enemies. I want it on posters and pamphlets. I want it on
front pages. Christ, I even want it on the radio. If they can't see
it, they can at least talk about it. By the time America wakes up
tomorrow morning and pours itself a coffee, I want it to have
seen this picture."

The people in the room looked at her. Dee smiled broadly.
She knew it made some of them afraid. She saw the looks in
their eyes: they had no idea what this crazy old dyke was going to tell them next, she thought. But she could not contain
herself. She was in complete control, just the way she liked it.
She saw the future and it was bright.

"Boys and girls," she said slowly, as if talking to a class
of school children. "This sorry ass campaign is finally going
places. Prepare yourselves for the big time. Your candidate is a
fucking American HERO."

———

DEE GRABBED Mike as soon as he walked into the headquarters, quickly dispatching his two student volunteers to start
blogging about the day's events.

"Come with me, buddy," she said. "We've got things to
discuss."

Mike ignored the jealous glances from other staffers as they
walked outside, and headed toward Walnut Street in downtown Des Moines. He thought back to when they first met at a
crowded bar on only his second night on the campaign. He and

Dee had hit it off immediately. He was one of the few people who dared to stand up to her and she appeared to appreciate that. He was older than lots of the other staffers and as a result he had real life experience. He also didn't scare easily. Down in Florida, among the immigrant shantytowns, he saw just how awful life could be. He was intimately familiar with stories of children working 16 hour days for a few dollars; of abuse and makeshift camps in which workers were locked overnight. Of the beatings and abuse that were commonplace. It took a lot to make Mike afraid and one of Dee's rants was never going to do it. Instead, he felt an immense respect for her. She was an outsider in political campaigning, for her gender and for her embrace of her sexuality. But also, in Mike's mind, because she grew up poor. Yet she took on the political world of privilege and bulldozed her way in. Now she was the mistress of her domain, perfectly at home, juggling a thousand tasks with the speed of a dervish and the grace of a ballet dancer. Mike knew she could teach him a lot about how to thrive in this bewildering world.

"Look at this," she said, holding up her Blackberry which was pinging at regular intervals as new messages kept arriving. "It has not stopped for two hours. And you know who's calling? *The View. Good Morning America.* Even Bill O'Reilly wants a piece of the action. I've busted my balls for months trying to get us a single mention on any one of those fucking shows. Now I've got my pick."

Her breath billowed out into the freezing air like plumes of steam that matched those from the huddled smokers crouched in each doorway, exiled from inside the downtown businesses. Mike shivered and pulled his jacket tighter around him. He had no idea why, but Dee always insisted on walking out in the freezing air. She ignored the warm, comfortable maze of walkways and passages that meant you could traipse from block to block in Des Moines without braving the winter cold. But Dee's Southern blood seemed immune to temperature. Or perhaps she simply felt like taking on the cold and beating it into submission with her will, just like everything else.

"This whole thing is perfect," Dee said with a broad laugh. "I can't believe I never thought of it before. What better way to get a campaign moving than almost having your guy killed? It's pure genius!"

Mike shivered from the cold. They were on their way to the Embassy Suites hotel, a little way from downtown, across the river. As they trudged over a bridge, Mike glanced at the gray, swirling waters barely visible in the darkness.

"What happens next?" he asked, struggling to keep pace with Dee.

"Textbook stuff," she said. "For the first time in this campaign, everyone wants our candidate. So we keep them hungry. Jack Hodges is the hottest thing in America right now and we've got to serve him up in small portions. We'll issue a statement tonight. Then tomorrow hit one of the morning shows. Then spread ourselves out over the next couple of days. We can ride this train for the rest of the week, right until the next debate."

Dee suddenly stopped in the middle of the bridge and

gazed out over the river. "It all changes now, Mike. I'm going to need good people near me. I'm going to need an opposition research guy. Someone good at digging up things on our opponents, maybe even on our friends, too. I know the sort of work you used to do in Florida. I've looked up some of your investigative campaigns. It seems like you had a knack for uncovering some of the nasty secrets of those big, old fruit firms down there."

She flicked her lit cigarette into the river, its little glow twirling like an out-of-season firefly until it was extinguished by the frigid water below.

"You want the job?" she asked. "Do you want to be my guy?"

Mike looked at Dee, trying to gauge what was going on behind that wide, excited smile and those mischievous eyes. But he could read nothing in her face. Opposition research? He knew what that meant. It meant being at the heart of the campaign, inside the bubble and close to power. A shield against attacks and a sword to be used against opponents. It sounded like a good deal to him.

"Of course," he said.

Dee grinned and extended her arm. She shook Mike's hand, held onto it and stared deep into his eyes. Mike fought hard not to flinch. Dee's grip was vice-like.

"Hodges is not just our man now, Mike. He is more than that. He is our cause. You know about causes. You proved that in Florida. And a cause is much more powerful than just a campaign. People *work* for campaigns, Mike, but they *believe* in causes. That's a big difference. But a cause is also something that needs to be protected. At all costs. You got that?"

Mike nodded. Dee released her hold. Together they marched across the bridge and into the lobby of the hotel.

JACK HODGES and Christine sat alone in their suite. They looked up as Dee and Mike entered. Hodges cracked a grim smile and nodded a hello, but Christine, her makeup smeared with tears, just buried her head in her hands. Hodges rested a hand on her shoulder, touching her lovingly, and squeezed.

"It's been tough on her," he said. "I guess everyone who runs for president thinks something like this might happen. You just never think it will happen to you..."

Dee sat down and waited a moment. She was clearly itching to talk but wanted to be polite; respect the enormity of what might have happened. A few inches to one side and the bullet would have hit home. Then they would be planning a funeral, not a talk show appearance. But it was Hodges, not Dee, who broke the silence.

"What happens now, Dee?" he asked. "I know you must have a plan."

Dee's face was serious. There was no trace of joy or thrill. It was down to business.

"I'll issue a statement tonight. Then tomorrow we'll have you do one of the morning shows. A day after that we'll soak up all the media we can get and it will be a lot. We keep it straight and simple. Make it personal. Make it all about how you stood tall when the shooting began."

Hodges laughed. "Dee, I've been a soldier all my life. That's not the first time I've heard gunfire," he said.

Dee pumped a fist. "Yes!" she said. "That's the sort of line you use. You're a natural, Jack."

"What about campaign appearances?" Mike asked. "We've got three town hall meetings set for tomorrow."

Dee nodded. "Good question. We stick to them. Do the TV around them. They'll come to us now. We don't have to change our schedule." Dee then turned to Hodges. "We keep you in the public eye."

A small moan cut through the room. Christine's shoulders shuddered up and down and her head sank to her breast. Hodges bent down and put his arms around her, whispering something in her ear. Then he looked up and shrugged at them. "She thinks there may be more shooters out there," he said.

Dee and Mike glanced at each other.

"Yeah," Dee said. "That's my next question. Sorry, to have to ask this. But you need to tell me everything you know."

A look of puzzlement crossed Hodges' face. He frowned and exchanged confused glances with Christine. "What do you mean?" he asked.

Dee was blunt. "Who tried to kill you, Jack? I need everything you know. I need the truth and I need it now."

Hodges stood up. He may have been wearing a politician's

suit but he looked a military man now. He paused before answering, just the same way that he worked a crowd before he spoke. "I have no more idea than the cops, Dee," he said. "They say it was a woman. But they have no idea who she is. She doesn't speak. She has no documents. They think maybe she's mentally ill or something."

Dee nodded. Something in Hodges' tone seem to imply that further questions would be unwelcome. She smiled. "That line is good enough for me. It keeps things simple. Just your average nutcase in a country full of them. But I tell you this, Jack, when you win this election, you're going to want to thank her for what she's done for you. You really are."

CHAPTER 3

MIKE SAT ON the bed in his hotel room in Des Moines surrounded by a fan-like spread of newspapers. It had all played out just like Dee predicted. Hodges had dominated the media for three days straight, right up until this night: the last Iowa debate.

The picture of the Senator, shielding his wife from a killer's bullet, was on every front page in America, before spreading across the world. Overnight, his public meetings went from a handful of bored farmers and a local journalist or two, to banks of TV cameras with standing room only. Through it all Hodges did not change a thing. He opened every meeting and every interview with his familiar phrase: "Let me tell you how we are going to save this country…"

Mike stared at the newspapers like he was hypnotized until a distant ringing in his ear grew suddenly clearer and he snapped into focus. It was his hotel phone. He picked it up and heard the clipped upstate New York accent of his mother.

"Hey, sweetie. I thought I'd just check in with you, before it begins," she said.

The debate started in a few minutes. The cable news shows were already counting down the minutes, a sea of talking heads filling the airspace with meaningless analysis until they had something actually concrete to discuss.

"It's a big night," said Mike. "Been a crazy few days." It was good to hear his mother's voice. Calming.

"So, is he all he's cracked up to be? Your Senator Hodges. Should he get your mom's vote for any reason other than out of loyalty to her son?"

He could feel his mother's warmth down the phone line, her tone gently mocking. She was always like that. Walking the line of tough love, with a joke and a twinkle in her eye. But he was surprised she was genuinely asking after Hodges. Moira Sweeney did not take politics lightly. She lived and breathed it. Always had. It was a way to rationalize their hardscrabble life in Corinth Falls, struggling to make ends meet in a factory town in the middle of New York, abandoned by a country that did not make anything anymore. She always distrusted mainstream politicians, damning them as *all the same.*

But now she was asking of Hodges: "Is this guy for real or does he just come in better packaging than the rest of his kind?"

He paused for a moment, before answering. He couldn't lie to her. He could not spin her the same lines that he did the student volunteers, the bloggers and the journalists. "He's the best

I've seen, Mom," he said. "I'm pretty close to him. They've made me the opposition research director and I see him every day. You should vote for him and not just because of me."

"That's wonderful, Mike," she said.

But Mike could tell there was something else behind her phone call. Her whirring mind was almost audible down the phone line; the cogs and wheels of disparate thoughts coming together. "What is it, Mom?"

She sighed. "It's Jaynie."

Those old, familiar words. His high school sweetheart. The love of his life who was now his ex-wife. It was a name he dreaded and feared hearing and yet still somehow, he longed for. It seemed there were few big moments in Mike's life that did not begin with someone saying: "It's Jaynie." Some were the happiest times of his childhood, others the worst nightmares of his adult years. His heart quickened.

"What's she done now, Mom?"

"Nothing specific. She just came around the other day, knocking on the door. She seemed kind of confused. I gave her some coffee and tried to get some sense out of her. But she didn't stay too long."

Mike knew what it was his mother would not bring herself to say. But the signs were clear enough. He would make the point for her.

"Do you think she was on something? Was she high again?" he asked.

"She didn't look good, Michael," she said. "I know you're

divorced now but you two have always been close and…well, I just thought you should know."

There was no hint of reproach, but there didn't need to be. Mike met Jaynie in high school, when they were both 15. Her family lived only a few blocks away and they formed a bond so close it seemed it would never break. She was the most beautiful creature he ever saw, and the most wild. She was like a crazy, free spirit, a shining light in the grim surroundings of their dying, little town. They were married by age twenty, but it was a disaster. Jaynie's crazy streak grew progressively more out of control and Mike struggled to contain it. Her drug problem began with pot which Mike dabbled in, but never found a taste for. But Jaynie didn't stop there. She quickly became lost in a maze of hard drugs and alcohol, trying to make meaning out of her life by driving it to the extremes. Mike tried to keep her grounded, struggling against her addictions like a boy clinging to a kite in a storm. But the tempest was too strong. He had to let go. To cope, Mike headed to Florida and flung himself into community organizing. Work became his own drug, but Jaynie was unable to follow him out of her chaos. The divorce came through five years ago, although they were separated long before that. Yet still Mike felt a responsibility; a sense that he failed her by grasping at escape and not being able to take her with him.

"Thanks, Mom," he said. "I'll get someone to check up on her and make sure she's okay."

His mom seemed satisfied with that and Mike glanced at

the TV. The screen showed a panning shot of the seven or so top candidates in the party, all of them, save Harriet Stanton, were men dressed in dark blue or gray suits. Hodges and Stanton stood next to each other, neither looking at the other, their heads down, reading their notes.

"The debate's about to start, Mom. I gotta go," Mike said, and he put down the phone.

Mike darted across the hallway and knocked on the door to Dee's room. She opened it quickly and ushered him in. A tight knot of campaign workers were already there, huddled around the TV like it was some sort of religious shrine. The atmosphere was tense and no one spoke as the on-screen moderator began introducing everyone. Dee smiled at Mike but he could tell she was feeling the strain. The lines around the corners of her eyes were pulled taught like fishing line on the end of a big catch – perhaps too big – and her forehead was deeply furrowed. She ran a hand through her close-cut graying hair, grasping for locks that were not there. For the first time, Mike thought, she looked every single one of her 52 hard-living years.

"I've done all I can with him," Dee said. "Now we let him fly."

She need not have worried.

The first exchanges were dully educational. Each candidate made a beginning statement and then the talk drifted between issues. Stanton and Hodges never looked at each other, though neither seemed ill at ease. Stanton, in particular, appeared relaxed and happy enough to let the debate go through the motions. After all, it was she, as one of the most well known figures in national politics, who stood twenty points up in the Iowa polls. It was she who assembled a fund-raising machine that out-raised every other candidate, *combined*. She stood by Hodges and did not even glance across at him. He was not there to her.

At least not until the final question.

It was about national security and each candidate gave a boilerplate answer. Stanton had just finished speaking when it came to Hodges. He was quiet for a moment – his usual trick to focus an audience's attention – and then he seemed to stretch himself taller. He cleared his throat and his voice was crystal clear. For the first time, he looked directly at Stanton and Stanton's face froze. She looked puzzled. Just a little. Just enough to indicate that underneath that calm visage, the ice was creaking a little.

"Unlike my fellow candidates, I am not a career politician," he said, keeping his eyes on her and letting the implication hang just a moment in the air. "I don't think of politics as a job. Seeing it that way makes every decision about polls. It makes every move you make about the next election. You fail to understand that there are problems in this country that need fixing and that are far more important things than any one politician's popularity. I view my candidacy the same way as my time in the army. I am here to serve my country. I'll take the hits for it if need-be. I'll stand in the line of fire."

He left the words hanging, the subtle reminder of the week's past events. Then he turned away from Stanton and back to face the cameras.

"I would ask the people watching at home: how many of my fellow candidates really know what it's like to serve their country? Or are they just serving themselves?"

In the hotel room Dee, Mike and the other staffers leapt to their feet. Hodges' attack was so unexpected but so perfectly delivered that no one saw it coming. Dee grabbed Mike and hugged him.

"Did you prime him with those lines?" he asked.

Dee shook her head. "I primed him with a bunch of others, but he didn't use them. I tell you, Mike, this son-of-a-bitch is a natural. I knew it when I signed on. We're going to be the headline news again after this."

She gazed upwards, seemingly seeing beyond the dull, cheap plaster of the hotel room's ceiling and far out, beyond, and up into the sky. "There's something special here. Do you feel it?"

Mike looked at Dee. Her face was utterly alive and animated.

"You know what it is, Mike?" she asked. "It's belief. People can believe in Jack Hodges. That's rare. That's special."

"I know," said Mike. "I've never felt this way about a politician before."

Dee laughed. "We sound like two high school girls discussing their latest crush," she said. Then she stopped and frowned. "But you know what else? It also makes me want to know why someone tried to kill him. I don't like not knowing who that woman is who wanted our Jack dead."

Mike looked at Dee. Her tone changed completely. Back to business.

"The cops said she was just some homeless kook," Mike said. "They don't even have a name. Just a crazy lady with a gun."

Dee grasped him by the hand and looked him straight in the eye.

"Jack Hodges is our man now. We need to be protecting him from nasty surprises. We need to know more about that woman than the cops do. It's time for you to take a little trip to jail, Mike. You need to pay her a visit."

WITH A sudden shove, Lauren O'Keefe was rammed back against the wall of the living room. She glared at the man who bumped his fat backside into her, but realized that in this crush of people she could do little more than silently curse him. It was astonishing, she thought, to see what happened to the Hodges campaign. As a political blogger, funding her coverage of the election on her own dime, desperately hoping to make it big, she regularly checked in with the former General's campaign. It was always the same. The good candidate playing to a tiny audience in half-full barns or school halls. He just gave his stump speech and moved on.

But now this.

It was meant to be a house party in Iowa City, but the suburban couple who invited Hodges into their home clearly had no idea what his campaign had become. Their spacious McMansion was big enough for 50 people. Maybe. Not 250. Every available space in all the downstairs rooms was rammed with bodies desperately crammed in, craning their heads to see Hodges, standing on a stool in the hall, giving his speech and taking their questions.

With the physical difficulty of a contortionist, Lauren managed to get out a notebook and pen and jot down a few quotes. But eventually she just gave up and watched Hodges listen patiently to a series of questions. He did not seem to have changed much with his new status as a political rock star.

One young woman, her voice almost impossible to hear, was on the edge of tears as she spoke of how job after job had departed overseas, leaving her struggling to find even minimum wage work. Hodges spoke quietly to her, touching her elbow and gently squeezing her arm like a concerned father. It seemed a moment designed for that single voter alone, not the TV cameras peering over people's heads.

Suddenly another body bumped into Lauren as Hodges bade a quick goodbye to the crowd. She delivered a sharp kick in the direction the bump came from. A yelp revealed her blow hit home.

"Excuse me," she said quickly and looked into the startled face of a youngish, red-haired man. He looked angry and then his face softened when he saw her.

"No problem. I think I bumped you. Hey, I know you.

You're a blogger, right? For the *Horse Race*? I'm Mike Sweeney," he said, extending his hand. "I'm with the Senator's staff."

The two shook hands awkwardly as the crowd moved around them like an ebbing and flowing human tide.

"Quite a change to your campaign, Mike. You must be delighted," Lauren said.

"It's certainly a bit different from a week ago. But, you know, the Senator deserves this. He's the best candidate by far."

"Yeah. But it all changed in Mount Pleasant. That was a very scary moment," Lauren said.

"Were you there?"

Lauren nodded. She noticed Mike's interest pique like he had suddenly extended radio antennae from his head. She smiled inwardly and told him how she had been in the sparse crowd, absent-mindedly checking emails, when she heard Christine scream. Then it was chaos. She crouched down, unsure of what was going on; her ears ringing painfully from the single shot.

"Did you see the woman with the gun?" Mike asked.

"I saw her get arrested. Two cops dragged her out. She didn't say a word. She was just blank, like she was high or something. I looked right into her face, but she just stared past me. It was spooky."

She shivered at the thought, partly just to hold Mike's attention, but also from the memory itself. Since then, she dreamed of the woman several times, always remembering how roughly she was dragged away, and her black, dense eyes, impenetrably staring out at some distant vision. The woman's face was like a statue's, sculpted out of unmoving rock.

Lauren snapped herself out of it and shrugged. "It's amazing to think some crazy like that could get so close to a candidate. But, hey, this is Iowa. It's all about pressing the flesh and getting out there with the people."

Mike laughed.

"Yeah. But not quite like that."

"Still," Lauren said. "Hodges is not the only one to benefit. My blog has seen traffic go up nearly a 100 times since the shooting. I might even be able to start earning money from this thing."

"But what about the woman?" Mike asked. "Did you get any sense of where she was from? Who she might be?"

Lauren stopped. Suddenly she felt she was the subject of an interview. She paused and ignored the question. "So, Mike. On the record, tell me about why Senator Hodges attacked Governor Stanton in the debate last night?"

Mike laughed. He looked at Lauren, saw her brown eyes widening innocently behind her blond fringe.

"I gotta go, Lauren," he said. "I'll see you around."

———

DRIVING AWAY from Iowa City and back down the long, straight overly familiar freeway to Des Moines, Mike could not stop thinking about Lauren. Or the feelings of guilt he had whenever he felt attracted to anyone other than Jaynie. Even five years after their divorce and Jaynie's continued run-ins with drugs, Mike still wasn't over her. He felt no clean break, just a ragged emotional tear. He couldn't believe it could take so long to get someone out of your system. It was as if their time together left them embedded in each other's flesh, picking out the hooks one by one.

He gripped the car wheel and kept driving, striving instead to think of what Lauren said about the night Hodges was almost killed.

"She was just blank."

That seemed to fit with everything else he heard. The shooter was an anonymous space. A nothing. A void. All the press coverage about the event didn't add much to the original police line. She was a kook, a nut, a roamer with no identity. Getting a gun was not hard in these parts, even for people like that. And wanting to kill a presidential candidate was hardly an original ambition. No, it was Hodges' heroism that was the story. Not the shooter. Now profile after profile looked at Hodges' service in Bosnia, Iraq and Afghanistan. His climbing of the career ladder right up to General, before breaking into politics rather than retire into the comfort of being military top brass.

Mike rubbed his eyes. This drive back to Des Moines was becoming increasingly dangerous because of the little sleep he was getting. With relief he finally pulled into the parking lot of the Embassy Suites and walked through the lobby. He wanted to go straight to bed but as he waited at the elevator he heard a familiar peel of raucous laughter from the bar area. He walked over and poked his head around the door to peer inside. Dee was sitting on the bar top, a whisky in one hand, holding court with a gaggle of staffers. They were giggling at one of her more lurid stories from campaigns past, like courtiers around a queen. Dee looked up and noticed Mike. She left her audience to pick up the pieces of the party without her for a moment, as she walked toward Mike. There was a swagger to her stride, just like some sort of cowboy. Mike smiled to himself.

Dee thrust a beer bottle into Mike's hands as he started to raise them in protest.

"Don't even think about not drinking it, buddy," she said in a tone of voice that immediately forced him to put the bottle to his mouth. "We've got some celebrating to do. Latest poll news came out. Guess what? We're up twelve points. Twelve fucking points!"

Mike did some quick mental calculations.

"Third place?"

Dee shook her head.

"Fourth. Stanton's on 30 still. Then Grady and Shaw are on 20 apiece. But we've gone from virtually nowhere to 15. And our trend is upwards. We're hot, Mike. We are HOT."

Mike swigged the beer and felt the cold liquid wash down his throat. But he had barely a moment to savor it before Dee carried on talking.

"I've got some other news too. I've swung you an interview with our shooter. Tomorrow morning you go to Evansville jail. The prison governor is all sweet on Hodges and I told him giving us access was a personal favor. It's not going to be a problem for you to get a bit of face time."

Dee stared at Mike and he nodded. Mike understood the sudden gravity of the task. "No problem."

"Good boy, Mike," Dee said. "Find out everything you can. Remember, we stand in the way between the Senator and nasty surprises. That's our job."

———

THE PRISON guard leaned on the wall opposite Mike in the tiny interrogation room. He regarded the campaign worker with the look of a school boy examining an ant. Curious, half-disgusted, perhaps thinking of the effort it might take to squash him. He had a slab-like face that looked like it might have been cut deep from the winter ice in a frozen Iowa river.

"So, you with the Hodges campaign, huh?" the man asked. "My boss likes him a whole lot. Seems to think he just might change the world."

Mike nodded. The man's expression softened a little as he hitched up his belt, on which hung an array of keys, a set of handcuffs and a can of mace.

"What do you think?" Mike asked.

"I hadn't heard of him until a week ago. But he seems like a good man," the guard said. "Leastways, I'm glad he didn't get shot."

Mike looked around him at the room, bare except for a table and two metal chairs. He had been waiting for someone to bring the prisoner to him for half an hour and he was praying there wasn't a problem: that Dee's links with the prison warden would hold up and nothing would go wrong.

"She's a strange one, though," the guard continued. "She hasn't said a word since she got here. Seems like a robot. Eats her food, does as she's told, not a moment's trouble. She just don't say nothing."

"Not a word?" Mike asked. He tried making his voice sound casual.

"Nope. Police think she's just a crazy. Only lead they had was that she stayed a night in that flea-pit motel, the Havana, up on Route 55. But the place didn't even ask her for a name. Apart from that she's like a ghost."

"A ghost or something else? What do you think?" Mike asked.

The guard looked at him warily, as if sensing some sort of trap. But he clearly liked talking about the mysterious prisoner and giving vent to his thoughts. He took a deep breath.

"What do *I* think? I think she's some sort of Indian. Off of one of them reservations out West. She sure looks like an Indian and God knows, they probably don't keep records that much. The cops have one thing right, though. She's crazy. Just take one look in her eyes and you see that."

Mike opened his mouth to ask another question. But at that moment the door to the interrogation room opened. He sat upright and the guard jumped off the wall to stand at attention.

She walked in.

The figure of the shooter – the would-be assassin of Senator Jack Hodges – seemed absurdly small. She was perhaps just over 5 feet tall with dark, tanned skin and jet-black hair. She shuffled forward slowly, between two burly guards. She wore a bright orange jumpsuit and her hands were cuffed in front of her. Her oval face was lined though, betraying that she was well into her 40s if not older. She did not look like a killer. But even here, dwarfed by the giant men around her, she had a presence. A sense of dead calm at the center of whatever was going around her, something quiet and foreboding.

Mike looked at the woman and a mix of emotions swirled through his head, fear and awe intertwined. She sat down at the desk and gave Mike a blank stare. Mike held her gaze for a few seconds, her eyes full of black, barely any white at all, like holes in her head from which her real eyes had retreated. Then he turned away.

"Okay," said the guard. "We'll get out of here. You've got 15 minutes."

The door clicked softly behind them, leaving nothing but a grim silence, like a grove deep in a forest, where even the fiercest wind cannot stir.

Mike looked again at the woman but he was unsure if she could even see him. He understood why the guard might think she was an Indian. Her darkness and her hair resembled a Sioux or an Apache from any old Western film. Or perhaps she was from further south, over the border down in Mexico.

"What is your name?" he asked.

Nothing came in return. The woman, ignoring him, turned her head to look around at her new surroundings.

'*Cual es su nombre?*" he tried in Spanish.

The woman did not even glance at him. He peppered her with questions, sometimes in English and sometimes in Spanish. But at no time did she even give a hint of understanding or listening to him. Perhaps, he thought with bitter humor, he should have brought along a Comanche phrase book. Just on the off-chance. Throwing questions at her in an Indian language could not have any less impact. His voice was the only sound in the room. Eventually, he just grew quiet. He leaned forward, his elbows resting on the table and his chin propped up by the tips of his fingers. Almost as if in prayer or supplication. A distant clang signaled the opening of a door across the hallway. The guards were coming back. Just for a moment, Mike saw a flicker of something cross the woman's face. She heard the sound too. She knew what it meant. There was something in there behind her mask.

"Look at me," he said firmly.

She turned her eyes to meet his, devoid of expression.

"I will find out who you are. I will find out why you wanted to kill a good man."

And then she was gone. With a burst of life, the guards entered the room, sucking the tight, taut air out of the chamber and filling it with the scraping of chairs and the stamping of boots. The woman stood up and left, without even glancing behind her, leaving Mike by himself. Silent. Contemplating a woman who seemed a human void.

CHAPTER 4

A CLOUD OF smoke hung over the half-eaten breakfast of General Rodrigo Estrada Carillo. His cigar, already burned down a third of its length despite the fact it was barely past 9:00 a.m., stuck out of his mouth like a glowing taper. He looked down with undisguised disgust at the plate of beans, fried plantain and round pink slices of sausage in front of him. His useless servant, Mohubub, never cooked well. But what could one expect of a Garifuna? Still, breakfast seemed to prove a singular challenge to him.

The General sighed, put his cigar to one side, and reached out for a bottle of violently spicy red hot sauce. He dashed liberal amounts of the scarlet liquid all over the meal and then took another bite. He felt the stinging burn light up his mouth. That was better. At least now it tasted like something. He took a few more mouthfuls, then pushed away the plate and poured himself a cup of coffee from the pot Mohubub brewed. He retrieved his cigar and got up to stand on his balcony and survey the day.

Carillo was a short man whose large belly sat uneasily on his frame, giving the impression that he was almost literally round. He wore a pair of faded pants and a shirt he had not bothered to button up. His face was covered with a tangled, dark, wiry beard, but his brown eyes glittered out of the mess with a fierce intensity. He stood on the balcony and looked out over the same scene that he'd viewed virtually every morning for the almost entire fifteen years he'd been stuck here. It was a view of exile: trapped on the Caribbean coast of Guatemala, hundreds of miles away from the capital of Guatemala City, where his family had lived for generations. He leaned forward and blew out a last plume of smoke. Then he let his cigar fall onto the street below where it joined the decaying husks of scores of others, similarly dropped each morning.

The ramshackle city that stretched out beneath him to the crystalline blue of a calm sea was a decaying tropical mess. Livingston. Home to a mix of Mayan Indians, descendents of African slaves called Garifunas and a handful of Latinos. Carillo viewed the place as a hellhole. It was always hot here. Stinking thick tropical heat that drenched his skin and left him constantly dabbing his forehead and cheeks in a losing battle against sweat.

What a strange place for a man like him to end up, he thought. A man whose family came to Guatemala more than three hundred years ago from the Mother Country of Spain. Who toiled among the ungrateful natives to civilize the place. Who won a great fortune in land and mines and had done so much to create a proud, independent country that they called their own. And yet his personal slice of it was now this faded old villa in Livingston. Rotting here among the Indians and the blacks, with their infernal drum music that kept him awake at night. It was exile. There was no other word for it. Forced to stay here by a government that did not understand that he had always acted in the best interests of this country. He felt a surge of anger, but closed his eyes and waited for the moment to pass. There was no point. He had endured this place for so many long years. It was his final patriotic sacrifice. He would do his duty. Many others met far worse fates.

He took a swig of coffee and immediately spat it out. *That fool Mohubub!* His coffee was even worse than his breakfast. It was far too bitter; it tasted like the black bastard cursed it before pouring it in the pot. The General straightened his back and started to button his shirt. He would walk into town this morning, he decided, and buy a decent cup of coffee from the little café on the town square.

"Federico!" he called and walked back into the breakfast room.

Almost immediately a tall, thin man entered. He had cropped black hair and a face covered with pockmarks, the lasting scars from a childhood marred by illness. The man nodded but did not say a word.

"Come. This morning I want to drink proper coffee. Not this vile stuff that Mohubub pisses out."

The General walked out of the house, his shirt now buttoned up. Federico walked about two feet behind him, his eyes darting from one side to another, subtly, but enough to reassure the General that he was always doing his job. Protecting him, watching over him, keeping him safe. Together the pair walked down a cobblestone road that led from Carillo's villa into the town and its harbor, near where a great river poured into the Bahia de Amatique. Carillo squinted against the bright sun, already feeling the sweat pouring down his back. He liked to watch the flowing waters emptying into the sea. He liked to tell Federico that he felt a kinship with it, so far from its familiar homelands, drifting out into the unknown, propelled by the irresistible force of gravity. But he did not feel the poetic mood taking him today. Today he just wanted a decent coffee.

The General and Federico marched on, earning a few nods from passersby familiar with their ritual forays into town. But others, especially the Indians, crossed the road as the pair walked forward, darting into homes and down sidestreets. The General pretended not to notice and Federico, relishing it as a sport, occasionally glared after them, or, in the case of fearful young children, sent them scurrying away with a sudden lunge in their direction, followed by a burst of harsh, grating laughter.

Finally they arrived at the Café Hermann and the General settled into a seat at the back, shielded from the view of the street. Federico perched himself by the door, sitting on a stool, casting an eye out onto the road. The owner of the café scurried over with a steaming pot of coffee and poured the General a cup and then carefully laid a folded newspaper by its side.

"Thank you, Don Hermann," Carillo said and he took a sip. That was better. Good Guatemalan coffee, straight from the highlands around Antigua and made hot and fresh. It was worth the walk, the heat and the stares of the strange people in this town, the General thought. He felt a brief and rare sense of satisfaction come over him, of being part of the world again. He glanced at the newspaper and then picked it up, scanning the headlines. The dreary news from the capital and the latest goings on of the government held no interest for him. He could not bear to read such things while he was stuck here. He flipped through to the foreign pages. After all, he was a man of the world. It would not do to become ignorant and it was far too long since he last read a newspaper.

He fished out a pair of reading glasses from his shirt pocket and perched them on the end of his nose. He peered at the picture on a page devoted to news from America. There was a sudden shock of recognition. The picture was of a man. A man with a solid jaw that Carillo remembered well. A man whose face Carillo had not seen in many years. He was standing, one arm thrust out, protecting a woman behind him. Carillo peered closer, his nostrils flaring as he began to feel his heart race. *Yes! It is her too. It is Jack and Christine Hodges.*

He read the headline. "*Presidente Hodges?*" it asked. He put down the paper. He did not need to read the story. He stared ahead of him, out into the street and beyond that, to the thin blue horizon of the sea. His hands clenched into fists and he felt, for the first time in a long time, a true surge of anger at his exile; at the unrelenting shame of it. He folded up the paper and finished his coffee in a single gulp. Enough, he thought. He needed his due. He deserved a reward for all his service and some compensation for his exile. General Rodrigo Estrada Carillo felt a sense of purpose come back into his life.

———

MIKE DIALED his hometown area code, tapping out the familiar numbers on his hotel room's phone with movements that felt ingrained into his mind. The phone rang twice and then he heard Sean's voice answer.

"Mike?" his old friend asked. "Is that you? Jesus, where have you been hiding?"

Mike felt a stab of guilt. It seemed that for the last few years his life in Florida left him no time for anyone except those he worked with. His schedule consisted of a non-stop series of court cases against huge fruit corporations, meetings and organizing drives. Now, if anything, he was even busier on the Hodges campaign, getting maybe five hours of sleep a night, if he was lucky. The campaign was all consuming and ate up time with a ferocious appetite that was impossible to satiate.

"Sorry, buddy," he said. "I'm a bad best friend."

Sean laughed. Mike knew Sean didn't really mind. Their families had been friends for years, since before they were born. And though Mike had moved away, Sean stayed in Corinth Falls. Still, their ties remained strong. Now Sean had a family of his own, scraping by on an electrician's salary.

"Your mom said you were on the Hodges campaign," Sean said. "Pretty exciting stuff."

Mike knew Sean would want to know all about it, get a glimpse of a life he suspected was more exciting and adventurous than his own. But Mike didn't have the time to get into it. "Yeah, it's a lot of work," he said. "But actually it was something my mom told me that I wanted to talk to you about. It's Jaynie."

The dreaded and loved words again. There was a pause on Sean's end of the phone.

"Mom seems to think she's on something again," Mike said. "Maybe she's in trouble. I was just wondering if you knew anything?"

Sean sighed. In the background, Mike heard the sounds of a child crying and the clatter of plates in a kitchen.

"I've heard a few rumors," Sean said. "Someone said they thought she was into meth again. Maybe even cooking some up. But I don't know anything concrete."

Mike closed his eyes. Cooking up meth? Jesus, Jaynie. He knew it was possible. The two of them knew about folks up in the hills outside of town who ran an entire meth-smuggling network, making the drug in trailers in the woods and running it all over the state. It seemed like a different world now, not just a different time.

"Could you check in on her?" Mike asked.

"Sure, I'll look her up," said Sean. "I don't suppose you're coming back this way anytime soon?"

There was a hint of reproach in his voice. Sean was a busy man too. Working a tough job and raising a family was every bit as demanding as the hours Mike was putting in on this campaign. Harder even.

"Thanks, man," Mike said. "I'll try and come back when I can and see her myself."

But he remembered the last time that happened. Two years ago, he took a break from his work in Florida and popped back to New York to visit Corinth Falls. He wasn't able to resist calling on Jaynie, just to check on her. To make sure she had not destroyed herself completely. It did not go well and ended with Mike fleeing Jaynie's rundown house – the one they bought together – with an array of pots and pans being flung after him. He still remembered the banshee-like wail that Jaynie screamed at him as he brought up her drug use and asked her to give it up. She immediately turned on him and he fled like a hunted fox.

A renewed bout of child's crying sounded in the background and Sean shouted something to his wife, before turning his attentions back to Mike. "Hey, sorry, family beckons. But don't worry, I'll make some time to check in on Jaynie and let you know. Don't be a stranger, Mike. Don't forget us."

Sean said the words lightly. Yet Mike took them hard. Forgetting would never be a problem. But he already felt like a stranger. He put down the now dead phone and gazed around his hotel room. This sterile space was his home now. At least for the moment. Before another hotel room would take its place; different, but just like it. He got up and walked over to the minibar and took out a tiny bottle of whiskey. He unscrewed the cap and began to sip it, just as there was a knock on the door.

It was Dee. She took one look at him, holding the tiny bottle, and laughed.

"Mike, my boy, how are you finding the pressures of campaign life?" she said with a sly wink. "We'll have you drinking from much bigger bottles than that before this show's over."

Dee did not wait for an explanation but just sat down on Mike's bed. She clutched a print-out of a blog entry. Mike could see it was from the *Horse Race*. It looked like Lauren had written up something about the mysterious woman behind bars in the local jail.

"Anything new in there?" he asked.

Dee shook her head. "Nope. Just a retread of everything we know. But I don't like it, Mike. So far the press has given us an easy time on this one. They've bought in so much to Jack as a hero that they're skipping over who this woman might be. Homeless crazy satisfies them at the moment. But it might not last and this blogger, Lauren O'Keefe, seems to want some answers. She might trigger others in to digging deeper. That means we've got to be one step ahead of them. You're my point man on this, Mike."

Mike shrugged.

"Does that article mention anything about a Havana Motel? The place she stayed at the night before she came to Mount Pleasant?"

Dee glanced at it again, her eyes darting over the page. "Not a word."

Mike smiled. "Then we're one step ahead. It's all I've got. But the police have already been there. No name was left."

That was not enough for Dee. "Check it out anyway. These Iowa cops ain't worth a damn on this sort of thing. I got a feeling this woman's a fly in our ointment, Mike. I want to know what sort of fly she is. Is she just a big ol' harmless house fly, or is she the biting kind?"

Mike put down the little bottle of whiskey. It was empty now anyway. He also put all thoughts of Jaynie, his home, and his past, out of his mind. There was no time for that. Not now. There was work to do.

———

THE HAVANA motel lay on the northern edge of Des Moines, just as the landscape broke up into a mix of new sub-divisions and square, brown fields edged with trees. It was a cold and gray morning as Mike pulled up, got out of his car and shivered against the weather. It was here that rural Iowa began, with its farms and gently rolling landscape hinting at the prairie that it once was – and, judging by the tall grass that grew up on any vacant lot, would quickly be again if ever given the chance.

The Havana was a one-story relic from the 1950s, arranged in a square horseshoe shape around a tarmac parking lot which long winters had disintegrated into a spider's web of cracks. At one end of the horseshoe there was an empty swimming pool, its diving board promising nothing more than a six-foot leap into bare concrete. At the other end lay a management office with a sign hanging on the door that read, optimistically, "Vacancies. Inquire within". The fact that there were only a half dozen cars in the parking lot seemed to indicate there was always room at this particular inn. Or that it played host to the sort of guests who did not need a whole night to carry out their business. Mike walked over and pushed open the door. An old man sat behind the desk, thin as one of the frozen telephone poles that lined the road outside. His chin was frosted with white stubble and his teeth were yellowed. In a voice turned gravely from cigarettes, he asked Mike if he wanted a room. Mike shook his head.

"I'm here about the woman who tried to shoot Senator Hodges. I work with his campaign."

The man looked him up and down with a barely disguised hostility. "The cops have already been here. We don't got nothing to say about her. No idea who she was."

"Mind if I look at her room?"

The man thought about it for a minute, casting his eyes back down to the paper, weighing his options. Eventually he shrugged his scrawny shoulders, got up and beckoned Mike to follow him. They trudged across the frozen parking lot heading to one of the motel's anonymous-looking rooms. It was number 37. The man opened the door.

"Ain't no different to any other room. She didn't leave nothin' behind neither."

Mike walked in. The room was sparse, with little more than a dingy bed, its faded linens pulled tightly around the mattress. An ancient-looking TV sat in one corner. Its walls were bare of any form of decoration and its bathroom tiles were streaked and stained. Yet, against his better judgment, against all rational thought, Mike felt he could sense the woman's presence here. The void that existed within her had been in this place too, sucking something from it, yet leaving a trace of its passing. He shook his head. He was imagining things, he told himself. "Anyone see her?" he asked.

The man shook his head. "I let her in. She didn't barely say a word. Just paid 20 bucks and took the room. I took her for a whore. But I didn't see no John with her and she seemed kinda old for that line of work. Still, wouldn't be the strangest whore I seen around here."

The man stared directly at Mike, daring him to be shocked at his words. He spat theatrically on the floor. "We ain't exactly the Sheraton, mister," he added.

Mike was about to give up, when suddenly a thought hit him. "The cleaner? The person who cleaned the rooms that morning. Who was that?"

The man shifted a little and shrugged his bird-like shoulders, so bony you could see his collar bone and his Adam's apple bobbed up and down like an elevator.

"I can't recall," he said.

Mike reached into his pocket and took out his wallet. "This must be a tough job. Pretty bad pay and some pretty mean customers."

Mike took out two 20 dollar bills and reached over to tuck them into the breast pocket of the man's shirt. He felt the man's bones poking through the skin beneath the material, hard and ridged, seemingly covered by skin as thin and brittle as parchment.

"Suppose I could look at the roster?" Mike asked.

They trudged back to the management office and the man hauled out a thick book from beneath the desk. He opened it and thumbed through the pages, peering at tiny lines of almost undecipherable inky handwriting.

"Ernesto. Ernesto Benitez was the guy who cleaned that room," he said, with the self-satisfied air of a man who just solved a puzzle.

"And where does he live? When's he next in?"

The man turned back to the book and flicked through pages of writing until eventually he turned over one sheet that was only half-full of scrawl. He snorted to himself. "Well, he lives over at a trailer park at Elm and Huntsville in Altoona. But he ain't been in since the morning he cleaned that woman's room. Looks like young Ernesto must have left our employment."

The two men looked at each other across the book laid out on the desk. Their eyes met, each perhaps realizing the significance of that information, or deciding to shy away from it.

"People leave all the time," the man said. His voice, though, was weak and by the time he finished his sentence, Mike was already half-way to his car, pangs of doubt starting to gnaw on the edges of his mind.

CHAPTER 5

GENERAL CARILLO SAT at his table and looked at his dining companion, the Livingston police chief, Antonio Alvarez Zaragosa. The last remnants of a bottle of red wine were dripping from Zaragosa's voluminous moustache like he had some desperate, alcoholic flu. Thank God he kept back the expensive Chilean stuff and served only Argentine table wine instead, Carillo thought. He was long familiar with Zaragosa's appetites and only a fool would waste good wine on such an oaf.

Zaragosa, who was taller than the General and less fat, was clearly drunk. His head hung down as he talked, almost half to himself, and then jerked up suddenly as he stumbled across some valid point. His words were slurred but he often broke into rapid fluency as his anger shone through the booze.

"Why are you here?" Zaragosa asked, warming to his favorite topic: the General's exile. He banged his fist on the table, prompting Carillo to hush him gently.

"But truly," the policeman continued. "It is not right. You

fought for our country against the communists. Against the bastards who would have taken our beloved homeland and turned it into a charnel house. Yet you are here, stuck in exile, as if you did something shameful. When all you did was make the hard choices to keep us safe in our beds at night."

Carillo shrugged his heavy soldiers. Though he had heard the speech a hundred times, he never truly tired of it. It did him good to be praised like this, called a hero. Just like Zaragoza did during the war when he was a mere private and Carillo was a colonel.

"You remember that time, in 1985, I think, near Chiquimula?" Zaragoza asked. "When the Reds thought they could just come into town at night and we waited for them. You remember their faces? The look of shock on those Indians. It was something you could never forget. They thought they were prisoners, huh?"

The General smiled. Of course, he remembered. He closed his eyes and savored the thought. The strength he had felt. The divine will of serving his country. The power he once wielded to make the right decisions to defend the nation.

"But we showed them, right?" Zaragosa said. "We don't take prisoners we know are guilty. Judge, jury and executioner. That's what you said. Take them out into the jungle where they came from. They were savages and we treated them like they deserved to be treated."

"Those were hard times and we had to be hard men," said Carillo.

The policeman thumped his fist loudly on the table again, sending their glasses into the air like jumping beans. He ignored the fierce look Carillo shot him.

"Exactly, my friend! Exactly! You deserve better reward then this! Hidden here by a government who should be grateful, not ashamed."

The General looked at his companion and decided that was enough. He got up from the table and rested a hand on the policeman's shoulder.

"Your words are true, Antonio," he said. "But perhaps the night is done now."

The policeman looked disappointed at his sudden downward turn of fortune. In truth, he had hoped for another bottle of wine. He himself could only afford beer or the moonshine that the Garifuna brewed, and that was no drink for a gentleman and a former officer of the armed forces of the Republic. But he recognized when he must cut his losses and the look on Carillo's face certainly suggested this night was at a close. He got up, banged into the table, thanked his host profusely and was led to the door.

When Zaragosa left, stumbling back down the road that led to town, the General walked back to the table. He picked up his own glass of wine and took a swig. Disgusting stuff, he thought. He walked into the kitchen and poured it down a sink, watching the bloody red liquid disappear down the plughole as the night's conversation came back to him. Had that night in Chiquimula really been more than 20 years ago? He looked in the sink at the wine splashes staining the white porcelain red. Images swam in his mind. Images he did not want to think about. Then anger rose in him again. The drunk policeman was right, he thought. He should be rewarded for his sacrifices, not condemned.

He washed his hands, which caused the last traces of wine to disappear, and then he stomped into the living room. He picked up the phone and dialed. It was a number he had not dared think about for a long time. At least not like this. The sound of the ringing sounded distant. Obscure. Calling across oceans of time as well as water. Then a male voice answered. Carillo introduced himself with a hello and his rank and name. The voice waited a second in silence, just breathing down the line. But the General already knew. The man remembered. Oh yes, he remembered.

MIKE DROVE down Huntsville Street in Altoona, just a few miles from Des Moines, and looked at the trailer park that Ernesto Benitez called home. It was typical of such places, just like many he had seen in Florida, trying to help the tens of thousands of immigrants who worked in the fruit plantations. It was half-hidden behind a junkyard, massed with towering skyscrapers of squashed cars, and consisted of a seemingly random scattering of trailer homes and shacks.

Mike parked the car and spied a group of Hispanic-looking men on the corner of the road. They stood huddled together against the cold like a group of Antarctic penguins, stamping their feet and blowing out plumes of steam with their breath. Day laborers, Mike thought. Desperate for work, hoping someone will have an odd job to give them in exchange for a handful of dollars. He walked over and greeted them in Spanish. No one even looked at him. He repeated his hello.

"Guys, I am not *la migra*," he said, using the nickname given to the immigration services. "I am with the campaign of Senator Jack Hodges. Have you heard of him?"

Mike took out his campaign ID, emblazoned with a red, white and blue logo. "Have you heard of the Senator? He wants to help make conditions better for guys like you."

One man, nervously looked at his compatriots and broke from the group. He peered at the ID and took it in his hand. He examined it carefully and flipped it over to read the back. He handed it back to Mike.

"I am not from the government," Mike insisted.

The man laughed. "But maybe you'll be the government one day," he said in Spanish thickly accented from some Mexican barrio.

Mike laughed too. "Hopefully. But for now I just need some help. I'm looking for a guy called Ernesto Benitez, or at least that's the name he used at work. He used to clean rooms over at the Havana Motel. You know him?"

The man regarded Mike for a moment and then went back to the huddle. The group talked quietly for a while, casting nervous glances over in Mike's direction. Then the man came back. "Why you want to know?" he asked.

"Look, this guy could be in real trouble. The hotel he worked at was used by someone who tried to shoot Senator

Hodges. He cleaned the room of the shooter. We need to speak to him."

There was silence between them. Mike tried again. "I'm not a cop. I'm ahead of the cops. I can help him. Senator Hodges can help him."

The man's face was a mass of contradictions. Mike had seen the expression a thousand times in Florida. These were people who feared any sort of authority, whose entire existence was based on staying below the radar, being anonymous, helping and trusting only each other. But the man clearly knew something else was going on here. Something big that could hurt his friend.

"He skipped town," he said at last. "He went to Kansas. Garden City. To the meat packing plants there. They're hiring at the moment. Tough work but the pay is okay. You can find him there, I think."

Mike offered his hand. The man took it, his grip firm. He looked Mike in the eyes. "I read about Jack Hodges," he said. "If you work with him, you must be a good man. When you vote for him, think of us."

Then he released Mike's grip and wandered back to the group, joining them again, looking up hopefully as a truck turned slowly into the street, offering briefly the prospect of work.

———

DEE SURVEYED the scene in the American Legion Building in Newton, a small town about twenty miles from

Des Moines. It was only 10:00 a.m., but already the room was packed with an exuberant crowd. Judging by the broad mix of ages, she guessed a good number of the crowd had taken off time from work. That was a hell of a good sign. She leaned on the wall at the back of the room behind the massed ranks of the press. Every so often a reporter or blogger approached her, notebook or tape recorder in hand, looking for a quote.

"Go on, git!" she said, waving them away like they were stray dogs, half-joking, half serious. "I'm not on the record. I'm on a break."

She inwardly relished the attention though and enjoyed sending the reporters away, tails between their hapless legs. It was incredible, she thought, what had happened. The campaign's latest internal poll numbers, which she devoured in her hotel room that morning, were still rising upwards. Now every day brought four or five campaign stops and each one was packed full. This was what she had dreamed of ever since she got in the game. To be at the heart of something big, something that could change the whole country. She closed her eyes a moment and listened to the local high school band striking up a welcoming tune and the deafening roar of the crowd as Hodges and Christine walked on stage. She opened them again and saw Mike standing beside her.

"Hey, buddy," she said. "What are you doing here? I thought you were making sure logistics are all good for tomorrow's run up to Sioux City?" Dee frowned. "And you've also got a little trip to the jail later, Mike. The warden is expecting you again. We've got to keep digging on our shooter. Keep interviewing her until we find something. It's top priority."

Mike looked past Dee's shoulder and saw Hodges trying to quiet the crowd that was loudly cheering his name. It seemed an impossible task.

"She hasn't said a word, Dee. Not a single word," Mike said.

Dee smiled thinly, her lips disappearing into a pencil-drawn crease. "I'm sure you are quite the charmer when you want to be, Mike. It'd be a good idea to get that charm working."

Mike nodded. "It's all in hand," he said. "I'm going back to the jail this afternoon. I just wanted to come by a campaign stop again. Soak up a bit of the feeling. I've felt a little too inside the loop the last few days."

Dee knew what he was saying. She sometimes got that way too. It was good to remind yourself of why you worked 20 hour days. Of why scores of people did not see their families, spouses and loved ones for weeks or months. She put a hand on Mike's shoulder.

"Good idea," she said.

Together they stood in silence and watched Hodges work the rope line that kept the people at the front of the crowd from storming the stage. Then he stood back, gave a few thanks to local dignitaries and launched into his stump speech. It touched all the familiar points: the need for jobs to help ordinary folk live the lives their parents had, to give them better health care, to restore the country's sense of dignity and possibility in the world. He seemed three feet taller than anyone else in the room as he spoke. His voice carried everywhere, full of dignity and purpose, warm, yet firm. It invaded the crowd, stilling them at first and then carrying them onwards and upwards, suddenly alive with possibilities. When it was over, there was a huge standing ovation. Hodges and Christine embraced, laughing and kissing like young lovers at a prom, beaming smiles and waving at the cheering throng.

"Those two must hug and kiss like that four or five times a day, but each time it still looks genuine," said Mike.

"That's because it is," said Dee. "You never seen love before, Mike? Real, honest true love? There's not much Jack Hodges does that isn't the real thing. I'm pretty sure his marriage is part of it. Thank God for us. I've had more than my share of campaigns ruined because the candidate was a horn dog."

They watched Hodges and Christine leave the room and then finally Dee gave an exaggerated wave of her arms as she called out to a waiting throng of reporters.

"Come on then, ladies and gentlemen, boys and girls, let's hear what you have to say," she said, and was immediately mobbed by a pack of reporters, clamoring with questions. Mike stepped back, eager to avoid the crush and attention. But one person followed him as he turned away. Lauren O'Keefe. She walked over and gently touched him on the arm. He looked into her open smile and stopped.

"Hi, Mike," she said. "How's the campaign treating you?"

Mike felt a flush of blood to his face. He could not help it and the sudden feeling caught him by surprise. "Good," he said. "Tiring though. Non-stop work."

"Did you see my blog post about the shooter? I was just wondering what you thought about it. Did it get any reaction from Hodges?"

Lauren's face was still smiling, but Mike shook his head. "I didn't see it, Lauren," he lied. "And I can't talk about stuff like that. On or off the record."

Lauren shrugged. She did not seem to mind. "No problem. You want to go for a coffee somewhere? I promise no campaign talk. I'm kind of sick of it for a moment. I haven't met anyone in weeks who has any kind of a personal life. I thought that was kind of sad and then I realized I was one of them." She smiled again.

Mike looked at her for a moment. She really was pretty and the thought of spending an hour talking about anything but the campaign was alluring. Her smile broadened and she touched his arm.

"Come on, Mike," she said.

FIFTEEN MINUTES later they sat in a little diner just off Newton's pretty town square. It was a quiet place, just a handful of tables, a paper menu encased in plastic and a threadbare carpet on the floor. A waitress poured them coffee and Lauren stretched her arms backwards reaching over her head in a manner that suggested, had she been at home, she would be kicking off her shoes.

"So what's the deal with you, Mike? Are you married to the campaign or do you have a wife and kids praying that Hodges loses and Daddy comes home."

Mike laughed. "Single as they come," he said, but he noticed his hand was absent- mindedly tugging at his ring finger as he said the words, feeling for a band of gold that had not sat there for years. She noticed too and raised an eyebrow.

"Divorced," he said. "Married too young and she's got a lot of... problems. Not her fault. She just didn't know to cope with the hand she got dealt."

Lauren looked sympathetic and instead of shying away from the issue she asked to hear more. To his surprise Mike found himself opening up about Jaynie, abandoning any pretence that this was some sort of date. He talked of the recent phone calls and his desire to help her. But he explained that he could not leave this campaign. Not now. It felt good to unburden himself, like letting the steam out of a kettle that was threatening to boil. Lauren listened and long before the coffee was cold in his cup, her hand was resting on his, telling him not to worry.

"It's okay, Mike," she said. "You think you're alone in this circus. But you're not. Everyone here is carrying their past behind them somehow, ignoring it while the campaign unfolds. Sometimes I think most of the people involved in this game are only doing it to run away from things in life. To throw themselves into causes bigger than themselves."

Mike had never thought of it that way. He always saw his intense attitude towards work as a savior, not an excuse. Life was a mess back in Corinth Falls. Jaynie hurtled down a path of abuse and crime and he failed to stop her. Now he thought his work filled the gap she left behind. But maybe Lauren had a point. Maybe it all just bandaged over a still bleeding wound, not actually healing it. He smiled at her and then caught a glimpse of the clock on the wall. An hour had already passed. He stood up suddenly, remembering that he needed to make his appointment at the jail. He felt his chest constrict at the thought.

"I gotta go. Important meeting and I'm a bit late," he said. He threw a few dollars down on the table and headed for the door. But then he stopped and turned around.

"Thank you, Lauren," he said. "I mean that."

———

THE WOMAN remained as blank as the first time he saw her. Her coal eyes did not even settle on him as she was led into the interrogation room. She sat just three feet away from him across a gray expanse of desk that might as well have been a vast desert, stretching out to some unseen horizon. She seemed unreachable. The prison guard from Mike's first visit remained in the room this time. Mike noticed the smack of the man's lips as he chewed on gum.

"She's a crazy bitch, son" the guard said, as if the woman was not in the room with them, but instead still locked in her cell. "She might as well be dead."

Mike felt a flare of anger at the words. It was disrespectful to talk about her as if she were not sitting in front of him.

"Perhaps it would help if you weren't here," Mike said, turning around to look at the guard. The man weighed his options, wondering whether to take offense.

"Suit yourself. You got 15 minutes again," he said. Mike waited until the door clanged shut and then turned to the woman.

There was nothing for him to do but to fill the emptiness with his own speech. "Where did you meet Senator Hodges? If you wanted to kill him, you must have had a reason. Did he do something to you? Or was it something he did to someone else?"

The woman stopped looking around the room and hung her head. For a moment Mike thought she might have drifted off to sleep.

"Was it Iraq? Or Afghanistan? Did you dislike him fighting in those wars?"

Still nothing. A blank wall of silence. Or was it sadness? There seemed a deep melancholia behind those eyes. Or perhaps Mike was reading too much of his own emotions about Jaynie into the situation. Seeing the prisoner as another lost soul in the world. Yet that puzzled him. He should be angry at this woman. She tried to kill a man he believed in. The one politician he thought might actually change this country for the better. But for some reason, he could muster no fury towards her. So he just talked. He talked of the campaign and how well it was going. Of how Hodges was being greeted by crowds of well-wishers. Of how the candidate won the debate and was climbing in the polls. For just a moment, Mike sensed a change in the room. Was it a quiver at the corner of her mouth? Or was it her lank, black hair, hanging over her face, suddenly twitching as she breathed out more heavily?

Mike pressed on.

Hodges, he told her, was a great man who would make a great president. America was waking up to his message. America was finally getting it and it all started here. In a campaign transformed by an act of violence that seemed like madness but that could change the world.

Mike paused. He leaned forward, his voice a whisper. "That change was thanks to you," he said. "He will owe it all to you."

The woman's face snapped up and Mike shot backwards, his chair scraping on the floor. She looked at him now. Her eyes flared up to the size of saucers. Her breath came in ragged heaves and her whole body tensed, like a cat about to pounce. Her arms were on the desk and seemed rigid, the muscles in her hands bulging.

Mike backed off, realizing with icy dread, something he had not truly understood until now. This was a woman who tried to kill a man. She waited patiently for hours upon hours with that sole purpose. The eyes looking at him now were those of a killer.

And then the moment passed.

Her head sagged back down and her body slumped. Mike, a cold sweat on his palms, sat there. It was his turn to be silent now. He remained so until the guard came back.

"She say anything?" the guard asked. He jerked his head in the direction of the woman.

"Not a thing," Mike answered. But she didn't need to. Mike learned something without words. This woman was not mad. She was not deranged and without reason. She was a killer with a purpose.

———————

OUTSIDE IN the cold, fresh air, Mike walked across the prison parking lot to his car. It was a relief to be out of the jail. His heart was still beating fast and he felt sweat freeze on his forehead as an icy blast swirled across the tarmac. He walked intently with his head bowed, so it was not until the last moment that he noticed a female figure leaning casually against his car, waiting for his arrival.

"Gotcha," Lauren said.

Mike opened his mouth but no words came out.

"I knew you guys were looking into the shooter. But I had to follow you to make sure it was true," she said. The note of triumph in her voice was unmistakable. Then she winced theatrically and shrugged her shoulders by way of apology.

"I'm sorry, Mike. You're not mad about this are you?"

Mike gathered his feelings, finally realizing that he was actually more impressed than angry. Not only did Lauren have the right sources in the campaign to get a lead, she had the balls to actually follow his car to see where he was going. *But did she know anything new?* He thought fast. She did not know about the cleaner at the Havana. She did not even know about the motel. She could follow his car but she could not follow his investigation.

"No," he said. He laughed before adding, "But I've got nothing for you. That woman in there hasn't said a word since she was arrested. She still hasn't."

He opened his car door.

"Come on, Mike. Gimme something. It's been cold waiting for you to come out."

Mike smiled again. He was actually enjoying this as long as he didn't have to give away any secrets. "I've got nothing for you, Lauren," he repeated. He winked at her as he shut the door and started the engine. Within seconds she was a shadow in his rear view mirror, gazing after his retreating car, no doubt already compiling her next blog post.

CHAPTER 6

THE ROAD ACROSS Kansas reached ahead of Mike like a rope stretched tight against some invisible peg past the flat horizon. He drove for hours barely moving the steering wheel, past Kansas City, past Lawrence and Topeka. Briefly the highway climbed up into the Flint Hills, where the old prairie grasses were never turned into farmland. The sudden beauty of the country shocked him and he pulled over at a rest stop, getting out of the car under a winter sky that suddenly cleared and bathed the landscape in beautiful sunshine.

He stood there for a moment of peace and freedom, untied at last from the heated atmosphere of the campaign back in Iowa. He felt the ever-blowing wind in his hair and the faint warmth of the winter sun. The sky felt big again; a gigantic dome of blue, not the glowering gray that seemed to have hunkered down in Iowa, barely above head height, for the last month. A sudden explosion of feathers in the brush took him by surprise and a prairie chicken hurtled into the sky. He laughed and got back into the car and started driving again. Soon the landscape of the Flint Hills was just a receding bump on the horizon and the road to Garden City beckoned again across the plains.

As his car ate up the miles and hours, the view gradually changed. The terrain, already virtually flat, seemed now to defy belief and become even more so. Western Kansas was a harsh landscape and ploughed fields surrendered to tougher soils that could only sustain herds of lanky cattle foraging on the short grass. He drove by Greensburg, Dodge City and Cimarron and finally into Garden City itself. It was a beaten down looking place, dominated by the hulks of the meat-processing factories on its outskirts and ringed by black-earthed cattle feed lots, where untold millions of cows from across the Midwest were fattened up on grains before being driven to the waiting slaughter houses.

Though small and isolated out on the plains, Garden City was a familiar name to Mike. The meat plants acted as a notorious candle, enticing thousands of illegal immigrants like moths to its flame. Even in Florida Mike knew hundreds of men and women who would suddenly abandon the fruit fields for a shot at labor they could not imagine being even more harsh than the work they already did. Usually, though, they discovered a deep disappointment. Conditions in the meat plants were dangerous, pay was low, and raids by *la migra* were a permanent part of life. Most workers soon found they had merely swapped the backbreaking toil of fruit picking for the equally-tough task of wielding huge cutting knives on a never-ending production line of cow flesh. It cost many a finger or two before they moved on yet again.

But Mike got lucky in his quest to find Ernesto Benitez. He knew a handful of union organizers and community activists out here, part of an informal network to which his own organization back in Florida belonged. One man in particular, Ivan Tobar, was an old friend who moved from Florida a year ago, following the trail of the immigrants. Tobar spent every waking hour of his week touring the trailer parks and cheap flophouses where the workers lived, informing them of their rights, calming their fears and trying to help them grasp at the better lives they sought. If anyone in Garden City knew of the arrival of Benitez – just another face in the anonymous flood of people flowing through town – it would be Tobar.

Mike checked into a roadside motel and then drove out to find Tobar's house. It was a collapsing bungalow in a dilapidated looking subdivision. A wire screen was half-hanging off the door frame as he knocked. He heard the rustle of someone coming into the door and then felt the firm grasp of Tobar sweeping him up in a bear hug.

"Mike! You made it! Welcome to my little slice of paradise. Sorry, the weather isn't as warm as Florida," he said.

Mike instantly felt the stress of the drive and his mission to find Benitez melt away in the warmth of his friend's smile. Tobar took him inside into the living room, a place almost devoid of furniture save for a beat-up couch and a flickering TV. It resembled the home of a student or unrepentant bachelor.

Tobar went into the kitchen and returned carrying two cans of beer. He popped open one and handed the other to Mike, before the two men settled on the couch.

"So, you're with the Hodges campaign, huh?" Tobar asked. "Didn't you hate all politicians?"

"Yeah, I know. But this guy feels different somehow."

Tobar raised an eyebrow.

"I know that sounds trite," Mike said. "But I mean that. He can change things. He can even change things in a town like this, make it better for people. Stand up for the little guys."

Tobar was silent a moment. "Really?" he said. "Because we sure could do with some change around here."

His voice was strained, carrying it with the unimaginable tensions and stresses of his work. "I thought Florida could be bad. But out here, it's like no one cares, man. This place is a machine and it chews up people more than the cattle. The immigrants come here, work for a pittance, then leave minus a finger or *la migra* sweeps them up. And the companies just roll on, raking in the profits."

Mike glanced out the window. Outside it was now dark. Tobar swigged his can and went to the kitchen to fetch another. When he came back he stood in the doorway and looked at Mike closely.

"So what can I do for you, Mike? It's good to see you but no one comes to Garden City on vacation."

Straight to the point. Typical Tobar. Mike did not beat about the bush either. He told Tobar he was looking for the cleaner of the room of the woman who tried to kill Hodges.

He said he just wanted to talk. Nothing else. "The guy's not in trouble. We're just covering our bases here."

Tobar looked at him warily. "You for real on this?" he asked.

Mike nodded.

"You know, if I can find him here, your candidate will owe us a favor," Tobar said. "If we get his back now, we'll want him to have our back in the future. These guys need a friend in the White House."

Tobar was striking a deal. But it sounded like a good one. Mike offered his hand and Tobar took it.

"I'll see what I can do," Tobar said.

———

DEE OPENED her eyes with surprise. She could not even remember falling asleep. But, as she glanced at her watch and saw that it was 6:00 a.m., she realized she must have dozed off at her desk. She was still in the back office of the campaign headquarters in Des Moines with the final polls and newspaper clippings spread in front of her. She shook her head and stumbled over to the coffee machine to make a cup of noxious, caffeine-laced liquid. Just before she put it to her lips, she paused and then fished in her handbag for a tiny bottle of gin poached from her hotel room's mini-bar. She poured it into the cup and gulped it down.

"Happy election day!" she toasted to herself and walked out into the room.

None of the score or so of people already there was surprised to see her. In fact, Dee collapsing in her office and spending the night was a common occurrence over the last two weeks of the campaign. Now, on election day itself, few expected her to be anywhere else.

Dee felt the distant buzz of the alcohol hit her system. It gave her a welcome thrill, drilling through the tiredness in her mind like sunshine poking through clouds. She felt her mood shift; her excitement begin to kick into gear and the adrenalin start to move through her veins. This was it. Everything in this whole race had been building up to this final hurdle and now they had to jump it. It was do or die time.

"Morning people!" she shouted. "Today I am going to make your lives hell. But tonight you will thank me for it!"

In a frenzy of activity she whirled from desk to desk, haranguing staff, shouting at volunteers, balling out aides. She had no time to think, she was just running on pure instinct. Everything had to go right. The volunteer teams carrying placards had to be on the street corners, the teams of drivers giving people lifts to the caucus venues had to pick up every single one of their targets, the weather reports were crucial. They needed sun. Without it, just the old and determined would show up. Hodges' appeal went to the young and the students too; the working moms; the unemployed and the immigrants. Sunshine meant those groups were more likely to turn out. One single mistake, one overlooked voter, could mean the difference between life and death for this campaign. It was Dee's job to make sure that did not happen.

Around noon, Hodges and Christine came into the headquarters. Unlike the staff members, the candidate and his wife had enjoyed a leisurely morning. Forbidden from directly campaigning, they had slept in and indulged in a late breakfast. They looked relaxed as they moved attentively through the frenzied room, stopping to thank volunteers and staffers alike. Finally, they got to Dee and she ushered them into a back room, clicking the door shut behind them. It felt like a little island of peace and quiet on a stormy sea.

"How's it going, Dee?" Hodges asked, settling down into the chair. There seemed something at ease about him as if, with judgment about to be decided, he at last felt liberated from the strain. He had done all he could.

"It's looking good," Dee said, and then flashed a grin. "But how the fuck would we really know? An Iowa caucus is one of the strangest elections in the whole of the free world. I'd be lying if I said I knew for sure what's going to really be on the minds of these folks."

That was the truth. Dee had worked and crafted this campaign in meticulous detail. She helped Hodges form himself into the very image of a president in the making. After the shooting, they ran a flawless campaign, dominating the headlines, attacking their opponents and rising in the polls. Nothing went wrong. She knew that. But did she really know what was going on? She was essentially just placing a gigantic bet. A bet that all their careers relied on.

Hodges shrugged. He reached out and grabbed her shoulder with his hand, something she had seen him do a hundred times with ordinary Iowans. Suddenly she felt his power and charisma; felt the blue-eyed gaze falling on her. It was like an electric shock. For the first time she understood what is it was really like to meet her candidate.

"I trust you, Dee," he said simply, his eyes boring into hers.

And, for the first time in weeks, Dee knew – truly knew – that it would be okay.

———

MIKE SAT on the bed of his hotel room in Garden City surrounded by the remains of a takeout pizza and a six-pack of beer. Both merely filled his stomach and dulled his head. They did not actually calm his nerves as he obsessively switched through the cable news channels as they covered the unfolding Iowa caucuses.

Across Iowa, almost 500 miles away, people trooped to school gymnasiums, town halls and even just people's private homes, to hold mini-debates about the candidates. They separated into different groups, backed a side and then tried to persuade each other to change their minds. Eventually, after a long excruciating delay, the final tallies fed through to Des Moines to be announced. It was an archaic process; a mad hangover from an earlier age. But it was how American presidents were born.

Mike sat up as he watched a shot of Hodges come onto the TV. The Senator sat in a roadside diner, somewhere in Des Moines, and waved to passers-by as he shooed away any TV news crew that got close to him. Mike sent Dee a brief email over his Blackberry and begged her for the latest news. He got a prompt reply:

"Trust in God and Jack Hodges (if you can tell the difference any more)."

Mike tried to laugh, but his throat was dry despite the beer and he felt a pressure building up in the front of his head. He got up and paced around the room. This was awful, he thought. If they did win, how would he cope with the pressure of New Hampshire or South Carolina and beyond? Let alone the actual presidential campaign. But he was getting ahead of himself. They needed to beat Stanton before dreaming of that. Suddenly, his thoughts were disturbed by his ringing phone. He looked at the screen. It was Tobar's number.

"I've got him for you, Mike," he said. "Ernesto Benitez. He arrived a week ago and signed up with the big Cargill plant. He's sharing a trailer with some other guys there I know. I'll email you the address."

Mike felt a glow of relief cut through his anxiety.

"Thanks, Ivan. I'll try and catch him tomorrow"

"Do it early. His shift will start before sunrise."

"I owe you one," Mike said.

"Senator Hodges owes us one," Tobar replied. "Let him know we helped. I hope this Benitez will speak to you, but nearly everyone here is skittish around outsiders. Good luck."

Mike glanced at the television and noticed with a shock that the first results were coming in and Harriet Stanton was well ahead. A handful of tiny caucuses had reported from rural areas and she already had more than 50 percent of the votes. Hodges was back in sixth place with just three percent. A stab of panic gripped Mike and he reached for his final beer. He flipped the tab and poured the liquid down his throat, not removing his eyes from the TV screen. He knew the first results were meaningless. They represented a few hundred voters. But he could not stop a primal thought from entering his mind. All of this work for what? We're in sixth!

Another slew of caucuses reported. Hodges ticked up. He hit eight percent now and Stanton slipped to 40. Hodges was in fifth place, bunched with a handful of other candidates. It was excruciating. But gradually the results flowed in, coming from bigger and bigger caucus meetings. They swept through the college towns where Hodges focused so much of his campaign's strength and out into the blue collar suburbs of Des Moines, Davenport and Sioux City. From fifth place, Hodges' numbers broke from the pack. Suddenly he was in third, notching up 15 percent. Then he was in second, just 12 points behind Stanton. Then ten points behind. Then eight points. Then five.

Then it was over.

Stanton won with 33 percent of the vote. But Hodges was second with 28 percent. It was an astounding result. Mike leapt up from his bed and called Dee. She answered the phone, or at least he thought she did. He could hear nothing on the other end but the sound of screaming, partying, cheering and cries of joy. He knew what she was doing. No words could describe their achievement so she held up her phone at their campaign headquarters and let the sounds travel down the line. Mike laughed and danced on his bed, fizzing his beer like a champagne bottle, giggling and whooping like a schoolboy.

———

THE NIGHT air was so cold that it penetrated the car's wheezing heating system as Mike steered it down a dark lane towards the trailer park address that Tobar emailed him. It was 4.30 a.m. and yet he realized he might already be too late. The men and women who worked the early shifts in the meat packing plants were already on the move, freezing half to death as they hitch-hiked to work or jammed themselves like sardines in mini-vans.

The road Mike followed was pitted and rough but broad and he was surprised to see a long line of cars and SUVs parked to one side. He drove slowly past them, aware also of shadowy figures milling about, adjusting clothes, putting on helmets. What the fuck? Mike thought. Then he understood. Immigration. *La migra.* There was going to be a raid. Shit.

One figure loomed out of the dark and put out a hand to stop the car. A flashlight lit up his face. Mike slowed the car and leant out of the window, making sure they could see his white skin and red hair.

"Pardon me, buddy. I'm late for work," Mike said, slowing but not stopping. The figure waved him onwards.

Mike did not dare speed up until he was out of sight. He could not give the impression he was about to warn anyone in the trailer park ahead. He drove slowly around a bend in the road and only then floored the gas, sending the car skidding off at speed and through the gates of the trailer park. Feverishly he looked at the address and wondered how he could find the right trailer in this mess. He got out, the cold blast of night air chilled him, but he was too panicked to feel it. He raced from trailer to trailer, checking the number, like trying to solve a puzzle. He prayed with each second that he would find it before the raid began. Finally, he got lucky. It was a tiny little trailer, tucked up against a thick line of trees and bushes at the edge of the park. He ran up to the thin, plastic-covered door and furiously knocked on it. There was no response. He rapped again, hissing Ernesto Benitez' name.

"Ernesto! Ernesto Benitez!"

He thought he heard movement inside. But it quickly stopped. He imagined the man, crouching low on the other side of the door, suddenly afraid at this intrusion into his already scary world. Mike knew there were only a few seconds left. He spoke in rapid Spanish.

"*Amigo, la migra* is coming. Soon. You have to get out. I can help you."

Silence.

"*Amigo.* I just want to talk. I promise. You can come with me now, or *la migra* will have you in a minute."

The door opened.

Ernesto Benitez was a slight figure, perhaps in his early 30s. His face was a golden brown and his eyes wide and dark. He looked terrified. The door opened just enough for him to peer out. Suddenly, his eyes widened and a flash of light, bright as the sun, illuminated the scene. With a roar of revved engines vehicles poured into the trailer park. The raid began.

"Fuck!" cried Mike.

He rammed his shoulder against the door and sent Benitez flying across the room. Mike grabbed him by the collar of the sweatshirt he was wearing and hauled him to his feet. He looked straight into his face.

"We have to get out of here," he said.

Benitez nodded and gestured to the rear of the trailer. There was another door there. They both ran and Benitez flung it open. It led straight into a thick patch of trees and bushes. It was so dark that they could barely see. But the flashlights shining from behind them, swinging low and high, like a crazed menagerie of lighthouses, spurred them onwards. Mike ploughed ahead first and plunged into the bushes. Twigs and branches, bare of leaves, clawed and ripped at his arms and legs and he put up a hand to protect his face. Behind him he could hear the grunting and footsteps of Benitez. But Mike did not dare to stop and look behind. He knew they had to put as much distance between themselves and the raid as possible.

"Keep close to me!" Mike said. Finally the lights and the sounds of shouting and crashing doors faded behind them, replaced by the stumbling of their own feet on the frosty earth. Eventually they stopped on the banks of a meandering stream that crossed their path. They both doubled-over in an effort to catch their breath. With his hands on his knees Benitez looked over at Mike.

"Who are you?" Benitez asked. They were the first words he had spoken. His Spanish was unusual, with an accent that Mike could not place. Almost as if it were a second language, too.

"A friend," Mike said and he stood up and plunged into the stream. His feet sank into the icy water and mud up to his knees. He gasped in sheer pain, but he hauled one foot in front of the other, like wading through thick, half-frozen treacle. The splashing behind him told him that Benitez was following, and as they finally reached the other side, Mike saw the glow of neon and the distant roar of traffic through another stretch of trees on the other side of the stream. Five minutes later they stumbled out into the forecourt of a truck stop. He saw a 24-hour diner. It looked dingy and dire, yet it was the most welcoming thing Mike could imagine. Mike stared at it, at last confident they had escaped.

"Come on," he said. "Let me buy you breakfast."

———

MIKE HAD never seen someone eat so fast as he watched Benitez wolf down a huge stack of pancakes, eggs and bacon. The immigrant's coffee cup went untouched as he ate and, after a while, Mike pushed him his own plate of food too. He never felt hungry this early in the morning and the hurried run through the night left his innards gurgling with nerves, not desiring greasy food. Benitez accepted Mike's plate eagerly and scraped off the food onto his own.

When the man finished eating, Mike explained he worked for Senator Hodges. Instantly Benitez froze. He glanced left to right, and back again, as if considering making a run for it.

"*Tranquillo*," Mike said. "You are not in trouble. But at the motel, the Havana in Des Moines, you cleaned the room of the woman who tried to shoot him. You know that right? That's why you left?"

Benitez bent forward and lowered his voice. "I knew she was evil. The moment I heard her speaking our language. I knew it from the look of her. She has the bad spirit in her."

Mike was puzzled.

"She was speaking Spanish?"

Benitez shook his head. Then he lifted his chin a little higher and seemed to grow in stature.

"No. Not Spanish. I am Mayan," he said. "From Guatemala. She is too. When I came into her room, she was praying on the floor, saying a prayer I remember from childhood, and she was speaking in my language, Kaqchikel."

Mayans? Mike was stunned. He knew next to nothing about them, apart from half-remembered history lessons and the images of lost cities in a jungle. Then suddenly Benitez spoke again and this time the words coming out of his mouth were like nothing Mike had ever heard before. They were low and guttural and transported them to a different world, far away from their surroundings in the Kansas diner.

"*Tek riyix niben orar*
tibana'jun oracion achi'el re'"

"What?" Mike said.

Benitez laughed.

"How do you call it? The Lord's Prayer, I think," he said. "That was what she prayed. She asked for help and guidance. I thought I was dreaming when I heard her. But she finished her prayer as I watched. She was on her knees and I saw it in her face. She had dead eyes. Empty. I have seen that look before, from people who fought or suffered too much in the war."

"Did you talk to her?"

Benitez shook his head. "I left her to her prayer. I never wanted to see her again. But then the next day I see what happened with your Senator. I see a picture of her. I ran for it."

Benitez looked at Mike with pleading in his eyes.

"You have to understand. My coming here is my family's last chance. I am illegal. I cannot afford to get in trouble. I cannot talk to police. I just want to work and earn some money to send home. Then maybe my cousins, maybe one day my own children, will go to school. That's all I want."

He paused again.

"These are not my problems."

He looked down at his empty plate and then stood up. "Thank you for the breakfast. But that is all I know. I have to get to work."

"What about *la migra*? The raid?'

Benitez shrugged.

"They will have gone by now. They only raid the trailer parks, never the factories. If I go to work I am safe. It is just a game show that you play in this country. Like those ones you have on TV. Today I survived to play another round. So I go to the factory. Goodbye, Mike."

With that he left and trudged out of the truck stop and headed for the freeway, looking to hitch a ride into town, his shoulders hunched, his head tucked into his chest against the cold wind, revealing nothing of the man inside.

CHAPTER 7

THE PLANE FROM Kansas City to New Hampshire flew right over Iowa. Mike looked down at the flat checkerboard landscape of fields and towns. It was hard to believe the intensity of the campaign down there could be switched off in an instant. It was a brutal process. But the moment after the last caucus vote was tallied, the various campaigns across Iowa calculated their chances and made their choice. Most folded. A few struggled on. Hodges and Stanton both declared victory and headed straight to New Hampshire. Not an extra hour was spent in Iowa. The state served its purpose and was now cast aside. Hodges and his top staffers touched down in New England before the clocks struck midnight.

"It's the best flight in the world. The one that leaves Des Moines on caucus night," Dee told him as he reported his findings in Kansas to her. "There are only two real tickets out of Iowa; first class and coach. Hodges is in coach at the moment and Stanton's still flying in style. But we've got our mind set on an upgrade."

Now Mike joined them.

The plane touched down in Manchester airport and he looked out over a landscape covered in ivory white snow. It lay in drifts up to four feet deep, with the runway carved out as a black scar, safe for the plane to land on. Different state, different territory, but the same awful, freezing cold. The same headlines too. Stanton may have won in Iowa, but Hodges' breakthrough was the main news. In the space of a few short weeks his campaign propelled him from nowhere to right on Stanton's heels. Columnist after columnist praised Hodges as a new sort of politician and smacked their lips at the coming battle against Stanton, the ultimate machine politician in the party. The official field of candidates still in the race stood at five. But everyone knew it was down to just two. Hodges versus Stanton. The Revolutionary versus the Old Guard. Mike drank in every word he read.

A beep on his phone indicated a message and he held the device to his ear as he trooped through Manchester Airport, looking for the campaign volunteer Dee said would be picking him up. But his purposeful march was dulled by the tinny voicemail and he slowed to a halt. It was a message from Sean.

"Hi Mike," Sean said. "I guess you're busy, but I thought I'd let you know about Jaynie. I went around to her old place and she's not living there anymore. Apparently she's up in some trailer in the Heights."

There was a pause, as Sean gathered his spirits to say more.

"It don't look good, Mike. People who've seen her think she's pretty messed up. Maybe you can get some time to come home for a spell? I know she's not your wife anymore, but it might do her some good to see you."

Mike could not listen. He stood there and his mind raced with a mix of guilt and pain. He felt Jaynie's hands reaching out to him, half in supplication, half trying to drag him down. Then he jumped as a hand tugged at his sleeve. It was a young man, wearing a Hodges campaign T-shirt.

"Mr. Sweeney, sir?" he said in a way that made Mike suddenly feel old. "I'm your ride up to Berlin. Are you all right?"

Mike smiled and pulled himself together.

"Come on, let's get going."

MIKE WAS eager to hit the ground running. This was new territory. Iowa was behind them and the battle of New Hampshire lay ahead. The car sped north out of Manchester and headed for the city of Berlin in the upper reaches of the state. It was an old logging town fallen on hard times; very different from the richer suburbs in the south of the state. That made it the perfect place for Hodges to kick off his campaign. He spoke for the voiceless and the ignored. He took the road less traveled. The student chattered excitedly as he drove and the icy, mountainous, forested landscape slipped by.

"Hardly any candidate ever comes up to Berlin," he was saying. "I can't believe the Senator is going to spend time up there. It's amazing."

Mike allowed the student to talk on and grunted every so often to keep him going. Outside he watched as the countryside slipped by. It was so different from Iowa's vast horizons and broad fields and tiny towns. Here the landscape was more crowded, dominated by thick, dark forests out of which reared mountains. The tidy New England towns they sped through seemed packed together tightly. It was more cramped, more intense and everywhere there were election placards. New Hampshire craved for Iowa to get out of the way. It wanted its turn in the limelight.

The drive lasted three hours and eventually they cruised into downtown Berlin, nestled in a wooded valley with a fast flowing river carving through the heart of it. The hulks of shuttered sawmills loomed over the city and reminded Mike of the landscapes where he grew up. The sun set but even in the twilight it was immediately obvious where Hodges' rally was being held. Crowds of people trudged through the streets towards the town hall. They parked the car and walked along with the crowd. Mike enjoyed feeling part of the throng of people; he was just one person being carried along. The cold air melted away in the face of the human warmth of the gathering, but it was a relief all the same to finally get inside the town hall.

Mike immediately saw the familiar faces of the staffers from Iowa who made the jump to New Hampshire. The same media too, now permanently trailing Hodges from event to event. Lauren was among them as she set up her computer at a crowded desk at the back of the room. She saw Mike and waved. He nodded in return and wondered if she noticed his election night absence – and whether she linked it to his investigating the shooter. But her smile seemed nothing but genuine and it felt good to be on the receiving end of it.

The crowd suddenly roared as Hodges entered the room and Mike felt the familiar rush of energy and anticipation. The candidate walked on stage like a man who knew he could win the state, exuding confidence. But his speech was humble and human. Each person in the room felt he asked them alone for his or her help, as he persuaded each individual that he or she really could make a difference. He took questions too, long into the night, for more than an hour and a half, as nervous aides twitched and fidgeted in the background. But Hodges never once looked at them. His focus was on the crowd, listening and debating, absorbing their concerns. At one point an old man, a logger long ago laid off who struggled against illness, stood up and spoke about a lifetime of poverty and a fight to get by that got worse with age, not better.

"I can't afford any more hope," he said at last with grim humor. "My heart can't take it."

There were a few laughs in the crowd but Hodges quieted them and walked to where the old man stood. He put the microphone down and grasped the man by the shoulder, clasping him in a hug, and whispered in his ear. Most could not hear what Hodges said. It was not a moment designed for the cameras. But the image of the two men was picked up and played back on TV. It was not a piece of political theatre. It was genuine. But what Mike saw Hodges' mouthing to the old man was a simple vow.

"I won't let you down," Hodges had said, and the old man started to weep.

———————

THE SMOKY little dive bar in Berlin looked exactly like the sort of place where a fight could break out at any moment. As such, Dee was perfectly at home. It was dark and a few groups of drinkers hung back in the corners while a couple of solitary men perched at the bar, nursing bottles of beer and chasers. That was Dee's drink of choice too as she chalked up another win at the pool table and sent a confused local back to the bar for another drink to comfort him in his latest loss.

"Come on, you rack them up this time, Mike," Dee said. "Local boys here can't shoot pool for shit."

Dee did not mind that her voice, with its Southern inflection, carried into the furthest depths of the bar. But, Mike guessed, the crowd in the bar had probably never seen anyone quite like Dee. This mannish-looking stocky middle-aged woman in blue jeans with a loud mouth and an even louder attitude. The bar crowd were the sort of guys who preferred to steer clear of such new and unusual things. Mike set up the balls.

"She's Guatemalan, huh? Mayan?" Dee said, whistling through her teeth. "You know, I have seen a lot of strange things in this business. Thirty years or more of strange things, truth be told. But this is up there with the weirdest of them. What do you think it means?"

Mike shrugged.

"You know Hodges' biography just like I do. We've always focused on his military career in the Gulf, in Iraq and then in Afghanistan. We never paid much attention to the things that happened in the 1980s. I mean he was all over Central America for some of that time, including Guatemala. He was a trainer at the School for the Americas, but it was all just routine stuff. He ran a few courses, he helped train a few colonels. I always thought it was a kind of a dull story."

Dee broke the triangle of pool balls with a mighty crack from her cue. Two of the balls sailed into the pockets and she swiftly lined up a third.

"Shit, I don't even know if he speaks Spanish."

She missed the shot and then paused for a moment.

"Though it would be useful. If he's fluent in Spanish that's going to be a big vote winner with the Hispanics in California and Texas."

"Are you really thinking that far ahead?"

Dee nodded.

"Hell, yes," she said. Her voice was firm, angry even at the suggestion. "This is no game, Mike. Look around you. Look at this sorry ass bar; look at this sorry ass town. Christ, look at this sorry ass goddamn country. Hodges can change that."

She softened slightly and put up her pool cue.

"Look, I don't mean to be hard. But I know the kind of

people in this town. They are good people. Hard-working folks who just haven't caught a break in a long time. I grew up in a town like this, except with hurricanes, not snow. We didn't have enough jobs to go around and life was just one long attempt to make do."

She took a deep breath.

"I'm sick of seeing people just get by, Mike. Believe it or not, these folks here are my people and I know Hodges will be good for them. He makes folks believe in him and then they believe in themselves. We harness that and we've got another Teddy Roosevelt on our hands. Or another FDR."

Mike missed a shot and Dee bent over to take her turn, effortlessly putting her ball in a pocket.

"Maybe it's a coincidence." Mike said. "Maybe it's nothing to do with his time in Central America. Perhaps the cops are right. The shooter is just crazy."

But even as he said the words he did not believe them. He remembered the look the woman gave him in their last meeting in prison. When he said Hodges owed his success to her. She looked angry, hateful, full of spite. But not insane.

"Nope. I don't buy it," Dee said. "I don't like coincidences. I don't believe in them. We got to keep digging. The stakes are getting higher every day."

And with that she cleared the rest of the table.

THE KNOCK on the door of Mike's hotel room woke him. He glanced at the glowing alarm clock on the bedside table; it read 1:43 a.m. He turned over, wondering if he dreamed the sound, when it came again. *Tap, tap.* Then a low whisper, seeping through the wood, coiled into his memory like a snake.

"Mike, Mike, Mike..."

Jaynie?

It couldn't be. Mike bolted upright. Then he stumbled over to the door and switched on the light. He kept the chain on, but opened the door a crack, and peered into the corridor.

She stood there, thin and forlorn, her brown hair, still parted in the middle as he remembered it and falling over her face. His Jaynie. But she was changed so much he drew an intake of breath. Her face was gaunt and lined, her cheeks shadowed by hollows. She looked ten years older than when he last saw her – when she hurled pots and pans and screamed at him to leave her alone. That Jaynie, at least, was full of fire and life. But the figure before him did not look like she could lift a plate, let alone throw it.

"What are you doing here?" he asked.

She smiled at his voice, her eyes lit up and her dimples, that he once loved so dearly, flowered at the corners of her mouth. For a moment, he saw his old lover there, standing in the shell of who she used to be.

"Mike!" she said. "Let me in. It's freezing out here."

She shifted her weight from foot to foot and held herself

with her arms. But Mike knew she wasn't cold. The hotel corridor was every bit as warm as his room. She was tweaking. She was high.

What else could he do? He opened the door anyway. She hugged him and he felt her twig-like arms grab him around his waist. She held him tight; her fingers dug into his back and triggered memories that flew into his mind. Of endless nights together. Of happy times. He wriggled out of her grasp and beckoned her to sit down. She perched on the bed and Mike sat in a chair. A brief frown, intended to be flirtatious, creased her brow and she patted the bed beside her. Mike shook his head.

"How did you find me?" he asked.

"Sean came around," she said. "He said you were working with the Hodges campaign and then I read in the paper that he was speaking here. So I just got in my car and drove. It's only a few hours and there aren't many hotels in this town. I knew you'd be in one of them."

She was always someone who went anywhere on a whim. Long before the drugs took hold, when they were just teenage lovers, she often took him off on wild goose chases, sudden hunting trips in the woods, or on inflated inner tubes down a river. She was a beautiful, carefree soul, who dragged him onto life's dance floor, always whirling and twirling, yet never seeming to get anywhere.

"It's good to see you, Mike. You look great," she said.

"You too," he lied. She knew it too. A tremor of her lower lip showed it for just a moment, like a cloud flitting across the sun, and then she continued with breezy cheerfulness.

"I can't believe you're doing this, Mike. Working on a presidential campaign! For a guy like Hodges too. What's he like?"

But Mike was in no mood to chat.

"Jaynie, it's the middle of the night. Why are you here?"

She looked at him and the light slowly faded out of her eyes. The cheerfulness evaporated. Her shoulders sagged and her head fell down.

"I just wanted to see you, Mike," she whispered.

Mike closed his eyes and felt his heart swell. He could not equate the girl he fell in love with and the woman he married, with this broken spirit. He went over to her and held her close. She rested her head on his chest and he stroked her back, kissing the crown of her head. Just once. Just like he had always done. His touch seemed to calm her. Whatever drug she was on, she was at the end of her high. The toxins left her system and she drifted off into sleep. When her breathing steadied and he knew she would not wake, Mike lifted her gently onto the bed and pulled the covers over her. Then he went back to the chair, used his jacket as a blanket, and tried to sleep himself.

———

GENERAL CARILLO sat on his patio and faced the ocean at sunset. The police chief, Zaragosa, was with him again. But this time Carillo felt no resentment about the presence of the drunken buffoon. It was sad, perhaps, but Zaragosa was as close as he got to a friend in these parts. Not just a friend either. A former comrade-in-arms, who respected him, who loved him and understood his fight for his country. So it was good that Zaragosa should share in this moment of celebration and longed-for reward. This time Carillo happily broke out the good Chilean wine and also a box of fine Cuban cigars. Puzzled but grateful, it was only after Zaragosa was on his second glass and smoking one of Carillo's fine El Rey Del Mundos that the policeman asked what they were celebrating.

"My reward!" Carillo proclaimed and raised a toast to the sun setting behind the hills behind them.

Zaragosa was puzzled but reluctant to press on.

"Let us just say, I have benefited from recent events and at last the true value of my sacrifices is being recognized. Livingston may be my home still, but I can afford to live a little more in the style of my forefathers."

Zaragosa smiled, his lips parting to reveal teeth now stained with wine too. He did not know what the General was talking about, but the old man appeared pleased. That could only be good for him and he tentatively reached out to fill his glass again. Carillo did not stop him and so Zaragosa greedily splashed the liquid into his cup.

"We both have been soldiers. We both have sacrificed much, my friend. Now God is smiling upon me at last for my struggles," Carillo said.

Perhaps it was the speed with which he drank the wine, or the sudden gloom as the sun finally dipped over the horizon, but Zaragosa felt a tug of melancholy pull at him. Emboldened by Carillo's hospitality, he got up and walked to the side of the patio and looked out over the restless sea, growing darker by the moment.

"Do you believe in God, General?" Zaragosa asked.

The General snorted in surprise. "What a question!" he cried. "The church is the mother of our souls. It grants us salvation. Of course, I believe in God. Sweet Jesus, don't tell me you have become like *los Indios* or the Garifunas. Are you a heathen, Zaragosa? Every week I go to mass. I do not see you there."

Zaragosa felt stung by the words.

"And then you must go to confession too?" Zaragosa asked.

As soon as he said it, Zaragosa knew it was a mistake. But the words were already out there, hanging in the thick tropical air that suddenly started to have a chill. The General stubbed out his cigar. He stared at Zaragosa and his nostrils flared. Then he sighed. This was a happy night; he would not let the drunken ramblings of an idiot anger him.

"For what reason should I go to confession?" he asked. "I have done nothing that needs confessing."

Inwardly Zaragosa breathed a sigh of relief and a silence fell between the two men. Carillo tried to regain his calm, drinking a deep draught from his wine cup. Do I believe in God? he thought. What a question indeed! But then, to his own surprise, he realized that perhaps he did have his doubts. Maybe he did not truly know anymore. He looked up into the skies and hoped to see a spray of stars, but the clouds glowered thick and dark above. Perhaps heaven was indeed far from guaranteed, he thought. Perhaps that was why he chose to take his rewards here on earth.

CHAPTER 8

LAUREN THOUGHT SHE was dreaming. The sound of rustling slipped into her mind, mingling with visions of a wind brushing through trees and hews of gold and red autumnal leaves playing against her subconscious. But, with surprise, she realized her eyes were now open, adjusting to the blackness of her Berlin, New Hampshire, hotel room, and the rustling sound was real.

She sat up in bed and the sound stopped. It came from her door and her eye suddenly caught a shadow move across the thin plank of yellow light that shone under the doorframe. She rubbed her eyes.

"Hello?" she called quietly to the darkness. Then she felt foolish and laughed nervously. She reached over to fumble for the bedside lamp, which stood by a radio alarm that glowed with the time. 4:34 a.m. She switched on the light and looked back to the door. A sheaf of paper had been pushed under it. It was yellow and folded in on itself. For a moment, she thought it was just the hotel bill, shoved there by a maid. But there was something about the paper that did not look like a bill. She padded across the room to pick it up. She unfolded it and immediately frowned. It was a bank statement of some kind: a photocopy of a Western Union money transfer order.

"What the hell?" she said, assuming it was pushed under the wrong door.

She examined it and walked back to her bed and pulled the covers around herself. She put on her glasses and peered at the rows of figures. She looked at the depositing account and read the words "Banco Nacional de Gautemala." She frowned and looked at the branch location. Livingston, Guatemala. For 9,995 dollars. In the name of Rodrigo Estrada Carillo. It made no sense. She scanned the figures again, looking for an indication about who sent it. Then she saw a name and she dropped the paper onto the bed with a little yelp.

Christine Maitland. Or, as Lauren knew her better, with the addition of a married name: Christine Maitland Hodges. Lauren stared at the paper again, making sure she was correct and that she was indeed holding a bank transfer agreement wiring almost 10,000 dollars to Guatemala from the account of Senator Hodges' wife.

She jumped off the bed and flung open the door, realizing too late, how ridiculous it would be if someone was still there. Nevertheless she looked down the empty corridor and half-expected to see a figure, her mind racing with a mix of fear and excitement. But it was silent and empty. Nothing but the dull, aching, dead artificial light of an anonymous hotel. Just another slice of life on the road. But a road now changed beyond recognition.

———

MIKE JUMPED at the sound of the ringing phone and stumbled through the darkness of the room to answer it. He worried that Jaynie, lying on his bed, would awaken. But she did not even stir. Whatever substance she abused left her in a vice-like sleep. He picked up his mobile. He glanced at his watch and his eyes widened at the time.

"Hello?" he whispered.

It was Lauren. She spoke in a lightning quick babble that he couldn't understand.

"Slow down," he said.

He heard her take a deep breath and when she spoke again her voice was loud, calm and clear.

"Mike," she said. "I've got a document that you should know about. It's related to Christine Hodges. It's a money order showing she has been sending money overseas. I think someone's trying to play dirty tricks on you guys and I want to talk to you before I go public with it."

Mike was awake now. Any trace of sleep was blasted out of his system by an adrenalin surge that coursed through his body at the mention of Christine's name. He needed to stay calm though.

"Okay," he said. "Let's meet downstairs. Ten minutes?"

"See you there."

Mike hung up. Dirty tricks? If someone slipped Lauren information, he was sure it came from Stanton's campaign. He pulled on some clothes, treading carefully so as not to make any noise that might wake Jaynie. But his mind raced as fast as his heart. He knew these things happened. Christ, he'd been the victim of endless plots and stunts in Florida. But this was national politics. This was a *presidential* campaign. The stakes were higher. Had they really rattled Stanton so much that they were trying such things now?

Mike headed for the door and glanced back at Jaynie. She was curled in a fetal position, her eyes closed, mouth half-open. He wondered how many times he shared a bed with her and looked across at her face. He gazed at her closed lids, watched the twitching movements of her eyeballs, hinting at unknown dreams within. He tucked the blankets around her to make sure she stayed warm. A sadness welled up in him and for a moment his throat felt dry. I've lost her, he thought. Years ago. Long before our divorce. Yet there she was, like a ghost in his bed, sleeping as peacefully as he had ever seen her. He watched the rise and fall of her chest as she breathed. He leaned over, kissed the top of her head softly, and got up to leave. He had work to do.

LAUREN WAITED for him in the lobby. She sat in the empty breakfast area across from a deserted reception desk.

"I think the reception guy is playing computer games in the

back," she said with a laugh. "So we have this place to ourselves."

Mike settled down opposite her. She looked calm and, he could not help notice, beautiful without her makeup. There was a flashy determination in her eyes that was at odds with the confusion and panic in her voice when she first called him. Clearly she had gathered her wits. Just as he had. This would not be a conversation. This would be a chess match. Two opponents, each wary of the other's intentions, yet each needing information from the other. Lauren smiled sweetly and pushed a paper across the table between them. He picked it up and scanned the figures and words.

Guatemala.

Shit.

His nerve-endings screamed like a tripped alarm. With an iron will, Mike kept his eyes trained on the page. He could not give away anything. He kept staring, moving his eyes rapidly up and down the sheet of paper. Lauren knew nothing about the shooter being Guatemalan, he thought. She couldn't. He was ahead of her. He looked up and shrugged.

"I don't understand what this is," he said.

Lauren looked at him.

"Christine Hodges has been wiring money to someone in Guatemala. Someone thinks that's interesting enough to slip this under my door at night. Someone wants this information out there," she said.

Mike felt a hint of relief. She was new to this game. She had nothing yet. She fired her shot too early. Mike would try to play dumb, even as he took in the implications of her words:

some bastard literally pushed this stuff under Lauren's door. And perhaps other doors too, hoping someone would have the balls to just put it out there and see where it went.

"So?" Mike said, trying not to sound abrupt. "They spent time there in the 80s, or maybe even the early 90s. I can't quite remember. It's probably some charity donation or something."

He looked at her face to see how she reacted. He watched her watching him for his own expression. Mike had a brief mental flash of poker games back in Corinth Falls, bluffing with Sean and his friends, laughing and joking as Jaynie took all their money. She was always best at convincing everyone she was on a bluff while she sat with aces in her hand. He sensed Lauren was like that too. He desperately wanted to ask if she planned to write something. But he knew to do so would only arouse suspicion. His only chance was to feign indifference.

"Someone on the other side thinks it's important," Lauren said.

"Maybe. But it's not enough to get me out of bed," Mike joked.

Lauren smiled an apology.

"It's just Stanton's people playing with our minds," Mike said. "I can understand why it might freak you out when someone creeps around a hotel like that. But I'll check it out and get back to you. Can you get me a copy of it, so I can run it by our people?" he asked.

Lauren nodded. "It's the least I can do for disturbing your beauty sleep," she said and jokingly added with a flirtatious smile: "I'll slip it under your door."

"You know this does show one thing," Mike said.

"What?"

"Stanton's campaign is scared. We must have put the fear of God into them in Iowa."

Lauren smiled. "I guess this is where the fight starts for real then," she said.

Mike walked back through the lobby, knowing she watched him from her seat. He did not turn around. He wanted to give away nothing. He yawned and stretched his arms, wanting to signal tired boredom. But as soon as he was out of sight he ran back to his room. He needed to get hold of Dee. He fumbled with his door key, his hands now in a cold sweat as he burst into his own room.

It was empty. Jaynie was gone. The blankets were rumpled on the unmade bed. He stood still for a moment, wondering how she got out of the hotel without going through the lobby. Wondering why she suddenly left. Then it hit him; an old familiar feeling of being conned. He saw his wallet open and empty on the bedside table. A handful of dollar bills that were inside it last night were gone. He noticed a note scrawled on hotel paper beside the wallet.

"I'll pay you back!! Love J." it read. She even scrawled a smiley face after her initial.

Fuck! Mike thought. The sun was not yet up and already two women tried to play him for a fool. He only hoped both of them did not succeed.

THERE WAS no disguising the look on Dee's face as Mike sat opposite her in her hotel room: stone cold fury. Her firm jaw, already broad and square, jutted out of her face and she rubbed her chin with her hand. Her eyes were wide and saucer-like, burning with anger. But she said nothing as Mike detailed what Lauren told him. Then he passed over the photocopy of the money transfer. She briefly glanced at it, just to confirm what Mike had said. Then she sat back in her chair. Mike studied Dee's face for any hint of her thoughts, striving to see the gears turning in her mind, knowing she'd make swift calculations as to what was going on and what she could do.

"You told her it could be a gift, right?" she asked.

Mike nodded. She smiled thinly.

"That was quick thinking, Mike. Real good. You're a natural at this."

Mike nodded at the praise but could not help wondering what she meant by "this." Telling a swift lie? Spinning a story that would buy some time?

"Fuck!" Dee suddenly spat, the cracks starting to show in her stern face.

"God, I hope this is not a sex scandal. We can't survive a John Edwards. There's nothing worse than that. It's a campaign-killer. The American public will take pretty much everything else but they have a Puritan streak a mile wide. If you screw someone who ain't your spouse, you're dead in the water."

Mike was taken aback. He felt suddenly naïve. He had not thought of that.

"You think Hodges might…" he said, but Dee cut him off with an ugly, sharp laugh and a comically raised eyebrow.

"He wouldn't exactly be the first to stray from the marital bed now would he, Mike?" she said. "I mean, as far as I can tell, he keeps his dick in his pants. But this is some strange shit here and in my experience when something's weird it's usually headed to the goddamn bedroom."

Dee shook her head and walked to the window. She looked out over the snowy white streetscape of Berlin. It was still early and barely a soul was moving outside in the half-gray morning light.

"What is it with you men? You can't trust a single one of you not to follow your cock into the strangest damn places. Ya'll ain't got the discipline that we women have. I mean we have the same desires. Believe me, I've been tempted by enough skirt in my time. But, by Christ, I've got my priorities straight. I know what's important."

Mike opened his mouth to protest, but thought better of it.

"It's especially true with big dogs like our Jack. I mean just look at Bill Clinton. That fool had the world at his fingertips and he let it all slide for a blow job from the office intern."

Mike did not know what to say. Dee turned around and looked at him. She sounded more puzzled than angry.

"But I tell you one thing, if this is somehow linked to a woman then I'm amazed Christine hasn't cut his pecker off.

She may look like she's just a country club blonde but that one's made of steel underneath those nice clothes. There's some cold, hard metal tottering around on those stilettos."

Mike was surprised. He did not think of Christine like that. She appeared such a typical candidate's wife. Perfect for any occasion, an asset in front of the TV cameras and also in private at any number of fund-raising dinners. Politically, the only disadvantage to their marriage was she and Hodges were not able to have children; denying them the picture-perfect image of the All American nuclear family. But Christine more than made up for it. She created a virtue of the issue by becoming a sympathetic and powerful spokesperson for childless couples and infertility clinics.

"But she sent the money, not Hodges," Mike said.

"Yeah," said Dee. "That's what gives me hope. I guess the truth is we don't know what this means. My guess is Stanton's people don't either. They just want to put the information out there and see where it goes. But I don't like the coincidences here. Our friend in jail is from Guatemala. Now it seems our candidate is sending money down there for God knows what reason."

Dee sat down again.

"We have to run a deeper game on our own man. I want you to get yourself back to Iowa. Keep digging on our shooter. Then follow up this lead. Go to this place in Guatemala on the money transfer… what the fuck is it called…? Livingston? Find this guy Carillo who collected the cash."

Mike knew this was coming. But still it felt like a shock. He was going to dig up dirt on Hodges himself. Investigate his own candidate. For the good of the campaign.

"You okay with this, Mike?"

Mike nodded. Dee came up to him and rested her hand on his shoulder.

"Jack can't know anything about it, Mike. We need to find out the truth if we are to protect him. Maybe even protect him from himself."

She held his gaze.

"You trust me, Mike, right?"

He looked back at her.

"I trust you," he whispered.

———————

DEE WATCHED from the back of the hall as Hodges walked into the high school gymnasium. It was the last stop in Berlin before they drove south for a lightning set of meetings in the rest of New Hampshire. There was not going to be time here for much of a speech, just a few words and a wave at the mob of school kids herded obediently into the room. Hodges walked a line of teachers and shook each by the hand as the crowd of children applauded and cheered. The youngsters actually looked interested, she thought, which was rare. Still, there was one sure thing that kids these days were impressed by: celebrity. Hodges was definitely that now.

She watched him carefully. She traced the lines of his face

and read his lips as he spoke with each person he met. Her mind still rang from this morning's bombshell. Perhaps if she peered hard enough she could read Hodges' mind, discover if any dark secrets lurked there. But, of course, there was nothing. Just Hodges flashing his winning grin, seducing people with his glow, giving them hope and making them believe in him. Dee folded her hands across her chest. A surge of anger stirred deep in her breast. Images of her childhood rose up; her family, mired in poverty struggling in Louisiana. She could almost hear her grandfather's native Cajun French whispered in her ear, swearing at the injustices of a forgotten world in the language of the bayou.

"Don't you let me down, *feet pue tan*," she thought. "Don't you ever let me down."

IOWA WAS different to Mike now. As he pulled up at the familiar gates of the jail he felt like someone left behind after the party ended. The streets were still lined with placards and posters. The gardens, covered in snow, still had yard signs poking out of the drifts. But many of them were for campaigns that had now collapsed. The lights were on, the glasses swept away, the floors mopped. The party was over and moved on to New Hampshire. Iowa was a state with a political hangover.

Mike even felt his own senses dull from being back here. He felt a throbbing ache pound at the back of his head that did not dissipate as he walked into the harsh light of the jail and smiled at the guard assigned to meet him. Mike was amazed at how easy it was. They could dodge normal procedure simply because the governor liked Hodges and Dee had the governor's private number on speed dial. But that was the way the world worked and Mike knew he must take full advantage of it. As a guard led Mike through the jail to the interview room he quizzed his companion. Prison gossip was hardly a reliable source of information but it had already paid major dividends.

"You guys got anything new on this woman? A name even?" Mike asked.

The guard shrugged his shoulders.

"We've been running checks on all the mental health institutions from here to Maine, seeing if any of them have a psycho missing. We've got nothing. No matches at all," he said.

"She spoken a word yet?"

The guard laughed. "Nope. She's a Grade A nutjob. They're the ones no one can legislate for," he said. "I just thank God she missed your Senator. Didn't get anyone killed."

"Well," Mike said. "I thought we'd give it one last try and see if we can get something out of her. She might prefer to talk to a civilian and not a cop or a guard."

The man held open the door to the interrogation room and ushered Mike in. The shooter was already there, her jumpsuit a flash of color in the bright, white room. The guard carried on talking about her as if she was not present.

"Maybe," the guard said. "But I doubt it. It's time to just shut the door and throw away the key on this one. She's not going to see the light of day again for a long, long time."

Mike didn't respond, but sat down and waited to hear the door clang shut behind him. Silence now filled the room. There was not a flicker of recognition as he looked at her. He waited for a few moments and gathered his thoughts. He came here with a speech planned, a monologue to tease something out of her, prompt her to react again like last time, with a terrifying flash of temper. But, facing her, it faded from his mind, sucked out of him as she ate up all the energy from the room. He sighed and closed his eyes. What did he have? Just one fact. Just one thing he knew that no one else did. No one apart from an immigrant meat plant worker in the frozen wilds of west Kansas.

"You are from Guatemala," he said. "You are a Mayan. You speak Kaqchikel."

She looked at him now. Mike felt the hairs on his arms stand up as she lifted her head and stared. It was like the temperature of the room plummeted to below freezing and he stifled a shiver that trembled down his spine. He forced out more words, half-expecting to see his breath freeze.

"Before you tried to kill the Senator you prayed. You said the Lord's prayer in your native language."

Her eyes were suddenly alive. Her mouth opened slightly and she seemed human, shrinking in front of Mike's eyes, her tanned skin warming. She hesitated and Mike nodded. His gaze never left hers and pleaded with her to break the silence. It seemed like a benediction and she opened her mouth.

"I meant to leave no sign," she said in slow but fluent English.

He had wondered what her voice would sound like. Imagined it as hard and full of menace. But it was soft and whispering, edged only by a harshness from using muscles that were silent for so long.

"Who are you?" Mike asked.

She shook her head. "I am an Angel of vengeance," she said.

Mike felt a pang of fear strike him and remembered the violence he glimpsed behind those eyes on his last visit. The words of the guard echoed back to him. Perhaps she was insane.

"Why did you try to kill Senator Hodges?" he asked.

"In my bible there is a description of this man. It says: "Be vigilant; because your adversary the devil, as a roaring lion, walks about, seeking whom he may devour.""

"You believe the Senator is the Devil?" Mike asked.

She laughed, a ragged sound. "After a lifetime of sin, I decided to finally obey my God," she said.

She reached out a hand, slowly, wrapping her fingers gently around Mike's wrist. Her touch was warm, but firm.

"You know nothing, *Americano*," she said.

Mike knew she would not speak again. He looked at her and it was like she had faded out of the room, appearing and disappearing in front of him. He stayed there for ten minutes more, looking at her, following her eyes as they wandered around the room, wondering at what she saw. He was certain it was not the same four walls that he did. Her mind doubtless gazed beyond the jail back down whatever unimaginable path brought her here. Eventually Mike got up and walked out, turning his back on her. The guard outside looked up from reading his newspaper.

"She say anything?" the guard asked.

"Not a word."

The casual lie barely left his mouth when he felt he heard Dee's voice in his ear, whispering her praise at his talent for deception. "You're good at this, Mike," she had said.

CHAPTER 9

DEE WALKED INTO McCordy's bistro still wearing her thick woolen scarf and hat that fought off the cold of the Manchester night outside. Yet the warm blast of air inside the restaurant made her wrap the clothes more tightly around her as she concealed her face. She nodded at a waiter.

"Reservation for Jones. Party of two," she said.

She followed the man through a bustle of tables thankfully devoid of any familiar faces. She did not want to be seen in this place, not with the man she was about to meet. It might set too many gossipy tongues wagging. But her dining companion insisted on this restaurant, smack in the middle of downtown, serving up its pricey steaks and blowing the cash gifted to them by donors with little idea it ended up being spent on such expensive meat. Still, at least he booked a private booth, hidden from prying eyes. The waiter pulled back a dark red curtain to a backroom and she saw that he was already waiting for her.

Howard Carver. Harriet Stanton's campaign manager.

"Good evening, Howie," Dee said. She could not resist using the pet name she knew he hated.

"Good to see you, Dee," Carver replied, though Dee fancied she caught a slight wince as he said the words. The thought thrilled her.

Carver was everything Dee was not. He was a patrician from the old school, part of a clique that dominated the party for two decades. He was born rich, the son of a congressman. Dee suspected, rightly, he never knew anyone like her until she forced herself into his world. It was not just her sex, or even her sexuality. It was that she was born with nothing. Everything she possessed, she had taken. Everything Carver had, he was given.

Yet each presidential campaign of the last six election cycles featured Carver prominently and win-or-lose he always came back into play. He was immune to the impact of actual results. He was the epitome of the establishment, exerting firm control over Stanton's staffing. Dee suspected – no she *knew* – he played a role in keeping her out of the upper echelons of Stanton's staff. The fact that she now headed Hodges' operation now must wound him deeply. Dee hoped so. She hated men like him. He was all machine with no fire in his belly for the actual voters. For him politics played out in smoky back rooms of restaurants like this. It was not on the streets or in the town halls. She sat down opposite him and ordered whisky and a burger. Carver, of course, had the steak. Rare.

"You must be scared shitless to want to see me, Howie," Dee said, relaxing back into her chair.

Carver smiled thinly, his jowly face sagging beneath a thinning shock of gray hair.

"Not at all, Dee. Our numbers are sound. We're going to win New Hampshire. Then we'll be two out of two."

Dee smiled. "Then why are you sticking notes under folks' hotel doors? That's a low move, *cocotte*," Dee hissed suddenly and then, struggling, she recovered herself. "Pardon my French. You can take a Cajun girl out of the bayou but not the bayou out of the Cajun girl."

Carver shrugged. "I don't know what you mean, Dee. We've done nothing like that," he said.

Dee looked at him. Nothing disturbed his cool demeanor. Not even his bold lie. "Really?" she snapped.

Carver looked away – just for a moment – as he sipped his drink and Dee caught the hint of a sly smile. That fucker, she fumed. Now she knew it. They were behind it. Carver didn't need to say a word more. She breathed deeply, keeping control. It was a useful reminder. Carver was dangerous and Dee ought to remember that. No need to poke a wasps' nest too hard just yet.

"Well, I'm mighty relieved to hear that," she said with thinly laced sarcasm. "Because whoever did circulate that little bank transfer paper is going to be sorely disappointed. It's nothing. A charity donation. Not very exciting to anyone. You're gonna have to do a hell of a lot better than that to knock us off course."

Their meals arrived and they stopped their jousting match

as the food was placed in front of them. Dee looked down and did not feel the slightest pang of hunger. But Carver immediately began slicing his steak.

"Just a shot across your bows, Dee. Just a little warning to keep things nice. It would be best for our future co-operation if things go cleanly here in New Hampshire."

Dee looked at Carver and the bloody red juice of the steak that dripped from one corner of his mouth. She hated this man. She hated him more than she hated the other party and the fool in the White House they both wanted to unseat. She was sick of sharing the same table with him. It was time to cut to the chase.

"Quit talking crap, Howie. You didn't invite me here for the pleasure of my company. What do you have to say?"

Carver stopped eating. He carefully put his knife and fork down on the white linen tablecloth and dabbed at his mouth with his napkin.

"Dee," he began quietly. "Governor Stanton is going to win New Hampshire. We know that. You know that. What I want to say is…" He stopped himself and rephrased it, smiling as he did so. "No, what *the governor* wants me to say is: when you lose here, you need to leave the race. Call it quits straight off. If you do that we'll make sure Hodges is a lock for the vice president's spot. The ticket will be Stanton and Hodges. In that order."

Dee looked at Carver. She said nothing and he frowned at her silence.

"Look," he said. "That's more than you could have dreamed of a month ago. Before some crazy bitch took a shot at your man."

That was enough for Dee. She saw it clearly. Carver was afraid. He was scared of Hodges and his campaign. His cozy world turned upside down. That meant Stanton was scared too. They read the same polling numbers Dee did and they saw the same thing: Hodges had a real chance. They could win New Hampshire. They really could. Dee felt a rush of pleasure. She picked up her burger and took a deliberate juicy bite and then spoke with her mouth full, holding the mess in one hand as she pointed at Carver. She was going to enjoy this.

"You know, Howie. That's a mighty fine offer ya'll are making. Perhaps a *couillonne* like me should feel pretty blessed for such attentions. But you know, Howie, I just ain't feeling it. I ain't feeling your love."

Dee looked at Carver's face and tried to read the mix of emotions struggling for control of his features. She felt sure no one had ever spoken to him like that before, especially not someone like her. It was a risk to anger him. But it was worth it. Her whole life she had worked to get a campaign in this position and now it was all or nothing time. Might as well enjoy it. Then, to her amazement, she started channeling Hodges. She could hear his voice in her head as she spoke. Christ, she thought, Hodges made a believer out of her.

"You see, Howie," she said. "We ain't about deals. We're about changing this country. We're about giving people back some hope. We're about actually making people's lives a little bit better, not just winning a goddamn race. If you ever got out of your little campaign bubble, you might see that. America is hurting, Howie, and we aim to fix that."

Suddenly she could not stand to be in the same room with Carver. She got up and threw down a wad of dollars on the table.

"We're going to fuck you boys up," she said.

Carver's cheeks flushed red.

"Let's keep this civil, Dee," he said. But Dee was rolling now.

"Fuck civil. Civil ended when you started pushing documents under hotel doors."

She turned and walked out the door. This time as she left through the restaurant she did not care who saw her. She had nothing to hide and when she hit the cold air outside she did not feel it. She felt warm, on fire almost, burning brightly from the light of making a stand.

"ALRIGHT, ALRIGHT! I'm coming," Mike snapped. The rapping on his door was so insistent he half-expected to see the hotel manager there. But it was Dee. He could tell something was different about her: a kind of frantic energy that radiated from her eyes as she barged past him. She looked like there was something inside her that she could not keep bottled up as she gestured for him to sit down.

She paced up and down a few times before she turned on her heel and casually tossed something small and plastic at him. He caught it deftly. It was a computer memory stick.

"Take this to your blogger friend, Lauren O'Keefe," she said with a grin. "It's time to give Stanton's team some pay-back from my little vault of secrets."

Mike looked at the tiny, white plastic in his hand.

"What?" he said.

Dee's grin grew wider. "That dumb son of a bitch Howard Carver started a war with his tricks. Well, now we fire back. For months, I've had teams of folks pouring over anything and everything related to Stanton – digging for anything we can use. I've got myself a nice little weapons depot now."

Mike put down the stick on his bedside table like it was a hot coal. But Dee ignored him and continued to talk.

"On that stick is a picture of Stanton when she was a student during the anti-war protests of 1974. She appears to be part of a group of people burning the American flag."

Dee let words hang in the air and then repeated herself. "Take this to your blogger friend."

Mike shook his head, suddenly realizing the scale of what she asked him to do.

"Hang on a minute," he said. "I don't want to be involved in something like this. It's not right."

Dee looked him up and down, as if taking the measure of him. Her expression softened. "Sorry," she said. "I know this is serious stuff. But that's what campaigns are made of; *winning* campaigns anyways. You've signed up for this fight, Mike. This is part of our job. We fight for our candidate. They shot first with that bullshit trick in the hotel. We have to protect our man."

Mike looked again at the memory stick. He had a queasy feeling in the pit of his stomach. "I don't know…" he began.

Dee sat down beside him and flung an arm around his shoulder. She ruffled his hair with her hand. "You're a good man, Mike. Most of the folks on this campaign are good people. That's why we are different. That's why when we win, it will make a difference."

She paused and then leaned in close to whisper in his ear. "This is how we *win*, Mike," she hissed.

She got up and did not look back as she left the room. Mike did not watch her go either. He sat in stunned silence on his bed, the tiny memory stick on his bedside table filling his vision and his thoughts.

"HOW MANY of you folks have heard this speech before?" Hodges asked as his iron-blue eyes twinkled above his craggy smile. He wore casual clothes, jeans and a heavy shirt, but still looked a military man. That bearing never left him. A forest of hands shot up in the tightly packed rooms and hallways of the suburban Manchester home in which he held his third house party of the day. Hodges grinned broadly at the response.

"Okay, then," he laughed. "I guess we have some real fans in here. So I'll just stick to some of the classic hits…"

Then he was off, riffing his campaign speech with the expertise and familiarity of a rock musician playing his greatest tunes. The sound was familiar and the audience knew what was coming, but he took to the task like he played it for the first time, and the crowd eagerly awaited their favorite moments. There was not an applause line in the speech that most of them had not heard before, but they waited for them all the same and clapped like school children.

Mike paused for just a moment to listen and marvel at Hodges' skills. The candidate – *his* candidate – was getting even better as the New Hampshire campaign took off. He was always good, bending crowds to his will, but he seemed to thrive on the excitement now. Hodges and his ever-larger audiences knew each other well and familiarity had bred love, not contempt. Mike watched as Hodges spent five minutes talking about the problems of just one crowd member, never hurrying the speaker along, giving her his focused attention, in a way that bonded the room together and forged them into one. They were not an audience and speaker, Mike thought, but something else. A movement. That was the right word. Hodges was building a movement. Mike reveled in the thought. For years he wanted to be a part of something like this, something with an impact. Now he was.

But he snapped himself out of the moment of reverie. He was not here to soak up the atmosphere. He was here to do a job for Dee. He saw Lauren tucked away in a corner of the room, tapping away on her computer. She looked up and caught his eye. She smiled and for a moment Mike felt the warmth of a pretty woman looking at him. Not a blogger. Just a woman. Just Lauren. He smiled back, nodded toward the door and tapped his watch.

"Five minutes?" he mouthed.

Lauren looked over at Hodges and evidently decided nothing new would come out of this particular meeting. Then she nodded back at him and closed her laptop.

Mike went outside and waited for her, hugging his arms against the cold despite the thick jacket he was wearing. He saw Lauren emerge and she kissed him on the cheek.

"Hey, Mike" she said. "What can I do for you? You got any news for me about the money transfer?"

"Let's walk," Mike said and they strolled down a sidewalk cleared of snow that cut a long black line through the white streetscape. Mike was silent for a minute and heard only the crunch of their footsteps on the salted, slushy path. He put his hand in his pocket and felt the memory stick in his palm. Lauren assumed Mike had not heard her.

"The wire transfer, Mike," she said. "Do you have any comment for me?"

"Yeah, that's what I wanted to talk to you about," Mike said, suddenly snapping into the moment. "We're still checking exactly what that's about. I'm 90 percent sure it's what I thought. Just a charity gift. But it's sensitive, so we'd still appreciate you holding off for a while."

Lauren pursed her lips and narrowed her eyes. "That sounds a little strange, Mike. I could just put it out there right now and see what happens."

Mike tried to keep his voice casual. "Of course," he said. "But this involves Christine and the Senator is fiercely protective of his family. He hates the fact that she has to be involved in the campaign at all." He decided to push that line a little further, sending a message.

"He's fiercely protective," he repeated. "You don't want to put this out there and then discover it's just some Guatemalan bake sale that's she been sponsoring."

Lauren was silent as she mulled over Mike's words. Mike felt a tinge of panic mixed with a rush of guilt. Had he over-done it? Made it too much of a threat? Still, that was the stick with which to beat back this Guatemala story. Now he had to get out the carrot.

"But we have found something that might be of interest to you," he said.

The pair halted. Lauren looked at him, puzzled. Mike could scarcely believe he was doing this but he heard Dee's admoni-tion. *This is your job. Protect the candidate.* He reached into his pocket and brought out the memory stick. He showed it to Lauren.

"On this stick is something we've found that disturbs us. It is a picture of Governor Stanton from an anti-Vietnam war protest when she was at Cornell. It shows her with a group of students, one of whom is setting fire to an American flag."

Lauren inhaled sharply, as she looked at the memory stick in Mike's hand, nestling there like a little nugget of gold. Or thirty pieces of silver. Mike willed Lauren to take it. It was a bribe. He knew it. Lauren knew it.

"This is some pretty dirty stuff, you're pulling here, Mike," Lauren said.

"We feel this is legitimate criticism. Senator Hodges is con-cerned that he is the only candidate who 100 percent supports our troops," Mike said.

Lauren giggled. But it was a sound devoid of mirth. She looked at Mike, straight in the eye, and searched for some sort of validation, or some sort of release to allow her complicity. Then she plucked the memory stick out of his hand.

"Why me?" she asked. "Why not Drudge or someone at the Huffington Post? My blog is growing fast but I'm not in their league."

Mike quickly put his hand back in his pocket, not giving her a chance to change her mind. He warmed his guilty palm against the heat of his body.

"You will be when you post that," he said.

They both knew his words were true. This was a quid pro quo deal. Lauren's silence on the mysterious Guatemala payment in return for an even bigger story. One that was sure to damage Stanton. It was an ugly, low blow. But Lauren did not have time for such thoughts. Mike had already turned and walked back up the road and Lauren's guilt was rapidly replaced by excitement. Her cheeks blossomed with color and her head felt dizzy and light. Mike was right. This was going to make her part of the story.

HODGES SLAMMED down his fist on the table of his office in the campaign's Manchester headquarters. His voice rang out and carried down the corridors, temporarily causing anyone in earshot to stop working. It was like a primal howl.

"I didn't want this!" he yelled. "Jesus Christ! I'm campaigning against this sort of bullshit."

In front of him was a pile of newspapers, all blaring the same story about Stanton and the flag-burning picture. It was a political firestorm that spread from Lauren's blog to the Drudge Report to cable news TV in just a matter of hours. It showed no sign of dying down.

But there was no denying Hodges' genuine fury as he stared at Dee, Mike and a half dozen other top staffers. He suddenly looked ten years older, his skin drawn tightly over his lean face as a vein throbbed at his temple. He put one hand to the side of his head and stared directly at Dee.

"Goddamn it, Dee!" he said. "I know Governor Stanton. She's a good woman. She loves her country and now people will think we've smeared her with this… this…" He waved a hand over the papers in front of him, all of them featuring a beaming 18-year-old Stanton standing near a burning American flag.

"This…bullshit!" Hodges said at last.

Dee withstood his withering gaze and let the storm die down, waiting for the dark clouds to stop fizzing with lightning and fury. Finally, she spoke. Her voice was firm and quiet.

"No one likes this," she said. "But look at these poll numbers." She pushed a sheaf of papers to Hodges.

He picked them up and scanned through them like the General he once was, picking out the positions of the opposing forces. He put them down again.

"Are these for real?" he asked quietly.

Dee nodded. "We're within three points of Stanton," she said. "If we play this right and make the last few days of this campaign about national security, I think it will give us four extra points. Maybe even six if we get lucky. It can push us over the top. We can win New Hampshire."

Hodges thought for a moment, glanced again at the poll numbers, and then placed them over the offending newspaper headlines. "Go on," he said.

Dee stood up. She saw she had her opening. "Let's drive this point home. Let's make it all about national security. You personally don't have to go anywhere near this flag-burning issue. You don't even have to mention Stanton by name. The press will do that for you. Just talk about your own record. Iraq, Afghanistan. Your service. You know what it's like to serve your country. That's all you have to talk about."

She left the rest unsaid but there was not a single person in the room who did not mentally add the words: "…and we'll take care of the rest."

Hodges stood up.

"Okay," he said. "I'm not going to touch any of this dirty stuff. This campaign is about me and my record. That's what I'm fighting on. Not bringing down this sort of shit on my opponent."

Dee nodded and Hodges headed for the door.

"Oh, just one more thing, Senator. Is there any other part of your service record we should be putting out there? Afghanistan and Iraq is solid territory and we tell that story well. But sometimes it's good to have something new. Perhaps from earlier in your career. Like in Central America? You were in Guatemala for a couple years. Should we be pushing that out there?"

Mike bristled inside, stunned at Dee's gambit. He scanned Hodges for any sort of reaction, any hint of something amiss or a distant pluck of conscience or fear. But there was nothing. Hodges mulled over the thought.

"Not much to tell, Dee. Let's keep it simple. Stick to more recent stuff and avoid ancient history."

"Simple is good, sir," said Dee.

As the group filed out of the door, Dee plucked Mike by the elbow and guided him into a backroom.

"That was a risky move," Mike said.

Dee shook her head. "I had to test the waters. See if I could get a rise out of him."

"And?" said Mike.

Dee did not bother answering. They both watched Hodges' face intently as hawks looking for prey. But there had been nothing. No reaction at all.

"The stakes are as high as they can be now, Mike," Dee said. "Things are going to get dirtier, so we need to know everything we can about our man."

She handed him a plain white envelope. "A ticket to Guatemala City," she said. "You leave tomorrow."

HIS MOTHER sobbed as Mike answered the phone in his hotel room. At first he could not understand who called him amid the soft moans and cries. But gradually he realized what was going on.

"Mom?" he said. "Calm down. Speak slowly."

There was a silence and then he heard the old, familiar phrase; the one he already suspected would be behind his mother's woe.

"It's Jaynie," she whispered.

Mike shut his eyes and held the receiver to his forehead. He held it so hard it felt like the cold plastic might bore through his skull.

"What is it?" he asked eventually.

"She's had an overdose, Michael. The poor, poor girl. She's in the hospital. The doctors say she'll be all right. But she's in a terrible state. You have to come and see her. It's not far."

Mike felt a shiver of emotion travel over his skin like the reverberations of a beating drum. His mind swam with a succession of terrible images: of Jaynie in a hospital bed, of her collapsed in the street or found in some dilapidated squat or vacant home. His chest tightened and a cold sweat broke out on his forehead. Then it was followed by something worse. He looked at the plane ticket that Dee had given him. It sat, accusingly, mockingly, on his bedside table.

"I can't," he said.

There was a stunned silence at the end of the phone.

"Michael, Jaynie is in the hospital," his mother said, her voice level and calm but accusing.

"I just can't, Mom. There are things going on here that I can't talk about. But I can't just up and walk away from them. Not even for this."

Again there was a moment of silence at the other end of the receiver. He could hear his mother breathe softly, her upset now replaced by an icy disappointment.

"Okay, Michael. I hope what you are doing is worth it."

After he put down the phone Mike sat on the side of the bed and held his ticket in his hand, while her words echoed in his mind in an endlessly replaying loop of guilt and speculation. He had no answer to her question and, as he searched his mind to justify his actions, he found no solace.

CHAPTER 10

THE PLANE SWOOPED into Guatemala City as its engines strained to cope with a shuddering series of spirals. Mike looked down from a window seat over a city that spread like a blanket among a series of high volcanic peaks and knife like gorges. For almost as far as he could see, he saw slums of ragged shacks and grimy concrete squares stretched out in a bewildering mess. It spoke of an unimaginable sprawl of humanity, collected together and dumped here, so far from the neat orderly suburbs of New Hampshire that he left behind. It was surreal for him to be here as the plane's wheels touched tarmac with a gentle thud. How could these two places possibly be linked? It seemed like some sort of fever dream. Yet here he was.

Mike passed swiftly through passport control and picked up his rental car, a tiny little red Fiat, that felt like driving in a rickety tin can compared to American cars. He guided it into the chaos of Guatemala City's streets, thick with choking traffic, like a river of metal, flowing in and out of the capital. As he pulled out into a phalanx of city buses painted a vibrant red, he gripped the steering wheel so hard that his knuckles turned white. The young woman at the rental counter had warned him about the buses with a laughing smile when he told her it was his first time in Guatemala.

"We call them killer tomatoes," she said.

He thought he misheard but now he understood perfectly. The giant red, rickety vehicles clattered randomly around the streets, swerving in and out of the traffic, oblivious to their fellow road-users. Aside from their color, they did not look like tomatoes, but killers they most certainly were. Mike thought about heading out into the countryside right away in an effort to eat some miles up on the long drive to Livingston before the sun set. But the traffic was such a shock that he decided against it. In a confusing series of U-turns and hair-raising loops, Mike finally spotted the gleaming skyscrapers of downtown and he emerged into a different world – one that he recognized. It was of tidy sidewalks, gleaming glass buildings and rows of neat shops. He spotted the imposing structure of a Hilton hotel and drove up to the lobby, gratefully passing the keys to a wait-ing bellhop. The man looked in puzzlement at the cheap, tiny car amid the hulking shiny SUVs that littered the rest of the forecourt, but gratefully accepted a handful of dollars as a tip.

"*Gracias, señor*," he said and guided Mike inside the hotel.

Immediately Mike was struck by a familiar sound. It was so jarring that he stood still, his mind struggling to comprehend what was going on.

"Let me tell you how we're going to save this country…"

It was Hodges' voice ringing out through the hotel lobby. Mike looked around and half-expected to see Hodges standing behind him. But the voice came from the TV inside the lobby bar. A group of people gathered around it. Mike sat down and nodded at the bartender for a beer. The TV played a CNN live package straight from New Hampshire. About half a dozen people in the bar watched a feed from the start of one of Hodges' rallies. Mike was stunned. These Guatemalans were just as entranced as the people back in America. Then, after about fifteen minutes of the speech, the coverage cut away to a news anchor who announced the details of the latest polls. It had Stanton at 35 points, with Hodges at 32. No one else in the chasing pack was even close. One or two of the Guatemalans muttered in disappointment at the numbers. But Mike knew better and smiled. They were closing in on Stanton. Just as Dee predicted, national security now dominated the last days of the campaign and was Hodges' strong point. He did not have to attack Stanton over the flag-burning picture. The media was doing that for him. He remembered handing Lauren the memory stick that Dee gave him, recalling the guilt he felt. But he was more sure of himself now. Dee was right, as usual. She saw it coming. If they could win New Hampshire, it would all be worth it.

"Are you American?" one of the young drinkers asked Mike.

He turned from the TV and noticed a pretty girl with long dark hair. She looked like a student. He nodded.

"What do you think of Senator Hodges?" she asked. "He is a good man, no?"

Mike began to speak, then stopped himself. He was on a mission. He needed to be careful.

"He seems so," he said. "But I try not to pay too much attention to politics."

———————

THE NEXT day Mike drove out of the city before the sun rose, hoping to beat the traffic. The road headed out of the central highlands where the capital stood, and down into a long central valley that wound its way to the sea. Even though Guatemala was a small country something about the journey felt epic. The countryside was breathtaking in its beauty, especially after the frigid landscapes of Iowa and New Hampshire. It was verdant and fresh, dotted with tiny fields and farms beneath a blue sky dotted with puffy white clouds. Green-shouldered volcanoes dominated the horizon and towered above the highway as it snaked over their flanks. Mike wound down the window, letting the warm air inside, and suddenly felt a surge of liberating freedom. Out of the campaign bubble, he found it easy to let his mind wander.

He already knew a sketchy history of the country from his work with Guatemalan immigrants in Florida's fruit plantations. It was a nation split between an indigenous population of mostly Mayan Indians, many of them still speaking Spanish as a second language, and the mixed blood descendents of Spanish conquerors who took local wives. The higher up the social ladder you went, the more white the population, until you got to a tiny elite of mostly pure blood whites. Conversely, the lower down you went the more Indian people became, until you hit vast tracts of impoverished farmers lorded over by absentee landowners and still tilling their ancestral soil as landless tenants. The divide often spilled into violence and in 1960 slowly burned into a civil war that lasted 36 years and became the longest and bloodiest in all of Latin America that cost tens of thousands of lives.

Although Mike knew the tragic history of the country, he could not square it with the landscape rolling out in front of him. It seemed so warm and peaceful. He stopped in a busy market town called Salama just before the highway dipped down out of the mountains and he bought an armful of meat-filled fried pastries for lunch. He leaned against the car as he ate and watched groups of Indian women, dressed in kaleidoscope-like dresses, sit at their stalls selling corn, vegetables, clothes and trinkets. A few noticed him and giggled and laughed among themselves. He caught a few snatches of what they said but they did not speak Spanish. Their tongue sounded alien to him, just like it had when he heard Benitez talk in Kansas. Yet it was also beautiful, full of incomprehensible vowels and consonants. This was the language's homeland, among these copper-skinned people and their soaring hills and deep valleys. He strained to hear more and smiled, trying to catch their eye and engage them in conversation, but they just looked away.

He glanced at his watch and continued the drive, heading downhill on the winding freeway into a broad and increasingly parched valley. It traced the flow of a meandering brown river heading towards the town of Puerto Barrios on the edge of the sparkling blue Caribbean Sea. Mike left his car in the town, trusting a local hotel owner to look after it in exchange for some much-needed US dollars. From Puerto Barrios he would have to continue by boat, since Livingston was not reachable by road. It was separate from the rest of country, kept apart by the sea and the thick, green forests of the coast.

The ferry to the city gave a hint of this world apart. It was filled with black-skinned men and women, many speaking thickly accented English. It was bewilderingly like being transported out of Guatemala and into Africa. An old man, his ancient black face wrinkled to an almost unimaginable degree, smiled at him and edged forward, nudging other passengers out of the way on the tightly packed boat. He reached out a hand and for a moment Mike thought he was going to beg for something. Then with an inner surge of embarrassment he understood the man was just trying to be friendly.

"Heading to Livingston then, huh?" he asked. "Welcome to Garifuna country."

Mike looked puzzled at the unfamiliar words. The man frowned. "Garifuna!" he said. "Do you know where you are?"

Mike shrugged apologetically and the man burst into a fit of hysterical laughter. The man passed a few unintelligible remarks to a few of his fellow passengers who shared his mirth. Then he turned back to Mike.

"We're a bit different from other Guatemalans. You've noticed that, *Americano*?" he said with a twinkle in his eye. Mike looked at the boat full of black men, women and children and felt suitably ridiculous.

"We are Garifuna. Our ancestors were slaves and Indians from the Islands. We ended up here. This is our own little country," the old man continued and pointed to the coast out to the left of the boat.

"*Yanquis*," he chuckled, in Spanish now. "They never understand where they are going."

———————

MIKE AWOKE the next morning in a fog of jetlag and fatigue. He had stumbled off the ferry and into the center of the ramshackle town where he found the Hotel La Plancha, a rundown old colonial building with half a dozen bungalows-for-hire in the back.

He quickly collapsed into a bed and awoke only now with the realization it was already past noon. He struggled to his feet, suddenly aware that a host of mosquitoes feasted on his bare arms as he slept and left a dense patina of red welts. He resisted the powerful urge to scratch them and attempted to gather his thoughts. He felt a world away from the campaign now. He could scarcely believe he was sweating. He had known nothing but cold for so long. But he knew that his sense of distance was an illusion. He still worked for the campaign and he must remain focused. He had one distinct mission here. Find the man Christine wired the money to and explore any possible link to the mystery shooter back in Iowa. Then get out and home, so they could prepare a defense should anyone else follow his trail.

He pulled on his clothes and walked out of the door, shielding his eyes from the sudden light and began to walk into the center of town.

The air was already thick and hot. Not even a breath of air blew in off a sea that was so flat it looked like a lake. Mike walked down streets populated with just a few pedestrians. He attracted a few stares at the sight of his white skin, but more often he was flashed a broad smile. A couple of young boys followed him briefly, tugging at his shirt sleeves and talking in a language he could not understand nor even place, a mix of vowels that sprang from Africa long ago.

The Western Union outlet was easy to find. It stood on the north side of a faded, colonial-era market square. As he walked into the building the kids following him stopped at the glass door, peering and pointing but not daring to follow. The see-through barrier was the gap between their home and the First World. They had no need to cross it. Mike welcomed a blast of air conditioning and walked up to the counter. He was the only customer and a young Latino woman snapped to attention at seeing him, straightened her back and hastily folded her gossip magazine.

"*Señor?*" she said.

Mike began his cover story. He spoke in Spanish and purposefully mangled the words like a harmless visiting American businessman would.

"Sorry to trouble you, but I am trying to track down a money order and speak to the recipient. We think there may have been a mistake. Can you find him for me?"

The woman smiled pleasantly.

"Of course, *señor*. Do you have the order details?"

Mike handed over a photocopy of the money order and returned her smile. The woman carefully unfolded the paper and spread it flat and typed into her computer. Then, suddenly, she stopped. She looked up at him, a flash of uncertainty in her eyes.

"I have to get my manager, *señor*," she said.

Mike opened his mouth to protest but she got up and walked out to the back office. Mike felt a stab of fear in his stomach, a feeling that only deepened when a tall, mustached-man burst in noisily from the back office. Mike glimpsed the woman cowering in the shadows behind him. The man, Latino like the woman, came around to the front of the desk. He grabbed Mike by the elbow.

"Go! Out of here!" he snapped.

Mike pulled free of his grip.

"What the fuck?" he said loudly. But the man did not hesitate or pull back. He pushed his face forward directly into Mike's face. Mike caught a whiff of his hot breath.

The man stared furiously at Mike. "Out!" he said in English. "You have no business here. Go home!"

Mike backed away and the man followed him, stood in the doorway, his hands resting on his hips and still glaring. Mike had no idea what was going on and he sensed suddenly that groups of people were looking at him. He felt confused and then also scared and vulnerable. This was the last thing he expected. He turned slowly and walked away as the manager shut the door and hung up a red "closed" sign in the window. Mike walked firmly forward, unwilling to give the impression that he was aimless. He just needed to sit somewhere and gather his thoughts.

Eventually he found his way back to the hotel. He sat on his bed and pulled the mosquito net over him to create a feeling of safety behind its white threads. He felt at a loss. He knew it was a name on the money order that had triggered such a response. Either Christine's or Rodrigo Estrada Carillo's. One of those two was famous enough in these parts to get people seriously scared. Mike closed his eyes. He felt suddenly lost. What was he doing here? He joined to work on a campaign. To work for Hodges and make a difference, to bring people into his cause, to get people out to vote, to convince them they could make their lives better. But here he was, thousands of miles away, running up against a mystery he did not understand. He felt like he was Alice after going through the looking glass, entering a weird world where the oddest things seemed important, and the day-to-day events of back home disappeared altogether. He closed his eyes, still feeling the disembodying effects of jet lag, and lay on the mattress while his head throbbed and his heart sank.

MIKE DID not know when he drifted off, but it was still daylight and as he opened his eyes he saw it was now dusk. His room was caught in a dusty half-light and he blinked a few times as his eyes slowly adjusted to the unfamiliar shadows.

Then one of them moved.

Mike sat up slowly, trying not to make a noise. A dark figure crouched over his suitcase, rifling quietly through his belongings. It seemed like a man, tall and thin. He was pulling the clothes out and checking the pockets. Mike's wallet and passport already lay on the ground next to him.

Then the figure stopped. Perhaps he heard the change in Mike's breathing from sleep to wakefulness. Either way, the man slowly stood up and turned around. It was still dark and Mike couldn't make out the man's features. But Mike knew one thing: the man was not afraid of being caught. Mike needed to act.

"Hey!" he shouted and jumped out of bed. The figure stood his ground. Mike decided to run for the door. He darted forward and ducked his head down as the man strode after him. Mike reached for the doorknob and yanked it open. Suddenly the darkness of the room was bathed in golden light from a lamp outside on the bungalow's porch. For a moment it was bright as day and Mike lunged forward. But he never made it. An explosion of pain detonated in the back of his head, followed by a brief shower of stars spraying in front of his eyes. Then he was aware of falling, tumbling down, and his knees buckled underneath him like a drunk. Then the world went dark.

THE POLICEMAN stood behind Mike and painfully prodded the bloodied bump on the back of his head with a finger. Mike yelped and angrily jerked his head away. The officer shrugged nonchalantly and went back to his seat and put his booted feet up on the desk.

Mike read his nametag: Zaragosa. The man stared back with indifference and disgust, like Mike was something that he found on the bottom of his shoe.

"We don't like this sort of trouble here in Livingston," Zaragosa said. "It disturbs the peace."

Mike rubbed a hand over the swelling bump on his crown. He could not believe what was happening. He had woken up collapsed on the floor of his hotel room and discovered his cash and his copy of the money order were both missing. The hotel manager fussed over his wound and told him to leave town and go to the hospital, but Mike refused. He felt more shaken than hurt and that led him to anger. He marched straight to the local police station and demanded to see the commander.

"But I have been attacked and robbed!" Mike said. "And I want to know what you are going to do about it."

Zaragosa examined his finger nails with feigned fascination. "Sir," he said with disdain. "Perhaps some people do not like Yankees like you coming around here and sticking their noses into other people's affairs."

Mike gasped. He did not want to come across as the outraged, blustering American, but he was furious. "There was a crime. You are the police. I want you to investigate it."

Zaragosa chuckled to himself. He sat up straight and shuffled the papers on his desk. "Yes, indeed. I will investigate. You can be sure of it." Then he stood up and gestured to the door. "Please leave. So we can immediately start our investigation."

Mike burned with humiliation. But he knew he had no choice. He stomped out of the police station and back to his hotel. But when he got to his bungalow, he found his hotel room locked. The manager stood in front of the door; Mike's luggage was packed and beside it.

"I'm sorry, *señor*," the man said with what seemed like genuine emotion. "But we have made a mistake and your room was double-booked. The hotel is full tonight."

The man spoke quickly and held his hands in front of him, refusing to meet Mike's stunned stare. "If you rush, you can make the last ferry out of Livingston. Perhaps that would be best?" he suggested.

Mike felt a wave of exhaustion crash over him and his head began to throb, the pain collecting where he had been struck. "What's going on?" he asked.

The manager paused. He weighed something in his mind and his eyes darted from one side to another. He let out a long, deep sigh.

"*Señor*, General Carillo is a very big man around here. His name means a lot to people and the army has much power in this country. With such people it is best not to enquire into their business. That is why you must leave. Even the police here are his friends."

Mike understood at last. Carillo was a General. A powerful man. But the manager continued. "You do not need to wonder who robbed you, *señor*. You just reported their own crime to them."

Mike stood statue-still. He felt so out of his depth.

The manager rested a hand on Mike's shoulder. His voice was soft and full of pity. "*Amigo*, I am sure I can find room for you for tonight. But in the morning, you must leave. Okay?"

Mike agreed. He had no choice.

CHAPTER 11

DEE SETTLED INTO the comfortable back seat of the town car headed to her Manchester hotel. She inhaled the sweet smell of the black leather and sank her flesh into its soft embrace. She was tired. She did not want to think about how little she had slept over the past three days as they prepped for the just finished debate. It was not more than five or six hours in total and she felt the strain now. It was a dull ache deep in her bones. She stretched out and closed her eyes. Her whole career built to this point; races won and lost, candidates picked and spurned, contacts made and worked. Girlfriends shed or shunned. Her personal life reduced to an addendum to her work. All of it to get a shot at the big one. She would not let her body fail her now, just as she was on the cusp.

And, my God, what a candidate she had. She allowed herself a smile. Hodges was magnificent in the debate. He came across as the firm, decent honorable soldier, desperate only to serve his country. All of it was in sharp contrast to Stanton, who went on the offensive, jabbing and prodding him. She labeled him a negative campaigner with no experience of politics. But it served to diminish herself and make Hodges look above the fray. As long as he, himself, did not hit back, he looked – incredibly – the bigger candidate.

The same sense of decent non-aggression was not true of the Hodges campaign, of course. For days now it hit hard at Stanton, running ads from allied groups and briefing reporters on Stanton's flag-burning photograph. Dee knew how to play reporters like a conductor in front of an orchestra. A whispered word here, a careful prod there, and then just sit back and watch the stories and angles play out while Hodges just smiled and talked up his own military career. It was Good Cop and Bad Cop, with Hodges the innocent front man for Dee's black operations. It worked flawlessly. They were taking Stanton down. She felt the truth of it in her aching bones and in the results she read in the ever-narrowing polls. She wished, just wished, to see Howard Carver's face right now. That old fart. She was handing his fat ass to him on a plate of her choosing.

Her phone rang and she toyed with the idea of ignoring it. For once she skipped the usual post-debate drinking with the young campaign staffers and the idea of her soft hotel bed was like Shang-Ri-La to her now. But as she tried to ignore the ringing, she knew she had to take the call.

The line crackled and it took a moment to recognize the frantic voice on the other end. When she did, she immediately kicked into high gear and banished the tiredness. Full alert.

"Mike!" she snapped. "Get a grip. Say that again. Slower."

Then she listened as Mike's story poured out. She listened as he described how Carillo was a retired General, of how everyone was afraid of him, of how the Western Union branch threw him into the street and finally of the burglary of his hotel room and the police who wanted to kick him out of town. Mike sounded panicked and paranoid. Dee was stunned.

"Mike, people getting robbed happens all the time in places like that. It must be a coincidence."

Mike shot back instantly. "It was no fucking coincidence, Dee. Besides you said you don't believe in them, remember?"

There was no doubt in his voice. Dee cradled the phone and her mind whirred. They could not afford this. They were just days from the election in New Hampshire. They were so close and yet the shooter and this Guatemalan story sat like a big, empty black hole at the heart of her plans. She knew she had no power over them and she hated that feeling.

"Dee? Are you still there?"

Mike sounded plaintive on the other end of the call.

"Hang tight, Mike. If you can, see what else you can find out. But don't take any risks. I'll work this end," she said.

She had shied away from this task for too long, she thought. She danced around things, hoping they would go away. You're a fool, Dee, she told herself. But she felt better now. She made a decision: it was time to talk directly to the source of the problem.

CHRISTINE HODGES opened the door of her hotel room with a look of surprise. Her mane of blond hair was tied back in a sharp bun and she wore no make-up.

"Dee?" she said. "Is there something wrong? Jack's not here."

Dee smiled at the platitudes. There was something sharp beneath Christine's homely perfect wife exterior. She could sense it, feel the edges underneath the skin like submerged rocks at sea, ready to tear the bottom out of a boat. Dee respected and feared that.

"Actually it's you I want to see. I hope you don't mind." Dee stood in the doorway, expectantly. She was going nowhere and she waited for that to sink in. Christine finally opened the door fully and gestured for Dee to come in. The candidate's wife perched on the bed and looked at Dee with a measured look of hostility. Dee knew she over-stepped boundaries by coming here like this, but she pressed on.

"Can I be upfront with you here, Christine?" she asked.

Christine nodded. "Of course," she said.

"Christine, Stanton's people have something they think they can use against us. They are starting to put it around. I didn't want to go to Jack. Because it doesn't involve him."

Dee let those words sink in.

"It involves you."

Dee watched Christine's features. There was nothing but a slight frown of puzzlement. The lines creased her forehead like rumpled sheets.

"Really?" she said.

"You have been paying money to a General Rodrigo Estrada Carillo. In Livingston, Guatemala. Stanton's people have a money order with your name on it."

Christine laughed and put a hand to her mouth. "Rodrigo?" she said. "Why on earth would that interest anyone?"

Dee was impressed. There was not a flicker of concern in Christine's voice.

"It is unusual, Christine, and nobody likes unusual when it comes to presidential campaigns. So I have to ask you what's going on. If the press decides to check it out and someone asks me about it, I need an answer for them. One blogger already has the story and we'd like to keep her from putting it out in the public domain."

Dee kept her voice firm. She would not play into Christine's casual attitude. "So give me an answer," Dee said.

Christine frowned again. "Rodrigo was a good friend of ours, back in the late 1980s, when we were stationed out in Guatemala City. We got to know him socially. He is a good man. A strong man and a great friend of America."

"So why are you sending him money?"

"Guatemala is a poor country, Dee. He has children who need to go to college. It's the least we could do. Rodrigo deserves our help. He phoned up and asked us for it recently, as a favor, and so we gave it to him. It was our duty, as his friends and out of respect for the service he gave to America."

There was a trace of rebuke in Christine's voice that started to cross over into anger. "You need to have a little more faith in people, Dee."

Dee smiled. True or not, that explanation would do. At least for a few days. She could use it to convince Lauren O'Keefe not to touch this story until after election day. By then – who knows? – they might be untouchable.

Dee turned to go. "Thanks for clearing that up, Christine. That's all I needed to know."

But as Dee walked back to her own room, she bristled at the tone of Christine's last comments. "Have faith?" Dee thought. She fought down an urge to spit. It was not her job to just *have faith*, she thought fiercely. Her job was to win.

―――――

THE CAB drove Mike in the direction of the jetty for the ferry back to where he left his car. But, as he watched the houses drift by, he knew he could not leave Livingston like this: in defeat. It was not his nature. He fingered the egg-size lump on the back of his head. This was wrong, he thought. He never backed down from a fight. Not in high school. Not in college. Not in long years of fighting the big corporations and their lawyers in Florida. He would not do it now. No. He was not leaving like this.

"Driver," he said, leaning forward to address the young Garifuna man whose battered car lurched down the potholed street. "You know where General Rodrigo Estrada Carillo lives?"

The man was silent for a moment. "Of course," he

eventually replied in halting Spanish. "But I am meant to take you to the ferry."

Mike handed him a crisp twenty dollar bill. "Change of plan," he said.

The driver did not hesitate. He took the bill with one hand as his other swung the car around. Now they headed the opposite direction, away from the port. The road went out of downtown and down the coast a little, going up a gentle rise and along a street lined with dilapidated once-grand villas. Most were surrounded by high walls and presented a blank face to the world. Few people walked in the streets. The car chugged quietly along and then rolled to a halt. The driver nodded at a building opposite. It was a square, ugly house, behind a compound wall into which was set an iron door.

"This is his villa, *señor*," he said.

Mike got out, still carrying his bags. For a moment he felt nervous. But he swallowed it down. He would not be intimidated. He put too much into this, too much of his personal life, too much of his professional life, to be treated like this.

He hammered his fist on the door. The dull clang deafened him. But there was no response. He thumped the door again. This time the door was flung open. A tall man with a pockmarked face stood there. For a brief moment, Mike had a terrifying thought: was this the man from his hotel room? He stepped back. The man also looked shocked. He opened and closed his mouth in surprise, like a fish gasping for air.

"*Señor?*" the man said gruffly.

"I need to see General Carillo," Mike said.

The man stared at Mike and said nothing. He stepped forward but then from behind him a jovial voice boomed and a short, fat mustached figure emerged from the shadows.

"*Americano?*" the man asked.

Mike nodded. "I work for Senator Jack Hodges," he said.

The man grinned and flung his arms wide. He stepped forward and caught Mike in a powerful bear hug that belied his stature. It was a strong grip and Mike's ribs cracked as he flinched from the man's powerful smell of sour tobacco and coffee.

"Come in! Come in!" the man said. "I am General Rodrigo Carillo and Senator Hodges is an old friend of mine."

The General took him by the elbow, looping his arm around him, and guided him back into the house. They walked into a dark and musty hallway that instantly shut out the blinding sunshine and blue sky outside. It was a different world, an older place, tinged by darkness. But Carillo was all warmth and charm. A pot of coffee, already warm, stood on a table and the General guided Mike to sit down. Mike was confused. He expected many things, but not hospitality.

"Why was I attacked?" he blurted out.

The General looked puzzled. Mike continued, fixing him with a fiery gaze.

"I've been sent here by the Senator's campaign to investigate a payment made to you and last night, in my hotel, someone came into my room. They knocked me out and then the police told me to leave town. You owe me an explanation, General," Mike said.

The General spread his hands wide and shook his head sadly.

"Ah *señor*. I am sorry for your troubles. The people here can be very over-protective of me. They are simple sorts. Peasants really, former slaves. So what can you expect? They don't like those who ask too many questions."

The General poured more coffee into Mike's cup. "What do you know of Guatemala?" he asked, but did not give Mike a chance to reply.

"For many years we had a war here. We fought to keep the Communists out of our beloved Motherland. To keep it free. I was a General in that war for a long time and I have many old comrades. They remember me and our sacrifices…"

The General's voice faded away a little, becoming something of a whisper.

"…and sometimes my former brothers in arms can be a little defensive. I offer my sincere apologies, if anyone has shown you discourtesy."

Mike was thrown for a loop. The General's garrulous demeanor was hard to resist. He seemed open and warm and eager to make amends. He got up and retreated into a backroom where Mike heard a distant clattering of pots. Mike glanced around the room. The wallpaper was faded and dirty, decades old, and everywhere hung photos and paintings. Some looked ancient and some were new. They were mainly black and white and chronicled the General and his ancestors – a succession of pictures of military and colonial life, all proud men bearing chests of medals or demure women, with ruffled dresses on the haciendas of grand coffee estates. Then the General emerged back into the room clutching a plate full of cheeses and olives and slices of fruit. He put it in front of Mike and signaled him to eat.

"Perhaps you can tell me now, why are you here?" the General asked.

Mike decided to confront him head on.

"It is my job to protect the Senator from his political enemies. It has come to my attention that you were paid money by the Senator's wife. That sort of thing concerns us. Are you an enemy or a friend of the Senator's campaign?"

The General stood up and laughed. "How ridiculous!" He guffawed and the sound echoed around the dark and lonely house. "I am Jack's old friend. This money? It is for my children and their education. I am just a poor man who has served his country well. Jack understands this and he was kind enough to remember our friendship all those years ago when he graced our lives with his presence. For him, this money was not so much, I think. But for me, in this poor country, it is a lot."

Carillo got up and took down one of the photos from the wall. He brushed off a patina of dirt with his sleeves and handed it to Mike. Mike peered at it, looking through the dust and back across the decades to the two men standing there. Age had changed both of them, but their identities were clear. Carillo and Hodges, both wearing dress uniform, and staring back at the camera, smiling.

"We defended this country for freedom and democracy," Carillo said.

Mike suddenly felt uneasy. There was something dark beneath the General's friendly demeanor; some hint of menace behind the smile. He could not put a finger on it but he knew he needed to leave and quickly. Mike thanked the General for his time and headed for the door.

"You will not stay?" the General asked.

Mike shook his head.

"But you had a bad knock on the head, you should not drive. Let my man Federico take you back to Guatemala City. He shall drive your car. It is the very least I can do to make up for your troubles."

The General spoke in a tone that suggested he would not take no for an answer. The pock-faced man appeared silently at Mike's side and followed closely as he left the house. Mike did not even try to resist further. The General was so open, so plausible. His story seemed logical. It explained everything and it was harmless. It was only on the ferry out of Livingston, as Federico sat wordlessly beside him, that Mike realized that on the walls of photos – detailing every facet of the General's life and career – there was not a single photograph of any children. Nor any sign of a wife. Carillo had no family to send to college. Mike also came to another conclusion: having Federico drive him back to the capital was not an act of kindness; it was to verify that Mike actually left.

———————

THE TWANGING accent on the end of her cell phone sounded familiar and terrifying and Lauren recognized the voice immediately. Dee Babineaux.

"How are you doing, *ma catin?*" Dee cooed. "I hope I'm not catching you at a busy time."

Lauren looked around the Starbucks café in downtown Manchester. It was full of students and a sprinkle of campaign workers and other bloggers. She stopped writing about a Stanton speech from a campaign stop in West Manchester that morning.

"No, not at all, Ms. Babineaux," she stammered.

"Call me Dee. Everyone does," Dee said.

"What can I do for you, Dee?" Lauren asked, trying out the name for size. It did not seem to fit. She was suddenly swimming in waters way out of her depth.

"I'm just getting back to you about that little matter over Christine Hodges making a money transfer to Guatemala that you asked about," Dee said. Her tone was casual and pleasant and betrayed no hint of stress.

"I'd been talking to Mike Sweeney about that," Lauren said.

"I know," Dee replied. "Mike's busy with other things so I thought I'd call you and let you know we checked it out. Seems the Senator and his wife spent a bit of time in Guatemala back in the 1980s, but you probably knew that. General Carillo is an old friend and they are just helping him out in some tough times. It's for a college fund for his kids, I think."

"Sounds like a nice gesture," Lauren said. "It would make a nice story even."

Lauren sensed a sea change on the other end of the phone even as Dee continued in her friendly voice.

"Doesn't it just? But here's the thing. The Hodges are a pretty private pair. They want to keep this campaign about policy, not personality. They're pretty jealous about their private lives and their family friends. You know what I'm saying?"

Lauren did. She knew exactly what Dee said and – far more importantly – what she meant.

"I understand. But a story is a story, Dee," she said as her heart suddenly raced with her own nerve at defying Dee's warning.

Dee gave a little snorted laugh and there was a moment's pause on the other end of the line.

"You liked getting that little flag-burning picture, didn't you, sweetie?" Dee asked. Dee's voice was calm and steady now. It filled Lauren's ear with delivered menace, an assurance it was Dee who was in control here, not Lauren. The sounds of the Starbucks faded out of Lauren's hearing, replaced by the hiss of Dee's voice in her head.

"We both know what that's done to your little blog's profile. The *Horse Race* is quite a big deal now. I've even seen you on the TV all dressed up and looking like the cat that got the cream."

Lauren's throat went dry. She knew Dee was going somewhere with this, but she was caught up in the words, pulled along like a riptide.

"Well, let me spell things out for you. You keep scratching

my back and I'll keep scratching yours. There'll be other little goodies in the future for you if you stay on the right side with this other thing. I've told you the Hodges want this campaign to be about politics, not their personal lives."

"Is that a threat, Dee?" asked Lauren.

Dee tittered down the line, a sound of genuine mirth, as if Lauren cracked a joke.

"Oh, Lauren. You're new to this game, honey, but once your hair gets a little grayer you'll come to understand that I don't make threats. I don't need to. I make promises."

"What's in it for me?" Lauren asked.

Dee laughed again. "I told you, *catin*, we like you right now. We appreciate the good work you've done. Maybe we'll get you a bit of face-time with the candidate. I'm sure I can arrange a nice big interview. Maybe we'll dig up a few other things about Stanton and pass them along. Just stick with us and you'll go places, Lauren. You'll go all the way. You're gonna be big, Lauren. Do we understand each other?"

"I understand," she whispered.

"Atta girl," said Dee, and with a click the phone went dead.

Lauren suddenly felt the real world around her come back into focus again. Her body fizzed with adrenalin and she felt herself literally shaking. She knew Dee opened a door to her, a gateway to a whole secret world where the prizes were enormous. She closed her eyes. "You're gonna be big," Dee said. For the first time in her life, Lauren believed it.

CHAPTER 12

THE GENERAL'S MAN, Federico, drove with no regard for anyone else on the road. He pitched the spluttering rental car down the highway back to Guatemala City with a grinding of gears and a groaning engine. He weaved in and out of the traffic like a football player racing for a touchdown, thumping down with an open palm on the horn and gesticulating wildly at other drivers.

Mike sat in the back and gripped the underside of the seat with both hands as his knuckles turned white while the scenery raced by. He looked in the rear-view mirror and tried to see Federico's face. He wondered if the driving was meant to intimidate him. But Federico's scarred visage betrayed no hint of a threat. Indeed he whistled softly to himself in between letting out violent expletives at the next crawling bus that slogged along the road.

"My friend. I am in no rush," Mike said. He reached out a hand to rest on Federico's shoulder. "Your country is beautiful. I would like to see it at a slower pace."

Federico glanced back at Mike and then looked sideways at the landscape rushing by outside. They had been on the road a couple of hours but already the highway started to climb into the highlands as the land crinkled up towards the clouds above. Federico shrugged, as if seeing the view speed by for the first time.

"Eh!" he grunted and wound down the window to spit out a gob of phlegm. "I need to get some fuel."

He jerked the car off the road and into a gas station. Mike got out with a feeling of relief. Finally, he was no longer thrown around like a rag doll by Federico's driving. They were in a small village that lined the main road with a strip of shops and restaurants. People milled around, mostly Indian-looking women in brightly-colored dresses and men in tattered work clothes. Mike breathed out and walked into a roadside restaurant while Federico began to harangue one of the attendants at the gas station.

A lone, elderly woman, her face wrinkled and round as a rosebud, stood behind a metal hot plate and fixed small round discs of dough into fat tortillas. She smiled at Mike as he walked in and bustled towards him, eager at the prospect of a customer. He glanced at the menu and ordered three chicken tacos by pointing at the words in a menu written on the wall behind her. Almost instantly the smell of frying meat filled the air.

He turned to the old woman and tried to engage her in conversation but she just smiled at him and nodded her head. He could not tell if she did not understand his accented Spanish or if she was deaf. She handed over a paper plate loaded with food that was doused liberally in chili sauce and accepted a few grubby quetzals in return. Mike took a bite and started to speak to the woman again when a sudden burst of Spanish outside cut through the air like gunfire.

Mike recognized the voice instantly. He swore, dropped the food on a table, and ran outside. Even from thirty yards away he heard Federico scream insults at a small, Mayan-looking man crumpled at his feet. Federico loomed over the man and yelled something about showing him some respect. He lifted a foot and delivered a sickening thud right into the man's belly that prompted the man to let out a piercing squeal. Around them a group of women skittered, clearly terrified of intervening.

Mike yelled out, "What's going on?"

Federico, poised to deliver another blow, suddenly stopped and looked up. His face was a bloated, twisted mask of rage, but the sight of Mike penetrated his temper. Federico's chest, which heaved like an ocean swell with each breath, calmed. He looked down at the man and then back at Mike.

"He was thinking of robbing me," Federico said. "I am sure of it. He was lurking around the back of the car when I went to pay."

The man beneath him moaned softly and put up his hands to protest his innocence. A thin trickle of blood leaked from a nasty tear in his scalp. Mike felt the urge to shout at Federico but he strangled the words. That could only make things worse. The two men stared at each other. Then Mike shrugged as nonchalantly as he could. "I have to make my plane," he said.

Federico smiled thinly. He understood. "Of course," he said and he gestured to the car.

Mike stepped over the man on the ground to get to the back of the car. The man held his head in his hands, not looking up, evidently praying that the monster who beat him would drive off. Mike thought to whisper an apology but he desperately wanted to hit the road again. Federico was at least halfway to a psychopath and there was no telling what he might do if Mike antagonized him by siding with his victim.

As soon as Mike was seated, Federico hit the accelerator and the car lurched forward and set off a blare of horns from traffic that swerved to avoid them. Federico looked at Mike in the rear mirror, caught his eye and flashed a grin.

"That bastard was a thief," he said. Mike understood, with a mix of shock and shame, that Federico saw him as an ally. As if Mike approved of the beating.

"This province is no better than down at the coast with all those black devil Garifunas," Federico said. "It is the same everywhere with all those low types. These ungrateful peasants who have no education or morality."

For a moment Mike thought to protest and make a stand. But he stopped himself. This was an opportunity. There was such real anger and emotion in his voice that Mike knew he could play Federico, push him to talk and see if he opened up. Mike felt a surge of energy: he was back on his mission.

"Where are you from, my friend?" he asked.

"Antigua," Federico said. "The same place as the General.

It is the old capital. A beautiful city. People come from all over the world to see it."

Mike asked him to say more and Federico soon talked in his gruff accent of his hometown where he grew up on a tiny farm just outside the city walls. Mike let him riff and hoped he enjoyed the experience of talking. It was an old trick that he learned while interviewing witnesses and sources for court cases down in Florida. He always tried to get his subjects to talk about themselves in the most general sense. Then as the river of information flowed he sought to guide them and fish for bits of words that floated by. It worked easily with Federico. Mike nudged his talk in the direction of Carillo. Federico revealed they met when he was a young volunteer in his first year in the army and the General was his first commander. They rose together, with Federico appointed his aide. He never left the General's side through the rest of his career.

"The General is a great man," Federico said, the pride in his voice obvious. He was like someone talking about a sports hero or an admired father. "He helped save this country and they repaid him by sending him down to live with the blacks in that mosquito-infested swamp. It is a crime! There should be statues of him all over Guatemala. But instead when peace comes he is sent into exile."

Federico's anger was very real. He spoke in a rapid-fire Spanish that Mike found difficult. His words poured from deep within him, like a hole in a dam that relieved a long pent-up pressure. The road climbed firmly into the mountains now and the countryside around them became green and lush. They sped through villages where Indian women lined the streets and sat at market stalls, their vibrant dresses like splashes of paint spilled against the tarmac of the roads. Their bronze skin and black hair also reminded him of another woman, thousands of miles away, in a solitary jail cell in Iowa.

"Tell me more about the war," Mike said.

Federico laughed, a crackling sound in the back of his throat like the sudden moment dry bark catches alight in a fireplace.

"You Yankees never really understand what happened here. It is like you forgot us and our struggles. But we have not forgotten." He shook his head and gestured out the window. "These people were all communists back then. All *los Indios* were Reds. They fell for that propaganda from Moscow and Havana and wanted to take this country back to the Stone Age. But we fought them hard. We fought them in the fields and the jungles. We even fought them in the churches."

Federico turned to look at Mike, driving without looking at the road ahead. His eyes were wide and their pupils dilated.

"There is blood all around here," he said. "Indian blood. Our blood. We fought for our country and have the scars to prove it. The General has especially. He fought the war harder than anyone. You Yankee liberals never understand it. They always say we went too far, but they never understood the price we paid."

Mike stood his ground, speaking softly. Suddenly the air inside the car felt full of electricity, alive and fizzing between them. Mike knew he was on dangerous territory but pressed on. "Is that why the General is in Livingston? He went too far?"

Federico stared straight ahead. For a long time he did not speak a word, but his eyes widened, as if he saw events long lost in time. A bead of sweat appeared on his forehead and trickled down his brow like a tear. "I tell you one thing more," he said, his teeth gritted and his jaw almost locked. "We did not go far enough."

They were the last words Federico spoke. For the remaining four hours to the airport, Mike stared out at the passing mountains, looking at their green folded shoulders shrug themselves into a cloud-strewn sky. They looked peaceful, beautiful, havens of life, dotted with tiny fields. But Mike only heard Federico's words describe the blood that ran down those same valleys just a few decades ago.

———

THE TWO students froze as Dee marched by in the chaotic mess that was now Hodges' Manchester headquarters. The boy, whose tousled blond hair suddenly reminded her of her younger brother, tickled the girl and nearly caused her to drop a sheaf of papers she was carrying. Dee's sudden appearance was like the arrival of a stern teacher in a classroom out of control.

"Get a room," Dee snapped as she walked by. But she could not resist a smile too. God, she envied their carefree youth.

She went into her office and slammed the door shut. She wore the same clothes for two days straight and was sure she smelled like she'd worn them for a week. Not that anyone would dare mention it. She glanced at her watch. It was past midnight and still the room outside was as busy as Grand Central at rush hour. The televisions blared the cable news shows, students placed fund-raising calls to the West Coast and abroad; plans were drawn up and arrangements made. There was just 48 hours to go now. No time to sleep. No time to waste.

She thought again of the two young students outside and remembered her own first campaign. She was at college in California. It was 1979 and Reagan was about to take over America. Looking back, you sensed it in the air, but she had no clue at the time. She threw everything she had into the campaign of a liberal congressman in Orange County, California. When he was swept away by the Republican tide, she was genuinely devastated. It was hard, she thought, for the first experience of a campaign to be such a loss. It was always good to taste the thrill of victory your first time. But it made her hard quickly and she was thankful for that. She sighed to herself. Had she ever really looked like one of those fresh-faced kids outside? That was more than thirty years ago. *Merde.* Still, here she was now. Ready to guide someone to the ultimate prize: the path to the White House. She could put Jack Hodges on that road. She knew she could. She just needed to win this race and then shake up this stuffy world.

A knock on the door disturbed her reverie. She looked up and shouted a "Come in." One of the flirting students walked in. The boy. He really did look like her little brother, Beau. Or the way she remembered him three decades ago when they scrapped and fought like bobcats down at their grandfather's farm.

"You look positively post-coital," Dee teased.

The boy blushed a deep red as he handed over a folder. It was the latest internal polling. She grabbed the sheath of papers, scanned the headline figures and plunged into the methodology and the detail. She drank in the lists of numbers and figures like it was spring water and she was lost in the desert.

Hodges was neck and neck with Stanton in New Hampshire. He was at 31 points to her 33, but with a margin of error up to four points. And he trended in the right direction. Independents broke to him by six points over the past few weeks. He was strongest among the young and students, but the elderly were warming up to him too. Stanton still led there by eight points. But a week ago it was a 16-point gap. She punched her fist in the air.

"Yes!" she said and got up from behind the desk. She banished her exhaustion and winked at the student. "We're on our way, sweetpea," she said.

She burst out of the office and headed down a hallway to a room used as a place to catch up on some of the many lost hours of sleep they all suffered from. Hodges lay in there now, resting on a makeshift cot. He had attended a whirlwind of house parties in the Manchester suburbs and had a 7:00 a.m. breakfast rally the next morning. There was little point in going back to the hotel. Dee knocked quietly on the door and pushed it open.

"Senator," she said. "You said to wake you when the latest numbers came through."

The light flashed on. Hodges was lying down, still wearing his somber blue suit. But he looked as alert as normal. He had an uncanny ability to go from sleep to wakefulness in an instant. He sat straight up, stretched and held out a hand. She gave him the papers. "This is good right?" he asked, his voice calm and measured.

Dee nodded. "We are trending strong in all the right places. We're moving into the independents and the old folks. Essentially that means we are now fighting on Stanton's home turf. Our tanks are parked right up on her lawn."

Hodges smiled. "You're doing a fine job, Dee. I knew I had a chance when we got you on board."

"It's what I do, Jack," Dee said.

Hodges stood up and looked down at the simple cot that he rested in. "Funny thing," he said. "I've been out of the military for years but I still sleep better in one of those things than any hotel bed I've ever found. I guess a body just does not forget certain habits."

"Neither do the voters," said Dee. "What's winning for us now is the oldest issue in the book: national security. That's where we hit them hard. That flag-burning picture hurt Stanton real bad."

Hodges shook his head. "You know I hated that, Dee," he said. "That's the sort of bullshit I never wanted near my campaign. In fact, I think we need to change tack for the last 48 hours. Try out something new. I want to talk about jobs and poverty reduction. Put some fresh policy meat on this campaign. We can brand it as a "Second New Deal for America." Speak out for ordinary Americans a bit more, address the things they care about in times like these and quit all these tacky political games."

Dee was silent. Hodges rested a hand on her shoulder and fixed her with a stare.

"I aim to change America, Dee. We can't do that if this campaign stays the same," he said. "Can you draw up a policy statement on that? We can announce it at a presser tomorrow afternoon. Get it out in time for the evening news shows."

Dee nodded. "Of course, Senator," she said. "But if I give you that, I want your permission to go after Stanton too. I know I can punch her out now if you allow me to keep playing my own game."

Hodges walked over to a window at the back of a room and pulled the thin curtain aside. Outside the city lights of Manchester twinkled in a cold, clear night. The streetlights reflected off the hard-packed snow.

"You have to *win* first before you can change anything," Dee said. "You can't *do* anything if you lose."

Hodges did not say anything. He just stared at the cold nightscape outside. Fuck it, Dee thought. I'm gonna take that as a yes.

"YOU PALE bastard. I thought at least you'd get a tan!"

Mike stood in the doorway of Dee's hotel room and still clutched his bags. He took a taxi straight from the airport and his brain felt fried from the drive with Federico, the jet lag and the lump on the back of his head. But Dee's raucous laugh and tight embrace brought him back. It was good to be here. Good to be back where the campaign was.

"No time for sun-bathing," he said. "I was too busy getting my ass kicked."

Dee winced sympathetically and pushed him down to sit on the bed. She positioned herself behind him and whistled through her teeth.

"Damn, Mike. You should have got this stitched," she said running a finger over the cut and lump, matted with strands of bloodied hair. She'd seen worse, mainly after Louisiana bar fights, but there was no doubt it was a nasty blow. Whoever dealt it was not shy about what they were doing. "You sure it was linked to this General Carillo?" she asked.

Mike shrugged. "I can't be sure. But it has to be. This guy is a piece of work. Seriously. He seems to be in some sort of internal exile, living in this out-of-the-way hellhole. Like they sent him there to forget him and what he did."

"What did he do?"

"I'm not sure. But his driver took me to the airport and from the way he was talking I would think Carillo was knee deep in the dirty war in the 80s. Tens of thousands of people got killed back then. Your classic Latin American shit show. Death squads, massacres. The works."

"And the shooter?" Dee asked.

"Most of the victims were Mayan Indians. She's a Mayan."

"Coincidence?"

"You don't believe in them. What do you think it means?"

Dee walked over to the mini-bar and yanked out two little bottles of Jack Daniels. She poured them neat into glasses and handed one to Mike, then downed her own. Mike sipped at his. He savored the burn of the liquid on his throat and the surge of warmth it brought him.

"I haven't got a clue," Dee said. "But I do know I don't like it. If it was not for this goddamn crazy bitch taking a shot at our man, I'd be happy enough to forget it. Just call the money Christine sent to Carillo school fees and leave it at that."

"If it was not for that "crazy bitch" we would not be in this position," Mike said.

Dee grinned wickedly. "Now that is surely true, my boy," she said. "But that great irony does not help us get out of our predicament. We need to know more about this man and what our candidate did down there on his stint in Central America. This is dangerous. It's military stuff and we built this campaign on the foundation of his service record."

She paused for thought. "We can't afford to have anything mess with that strategy. He must remain pure on national security. So we need to you to find out more about what Carillo did during the war. See if there's a link from him to our shooter. Perhaps you should look up some of Hodges' old colleagues from his army days. Just sniff out what you can."

Mike sighed. He wanted back out on the streets; he wanted to give speeches to teams of students, eager for the fight; he wanted to see the look on their faces as they shifted from skeptics to believers. He was sick of skulking in shadows, digging in obscure corners.

"This is not what I signed up for, Dee," he said.

Dee looked at him with sympathy. She handed him another little bottle from the mini-bar. "You're a soldier now, Mike. You follow orders. But you do it because you believe in Hodges. You do it because our cause is just. Because when we win this thing, we are going to get a chance to really change things."

Mike looked at Dee. There was not a trace of doubt in her voice. She was straight with him, like a mother to a son, explaining the lessons of a hard, unforgiving world.

"That's why you're here, right? You want to make a difference. Let me tell you a story, Mike. Where I grew up there was a big appliance factory in my town. Just about everybody worked in that place, including my daddy. Then one day the company that owned it discovered they could make things twice as cheap if they shipped everything off to Mexico. My daddy's job went south overnight. Literally. So did our nice little home. We ended up moving from place to place for a while. My daddy started drinking and he swatted us kids around and my mama too. Nothing serious, but enough that these days they would've put him away."

The room was quiet. Mike never heard Dee talk like this. She stared off into that distant place, back to a past he never really guessed about. It was hard to think of Dee as a young girl, vulnerable and scared, wondering what turned her daddy into a figure of fear and violence.

"You see, Mike, my daddy ended up mean and for a while I hated him for that. But when I got a bit older and, God forgive me, long after he died, I came to understand one thing: he didn't begin that way. It was his life that made him mean. Some faceless bastard took away what little he had for a bit more profit. It humiliated him, made him think working with his hands was useless. Told him he was just something to be exported overseas. It made him poor. I'm in this to try and stop that happening to folks anymore. To try and make this country a little better for people whose families are like mine."

She smiled wanly. "Now ain't that a story for ya? Ol' Dee the bleeding heart. Well don't be fooled, Mike, because ol' Dee will still castrate any living mother fucker who stands in her way."

Mike laughed out loud and raised his drink to her. They clinked their glasses.

"We have a bit of common ground, Dee. My ex-wife Jaynie. She's in a heap of trouble. Some of it's her own fault. She's into drugs and a bad crowd. But Christ, you should see where we grew up. There's nothing left of that town. The jobs went. The downtown's a mess. The police aren't worth a thing. There's nothing for her there. No wonder she gets high. She overdosed a week ago. She's lucky to be alive."

Dee ran a hand through his hair, protectively. "That's why we have to win, Mike. Politics is power. When we get power we can rewrite the rules. That's why I need your help with another thing."

Mike looked up at her. She walked over to her bag and dragged out a laptop. She fired it up and gestured for him to come over as she slipped a memory stick in its side.

"I've been back into my vault," she explained. "In times of need we have to dip our paws into the mud and get them a little dirty. Hodges wants to launch a new policy initiative on poverty, which is great. I'll do it. But we need a good jab to Stanton's jaw before the bell rings and that's where this comes in."

Her fingers danced over the keys and suddenly a video played. It was grainy, perhaps from some sort of conference, and there was no date. But the figure of Stanton was clear. She listened to questions from a crowd of people behind the camera. She nodded her head and then got up to a lectern to speak.

"That's a very good point you have there. You know I think that a lot of military wives and families think that's true. That they have a tough time at home when their husbands and fathers are away. I've heard some people say there's too much emphasis on the problems the soldiers face. Sometimes the war at home is much harder to speak up for than the one being fought by the troops. We need to make sure our military families are looked out for every bit as much as our wonderful veterans."

Mike was puzzled.

"I don't get it," he said.

Dee laughed. "Now watch the edited clip that you are going to pass onto your new friend Lauren at the *Horse Race* blog."

The clip ran again, this time cutting straight into the middle of Stanton's speech. It was shaved to just a few seconds long.

"There's too much emphasis on the problems the soldiers face. Sometimes the war at home is much harder to speak up for than the one being fought by the troops."

The new video ended there.

"She just doesn't seem to understand our boys in uniform," Dee said and shook her head. "She seems to have a real problem with those fine Americans soldiers. Thinks perhaps they get the kid gloves treatment. I find that very disturbing."

Dee yanked out the memory stick and handed it to Mike. "Now make sure that gets in the right hands by tomorrow morning. You understand?"

Mike nodded. He understood his orders perfectly.

CHAPTER 13

LAUREN HUNCHED OVER her laptop and tapped furiously at its keyboard. Suddenly in the dim reflection of the computer screen she spotted a figure standing behind her in the busy downtown Manchester coffee shop. She could see his silhouette shadowy and blank. Then she recognized him.

"Mike Sweeney," she said and turned around with a smile. "It's been a few days since I saw you. Where have you been?"

Mike looked stressed and even his quick grin did not hide an itchy unease that Lauren immediately picked up on as he sat down. He appeared uncomfortable in his skin, wearing it like an ill-fitting second hand suit.

"Oh, busy, you know how it is. These are crazy times," he said.

Lauren leaned her face into his. Her eyes scanned him like she was checking out a passport picture. "Is that a bit of sunburn on your nose?" she asked. "How did you manage to get that in New Hampshire?"

Mike felt a hot flush spreading over his face. He was

flustered at her immediate questioning of him. She was far from just a pretty face, this woman. Nothing got by her.

"I've got something for you," he said, ignoring her question and fishing into his pocket. He brought out Dee's memory stick and reached over and plugged it into her computer. Lauren held his gaze, She was calm and completely in control. It was not meant to be like this, Mike thought. He should be in charge.

"Check out the video file marked Stanton," he said.

Lauren opened up the file. An image flickered onto her screen and she bent in close to hear the audio of the brief clip of Stanton speaking. It was the edited version that Dee produced from her vault. The tinny voice echoed from Lauren's laptop.

"There's too much emphasis on the problems the soldiers face. Sometimes the war at home is much harder to speak up for than the one being fought by the troops."

Lauren pressed repeat and played the clip again. Then a third time. Then she settled back in her chair and folded her arms across her chest. She did not smile.

"Why are you doing this, Mike?" she asked evenly. "This is the second time you've given me something on Stanton. First the flag burning picture and now this recording. I don't like feeling I'm being used as part of a dirty tricks operation."

Mike tried to shrug casually as if to pass it as simply nothing at all. Trying to disguise the knife he wanted her to plunge into Stanton's back.

"We just think it highlights a difference between the Senator and Governor Stanton. She just does not seem to get the importance of our national security. We do. We don't think…"

Lauren put up a hand and his words died on his tongue. "Cut the crap, Mike," she said. "How do I know where this comes from? What is she really saying? What's the context? This is some pretty low shit, Mike."

Lauren looked down at the clip and played it again. Mike watched her face though and, despite her words, he knew she would take it. Briefly he was disappointed. He almost relished her admonishment and her harsh words. They were righteous, even if only for a moment, and that was a feeling he now only dimly remembered. But it was gone now. Lauren's eyes widened as she watched the clip again and the tip of her tongue touched her top lip. He knew she thought of page views, headlines and appearances on cable news shows.

"If you don't want it, we can put it out elsewhere," Mike said and reached for the memory stick. She playfully slapped away his hand. Then in a whir of fingers she copied the file and handed the stick back to him. Her disapproval was gone.

"No, you're right," she said. "It's all part of the national security debate."

Mike stood up. They were on the same side now, co-conspirators in this thing that neither of them felt sure of, clinging together on shifting ground. They did not look directly at the other.

"See you around, Lauren," Mike said. She grunted, not lifting up her head from her screen, but as he turned around she called his name. She smiled as her hair crowned her face.

Once again he marveled at how pretty she was. "Yeah?"

She opened her mouth but no words came. She paused, turning something over in her mind, then she shook her head. "Nothing," she said. "See you around."

———————

AS MIKE drove out of Manchester his head felt it might explode. He hated himself for passing on a snippet of video that he knew was bullshit. He hated even more that Lauren spotted the ruse and then grasped at it anyway.

But as the car began to eat up the miles and Manchester faded away behind him, slumping into strip-malled suburbs and then crowding thickets of dark green trees, his mind eased with thoughts of a new mission.

Jaynie.

He had to see her.

It was too long since his mother's phone call alerted him to her overdose and he had done nothing. He put his private life aside in favor of Hodges' cause. But not now. Corinth Falls was just a four hour drive from here, across Vermont and into upstate New York. He would start to make it right. He was supposed to head straight to Washington to look up some of Hodges' old army comrades from the 1980s. But that could wait until after he took this detour. Swinging by Corinth Falls would not even take him far out of his way.

Normally Mike drove with the radio on to relieve the tedium of the journey with the sounds of music or chat. He caught up on the news or even tuned into a religious channel, lulled by the mesmerizing rhythms of some far-off pastor's voice. Not this time. Now he relished the simple silence of the car, the straightness of the road ahead and the sense that he escaped the bubble that held him in its grip for countless weeks. Now he felt he could think properly again at last, not just about the latest development in the campaign. He wondered what lay ahead of him in Corinth Falls' hospital. What would Jaynie be like? He dreaded to think of her lying in some awful ward, tubes coming out her arms. But it would not be the first time. He wondered if she used the money she took from him to buy the drugs that almost killed her and his foot slowly sank onto the accelerator and sent the car racing down the road ahead, forward in time but back into his past.

The outskirts of Corinth Falls, nestled in its little river valley, looked like they always did. He took an early exit so he could enter on an old country road and not the main drag. He always liked cresting the rise of a hill above town that gave a view of the place, snaking along its valley, still dominated by the giant hulks of a half dozen factories and steel mills long since closed. Mike pulled the car over onto the side of the road. It was too cold to get out but he looked at the lights below him as the sun – hidden somewhere behind a thick blanket of cloud – dipped below the horizon. The city lights switched on, twinkling in the growing twilight, and he absorbed the view, as familiar to him as his own face. He closed his eyes and remembered his childhood here as a bright and distant land despite its troubles. For a long time Jaynie was the sun that illuminated it.

He leaned his head forward onto the steering wheel and shut his eyes. Suddenly the task ahead loomed like a mountaintop. He did not want to do this, he thought. But, with a physical heave, he put the car into gear and drove towards home.

―――――――――――

THE HOSPITAL waiting room was quiet. The white-washed walls were faded, though clean, and the smell of fresh disinfectant pervaded the air as Mike walked into reception. Only a handful of people sat in the chairs either sitting alone or huddled together. There was no rush of patients here, not until the bars closed and the casualties from the fights started to trickle in. The receptionist glanced up from reading a paperback novel, looked at Mike quizzically, and perhaps sensed immediately he was now an outsider.

"I am looking for Jaynie Collins," he said. "She was admitted a few days ago."

The receptionist glanced at her computer. "She checked herself out this morning," she said, with a tone of disapproval. She had obviously seen the reason Jaynie was admitted. Drug overdoses were not exactly uncommon here but old moralities held hard.

"I can't give you her address," she said, a sharp edge in her voice.

Mike turned around and stalked out. "No need," he muttered.

He got back in the car and drove out into the hills above the north side of town. There were a few scattered subdivisions and trailer parks up there and that is where Sean said Jaynie lived for the past year. She moved there after selling their old marital home to buy a dilapidated trailer out in the woods. The rest of the cash, he knew, she steadily blew on her habits. He drove up a narrow road, eventually slipping and sliding on an icy track crowded overhead with black tree branches stripped of leaves. Mike fought with the steering wheel as it lurched from side to side and gradually brought the careering car to a halt outside a white half-wide trailer. There was a beat-up Ford outside that Mike recognized as Jaynie's sister's old car. The place looked a mess, but he expected that. At least a light was on. He got out of the car, pulled his jacket tight around him, and walked up to the cheap, plastic door.

Mike was possessed with a sudden doubt. What was he doing here? It felt like picking at a wound, peeling off a thick scab of pain, just to see how it felt. And at this moment it felt bad. But he walked on and rapped on the door. There was nothing; just silence and a chilling wind buffeted his ears. He turned to go when the door creaked open and Jaynie's face appeared, blinking her eyes slowly as if she had just awakened. She looked startled to see Mike and for a second he thought she would smile, that the sweet Jaynie who appeared at his door in New Hampshire would emerge again. But, like a thundercloud sprouting from a summer sky, a look of fury creased her brow.

"Mike! What the fuck are you doing here?" she asked.

Mike stepped back. "I heard you were in the hospital. I thought "

She did not let him finish his thoughts before she attacked.

"Get out of here. What do you care? People should mind their own business."

Behind her Mike thought he heard a thud back inside the trailer, the hint of someone moving around. Jaynie heard it too and a look crossed her face, part fear, part something else Mike could not explain. A dealer? A lover? Someone was back there. Jaynie saw Mike react and reached out a hand to push him in the center of his chest.

"Get out of here, Mike," she said. "I don't want to see you."

He stepped back, but his foot caught on a patch of ice and he fell backwards. He tried to twist around but he only skidded more and the wind was knocked out of him as he fell onto the ground. An explosion of color filled his mind as the wound on his head from Guatemala sprang open anew. His eyes lost focus and when they found it again he saw Jaynie look down at him in horror. A trickle of blood crawled down his forehead.

"Mike?" she said and when he blinked and looked at her a momentary expression of relief crossed her face. It was rapidly replaced by a sneer.

"Go away." She slammed the door and from inside Mike heard the heated sound of raised voices. He hauled himself to his feet, feeling frozen and bruised, and staggered back to his car, certain in the knowledge he made a terrible mistake coming back to Corinth Falls. He got in the car, shivering, and slowly guided it back the way he had come, headed towards the distant blinking lights of a world far away from Jaynie's trailer.

MIKE STOOD in front of the White House surrounded by camera-toting tourists. The thought was surreal: could this campaign really end up here? This small building with its familiar ivory façade was what they fought for. Every speech, every dirty trick, every sacrifice of friend and family, aimed at finally getting inside this place. He could scarcely believe it. Then a nudge from a careless tourist angling for a better shot jolted him from his daydream.

He turned and walked back through Washington's streets. He trekked down the cold sidewalks until he hit K Street, the heart of lobbying in the capital. It was a soulless boulevard flanked by mirror-faced office buildings and busy with traffic. But it was home to countless consultancies and PR firms that all fed at the trough of government. Mike walked through the door of one of them, an anonymous eight-storey edifice that sat on a busy intersection. A long list of corporate names ran down a board behind the head of a bored-looking security guard. Mike saw the name he was looking for: Andersen Security Solutions. It was founded and run by General Arnold Andersen, a name that he dug up from Hodges' past as a fellow instructor at the School of the Americas and someone who was also posted throughout Central America in the 1980s. Dee then made the call and persuaded Andersen they were just collecting details for Hodges' biography. The General turned security consultant was only too happy to have Mike come in for a talk.

Andersen Security was on the fourth floor and the elevator whooshed Mike soundlessly skywards with doors that opened directly into the firm's plush lobby. He was barely out of the door when a tall, barrel-chested man in a dark blue suit hailed him from a side-office.

"Welcome! You must be Mike Sweeney!" he called and stepped forward to grab Mike's hand in a grip so tight that Mike reflexively massaged his fingers afterwards.

"General Andersen?" Mike asked.

The man nodded and stepped aside to let Mike into his office. It was a huge open space in the corner of the building. For a moment the view took Mike's breath away. With Washington's low-level skyline, you could see across the rooftops of the city to the Washington Memorial sticking needle-like into the sky, puncturing the gray clouds above.

"Ain't she something?" Andersen said, walking up behind Mike. "That view looks out over the most powerful square mile in the world. There ain't nowhere that even comes close to it."

Mike sat down and sank into a leather chair opposite Andersen's enormous desk. On the wall behind the General were photos from all over the world. Most featured Andersen in numerous shades of camouflage or elaborate dress uniforms. For a moment Mike thought of a different room: a dark, musty place on the shores of the Caribbean, where another military career was held in a similar but more secretive regard.

"So what can I do for you?" Andersen asked. "Jack Hodges is an old friend of mine and I'm happy to help him out.

Christ, the way things are going he'll be coming down here to Washington as goddamn president."

Mike fed Andersen the explanation that they were gathering biographic material as the campaign went on, looking to meet reporters' demands for fresh stories, keep the focus on his military record and hammer home their advantage on national security.

Andersen nodded. "Jack Hodges knows what it's like to fight for this country. Really fight. He's shed blood for his flag. I was with him in Iraq, the first time around. Back in '92. I've seen that man under pressure and under fire and let me tell you, there's no one you'd rather have with you in a fox hole."

Andersen's speech was emphatic and from the heart. Mike let him speak on. He and Hodges clearly went back decades, their careers zigzagged around each other as they rose through the ranks in an intricate game of tag. Andersen got out first and set up his consultancy in the wake of 9/11 and the war in Afghanistan. He worked from the lucrative sidelines as Hodges served two tough tours in Iraq and cemented his reputation as a man who got the job done. Mike listened patiently and prodded Andersen into one anecdote after another, dutifully taking notes, playing the role of a court stenographer to his testimony. Andersen, like many of his ilk, loved the sound of his own voice describing past glories. With such men it was always best to hear them out before striking. But eventually Mike needed to make his move. He waited for a lull in Andersen's monologue and then casually tried to shift things back in time.

"When did you meet the Senator though? That was at the

School of the Americas, right? You were both on the training staff there?"

The General nodded. "That's right. Can hardly believe we were training people who were mostly older than us."

"It gets some bad press though, that program," Mike said. "Lots of people said it encouraged some pretty nasty practices in some of our allies."

For the first time, the smile dropped off Andersen's face. "That's what some people say. People who know nothing about what we did there. We trained good men to fight some horrible, little wars. But we taught them to win and that's what they did."

"Then the Senator spent some time in Guatemala. Did you work with him there?" Mike asked. "We're trying to flesh out that part of his story, it seems a little sparse. What was the nature of his work there?"

Andersen leaned back in his chair and regarded Mike with a studied look of disdain. "What are you getting at, young man?"

Mike was stunned. He didn't think he had even begun to push Andersen's buttons, but the General came out swinging. Mike did not need to feign surprise.

"Nothing at all. It just seems a blank in his CV."

Andersen stood up. "We saved that country from communism. We stopped the goddamn Soviets and the Maoists and God knows what else from taking over that place. We did it for America and people seem to have forgotten that."

The General walked to the door and opened it. "This interview is over," he said.

Mike got up and smiled in as friendly a way as possible. "Thank you for your time," he said. He knew Andersen thought it was a clever trick to shut down the conversation. But Andersen was an army man and thought killing something made it go away. Mike knew better. Andersen miscalculated. Mike now knew he was onto something. Again he thought of General Carillo, giving the same sort of speech, about fighting communists and saving a country. He also spouted words of duty and of honor. More linked these men than just words and sentiment. Mike was sure of it.

————

HODGES WAS furious again. There was no getting away from it as Dee sat in her office chair and endured the withering blast of his rage. He towered over her, his eyes wide with anger and his usually delicately combed hair suddenly disheveled.

"Where the hell is the coverage of my anti-poverty plan? Where is it?" he screamed. "Instead we have nothing but this bullshit!"

Hodges jabbed at the remote control in Dee's office and turned up the volume on the television that was permanently tuned to CNN. As the words of a panel of talking heads leaked into the air it was clear they were still discussing the latest Stanton tape.

Dee said nothing. She knew Hodges needed to blow out his fury but at the same time she had no doubt at all that she did the right thing. The tape worked like a charm as soon as Lauren posted it up on her *Horse Race* blog. Drudge picked it up within ten minutes and Dee suspected Lauren herself had emailed in the link, which was useful, as Dee had been preparing to do just that when she saw it was already the headline. Then it spread over the rest of the web like wildfire. She watched it burn through the blogs and eventually onto Fox News and the rest of the cable TV universe. Tomorrow, she knew, it would be the front page of the newspapers. But there was no denying Hodges' genuine fury. He leaned in close to her, like a General at a rebellious Private, looking at her with eyes set deep in a face that was now red, its veins pulsing with blood.

"I told you," he said, the words grinding out through clenched jaws. "I did not want this sort of campaign. Where's the coverage of my Second New Deal? Where are the headlines on that? I gave a goddamn press conference about it and no one seems to give a shit."

Dee backed off slightly, staying seated but rolling away on her chair, gliding out of his zone of control.

"We're putting it out there, Senator," she said. "But we don't dictate what the media does. They make their own story choices and they're going with this instead."

She chose her words carefully. She wanted him to calm down, but she also wanted control of her own emotions. She was not used to getting balled out like this. Not by anyone. One of her toughest fights was to keep her own temper in check as well as monitoring that of her candidate.

"It's unfortunate that it's been drowned out by this other thing," she said.

Hodges gave a violent groan that seemed to well up from deep within him, wordless and full of anger. He stalked over to the other side of the room and his hands grasped at his tightly cut hair. Dee had never seen him like this. He cared about this campaign so much, she thought. More than any of them understood. She felt a little humbled. Other candidates exploded over losses, despaired over poor polls, but she had never seen one go off the deep end over a low blow at an opponent. Especially not a punch that landed so effectively.

"I did not want this," he said again and flung himself into a chair, looking deflated, like a suddenly burst balloon.

Dee stood up and walked over to him. She put a hand on his shoulder and squeezed her fingers into the tightly knotted muscles. They felt like girders of tense steel.

"I'm sorry, sir," she said. "But this is going to be worth two points to us. Four points if we get lucky. It's a 48 hour story that will take us to the finishing post."

Hodges did not react. Dee knelt down in front of him. She looked at him straight.

"Jack, you are in sight of winning New Hampshire. It won't be like Iowa. We don't have to come in second this time."

CHAPTER 14

MIKE OPENED HIS eyes and waited for the world of his Washington hotel room to swim into focus. It was past 8:00 a.m. which was obscenely late after endless months of rising before the sun. The campaign trail scrambled his body clock, which now thought nothing of existing on four hours sleep. But deep within him a well of exhaustion sometimes bubbled to the surface. He rolled over and stared at the beeping alarm clock. It went off for perhaps an hour before it woke him. He reached out and whacked it with the flat of his hand and sent it skittering onto the floor, still squawking forlornly. With a grimace, Mike hauled himself out of bed and switched it off.

Perhaps it was his reaction to the meeting with General Andersen yesterday that triggered his exhaustion. He felt he got nothing out of it apart from a sense he was on the trail of something awful, something that dragged him further and further away from the campaign. Last night he phoned Ivan Tobar out in Garden City and asked him who in Washington might know something about Central America in the 1980s.

He danced delicately around the reasons why he needed to know. Tobar provided the name and address of an immigrants' rights group, The American Center for Latino Justice. Now Mike looked at the scribbled words on his hotel notepad and saw the address lay way outside the center of Washington, far out in the sprawling suburbs of northern Virginia. It would be good, he thought, to get away from K Street and Andersen's gleaming office with its pictures of military parades.

———————

THE DRIVE there took him on a painfully slow crawl through the traffic-clogged suburbs of Fairfax County that emerged from Washington's downtown in a formless mass of malls and business parks. Only a few decades ago most of this area was rolling Virginia farmland but it was eaten up by the business of government. Now it stretched to the horizon as a tangled grid of roads and vehicles. Mike was in a daze as he pulled the car into a parking lot outside a non-descript business park by the side of a two-lane highway that roared with traffic. He checked the address and looked at the building's black darkened windows, like a vast screen of unseeing eyes. The ACLJ was on the top floor. He trudged across the parking lot and went inside.

Tobar said to ask for a woman named Jenny Gusman, the group's chief researcher, and she appeared quickly from a back office to shake Mike's hand. She looked him up and down and asked where he was from.

"I'm a friend of Ivan Tobar," he said. "I'm doing some research for an academic project. He said you guys were the people to speak to when it comes to U.S. policy in Guatemala in the 1980s."

Mike deliberately kept his words vague and hoped her curiosity would not be too piqued. He looked around the tattered-looking suite of offices, full of young people dressed in jeans and T-shirts answering phones that never stopped ringing. It looked like a campaign office. Gusman, a pixie-ish woman and full of energy, smiled.

"Any friend of Ivan's is a friend of ours. We mainly do work with immigrant associations in the Washington area, but we have a little human rights section that we keep updated," she said and she beckoned Mike to follow her.

They went into a converted storeroom at the back. It was lined with shelves packed with thick files of papers. On the wall were black and white photographs of bodies lying in front of burnt-out huts or splayed out in fields. Gusman gestured at the mass of paperwork.

"What do you want to know?"

Mike was at a loss. He realized he had no idea what he was really investigating. He pulled up a stool and removed a pile of papers, putting them gingerly on the floor and hoping they would not topple down. He felt a wave of exhaustion wash over him again, swamping him, and decided he should be as honest as possible.

"Look," he said. "I can't say exactly who I work for. But I am researching a topic that leads back to the late 1980s in

Guatemala and US involvement in the civil war there. It's not my area of expertise. I just need help."

Gusman narrowed her eyes and regarded him for a moment. Though he dwarfed her in size, Mike suddenly felt small. Eventually she gave a little laugh.

"It's about time some *Americano* took an interest in what your country did there."

She took down a large folder from one of the shelves. She spread it out in front of him. It contained numerous pieces of white paper that appeared to be some sort of incident reports. They were interspersed with dozens of the same kind of black and white photos that were pasted up on the wall. Bodies upon bodies; men, women and children. The effect numbed Mike.

"This is the file for one province from 1987," Gusman said. "We are trying to build a database of incidents. We get a lot of folks from Guatemala coming through here and we try and ask them about things they may have seen. A lot of them say nothing. But others can help us fill in the details."

"Who are these people?" Mike asked, gesturing at the pictures of the dead.

"Farmers, peasants and, most likely, a few guerrillas too. The Americans trained the Guatemalan army to fight communists. The army did just that, but they did not care too much about the details. Nuns, social workers, union organizers, journalists… the definition of communist became pretty broad."

Gusman saw the look on Mike's face.

"Americans are never so good at looking at their past, especially beyond their borders. It is a talent you all have," she said.

"What was the School of the Americas?" he asked.

"Was? It still exists. It is a military training school for Latin American countries. Thousands of army soldiers from Central America passed through its ranks in the 1980s. When you look at those photos you can see their handiwork."

"And in Guatemala?"

"America feared a communist takeover, just like happened in Cuba," she said. "So they helped the government murder and torture anyone with leftist sympathies."

Gusman put more files down in front of him and began to go through the years, one by one. It was a litany of horror. The massacres, the torture of thousands in grimy prison cells, the CIA advisors and trainers who marshaled local thugs to keep the army in power. The pillage of vast areas of the country-side and the spilling of rivers of blood. Two hundred thousand people died or disappeared by the time it ended in 1996. The vast majority of them were Mayan Indians.

Finally, Mike could not take the endless lists of the dead anymore. "Do you know the name of General Rodrigo Carillo?" he blurted out.

Gusman nodded slowly. "A senior commander in the Lake Atitlan area. He was involved in the church massacre at Santa Teresa in 1987," she said, realizing that Mike knew a little more than he was letting on. "The army killed 75 or more peasants around a village church after a guerrilla raid wiped out one of their patrols. It's a relatively little known massacre."

She paused, noticing the blank look on Mike's face. "It's well known to us. Just not many others seem to care."

Mike could not miss the sadness and reproach in her voice. "And Carillo was responsible?"

"Carillo was hardly the only brute working for the army who broke the rules of war," Gusman said. "But he was one of the most enthusiastic. He killed peasants, he tortured suspects…"

Suddenly Gusman shut the file with a snap and stood up. "I can do better than just tell you about him," she said. "I can take you to someone with a more personal story. Come on, let's go."

Gusman took Mike by the arm and led him out of the office to her battered white Toyota sedan. It was a mess inside, full of Coke cans and scraps of paper. She grinned an apology and they set off. They drove for twenty minutes down blocks of increasingly scruffy-looking suburbia. Gradually all the shop signs in English switched to Spanish. Mike saw groups of men hunkered down on street corners, waiting for day laboring jobs that rarely came. Eventually Gusman pulled up outside a dilapidated ranch home surrounded by a half-dozen beat-up cars. They got out of the car and they walked up to the front door.

Gusman knocked and a small, dark-haired man peered out. His eyes blinked wide as if just awakened. There followed a burst of chatter in Spanish that was so quick Mike could not follow it. But at the end of the conversation, the small man cast a glance in Mike's direction, nodded imperceptibly and opened the door to let them in.

Inside the living room was entirely bare except for an ancient television set and a couple of grimy-looking mattresses on the floor. The man sat on one of them and gestured unself-consciously for Gusman and Mike to do likewise. Mike settled himself, and tried hard not to look at the stains.

"This is 'Jose'," Gusman said. "You don't need to know his real name. He was a villager from the Atitlan area, near where the Santa Teresa massacre happened. He was picked up for interrogation by Carillo's unit back in 1989. He can tell you what sort of person the General is."

Mike looked at the man. He could not guess his age. He must be at least 40 or so, he thought, but you could put ten years on either side of that and he would not have been surprised. His face was lined with the harsh kisses of the sun and the stresses of hard work, but his eyes sparkled and his black hair shone like it had been polished. His hands, which seemed large for his body, were thick and muscular, a product of a lifetime of labor. They looked like they could strangle a horse.

"Tell me what you know about General Carillo," Mike said.

Jose nodded and spoke slowly in thickly accented English, while Gusman helped him along when he got stuck. He talked of his village, San Diego, deep in the Highlands, surrounded by thick jungles and farms. Of how the guerrillas came down from the mountains and took food for their supplies; of how the villagers begged them not to come, but could not refuse their requests. They were just peasants with no weapons and, besides, many of the guerrillas were cousins and brothers.

Then, one day, Carillo came to their village and lambasted them as communist-lovers. He ignored protestations that they were simple farmers. He singled out five of them for interrogation, including Jose. They were put in the back of a jeep and taken to an army camp.

Jose stopped talking. Mike could see the man's bottom lip quivering and his breath came in deep gasps. Gusman reached out and rested a hand on his arm.

"Perhaps this was not a good idea," she said. But Jose jerked his arm away and shook his head fiercely.

"It's about time someone asked about this," he said. "Carillo was beloved of the Americans in Guatemala City."

Mike said nothing. It seemed there was a spell in the house that gathered in the shadows from the far corners of the room and reached out to throttle the light.

"I was kept in a dirty room for seven days. I was tied to a chair and they beat me three times a day. Each morning, noon and night, they beat me. Their fists fed on me."

Jose spat the words out angrily, his eyes shining and defiant as they tumbled out of his mouth. "Carillo was the worst," he said. "He asked the same questions over and over again. Where are the guerrillas? Who are they? Give me their names. It did not even matter what I told him. Whatever the answer he would take one of his big, fat Cuban cigars and stab it out on my flesh."

Mike winced at the thought and remembered the smell of smoke that permeated Carillo's villa. He wondered how the stench changed when mixed with burning skin and muscle.

Jose stood up and lifted his T-shirt to reveal a long line of old, blistered white scars that marched across his chest like a line of lunar craters. "In the end I told him what I knew. Everyone did," he said. "They made a few arrests and they let me go."

His voice faded away and he looked down at the ground. "But I survived," he said. Then more loudly: "I survived."

There was a sudden knock on the door which broke the dark spell in the room like a snapped twig. Jose rushed to open the door. Again there was a burst of staccato Spanish and he looked back. "There is a job," he said. "A lady in Georgetown is moving house. It's a half-day's work to lift her furniture. I'll get twenty dollars."

Gusman and Mike got up and Jose brushed past them as he left. He barely acknowledged them as he collected some warm work clothes. A flat-bed truck idled outside and its exhaust sent plumes of smoke into the cold air. A half-dozen other Latino men sat on the back of it, wrapped up warm, their faces dark or light, young and old, betrayed different nationalities and stories. Jose jumped on the truck to join them. It trundled slowly down the street. Jose did not look back. But Gusman and Mike stared at it until it disappeared from view, carrying its human cargo, his scars hidden beneath cheap clothing, onto the highway heading north.

AS he drove back from Washington to New Hampshire, Mike decided to visit Corinth Falls again. It was a whim, borne of the long drive and a longing to see Sean. He desperately needed someone to just relax with, free from the campaign, free from Guatemala. Just an old friend. He punched in his phone number and, when Sean answered, simply named their old, favorite local bar.

"I'll see you in two hours," Mike said and hung up without waiting for a reply.

Then his foot hit the gas pedal and he was there in ninety minutes.

The bar had not changed one bit. O'Rourke's squatted on the corner of Locust and Main. It was a dark, seedy dive where daylight never penetrated and the same selection of 80s hits that Mike remembered from so many wasted evenings of his youth still played on the Juke box. Sean waited inside. They embraced each other and then burst out laughing and ordered a round of beers.

Mike listened patiently first while Sean updated him on his family life and the struggle to find work. Then it was Sean's turn to play confessor and listen to Mike unburden himself. He talked about his trip to Guatemala and Washington but kept the details a little vague. He trusted his old friend with more than he told anyone else so he mentioned Hodges' links to Central America, the visit with the General and Jose's horrible story. Sean grimaced and shook his head.

"The only good thing to come out of the 80s was the music," he said, as a *Guns'n Roses* hit played for the fourth time. "The politics stank."

"Yeah, I know. But don't you think it all seems like ancient history now? I mean, it was the Cold War."

Sean shrugged. "Doesn't seem like ancient history to you. Nor that Jose guy in Virginia," Sean said.

"Yeah, but what if Hodges was involved in something really bad? What if the woman who tried to shoot him wasn't just some crazy person? But was out for revenge. I mean, Jesus, what could Hodges have done that means you would still want to kill him 30 years later?"

The pair fell silent. Mike had finally voiced his innermost fear, the burden that grew heavier and heavier the more he delved into Hodges' background. Sean breathed a deep sigh and took a swig of the whisky chaser that nestled snugly beside his bottle of beer.

"Fuck," he said. "I can't think like that, Mike. Hodges gives a lot of people around here a bit of hope. People talk about him all the time. They're rooting for him to win in New Hampshire. They don't want the same old bullshit from some career politician like Stanton," he said.

He paused for a moment. "They want a chance to vote for Hodges, Mike," he added. "Not just in the primaries. But in the real election against that prick we've got in the White House right now. They want to vote for Hodges to be president."

Now it was Mike's turn to have a drink. He could hear Dee's voice, delivering her favorite lecture: we're here to protect our man. Even from himself. From his own past. From his own sins. Mike was a soldier. Trust in the righteousness of the cause. And it was righteous too, he thought. The hope and inspiration that he read in people's faces when they heard Hodges speak, when he spoke to them directly, like a man, like a fellow American, not just another politician angling for votes. He felt it himself, too. That was, after all, why he first signed up.

"Oh shit…" Sean breathed suddenly and Mike followed his gaze to the bar's front door where a slim, female figure had walked in out of the cold.

Jaynie.

She cast her eye around the bar and when it settled upon Mike's surprised face, her expression lit up like a pinball machine. Mike could almost hear the bells and whistles going off. She smiled a heart-breakingly familiar grin and bounded over.

"Mike!" she cried. "Goddamn! What are you doing here?"

Mike looked at her, trying to see if she was high on anything. But her eyes were clear. She pulled herself up a few feet away from them. Mike wondered if she remembered how just two days ago she slammed the door on him and left him sprawled on the ground.

"Can I join you?" she asked, an acknowledgement that now she needed to be invited.

Mike strained to say no. He knew he should. He did not have the strength to deal with Jaynie right now. But he felt his resistance melt at the softness of her touch, at the pleading at the edge of her voice. He said nothing and just made room for her in the booth, scrunching up to create space for Jaynie at the table. It was always like that.

THREE HOURS later Mike stumbled along in a dizzy, drunken haze, immune to the midnight cold that caressed his skin. Jaynie walked by his side and giggled as they slipped and slithered down an earthen bank towards the railway tracks that were a shortcut back to Jaynie's trailer.

The evening was, in the end, just like old times. Jaynie was funny and flirtatious and the three of them sank into an orgy of reminiscence. They relived their school days, their college vacations and all the tales they relegated to a half-remembered past, like it was a foreign country. They shot pool and slammed whiskies, put their favorite songs on the juke box until well past midnight when Sean finally declared that he needed to leave and get back to his family. Jaynie raised a single eyebrow at Mike and wordlessly the two left the bar. Mike shed his jacket and placed it around her shoulders to ward off the freezing air. Now they bumped along the train tracks, like off-kilter dance partners, laughing loud at each stumble and pratfall.

"You remember the prom?" Jaynie giggled. "Didn't we come down here that night?"

"Yeah. I don't think I've ever been as drunk as that," he said and laughed. "Nor as happy." He remembered that far-off evening when they were both 17, already dating for two years, and the sweethearts of their class. They got drunk on a bottle of moonshine from one of Jaynie's country uncles and flung themselves around the dance floor like whirling dervishes. Then they came down to the railway tracks to watch the stars madly circle overhead and make love in the heat of a summer night.

"Feels like a long time ago now," Jaynie said. Suddenly she seemed more sober than he was. She steadied him and helped him off the tracks as they neared the spot where they could scramble up into Jaynie's back yard.

"You know. I owe you so many apologies, Mike," she said. "I know I've got into more trouble than anyone ever thought possible. I know I was impossible to be around, let alone stay married to. I don't blame you for leaving."

There was not a trace of bitterness or rancor in her voice, just a whiff of regret and melancholy.

"We were just kids, Jaynie," Mike said as they clambered up the slope towards a copse of trees behind which the dark hulk of Jaynie's trailer could be seen.

She slipped her arm through his and helped him along. She felt warm beside him and he thought of the touch of her flesh alongside his. It had been a long time, he thought. He looked at her and traced the line of her face, still beautiful in this half-light. She was still in there; his Jaynie. Through all the time and the drugs and the booze and the hopelessness, somewhere in the core of her being, a little diamond shined on.

They arrived at the trailer and Jaynie ushered him in. It was dark, musty and chaotically littered. It smelled like a troop of cats lived there. He scrunched up his nose.

"Since when did you get a cat?" he asked.

Jaynie did not reply but pushed him down into a sofa. "I'll get something else to drink," she said and went into the kitchen to rummage around in the cupboards. Mike settled into the sofa. It was soft. He felt the ceiling above begin to whirl, like the night sky did years ago. He tried to focus on the light in the center of the room, but it was a lost battle. By the time Jaynie returned, clutching a half-drunk bottle of bourbon, Mike was already snoring. He never felt her lean over and kiss him gently on the top of his head or her lips brush over his forehead like a benediction. She snuggled down beside him on the couch and nestled her head against his shoulder. Within seconds she too slept.

———

THE SOUND exploded into the front room of the trailer like a bomb going off. The door burst open, half-shattered and hanging off one hinge. A tumble of figures burst through into the room and screamed and shouted as Mike and Jaynie flailed into rude consciousness, untangling from one another on the couch in a whirl of knotted limbs.

"Police! Police! Get down!"

Mike, stunned, looked around at the black-uniformed figures coming towards him, pistols grasped in both hands. He barely registered the sight before a blow caught him on the back of the head and he hit the floor, his mouth open, and tasted the bitter, ashy carpet. He was facedown and he felt a knee plant itself in the middle of his back and his arms hauled forcefully behind him. Then he felt a caress of cold metal around his wrists and heard a faint click. He was handcuffed.

He twisted his head to his right and saw that Jaynie lay there too, trussed up like a turkey dressed for a Sunday dinner. She struggled hard, her head rocked from side-to-side and the veins in her neck stood out like pipelines and pulsed beneath her skin. She wailed and screamed, a banshee-like sound, as the police began to search through the trailer.

"Jaynie! Jaynie! It's all right. Calm down," said Mike. But she did not hear him. She was frantic and roiled on her belly like a run over snake.

"Better watch that one. She's feisty," one of the cops said, as he emptied a cupboard that overflowed with plastic dishes and pots and pans.

"What the fuck is going on?" Mike asked.

One of the cops cast him a sideways glance but did not answer him. Instead he sniffed the air and grimaced. "Sure smells like a meth lab in here," he said.

Mike closed his eyes. Fuck, he breathed. Then to himself, loudly in his mind, he screamed the words he could not express out loud.

Fuck! Fuck! Fuck!

Jaynie did not have a cat. The sour, rotten smell in the trailer was from her cooking up meth. He suddenly thought of her reaction when he came here before, pushing him away, certain of someone else with her. She was not hiding a lover. She hid her drug-making partner.

One of the cops roughly pushed open a door to a back bedroom and the sour smell suddenly got stronger.

"Bingo!" the cop said and held open the door. Mike craned

his neck up from the ground and saw a complex tangle of piping and pots, like some crazed hillbilly scientist's perpetual motion machine.

He turned to Jaynie. She was quiet now and would not look at him. She faced the opposite wall, even when the cops hauled them both roughly to their feet.

"I've no idea what this is…" Mike said to the cop who held his arms. But the expression of naked disgust on the man's face caused the words to evaporate. The cop glanced over at Jaynie.

"We'd heard you'd been hooked up with those Callaghan boys and their crew," he said. "You've had plenty of chances, ma'am. Now it's time to do a little time."

They were frog-marched out of the trailer and pushed outside into the bright sunshine. Mike instinctively raised his hands to shield his eyes form the light. But they were caught behind his body by the cuffs and he yelped at the unfamiliar strain in his triceps. Then he was shoved forward to a trio of squad cars parked outside the trailer, like wagons drawn up on the prairie. They were placed in the back of one of them and the car's engine hummed into life.

Mike stared ahead and his mind whirred with panic. Things had happened so quickly he could barely think.

"Mike… Mike…"

Jaynie sounded desperate and pleading. He turned around. Jaynie looked at him now with eyes full of fear and tears. "I don't want to go to jail, Mike," she said.

Slowly, and painfully, she moved her handcuffed hands from out behind her and twisted her back. She inched a finger over to touch his side and rested it there. Mike felt a rage rise inside him. He turned from her and moved away, shifting out of reach of her desperate touch, the gulf between them just inches, but now as uncrossable as an ocean.

———

MIKE PUT the phone receiver to his forehead and paused for a moment before dialing the number. He looked around at the bars of the holding cell while three other listless male prisoners returned his gaze. He could not believe his situation. He had one phone call. It felt like a movie even just thinking that. But it was the truth. He was arrested for aiding and abetting the production of illegal narcotics. He told the cops he was just visiting his ex-wife but they seemed uninterested.

"Tell it to the court," one said.

He dialed a number now and prayed it would not go through to a voicemail. That she would answer. That she would help.

"Hello?"

Dee's voice never sounded so good. Mike blurted out his story and quickly rattled off his whereabouts and what happened. The entire time he spoke he heard Dee's measured breathing get a little quicker on the other end of the line. Eventually he finished. There was a pause.

"Just one question, Mike. You were just visiting, right? You're innocent?"

"Yes!" Mike insisted. "Jesus, Dee. For the past three months

I've been nowhere that you didn't know about. I haven't a spare second to shave, let alone run a fucking drug ring."

He sounded hysterical, wild even. But then he heard Dee chuckle and her Southern drawl got a little thicker. "Yeah, I guess you have a point, Mike," she said. "Sit tight there, fella, and try not to get too friendly with anyone in the showers. I'll see what I can do."

Mike heard the click of Dee putting down the phone. He felt like he just flung a Hail Mary pass the entire length of the field and was watching the spinning football twirl towards the horizon without the slightest sense whether it would make its target. He slumped onto a bench and held his head in his hands and a tide of despair filled him. He was still like that three hours later when the door to the holding cell opened and a burly cop walked in.

"Sweeney. Your story checks out. You're outta here," he said.

Mike got up and stumbled forward. As he walked past the cop the man grabbed his elbow and leaned in close, whispering words with a mix of admiration and envy.

"You've got some powerful friends," he said.

CHAPTER 15

DEE RESTED AGAINST the lamppost on the corner of Main Street and Elm in Manchester and sucked in deeply on her cigarette. She felt the nerve endings jingle in her brain as the nicotine rush hit its target. They lit up one by one as if someone was turning on the Christmas lights. It was early on polling day but she wanted to step outside the campaign head-quarters and watch the New Hampshire streets a little.

She leaned against the cold metal, her skin protected by a thick overcoat, and looked at a posse of student volunteers gath-ered on the opposite side of the street. They carried Hodges' placards, crudely drawn in crayon that they churned out for weeks in the headquarters like some campaign version of a Chinese sweatshop. Now they waved them high in the air as each car drove down the street and they cheered loudly at any motorist who bothered to press their horn. Many did. It was like the sound of a mini-traffic jam amid the cries and shouts and laughter.

Dee did not allow herself to take that as a sign. Long years in the game told her not to trust things like a straw poll of horn honkers. What she trusted was the poll that landed on her desk last night. It was the final snap shot of the New Hampshire campaign and it spelled out in black and white the one thing they needed to know: Hodges and Stanton were neck and neck. The dirt they poured all over Stanton's campaign had kept the opposition down. But Hodges was not decisively ahead. He and Stanton were like two fighters in some old cliffhanger movie. They slugged away at each other on the edge of a chasm and each hoped that only one would topple over, not both. Dee drew in a deep blast of her cigarette and puffed out the smoke until it wreathed around her like an ashy halo and billowed in the freezing air. She had done all she could, she reflected. She knew that. And yet… she hated the thought of getting this close and losing. They had their single piece of glorious luck in Iowa and rode it for all it was worth. Right to this point of potential victory. If they won here, Stanton was firmly on the ropes and headed to South Carolina for a last stand where they could knock her out. But if Stanton won New Hampshire, then the narrative changed. Suddenly she would be the "comeback kid" story for the media to latch onto, fighting off a scrappy but over-reaching interloper.

She watched the students opposite her, fixing on their smiling faces, their sheer joy and belief in what they were doing. She narrowed her eyes and focused in on two girls with their arms wrapped around each other as they held placards in their other hands. They jumped together at each car horn and laughed so hard it looked like they were drunk, despite being just after 7:00 on a freezing January morning.

"High on goddamn life," Dee muttered and then smiled to admonish herself for a sense of sour envy. "What was that about, *catin?*" she thought. "Come on. Remember why you do this."

She felt a sudden flash of heat in her hand and instinctively dropped her cigarette butt which had burned down to the filter. She stamped on it to put it out in the slushy snow and headed back to the headquarters where her car was parked. It was time to see her candidate.

———

SHE FOUND him in the hotel swimming pool. A security detail closed it to keep out the prying eyes of other guests while he swam a series of lengths. She walked into the room, breathing in the unexpected humidity and warmth of the air. Hodges was in the water, perfectly in synch as he scythed through the blue, chlorinated pool. She had no idea whether he saw her. His stroke did not alter. Just back and forth, back and forth, like a shark, moving all the time, never slowing. She settled into a faux beach chair and waited, not taking her eyes off him, noticing his body was lean and muscular and looked a good twenty years younger than the calendar told her it was. She never found male bodies attractive. She hated their hardness, their muscles, their hair. The softness of a woman was so much superior, so inviting and warm. But even she admired Hodges' physique. He looked carved from marble. Eventually he finished his laps and emerged from the end of the pool dripping wet and taking off his goggles. He nodded hello to Dee and walked over.

"What's up, Dee?" he asked.

She stood up, feeling suddenly like a private standing to attention. He naturally commanded respect. "I got the final numbers last night. We're even, maybe slightly ahead."

Hodges absorbed the information and picked up a towel to dry his tightly cut hair. "It's going to be a tense day then," he said.

Dee nodded. "I'll get more feedback later in the afternoon, but I don't imagine it will change much. We just have to wait for the result."

Hodges wrapped the towel around his waist. He was silent for a moment, lost in thought, and then he smiled. "Hell, two months ago, slogging our ass through Iowa and getting nowhere, we never dreamed of being here, Dee. But I'd have given my life for it."

"You almost did, sir," Dee said.

Hodges chuckled. But it was a distant sound. "It's the strangest thing," he said. "I wanted to get here because of what I believed in. Because I know that I could make this country right. But it took some crazy woman trying to kill me to get me noticed."

Hodges grunted a brief, bitter laugh. "That's not how it should be," he said.

Dee put a hand on his arm, felt the rigid muscle on his forearm still flush with blood after the swim. "It's a game, Jack," she said. "It's a vicious, nasty game. That's why you've got me. Then once we're done, you can rip up the old rule book and change the way it's played."

Hodges seemed to snap out of the moment. He resumed toweling his hair dry again. "We've got to win first," he said and turned around.

Dee watched him go. She never had a candidate like him. Anyone else would be in a feverish mood now, veering between the thrill of a dreamed for victory or the pitch-black despair of a feared defeat. They tally all the long years, the thousands of days and tens of thousands of hours that brought them to this point. But not Hodges. He had the nerves to get reflective. The iron will to look at his own ego and understand this was about more than him. She looked at the pool. Its rough waters were calm now that Hodges was out and the ripples and waves smoothed back in to a mirror-like flatness.

Her phone rang. She looked at the number and felt a stab of surprise. Howard Carver. She weighed whether to answer it. That fat bastard would not have anything good to say. But she could not resist. She flipped open her phone.

"Howie?" she cooed. "You're the last person I thought I'd hear from today. How's life over in Camp Stanton? You staying warm by burning some more flags?"

She heard Carver's heavy breathing on the other end of the line. He was clearly flustered about something.

"Fuck you, Dee," he said. Dee grinned. She had not really expected her crude remark to hit home. It was too easy with him. "You bastards have dragged this campaign through the mud. But it's not over. When we get to South Carolina we are going to tear you apart. We are going to blow you out of the water."

His tone was spitting and vicious.

"What's got your goat, Howie?" Dee said, barely able to keep herself from laughing. This was like being back on the schoolyard.

"Just wait, Dee. Just wait," he said and hung up.

Dee stared at her phone as a growing feeling of realization surged through her body like a warm glow. She bit her lower lip to keep herself from letting out a little squeal. Carver's team and Stanton must have got their own last set of internal polls and whatever it contained was different from hers. It was bad news for them. Perhaps, very bad. She slipped the phone back into her pocket.

"*Pic kee toi*, Howie," she said under her breath. *Fuck you.* At last she let herself begin to laugh.

———

MIKE FOUND Dee in her office at the campaign headquarters. She glanced up at him as he came in and gestured with her head for him to close the door. He flopped down in front of her, a look of panic across his face. He had no idea what she would say about his arrest at Jaynie's trailer.

Dee sat on the edge of her desk and looked him up and down. He could not take the silence any longer.

"I'm sorry, Dee!" he said. "I just went home to check up on things and ended up at my ex-wife's place. She's a junkie and apparently a dealer now and I choose the morning she gets raided to spend the night there."

He put his head in his hands and stared at the floor. Then it slowly dawned on him that he could hear Dee laughing. He looked up. She smiled like a Cheshire cat.

"Relax, Mike. I know you would not get involved in anything like that. So I made a call to the cops. It's going to be fine."

"But what happened?"

Dee shrugged and spread her arms out wide. "Jesus, Mike, it ain't a crime in this country to be in the wrong place at the wrong time. Least it ain't yet anyway. I spoke to the Sheriff – he's a big fan of Hodges apparently – and explained the situation. He was very sympathetic to our point of view."

She went back and sat in her chair. "The cops ain't your problem, Mike. What about your ex-wife? Jaynie, right?"

Mike nodded. "She's in jail. They found a meth lab in her trailer...."

His words trailed away. He could scarcely believe it. He thought of her behind bars and to his shock felt all his anger towards her melt away. Jaynie, his Jaynie, was in *jail*. How did it come to this? He felt an almost overwhelming sense of guilt. He left her, first for Florida and then for the Hodges campaign. Now she was behind bars and alone.

"Good," said Dee.

Mike looked up in shock. She raised an eyebrow; dared daring him to say something.

"I haven't got time for any more shit, Mike," she said, her voice cold and low. "Neither have you. Neither has this campaign. She's where she needs to be and there's nothing you can do about it. Now you need to get your head right. Focus on the job in hand. Tell me about your trip to Washington? What did you find there?"

He looked at her with a mix of horror and shock. But her expression did not change. Dee was all business. Stuttering, he told her of meeting with General Andersen and how he stone-walled over Hodges' time in Guatemala. Then, picking up speed, he described his trip to the American Center for Latino Justice and what he found out about the dirty war in Guatemala and General Carillo's role in it. Dee listened intently and occasionally thrummed her fingers on the desk. When he was finished, she let out a loud sigh and puffed out her cheeks.

"Jesus, Mike. I don't like this. Whatever happens here in New Hampshire today, Stanton is going to start getting ugly with us. Howie Carver's already been threatening me with all sorts of hell to pay down in South Carolina."

Mike grimaced. South Carolina was legendary among political campaigners. The third stop on the nomination race and the one known to every campaign insider simply as The Swamp: a hot bed of dirty tricks and racial tension that could blow up even the most stable campaign.

"You've got to nail this down, Mike," she said. "We've sedated the link between Hodges and Carillo with that bullshit about donating to his kids' college fund. But that ain't going to hold. Lauren O'Keefe is not a fool. Nor is Carver. Our best shot is to get the dirt before they do. Then we can spin it our way. It's better to wash your own laundry then let someone else get all up in your underwear."

Mike knew what was coming next. He bowed his head.

"Go back to Iowa. Confront the shooter about Carillo. See if there's a link. Then get back to Guatemala and dig up everything you've got on this Carillo bastard. If he's got something on Hodges, then I want something on him."

Mike nodded. He would obey his orders.

Dee watched Mike as he got up to go. Just as he was about to open the door, she spoke. "Mike," she said. "I know it is hard. I know you feel like you're not doing proper campaign work. But, believe me, you are doing so much more than that."

Her voice was soft. Mike looked at her and he could see that she cared, that she read his doubts like he was an open book. That she understood them too.

"Trust me, Mike," she continued. "When the results come in tonight and we win this damn thing, it will be down to you as much as anyone else. What you are doing in secret is just as important to this campaign as anything that happens in public."

———

THOSE WORDS were still in Mike's mind as he watched the first vote tallies come through on a TV monitor on the crowded main floor of the campaign headquarters. The tension was unbearable. The entire staff stood or sat around the television like worshippers at a church, or star-struck country folk being visited by a UFO. Their eyes glazed over and their faces shone in the reflected glow of CNN. No one moved a muscle. Or spoke a word. Everything hinged on this. It came down to a ticking counter at the corner of the TV screen that showed Hodges and Stanton neck-and-neck.

It was agonizing. The first flood of returns arrived and Stanton led 40 percent to 31 percent. Mike shot a feverish glance at Dee, but she just shook her head.

"It's nothing," she mouthed as she leaned against a water cooler, but he noticed her fists clenched into tiny balls of tension, her finger bones strained white against her skin.

Then Hodges began to climb. After a third of the vote was counted the lead narrowed to just two points with Stanton at 37 percent and Hodges at 35 percent. It remained that way as the tally moved past 50 percent, then 60 percent, then 70 percent. Then they were both at 36 percent with Stanton just a few thousands votes ahead. Mike muttered under his breath, like a rabid sports fan, watching his team just behind in the final innings, stepping up to the plate with just a few at-bats to go.

"Come on, come on, come on," he said. He uttered the words like a prayer of want and longing, afraid almost to blink lest he miss an update.

A huge cheer went up. The ticker finally showed they were ahead. With 80 percent of the results in, Hodges and Stanton were still level at 36 percent but Hodges was in front on the count by just over 200 votes. Mike looked over at Dee again. She was transfixed by the screen nearest to her and he could almost see her thoughts as her eyes scanned the maps displayed on the TV, desperate to see where the remaining votes would come from. She suddenly turned around and raised her fists in the air.

"It's mostly Manchester that's still to come! That's our turf!" she yelled.

Manchester meant one thing: college kids and the working class. Hodges voters. Mike felt adrenalin go through his body like an electric shock and his vision dimmed as if someone in the room switched the lights on and off. He reached out a hand and steadied himself against a desk.

And then it was over.

"CNN newsbreak: Hodges wins New Hampshire"

The words flashed over the screen like a long-awaited Second Coming and pandemonium broke out. Mike felt a strong pair of arms grab him around the middle as a scrum of student volunteers and staffers all yelled and screamed at once. He was hauled into the air and thrown around and he punched the air with his fists, shouting at the top of his lungs, his mind devoid of any thought but simple, pure elation. They won. They did it. It was like fireworks exploded in his mind. Every lost night of sleep and every moment of exhaustion disappeared, burned out by this moment of triumph. His doubts vanished for a moment, exorcised in the pure thrill of victory.

Gradually, like a referee's whistle sounding through the cheering of a crowd, a lone voice cut through the noise and tried to calm down things. It was Dee, shouting against the tide. Eventually, she stood on top of a desk, an open champagne bottle in one hand and a lit cigar in the other. The cheers rang out even louder for a while but eventually subsided as she waved her arms for quiet. She took a swig of the champagne and puffed on her cigar like some political version of General

Patton. Eventually the noise died down enough so Dee could begin to speak.

"Ya'll here know I'm not one for emotion," Dee began and prompted a loud chorus of laughter and whistles. She paused, gathering herself and breathing out. Her eyes glistened slightly. She felt a deep hollow in her breast that swallowed up her breath, strangling the words in her throat. She paused and then carefully allowed herself to speak.

"We've all been working for this moment for a long time and I want you to know that ya'll deserve to feel on top of the world right now. No one ever believed we could do this. No one ever believed in our candidate but us…"

Her voice tailed off slightly as she took another deep swig from the champagne bottle. She gave a laugh and started again, wielding her bottle like a baton.

"You know," she said. "Politics can be a shitty game. I know that better than most. But every once in a while, something happens that makes you thankful that you put up with all the shit. This is one of those moments."

She pointed up to one of the TV screens that showed Hodges walking out in front of a cheering crowd at the victory rally held in a hotel a few hundred yards away.

"That is our man right there," Dee said. "He's special. He can change this country. For the first time America will care for its poor. For the first time it will look after its veterans. It will clean the lobbyists out of Washington. Hodges can do all that and he is getting that chance because of the work that you have done…"

Dee stopped talking and looked at the screen. Hodges was trying to quiet the crowd, Christine by his side, and he waved amid the cheers and confetti and placards with his name on it.

Eventually the noise died down and Hodges spoke. He stared past the crowd and into the massed ranks of TV cameras that lined up in front of him like a friendly firing squad. He paused. For a long time he looked out at what he finally knew was an entire nation watching him. There was not a hint of stress or pressure on his face. Just a man in control of his moment, taking the first steps on the stage of history.

"Let me tell you how we're going to save this country…" he began.

CHAPTER 16

AT LEAST SHE was surprised to see Mike again. In the hollow glaring light of the interrogation room she sat opposite him in her red jump suit, her black hair tied in a tight bun. She could not hide a sudden widening of her eyes and a crease in her brow as Mike walked in. Perhaps she expected yet another fruitless lawyer visit or a cop. Not the suited figure of Mike visiting as if from another world. She moved back in her chair slightly and the legs dragged a little on the floor sending a grating echo into the room.

Mike sat down and nodded a hello. But now she had no reaction. No response. Her eyes did not leave him as he settled himself opposite her.

"*Hola, como estas?*" he said.

She said nothing. Not that Mike expected her to. He knew this was his last chance to get anything out of her before he headed back to Guatemala. A simple greeting would not cut it. But now he had ammunition to fire at her.

"It's been a long time since I last came to see you. The

guards here say that you still have not spoken to anyone else. That's your choice. But I bet it gets pretty lonely living without words, locked up in solitary with no news of the world outside. So let me tell you what's been going on…"

Mike watched her face, but she looked up at the ceiling now with her hands placed flat on the table between them, not moving a muscle.

"Senator Hodges is doing well. The man you tried to kill is winning his party's nomination race. What do you think of that?"

Nothing. That line had worked before, getting the only reaction he ever saw in her. It would not work a second time.

"But did you know the Senator's wife is giving money to someone from your homeland, a General Rodrigo Estrada Carillo? Do you know him?"

He watched her intently. Nothing.

"I went to visit him. I met with him at his house," Mike went on. He felt something now. Some presence entered the room, some ghostly thing seep through the walls. It was if the temperature rose to match a Caribbean heat and he caught a whiff of the General's cigar smoke in the air, like a whisper of sulphur. He noticed a vein start to throb at the woman's temple. Her top lip quivered slightly.

Bingo, Mike thought.

"He is an interesting man. He lives by the beach in a beautiful house."

The woman looked back at him now; her eyes bored into his and he remembered the last time he was here. He edged back in his chair. He was suddenly aware that none of this was a game. Not here, alone in the room with the woman who tried to kill Hodges; someone who willingly pulled the trigger on another human being. But he pressed on.

"Yet I don't think General Carillo is a good man. I have spoken to people about what he did during the war. He is a man who did some very bad things."

One of the woman's hands trembled, like a pressure kettle starting to boil.

"I've been talking to people about the war in your country," Mike said. His voice was quiet, slow and deliberate. Static electricity prickled along his back as if Carillo himself stood behind him, looming over his shoulder at the woman in front of him.

"Someone told me about a massacre at Santa Teresa."

The woman visibly flinched and a hissing sound escaped from her lips. Her head dropped as her eyes sought the floor and she brought a hand up to her forehead and kneaded her brow like bread. The knuckles scraped across her skull and bruised the skin underneath them. Mike winced and leaned forward in sudden shock.

"Were you there?" he asked, half in disbelief. "Were you a victim?"

Her head snapped back up.

"Who are you?" Mike asked.

She let out a snort of derision. "Get out of here," she snapped. "Go back to your life and leave all this alone," she said, her voice grating with lack of use, the vocal chords ringing like a guitar strummed out of tune.

"Why did you try to kill Senator Hodges?" he asked.

She held his gaze for a moment and then spoke in a dull monotone. "The righteous shall rejoice when he seeth the vengeance: he shall wash his feet in the blood of the wicked," she said.

Mike shook his head. "Cut out that Biblical stuff. You know Carillo. You know about Santa Teresa. I will find out who you are. You know that," he said.

The woman smiled thinly. "*Si*," she said, switching to Spanish. "*Es claro.*"

Then she leapt at him.

The table jumped up into the air as she sprang like a cat across the short distance between them. Mike barely registered that she was not in handcuffs when he felt one of her hands strike him in the throat. The strength behind the blow was astonishing. She was like a coiled steel trap suddenly unsprung. He reeled backward and his chair toppled over. She was on top of him as he hit the floor, her face a mask of fury and both hands reached for his neck. Mike felt them squeeze, a vicious constriction around his throat that made him gasp as the breath was forced from him. He was helpless. He could not move. He could only look up into her eyes, aware at the dimming limits of his consciousness that somewhere his arms and legs flailed uselessly; flopping like a fish out of water. Now he could barely feel anything, just see those eyes bore down into him, filling his vision, even as the shadows at the edge crept in like a camera lens closing, narrowing the light down to a point, leaving just the brown eyes, burning with fury.

Then there was a sudden flash of light and a dreadful scream. The hold was suddenly released. Mike felt a huge gasp of air rush into his lungs and his chest expanded like an inflated balloon. At the same time a crippling wave of pain washed over him and burned his throat where her hands crushed in on his windpipe. He dry-heaved and felt like his lungs were on fire. He sat up and saw the woman writhe in pain on the floor as two wires protruded from her back. She screamed as the smell of burning hair filled the room. A guard stood over her, Taser in hand, and watched her squirm. Eventually he stopped and looked across at Mike.

"Jesus Christ," the guard said. "Are you all right?"

Mike tried to speak but his throat hurt too much to even croak a reply. He nodded instead. Another guard burst into the room and whistled at the scene of carnage.

"That bitch," he said. "You got her under control, Jake?"

The first guard looked down at the woman laid out on the floor. She was unmoving, save for her chest, which heaved up and down like an ocean wave. "She ain't going to be any more trouble. I told you she was just a psycho," the guard said.

"Yeah?" the second guard said and he too brought out a Taser. He aimed it at the fallen woman.

"Let's see about that," he said and he fired. The darts struck the woman on the leg and immediately she buckled off the floor, screaming and yelling. It was an awful sound, filling the rooms with words in a language that was not English nor Spanish. Loud, desperate, animal words that Mike did not comprehend. He staggered to his feet and grabbed the guard.

"Enough," he managed to rasp. "Enough."

The guard released his grip on the Taser's trigger and the unholy noise subsided. The woman gibbered quietly on the floor, curled up into a fetal ball. She spoke her native tongue, keening softly as tears and phlegm poured down her face like a gruesome, sickly waterfall. Mike staggered outside. He slumped against a wall and held his head in his hands. Two words had changed it all. Just two words.

Santa Teresa.

He knew where he would be going next.

———

DEE COULD not help herself. It felt good to be back in the South. As the black limousine carried her and Hodges slowly though the streets of Columbia, South Carolina, she finally felt on home turf. She was at last out of the frozen battleground of New Hampshire and in a place where her accent would not be marked as unusual. She regarded the suburban homes rolling by, looking more and more faded as they approached downtown. Outside a dim sun shone from the sky. It was winter still, hardly warm, but there was no snow on the ground. She shed her thick woolen clothes like a snake casting off a skin. Finally, smoking outside on the streets would not involve almost freezing to death. She looked over at Hodges, sitting beside her in the car. He silently watched the buildings slip by. Did he know what he had done by winning New Hampshire? she wondered. He was on the cusp of beating Harriet Stanton and pulling off one of the greatest political upsets of all time to secure the party's presidential nomination. Yet he was perfectly calm. Dee shook her head and instantly regretted it. She still had a hangover from all of the drinking the night before. She could barely remember getting on the plane. But Hodges was as fresh as a daisy. Must be that military constitution, she mused.

"This is where we end it, Jack," Dee said, breaking the silence.

Hodges did not stop looking outside the window but he spoke, his voice level and measured. "You think we can?" he asked.

"We're on a roll," Dee said. "It doesn't matter that New Hampshire was a squeaker. Americans don't care about margins, they just care about winners. We've made Stanton a loser now. If we pull it off again, then she is dead in the water. She'll never make it to Super Tuesday."

Finally, Hodges pulled away from the view outside the car. He drew his jacket around him, though it wasn't cold. He smiled thinly. "I know South Carolina's got a bit of a reputation, Dee, and if Stanton's desperate, how bad do you think it can get?"

Dee chuckled. They were in downtown now and they passed the State Capitol, in front of which stood a memorial to the war dead of the Confederacy, still proudly flying its battle flag. Memories were long here, the wounds of race never far from the surface, still crisscrossing the surface like a network of scars left by whips of a different age. Dee remembered those same monuments in the towns of her childhood, hearing conversations in bars and around barbecues of the War Between the States. It was a different world down here and it played by different rules. But, by God, she was going to enjoy trying to drag it into the 21st Century.

"It will get bad," she said. "Hell, if I were Howard Carver I would make this the worst experience of your life."

"Don't sugar coat it, Dee."

"Never have, never will," Dee said. "There are people down here who will try anything to rock your boat and most of them signed up with Stanton's campaign months ago when she was sitting pretty. We have to be prepared for anything to come up. Because whatever they have, they will throw it at us."

Hodges nodded and then looked puzzled as Dee held his gaze.

"So if there's anything you need to tell me, Jack. Anything at all, now would be a good time. So we can prepare for any possible contingencies."

Hodges laughed, at first a chuckle, and then longer and out loud. "Dee," he said and he put a hand on her arm. "You know all there is."

There was no hesitation in his voice. Dee smiled back at him as she marveled at his ability to lie like that. Or at least she thought he lied. He had never mentioned anything about his time in Guatemala to her except when she asked. What the fuck was going on here?

"Nothing at all?"

"Nothing," he repeated.

"That's why you're my guy," Dee said as the car stopped

outside the downtown Marriott hotel. Their latest home away from home.

Hodges opened the door of the car and stood aside to let her out. The air was gratifyingly warm and the sun's rays caressed her skin. Her headache evaporated as adrenalin once more dripped into her bloodstream. They had barely a week here. Just six days to win this race. Six days to knock Stanton to the mat and count her out.

"Let's get to work," she said.

———

MIKE FELT her hands tighten around his throat again, throttling the life from him. She was so small, so light, how could her grip be so strong? Her fingers were like iron; cold and firm and unbreakable. He looked up, desperate to stop her and her face swam into view as, her fingers dug into his flesh, exploring deep into his body as she whispered in his ear.

"I love you, Mike. I love you, Mike."

Now Jaynie's face swam in front of him. She was strangling him, dragging the life out of him. If only he could tell her to stop. He opened his mouth and finally began to scream…

He woke with a start, alone in his hotel room. Sweat covered him and the only sound was the whirring hum of the air conditioner. He breathed heavily as he waited for his eyes to focus in the darkness. Then he flung off the sheets and padded over to the window and drew back the curtains. Outside it was still dark and the lights of Guatemala City twinkled below him, spread out like a rolling carpet of fireflies fleeing to a broken and jagged horizon of dark mountains. He was back.

"Jesus Christ," he muttered to himself.

He put a hand to his throat and felt the swelling where a ring of purple circled his throat in a mottled necklace of bruises. He winced and remembered the eyes that looked down on him as her hands tried to kill him. He felt a twinge of emasculating shame that a woman older and so much smaller than himself was able to take him down. But her sudden attack was so brutal he barely knew what was going on even while it was happening. She would have killed him too; he did not doubt it.

He shivered and turned down the air conditioning. Immediately the heat and humidity of the tropical night invaded the room. There was no going back to sleep so he brewed a cup of coffee and sipped it in front of the window while a slow dawn crept across the mountain horizon to begin a new day. He was jittery and it had nothing to do with the caffeine. He had looked up Santa Teresa on the map and planned to head straight there, armed with little more than a police photograph of the shooter and a long list of questions.

The tiny village was about five hours drive away, along winding roads through the volcanic Mayan heart of the country. It was up in the Highlands that formed the central spine of Guatemala, far from the hot and sweaty Garifuna coast where Carillo now lived. It would be yet another different world. Mike sighed. It felt like an insane expedition and far removed from the campaign he joined. He made a second cup of coffee and watched the dawn break. It was time to go.

AS HE checked out Mike failed to notice the pretty woman standing beside him until he turned around to head for the door. Even then, as he stared into the familiar face, it was so unexpected, it took a full two seconds of gawping before his brain comprehended with startled recognition.

"Hi Mike!" the woman said with a grin full of triumph and satisfaction.

Lauren.

Mike's mouth opened and closed like a gasping goldfish. He dropped his bag and searched for words but managed to stutter out only a stunned response. "What… what are you doing here?"

Lauren kept on grinning. "Now that's really my question to you, Mike," she said and she stood in front of him, hands on her hips with her head cocked quizzically to one side.

Mike said nothing. He struggled to gather his thoughts. She caught him again. Just like outside the prison in Iowa, she tracked him down. He was flabbergasted.

"Come on, Mike," Lauren said. "I didn't follow you again just to have you clam up on me."

He could barely speak. "How…?" he stammered.

"You think you're my only source? You guys have

downplayed that Guatemalan money transfer, but then I heard a whisper among some of the student volunteers in Manchester that you visited down here on a trip. Didn't take long to figure out there must be a link. Then I start digging around with the folks who arrange travel for you guys. Seems you've not been spending much time on the campaign trail at all recently. You're on your own mission, Mike, and I'd like to know what it is. So when I heard you were heading down here again, I figured I needed to know why. So I took another risk. I followed you. Here I am."

Mike was floored. But also impressed. He had no idea she was on his tail.

"What's going on Mike?" she repeated. "What's the link with Guatemala? What's to stop me putting a blog post out in the next hour saying you're down here?"

The threat was clear. Mike put up a hand and took out his phone.

"Okay," he said. "You got me. But wait a moment. Let me make a phone call. See if we can make a deal."

Lauren shrugged. "Sure. But don't leave my sight," she said.

Mike walked a few yards and punched in Dee's numbers. He blurted out the news in a frenzied whisper while covering his phone with his hand and glancing at Lauren who watched him like a hawk eyeing up a rabbit. There was silence on the other end of the phone. Then Dee spoke.

"What the fuck?" she screamed.

Mike shut his eyes. He had never heard Dee lose her cool like that. Not at any point of the campaign. But she lost it now.

She shouted a long list of expletives and Mike heard a distant smash as something crashed to the ground in whatever room she was in. Mike weathered the storm and prayed for it to end. He needed Dee to tell him what to do. Eventually there was quiet on the other end and he heard Dee struggle to regain composure.

"We are in a heap of shit here," she said. "We've got six days until polling starts in South Carolina and we don't need any mistakes. You must keep her quiet until the voting is done and dusted. After that we can deal with any shit that's going to come out. But *not* before. You got that?"

"Fine," Mike said. "But what the hell do I do?"

Dee thought for a moment. "Keep her close. We want time and she wants information. So we trade that. Take her with you. Work with her. But tell her that what you discover is embargoed until after South Carolina votes. She can't run anything about what you find out down there until the last vote is counted. Got that?"

Mike nodded and Dee hung up without a further word. He walked back to Lauren who looked at him expectantly.

"Let's grab a coffee," he said. 'I've got a proposal for you."

CHAPTER 17

"SO, WHERE ARE we going, Mike?" Lauren asked as they at last drove past the final suburbs and slums of Guatemala City.

Her voice was playful but laced with a trace of triumph she could not resist. Mike did not blame her. After all, her journalistic gamble paid off. Both he and Dee seriously underestimated her by assuming stalling tactics would make her lose interest.

"Santa Teresa," he said. "It's a village up in the mountains. There was a massacre there back during the war. We are not sure, but we think the shooter witnessed it. She may be a survivor. It would certainly explain a lot. Maybe she went a little crazy and just hates the American military."

Lauren nodded and jotted down a few things in her notebook. She agreed to Dee's proposal easily enough. Lauren would get the inside scoop on this investigation but she could not publish it before South Carolina was over. Quid pro quo. But Dee also gave Mike other instructions.

"Don't let this bitch out of your sight, Mike, and keep her on a strictly need-to-know basis. She's not your friend. Remember that," she said.

Mike glanced again at Lauren as she scribbled in her pad in a spider-like shorthand. *Christ, why did everyone have an agenda?* He just tried to do his job and somehow it led to this place, juggling more cover stories and deceptions than a spy. What happened to playing it straight? Lauren looked at him and cocked her head to one side.

"And General Carillo?" she asked.

Mike shrugged as nonchalantly as he could. "We told you about that. He and the Hodges are friends. He's just helping him out financially. Not everything is a story, you know. We're following the shooter's trail here, not Hodges'. You journalists are too damn cynical."

Lauren raised an eyebrow, but Mike pretended not to see and concentrated on the road ahead that climbed into a rumpled fold of mountains and soared into thickly-clouded skies ahead that steadily darkened.

THE DRIVE was spectacular. Traffic thinned out between villages and Mike took his eyes off the road for a few precious seconds to admire the scenery. They passed through a series of deep valleys lorded over by a line of perfect cone-shaped volcanoes so symmetrical in their slopes that Mike was reminded of his high school geography text books. At every village Mayan women carried trays of fruit and fried pastries and approached the car when they stopped at junctions. Young children clamored at the windows to sell CDs or newspapers or just beg for a few grimy quetzal notes.

Lauren stared out at the window, entranced by it all. She waved at the people and bought far more food than they would possibly need. From one young, grimy-faced kid she bought a CD of Guatemalan rap music and shoved it into the car's archaic sound system. Immediately a melody of tinkling, electronic pop blasted into the car amid a howl of Spanish. Mike jumped and the car swerved violently. Lauren burst out laughing.

"Lighten up!" she giggled.

Mike shook his head but could not help but smile. He had to relax and try to enjoy this odd pairing up. Forget the games played behind the scenes and skim along on the surface. Lauren started to dance in her seat beside him, moving her head to the strangled sounds coming out of the stereo. Mike laughed too. She rested a hand on his arm. Her touch felt warm.

"That's better," she said.

The car crested a steep mountain pass and they looked down over a landscape of astonishing beauty. In front of them stretched rumpled folds of hills dotted with forest and a patchwork of tiny maize fields. It looked like an immense quilt flung over the earth. In the center of their vision was a shallow volcano, whose low walls were notched, like a broken saucer, and through the gaps they glimpsed a shimmering silver lake. Santa Teresa was one of half a dozen villages inside the crater that clung to the shores of the lake. The previous day Mike had again spoken to Jenny Gusman at the American Center for Latino Justice and she promised that someone would be waiting for them when they arrived. She was so casual that Mike had no idea if she would follow through. But as they drove down into the lip of the volcano he understood how dependent he was on Gusman's help.

The road zigzagged up the slopes of the volcano and then repeated the pattern heading down into the enormous crater. In a series of switch-backs it descended until the lake at last spread out before them, sparkling in bright blue sunshine like a vision.

"Christ, it's beautiful," Lauren said.

Mike's silence signaled his awed agreement. He drove slowly as the tattered tarmac gradually reverted to dirt and the car lurched over huge potholes. They circled the lake and a cluster of whitewashed buildings came into view around the curve of the crater wall. It was a tiny village with buildings scattered like shaken dice, some on the shore, and others up the gentle slopes of the crater wall near a thick band of forest. A gabled church stood in the middle and looked like the only really solid building. The car crawled on past fields of tall maize worked by women all wearing bright dresses. A few glanced up but most continued their backbreaking labor, enormous baskets carried on their shoulders.

Mike thought, suddenly, of his time in Florida, trying to fight against the dreadful conditions on the plantations. For the first time he knew why it was so hard to get people organized there. If this was how they grew up, how could they even know they were exploited? He glanced in the rear-view mirror and saw a gaggle of young children trailing the car, smiling and running along, trying to catch it as they pulled into the village.

Suddenly, an older man, who waited by the side of the road, walked out into the middle of their path. Mike braked quickly. The man came around to the side of the car and tapped on the window with a gnarled looking walking stick. Mike had no idea how old the man was. His features looked like he was in his 50s, but his skin glowed flawlessly and smooth, stretched over an angular face and a prominent nose. He appeared to be pureblood Mayan, like he stepped down from the murals of some ancient pyramid. Mike wound down the window.

"*Señor* Sweeney?" the man said and looked suspiciously over at Lauren.

Mike nodded. "You know Jenny Gusman?" Mike asked in Spanish.

The man nodded and signaled them to park the car next to a nearby house. "I got a message from her last night. I am Rodolfo," he said. "Follow me."

The man disappeared into a low building outside which they parked the car. Mike and Lauren followed Rodolfo inside and were immediately assailed by the strong, acrid smell of brewing coffee. It was dark and the ceiling was low. Rodolfo busied himself over a wood burning stove with a bubbling black cast iron pot. He gestured at two plastic chairs and they sat down. A minute later the man brought them small cups of thick black liquid. Mike and Lauren sipped at them. Their lips stung from the heat and their brains suddenly fizzed with the injection of strong caffeine.

"Welcome to Santa Teresa," Rodolfo said in Spanish. "I am glad you have come to pay testament to what happened here."

Mike looked at Lauren. He could see she did not entirely understand what was being said. Her Spanish was not quite good enough to cope with the fact that Rodolfo's first language was a Mayan dialect. Indeed, Mike needed to concentrate hard to make sure he understood all the old man said. Mike felt pleased he had this advantage over Lauren. It helped control the amount of information she would get.

"Thank you, Rodolfo," Mike said. "If I could just start by asking…"

But Rodolfo cut him off with a raised hand. "Wait. Before we begin we must seek the blessing of Maximón," he said and he got up and signaled for them to finish their drinks. Lauren frowned.

"What's going on?" she asked Mike.

Mike was prepared to lie. But there was no need. "I have no idea," he said.

———

RODOLFO WALKED out of the house and they followed him. By now a small crowd of people, mostly children and teenaged boys, gathered again. They followed at a respectful distance as the trio headed into a maze of buildings. The street was paved with rough-cut stone and led into a series of alleyways so narrow that the sun was shielded from sight and it grew dark, despite being the middle of the day. Eventually they stopped outside a non-descript looking wooden door. Rodolfo disappeared inside. Mike hesitated and looked at Lauren.

"I guess we have to just go with the flow," she said.

Mike pushed open the creaking door and they went inside. It took a few seconds for their eyes to adjust to the gloom and when they did they stared in shock at the sight in front of them. In the darkness two men lounged in plastic chairs against a wall and in the middle of them was a human-sized wooden statue. Its face was unsmiling and jammed in its mouth was a smoldering cigar, whose smoke curled upwards in a spiral of white, filling the unventilated room and stinging the eyes. The statue wore a black wide-brimmed cowboy hat and was festooned in colorful ribbons that looked like neckties. At its feet flickered a dozen large candles that stood among thick bunches of flowers. It felt like stepping through a mirror into another world. Hidden behind the dirty walls of this forgotten little village lurked Gods whose stories stretched back thousands of years.

Rodolfo walked up to the statue and spoke to it in Mayan, the low sounds of the language being swallowed up by the thick air. One of the attendants stood up and proffered his hand. Rodolfo looked around at the stunned figures of Mike and Lauren.

"You must give him some money. Maximón is often angry at those who visit the village from outside," said Rodolfo.

Mike fished into his wallet for a handful of dollars. He handed them over to the attendant, who stuffed them into his pocket, walked back to the statue and reached behind his chair. He pulled out a clear bottle of white liquid and took a swig from it. Instantly the smell of strong alcohol mingled with the stench of tobacco. Then the man reached over and poured the bottle into some hidden hole in the statue's mouth. A splash hit the lit end of the cigar and a small tongue of blue flame erupted from the statue's face. The other attendant let out a harsh laugh. Again Rodolfo spoke to the two men in Mayan and turned to Mike.

"Maximón is appeased. Now we can begin," he said.

———

GENERAL CARILLO sat in his chair and lit a cigar. He had just returned from the center of Livingston to pick up another cash transfer from America. He went to the bank and put it directly into his savings account, reading the numbers of his balance with a thrill that he had not felt in many years. He always told himself that he did not put a huge store in great wealth: he wanted to be comfortable, for sure, but never rich. Not like those parasites in Guatemala City. The new government ministers with their big cars and fancy penthouses. But now, with his savings growing and growing, he luxuriated in the feeling of security. It was reward for years of difficult service during the war, followed by his exile here that, in many ways, was harder.

Now it was worth it. The Lord now smiled upon His humble servant and saw that he would not have to wait until heaven for happiness. Carillo sat and relaxed in his front room, lined with the photographs of his past, and day-dreamed about returning to the Highlands and buying a coffee estate. He knew the government would not want him to leave Livingston, but he would splash his new wealth around a little and oil some of those stuck wheels with a bribe or two. In a few years he would be out of here with more than enough to buy a plot of land and a ranch house.

He got up and walked over to one of the photograph-lined walls. He saw the old pictures of his passing-out ceremony at the School of the Americas. His smiling youthful shade looked like a different person entirely. Carillo frowned. He expected to feel a connection to that young man, so full of promise and ambition. Instead he walked farther down the wall to an old black and white picture of his grandfather, standing proud as a peacock in a ceremonial uniform that looked cartoonish in its extravagance and aping of European styles. But for Carillo this was more like it. The man, with his huge bushy whiskers and feathers streaming from his cap, looked the epitome of style and honor. Carillo ran a finger through the coating of dust on the picture. He did his ancestors proud, he thought.

The dim ring of his telephone disturbed him from his moment of reverie. He ignored it. But then it began again. Someone wanted him urgently. Cursing under his breath he walked out into the hall and picked up the receiver. He barked a hello.

"Many apologies for disturbing you, my General," came the voice at the end of the line. "It is Enrico and I have news I think you will be interested in."

Carillo thought for a moment and then recognition struck him. Enrico Lopez. An old comrade who worked in the immigration department in the capital.

"Federico asked me to keep an eye out for a certain man at customs in the airport. He said you would want to know that he left the country."

Carillo shut his eyes. He knew this was bad news.

"He is an *Americano*. A Mike Sweeney. Well, he left okay. But now he is back. He came back through yesterday."

Carillo allowed the news to sink in and sought to calm his racing heart, before he uttered a word. He counted to five, slowly, an old routine from his military days when he wanted to cool his blood. "Thank you, Enrico, old friend," he said. "Where was he going?"

"He left a telephone number at the Marriott Hotel in Guatemala City as his contact. He also rented an Avis car. That is all I know."

Silence again.

"My General…'"

"That is good, Enrico. You have done well. I shall see that you are rewarded," he said. He put down the phone and cut off the man's fulsome thanks.

Carillo walked back into his lounge and sat down again. The room was a much darker place to him now. This American was like a stinking fly in his soup, he thought. An ugly thing that spoiled everything it touched, even though it was so small and puny. His mind lit up with a feeling of anger and his breathing grew ragged as he stubbed out his cigar. Why was he being investigated like this by Hodges' people? Was he being played like a fool, given his reward only to have it used against him? He did not understand the ways of Americans. Never had. They always said one thing and did another.

"Federico!" he called and instantly heard a door upstairs open and the sound of footsteps. Federico always knew when to respond quickly and the General's tone left little doubt. He burst into the room to face his master.

"The American that you took to the airport has come back. He arrived in the capital yesterday. I want you to call Enrico at Customs and get all the details from him. Then leave immediately for Guatemala City. Find him and see what he is doing here. I want to know who he is seeing and what he wants."

Federico nodded. "Should I take care of him?" he asked, his face unmoving but his implication clear.

Carillo thought for a moment. It was tempting, he knew, to deal with such a problem directly and in such a decisive manner. But this man was an American and that was bound to cause trouble. He did not want to act hastily. He wanted his chance to leave this horrid exile and go back to the clear air of the Highlands. He looked at Federico. The man was like a human guard dog, utterly loyal and trained to his will. All it would take was a word and he would kill. But the General would not make such a decision now.

"No," Carillo said, shaking his head. "Not yet. Just watch."

MIKE AND Lauren emerged from the room where Maximón was kept. They were silent and unsure of themselves. It was a glimpse into an entirely unexpected world, one that lurked beneath the façade of the Guatemalan village. The heat and light was suddenly unfamiliar and the faces of the pack of small boys that followed them became less innocent and joyful. Not sinister. But different and alien. Rodolfo, however, seemed brighter and more cheerful, as if relieved from some burden that worried him. He led them though the streets of the village and past the church that towered over a tidy but ancient town square. Rodolfo gestured at the pack of kids behind them with his stick and shouted a few harsh words in Mayan and the children scattered back into the village. Rodolfo flashed a boyish grin that belied his years.

"They follow anything new in the village," he said. "They are like little mice in the kitchen who catch the smell of fresh bread."

The trio climbed away from the streets and a little ways up to a gentle slope above the village. Rodolfo sat down on a patch of rocks and tucked his knees up and rested his chin on them. "Here is a good place," he said. "We must keep talk of evil things away from the village. For the good of us all."

Mike and Lauren sat in front him. Mike felt almost like he was back at a church meeting from his childhood. Rodolfo inspired that sort of feeling; that of a wise man and a teacher. Like an old pastor Mike knew back in the dim-remembered days of his childhood. He looked over at Lauren and saw her get out her notebook.

Rodolfo looked off into the distance, his eyes a little glazed. In front of them the landscape stretched out like an oil painting of vivid colors and life; the white of the village houses, the deep blue of the lake, reflecting the sky above, and the lush, tropical greens of the forest-draped crater walls. It seemed that nothing bad could ever happen in such a place.

"We have a few questions about the massacre that occurred here during the war," Mike began. "We are investigating someone in America who may be involved in things that happened that day. We would like you tell us about it."

Rodolfo waited a moment and chewed over the thought in his mind; then he spoke slowly and deliberately. Mike understood him perfectly and looked over at Lauren who jotted down notes. Evidently her basic Spanish was adequate to get the broad outlines of the story.

"It began on a day much like this one," Rodolfo said, and stretched out his stick to point back to the road to the village that they drove in on. "Soldiers came in on a jeep. Just four of them. They were looking for rebels, the men who took to the jungles to fight the government and the army. They said some comrades were attacked and killed while on patrol. We knew nothing of this. We told them we have nothing to do with the guerrillas. They did not believe us."

Rodolfo shrugged. "But they were right not to. We were lying. The men in the jungles were our brothers and our cousins. But we wanted a quiet life. We wanted no trouble. We are simple farmers and fishermen. But how could we refuse our relatives help when they asked for food or shelter?"

"What did the soldiers want you to do?" Mike asked.

"They wanted us to tell them when the rebels came. They gave us names of people they wanted and told us to alert them when they came to our village. Our village leaders said we would do this. But, of course, we did not. We cannot betray our own. Not to those monsters who hate us for the color of our skin and don't even speak our language. We thought they would go away and leave us alone. They had done so before. But that was a mistake."

Rodolfo's voice faded. A wind whipped across the lake, spurred by the late heat of day. It rustled past the shore and reached up to the craggy crater walls above. It seemed to whisper something as it went, twirling around Mike and Lauren like fingers made of air.

"A week later they came back. They said they knew the rebels who attacked the patrol were in our village and that we did nothing. This time, they said, we would be taught a lesson. We begged and pleaded but they made us wait for a new unit of soldiers to arrive. These were soldiers we did not know. They had not been in our village before. They came in a convoy of trucks and jeeps. Everyone in the village was herded into the town square. We went like sheep to the market. Even then we did not know what would happen. It was only when they picked out twelve men and put them against the church wall that we understood. They shot them all down right there."

Mike sucked in a sudden breath. He saw that Lauren

understood too. Her face grew pale. Mike thought of the church below. It looked sleepy and innocent enough. Just a simple place of worship, not of murder.

"Our young men were killed before our eyes and so we began to fight and run. That is when the soldiers turned on everyone. Man, woman and child. Old and young. They did not care. We ran into the fields. We hid among our corn and prayed to Maximón to save us. On that day he answered some of our prayers. But not all of them.

There was silence between them now. Mike already knew the simple facts of the killings. At least 75 men, women and children mowed down in cold blood by the army. But those were just statistics. Now he looked down at the spot where it happened, talking with someone who witnessed the deaths of his friends and loved ones. Perhaps only yards from where they sat people were killed. Perhaps this very spot was drenched in blood; the full stop to someone's life, dying suddenly and terrified. Mike felt the hair stand up on his arms. He reached into his wallet, unfolded a black and white picture of the shooter and held it out to Rodolfo.

"Who is this woman? Was she there that day?"

Rodolfo looked at the picture. Mike did not expect him to recognize her. But he hoped against hope he would. That he would spot some long-lost cousin or distant childhood friend. Someone who witnessed the terrible killings and thus provide a reason for the dreadful things that he saw lying behind the shooter's eyes; explain the terrible death grip he felt constrict around his own throat.

But Rodolfo reacted like Mike handed him something infected with a deadly disease. As soon as Rodolfo saw the face in the photograph, his eyes widened in shock. Fear even. He looked back at Mike and spat out angry sounds in Mayan. He jumped to his feet and raised his stick above his head. Mike backed away and Lauren scrambled to her feet. Rodolfo screamed at them, one clear word in Spanish, which left no doubt as to what he wanted them to do.

"Go!" he yelled. "Go!"

CHAPTER 18

THE MAIN STREET of Dawson, South Carolina, was lined with empty lots and shuttered storefronts. Hodges' convoy drove down it at a leisurely pace and formed virtually the only traffic. A red pick-up truck passed by them on the other side of the road and its bearded white driver craned his neck to stare at the procession, while keeping one hand firmly on the wheel, ensuring the vehicle did not drift even an inch from its course. Dee watched him with a grin and let the wintry southern sun warm her face.

Dawson was a shit hole. There was no getting away from that. The only large town in a small Low Country county it was part of the "black belt" of the South. A wide swath of former plantation land sandwiched between the coast and the mountains, it was a region of dire poverty and tense race relations where time moved at a different pace from anywhere else. But also, for Dee, it reminded her of home. She grew up in a little isolated burgh like this in Louisiana. Like her hometown, the black and white communities lived largely separate lives, divided by a railway track. The only place where they really met was in the few surviving shops in the battered downtown and the Piggly Wiggly out by the highway.

Hodges seemed to sense Dee's thoughts. "See anything familiar?" he asked.

"Lots," Dee said and she surprised herself at how hard that word was to get out. She felt a huge pressure in her head and a rush of memories and images. She pictured the rundown house of her early childhood and watching her momma do a towering stack of dishes at a filthy sink. The fights at high school. She also remembered the endless heat of summer and the cool of an afternoon storm. The steady understanding that she was different from the other kids at her school. The taunts of her peers, that she first endured and then learned to counter, giving every bit as good as she got. She felt a flush of blood to her cheeks – a mix of shame and defiance – just as when her father started coming home drunk after he lost his job.

Hodges put a friendly hand on her shoulder. There were not many people who would dare to do that to Dee. Fewer who would get away with it. But the gesture from Hodges not only felt genuine, it felt welcome. Comforting.

"We've come a long way, Jack," she said. "But South Carolina ain't Iowa or New Hampshire. Folks here been down so long, they've gotten used to it. It's going to take more than pretty words to get them excited."

Hodges nodded. The convoy approached a red brick school building at the end of Main Street. It was a huge structure but even from a distance it was clear it was in a dilapidated state of repair. Its brick walls were a patchwork of repairs and cracks and its roof looked ancient. Its playing fields were a worn scrub-brown, more dust than grass.

"Martin Luther King High," Dee said, looking down at a sheaf of notes on her lap. "Intake 3,500. Average class size 41. Dropout rate of 56 percent."

Hodges whistled through his teeth. Dee ploughed on.

"That's not all of it. The gymnasium's been out of action for two years. Hole in the roof means it floods every time it rains. The railway goes right around the back of the building and messed with the foundations. The whole building shakes every time a big freight train comes through."

"I don't know how the town puts up with it," Hodges said.

Dee fixed him a glare. "The white part of town doesn't. Most white folks send their kids to a private school in the next county. This place is just for poor cracker trash and the blacks."

The car pulled into the school grounds and they saw a crowd of people snaking out of the main entrance. Several hundred people, many of them carrying placards with campaign slogans, broke into a cheer and a frenzy of waving. The car swung around the rear of the building. Dee and Hodges got out and were greeted by a small throng of people. One young black woman introduced herself as the principal, Mary Sloane. Hodges kept hold of her hand after she proffered it.

"Principal Sloane," he said. "It's an honor to meet you. It really is. Dee told me of the difficulties you guys face here. I have to say, I was shocked."

Sloane looked like someone caught in the headlights of an

oncoming car. The tone of real anger in Hodges voice clearly caught her off-guard.

"We've got some good kids in this school," she said. "We just want to give them a chance."

Hodges looked at his watch. "Look, I'm not due on stage for twenty minutes yet. Why don't you show me around? Dee said your gym is out of action. Why don't you show me that hole in the roof?"

Dee made a move to stop him. She had a list of local dignitaries Hodges needed to meet. The local mayor, a half-dozen ministers from the black churches and the editor of the Dalton Gazette. But Hodges stopped her with a fierce look.

"Let's go," he said to Sloane and he strode into the school, leaving no one any choice but to follow.

———

THAT NIGHT Dee sat cross-legged on the dusty bed of the highway motel they ended up in and poured over the latest poll data emailed to her on her Blackberry. The figures blurred in front of her. They were in a dead heat with Stanton. Forty points each. Not as good as she hoped. But not bad either. She scanned the deep data, running her eyes along columns of figures and breakdowns of social type. Independents, blacks, whites, the college-educated, the conservatives and the liberals. She needed to master what trended up and trended down in order to tweak their message and deliver the election. But she could not shake the afternoon's events out of her mind.

Hodges stalked around the school in Dalton for 30 minutes, eventually dragging an entire retinue of local big wigs around with him. They traipsed through the corridors to look at peeling paint, toilets more suited to a prison camp, metal detectors at the main door to stop students with guns, a library of worn and used books and, finally, the mildewed gymnasium with a hole torn in its roof through which peeked a square of blue sky. Then Hodges walked onto the stage of the school hall and tore up his speech and launched into an impassioned monologue on his Second New Deal for America. Perhaps it was revenge for Dee's taking the wind out of his plan's sails when he announced it in New Hampshire, but she didn't think so. She thought he really believed his ideas would help here. He genuinely thought he had answers that would make places like this a thing of the past.

By the end of it all, the entire hall stood and applauded as if they had won a state football championship. They chanted his name and tried to rush the rope line. In all her long days, Dee had never seen anything like it. Never seen a crowd react like that. Yet Hodges barely recognized it. The words just poured out of him in an impassioned torrent and at its end he stood statue-like, as surprised as anyone by the reaction.

"He's a natural," Dee breathed to herself.

She could not concentrate now and she closed the file of numbers. She would get up early, with a fresh mind, and study them in the morning. There were four campaign stops tomorrow, ending up in Charleston on the coast. That was plenty of opportunity to try out some fresh messages and roll out a few new tricks. She put down her Blackberry on her bedside table and lay back on the lumpy mattress and stared at a spider web of ugly cracks that traced their way across the dirty white paint of the ceiling. She felt the tug of deep exhaustion at her mind's edges close in like a lengthening shadow.

Ping!

The sound of her Blackberry's message alert jolted her back from sleep. Groaning, she reached over and glared at the tiny screen. At first the name on the new message was unfamiliar to her. Sheriff William Jackson? From Corinth Falls, New York? Then her mind flared with recognition and she clicked on the attachment. She forgot she called in this particular favor.

The PDF file downloaded and she scrolled down. It was an arrest report. The full case history of two people arrested in New York on drugs allegations. One charged and the other let go. She stared at the mug shot pictures and smiled grimly. In one picture a thin-faced woman stared sullenly into camera. In the other, a red-haired man glared angrily back with a mix of fear and confusion.

"Damn, Mike," she said. "You gotta smile for the camera."

Then she began to read the arrest reports, the thought of sleep forgotten.

RODOLFO GLARED at Mike, his arm raised high, holding his gnarled walking stick in his hand. Mike edged in front of Lauren and they backed carefully away. The old Mayan was at least thirty years older than them, but the look in his eyes made them back away.

"Wait.. wait…" Mike said.

Rodolfo's eyes bulged out of his sockets and he looked half-possessed. He stared at them wildly and muttered under his breath in Mayan. Then he stalked back down the hillside in the direction of the village. Mike and Lauren looked at each other. Lauren was breathing heavily and looked terrified.

"What's going on?" she asked.

Mike shook his head and watched Rodolfo's back retreating down the path towards the village. He grabbed Lauren's hand and started after him. "Come on," he said.

Mike shouted at Rodolfo, but the old man kept striding onwards, nimbly striding down the rutted path at a pace that belied his age. Mike's mind whirred. Why did he react like that to the photograph? Who was the woman? Based on Rodolfo's response Mike felt certain she was not a victim. But maybe something so awful happened to her that she was shunned by her former neighbors. The answer to the puzzle was walking rapidly out of sight.

"Rodolfo! Wait!" Mike yelled.

Finally, Rodolfo stopped and faced them. With his arms folded across his chest and clutching his stick like a scepter, he waited for Lauren and Mike to catch up to him. When they did, he glared at them.

"Who is she?" Mike asked waving the photo at him. "You need to tell me who she is!"

Rodolfo breathed heavily, like a bull at bay in the bullring. Mike would not have been surprised had he started to paw the ground with his feet. But eventually he spoke.

"She is the bringer of death!" he said. "She is one whose name should not be mentioned here."

"But Rodolfo…" Mike began but the old man cut him off.

"Enough! Go! Maximón blessed you but perhaps it was a curse on us."

Rodolfo lurched forward and Lauren retreated down the path. Mike stood his ground. "This woman is in jail in my country. She is many miles away. But she is important to me. I must know who she is."

Rodolfo stopped mid-charge, as if suddenly confused by the insistence of the matador on staying still. He seemed a little calmer now. Finally, he spoke, in slow and deliberate Spanish. "If you want to know of her you must see the priest, Father Gregorio Villatoro. He was here before and after the massacre. He is at the San Gabriel mission in Guatemala City. He can tell you about this demon. But not us!"

Mike was aware a crowd was gathering. Like ghosts emerging from the shadows, a handful of laborers appeared from the cornfields. They stood and stared, machetes and hoes in their hands. Mike tried to read their faces but they were blank and silent and just stared at them. A few young boys, who earlier were full of chatter and laughter, were now silent and still, taking the lead from their fathers and grandfathers. The children's eyes were dark and glowered like the hint of thunderclouds on a far horizon but getting nearer. Mike opened his mouth to speak but stopped when he felt Lauren tug at his sleeve. Her face was pale with fear.

"I'm scared," she whispered.

Mike looked around. More figures emerged from the fields. About twenty people stood around them with Rodolfo at their head. Mike took Lauren's hand and slowly walked through the crowd, trying not to catch anyone's eye, back through a village as threatening and alien as anywhere he had ever been; full of mystery and an angry cigar-smoking God.

———

THE VILLAGE rapidly receded into the distance in the rear view mirror but still Mike looked up to check no vehicle was following them. It seemed insane, but he would not be surprised to see Rodolfo drive after them in some beaten up old truck with a mob of machete-wielding Mayans in the back. Beside him Lauren sat and stared straight ahead. She was on the edge of tears. Now that he had calmed down and was over his fear he began to worry about her.

"Are you okay, Lauren?" he repeated several times and she nodded each time in a way that fell far short of convincing.

Mike resisted the temptation to simply floor the accelerator and speed away as fast as possible. The road back to Guatemala City climbed out of the crater in a series of terrifying switchbacks. He needed to take it easy. Not panic. Not kill them both in some stupid car crash. He glanced again at

Lauren as they finally climbed out of the crater and saw again a broad panorama of mountains ahead of them. She looked silently out of the window, keeping her thoughts to herself. He surprised himself by feeling responsible for her. She was the one who came out here, practically sabotaging his mission, but now he simply and guiltily thought: what had he dragged her into?

He had no answer. It was a hard confession to make. He felt he was on a roller coaster. At first the shooter was a violent, evil mystery. Then she seemed a traumatized victim. Now it was clear Rodolfo and the others feared and hated the very sight of a photograph of her. And still he did not even know her name. Or have a link back to Hodges. He felt lost, and a long way from South Carolina where the political battle was being fought. Caught in his own thoughts, he heard Lauren speak at last.

"What's going on, Mike?" she asked. "Who the hell is that woman? Why did she want to kill Senator Hodges?"

Mike shrugged. Despite Dee's instructions to keep Lauren in the dark, he found himself telling her the truth.

"I have no real idea," he said.

THEY ARRIVED back in Guatemala City that night and headed straight to the bar of the Marriott. They sat in a dark corner with a pair of strong drinks and relaxed. Finally, returned to the familiar environment of a modern hotel bar, they were at ease. It was a whole world away from the village of Santa Teresa with its massacre and strange pre-Christian Gods. That was a glimpse into an alien world, one that unsuspectingly lurked just under the surface. Always there but hidden. Even though they saw that now, and knew it existed, the surroundings of the hotel bar allowed them to convince themselves they were again on safe ground.

For a while they talked about themselves and ignored the wider world. Mike talked passionately about the campaign and Hodges and his desire to make a difference. As the words poured out, they helped him ground himself in his purpose here. It reminded him why he joined Hodges' cause and agreed to what Dee asked him to do.

"I believe in him," he said. "I've spent my life trying to make a difference with people's lives. I've had my triumphs but mostly it's a struggle just to keep things from getting worse. But this? This is different. If Hodges wins and he follows through on even half of what he's promised, it'll change our nation."

Lauren smiled. "You really believe that?" she asked. She seemed genuine and Mike was genuine back.

"I honestly do," he said. "Nothing is as important to me as getting Hodges elected. He'll make people's lives better. I've never really believed that before."

They sat closer together now and drew in to each other as they talked.

"But who is that woman?" Lauren asked. "It makes no sense she would want to kill Hodges."

Mike shook his head.

"No idea. But she tried to kill me too," he whispered and unbuttoned the high collar of his shirt to show the purpling bruise around his throat where she tried to throttle the life out of him.

Lauren blanched.

"She attacked me when I saw her in jail a few days ago," he said.

"Jesus," Lauren said and gingerly caressed the damaged skin of his neck with a brush of her hand. Mike closed his eyes and luxuriated in her touch. But then an alarm bell went off in his mind. Stop! Get a grip, he thought. He opened his eyes and edged away.

Lauren withdrew her hand. "So what next?" she said as if nothing were amiss.

"We do what Rodolfo said," Mike replied. "We go and see that priest. I asked the concierge. San Gabriel is a church out in the slums. We find the church and we find him. It's our only lead really."

Lauren sensed any moment of flirtation had passed. She yawned theatrically and stretched her arms. "I'm beat," she said.

They headed upstairs to rooms that were opposite each other on the sixth floor. Mike closed the door to his room and breathed out a sigh of relief. He needed to keep self-control. This was too important to mess up and Lauren represented a time bomb on this story. He did not want to complicate things any further simply because he was attracted to her. He walked over to the window of his room and flung back the curtains exposing the nightscape of the city stretching out below.

His phone buzzed in his pocket. It was Dee. Her Southern drawl, more pronounced than he remembered, carried down the line.

"What's up, Mike?" she asked.

He told her about the experience in the village. To his surprise she was not outraged or shocked. There was just a measured response.

"I always thought that shooter was just a plain old nut job. Some scary psycho," she said.

"You did not see these people's reaction. It was more than…" Mike began but she shushed him.

"Keep digging. We need to know her identity and the link with the General and Hodges. Every time I look at Hodges I see a man I believe in. But then I remember the money paid down to this goddamn Carillo in Guatemala and it's like an itch I can't quite reach. It's bothering the heck out of me, Mike. I need you to scratch it."

"There's a priest here who should know who she is. We'll try and find him tomorrow."

"Good. But how's our little blogging friend? Are you keeping her close by? Not too close I hope."

There was a hint of playful accusation in Dee's voice. Mike ignored it.

"It's all under control," he said.

Dee laughed. "Remember, Mike, men always mess things up because of their peckers. Keep yours in your own pants."

Mike spluttered in embarrassment but Dee just steamrollered on. "There's one other thing," she said. "My friend on your home town sheriff's department just updated me on Jaynie's case. He sent me her arrest report and case file. It's pretty bad."

Mike felt struck in the stomach. Jaynie. He thought of her screams when the police burst in. They were animal-like: pure anguish and fear. On instinct alone she must have known that moment was the end of freedom.

"How bad is it?"

"She's been mixed up in some pretty nasty stuff, Mike. She's brewed meth for a crew of dealers for a year or so. The cops have her red-handed with a still in her trailer and enough meth to float the boats of half of New York's cracker population. She's staring at five years, minimum. Maybe a hell of a lot more."

There was nothing left to say.

"Thanks for letting me know, Dee," he said and he hung up the phone.

Five years inside? Jaynie would not survive that he thought. He remembered the last time he saw her, in the back of the cop car. She had reached out to him with her bound hands and he edged away from her. He felt a terrible rush of guilt and he pulled down the blinds on his window, blocking out the sparking lights of the city in a series of shadows that looked like the bars of a cage.

CHAPTER 19

DEE WATCHED BOB "Swampy" Murphy lift the tumbler of expensive scotch to his mouth and down it in a single gulp. He smacked his lips with loud theatrical effect and settled back in the comfy leather of his chair. They sat in a back room at Magnolia's, one of the finest restaurants in Charleston, which took the common food of the South and gave it a haute cuisine twist. Dee hated the place. But Murphy insisted. After all he wasn't the one paying the bill.

"So will he agree to it? Has this candidate of yours got what it takes to win down here?" Murphy asked.

He was almost a parody of the dark side of South Carolina politics. Obese and short with what seemed a permanent sheen of sweat on his forehead, Murphy ran a small political consultancy in the state. He had done so for decades. Just like his father before him and his grandfather before that. Down in the South even dirty politics were passed on in families like a real sweat-and-blood trade and no game-player was dirtier than Murphy. For a fee, he arranged rumors to sweep through an election. Fly-posters appeared over night in any neighborhood in the state. Untraceable stories popped up on the Internet or in gossip columns. Push-polls planted the most outlandish stories about an opponent. It was a dark, seedy underbelly of "The Swamp" and Murphy was its master practitioner.

Dee poured him another glass from a whisky bottle the waiter left on the table along with a carafe of expensive red wine.

"I do believe he will, Bob," she said. "But we have to convince him it is the right thing to do. Not just tactically. But morally."

Murphy chuckled, his fat cheeks inflating and deflating. "Oh boy, Dee. Have you got yourself lumbered to a candidate with a serious case of morality? For a campaign that hopes to win anything, that can be a very debilitating condition."

A warm glow of dislike rose up in Dee. She needed Murphy. She would sanction anything he would do if it destroyed Stanton and won this fight. But she baulked at his casual joy in the dark arts of their craft. Dee still believed in a cause. She was a means to an end. Murphy lost any notion of an end long ago. He was all about the method. She sighed inwardly. She disliked Charleston, she thought. It was genteel and Southern and wealthy, but it masked its ugly side. The terrible race relations and the ghettos just a few miles from the mansions of Broad Street were all hidden under the surface. Like this restaurant, she thought. Dress up chitterlings with some fancy sauces and slap a high price tag on it and call it gourmet. But at the end of the day you still ate pig belly.

"He's a good man, Bob," she said quietly, gritting her teeth.

Murphy failed to notice anything amiss. "They're the worst," he said. "What do you need?"

"To undermine Stanton's support in the black community. She's from Virginia. She knows her way around this territory better than Hodges. She's got a long record of support from black churches. We need to chip away at that. Splinter off some of her base. If we do that we can take her down."

Murphy nodded. "Go on," he said.

"Nothing too extreme, Bob," Dee said. "I don't want a repeat of the McCain fiasco when everyone thought his own adopted daughter was a black love child."

Murphy gave an impish grin.

"Just kick up a bit of doubt," Dee said. "If we can puncture Stanton's black support, then all the air will go out of her campaign. It's her weak underbelly," Dee said.

Murphy smiled and revealed a mouth of stubby off-white teeth. Dee had a sudden mental image of some ugly, bottom-dwelling fish that lurked deep in the ocean far from sunlight.

"Creating doubt is my specialty," Murphy said. "I can push-poll some stuff about her comments on cutting welfare and portray that in more racial terms. She's been close to a few evangelical leaders in her time. I bet a few of them have some associations on the extreme right I can use. Colored folks don't have too much time for the Jerry Falwells of this world."

Dee smiled. Murphy was a son-of-a-bitch. But, for the right price, he was going to be *her* son-of-a-bitch. She began to speak again but just then the door to their semi-private dining room opened and Hodges and Christine walked in, arm in arm, accompanied by a blast of sound and laughter from the main dining room outside. It was like a light switched on in the room.

"Dee!" Hodges said, striding forward. "This place looks fantastic. Christine and I have been blown away by Charleston. It's wonderful."

Dee made her introductions. She described Murphy as a trusted political consultant and poured out the wine. She filled four glasses until they almost over-flowed as she listened to Hodges and Christine praise the delights of the city. Murphy played along and oozed his local charm and recommended a series of other restaurants they should try. Then he offered the use of his weekend beach house the next time they were in town.

"It beats hotels," Murphy said. "It will save your campaign some money down the line too."

Dee interjected. "Yeah, well, we have to win here first, Bob," she said.

Now was her chance. She looked at Hodges. "Jack. Bob has offered to run some polls for us, maybe take the fight to Stanton a little. He thinks he can knock five points off her in the next week by going for the black vote."

Hodges put down his glass of wine. "What sort of polls, Dee?" he asked. "You've been telling me Stanton's pretty solid with African-Americans here."

Murphy spoke up. "It is my belief that there are some serious doubts to be raised about Governor Stanton's commitment to minority rights. It's time someone started asking some tough questions of your opponent."

Hodges was not fooled for a moment. He ignored Murphy and fixed Dee with a stern glare.

"Push-polls?" he said. "I told you this campaign did not want to go down that route."

Dee opened her mouth to speak. But Christine suddenly spoke up.

"What are push-polls?" she asked.

Hodges turned to her angrily. "That's when you ring someone up to ask: would you still vote for Candidate X if you knew they were beating their wife? It does not matter that they haven't been. Just asking the question suggests they might have."

He turned to look at Dee again and ignored a blustery protestation from Murphy.

"Stanton deserves better than that," he said.

"We would raise legitimate issues," Dee said, repeating Murphy's line. "We won't take this into the gutter."

Stanton continued to glare at her but he said nothing.

"Jack," Dee said softly. "We've got one more week of campaigning in this state. If we beat Stanton here, it's over. We have the party nomination. Then we can run for the White House. Then we can make you President. But we can't get there by playing softball."

Hodges drained his glass of wine as if possessed of a desperate thirst. Then he stood up and stalked out of the room. They watched his back disappear out of the room. To Dee's surprise Christine remained seated. She ran a finger along the top of her own glass to create a distant buzzing sound.

"You think this will work?" Christine asked quietly.

Murphy nodded. "Ma'am," he said. "I know my business."

Christine looked at Dee.

Dee nodded in agreement. "It's time to get a little dirty to get the job done. Do you think you can persuade him?" Dee said.

Christine took a deep breath and then let out a laugh. She was fully composed, in control. Her eyes sparked like icy wells in the middle of her face, hard and firm.

"Oh, Dee," she said. "Did you hear Jack actually say no?"

Then she got up and followed her husband.

Dee watched her leave the room, her trim form sashaying in her tightly fitting dress. Dee could not stop herself from casting an admiring glance over her body. The door closed with a soft click.

Christine called it exactly right. Hodges gave them the green light without actually having to say anything. To Dee's surprise, she felt a stab of disappointment. He was compromising his stance. He was doing what he needed to do to win, not just what he thought was right.

But Dee got what she wanted. Or at least she thought so. What did the CIA call Hodges' tactic? Plausible deniability. Hodges did not explicitly say yes, but he got all the gain if it worked. Meanwhile, they took all the pain if it didn't. She looked at Murphy and saw that he thought the same thing. His slack jaw broke out in a blubbery grin.

"Damn, he's good," Murphy said.

MIKE AND Lauren were in a slum about ten miles from the center of Guatemala City. They followed a handwritten set of directions from the hotel concierge to the mission of San Gabriel. Lauren read them and tried to direct Mike's driving, but both of them were too distracted by the sights and sounds around them to be sure they were on the right route. The slum was like nothing they ever saw before. It was vast. It began on a flat plateau and then tumbled down the sides of a series of steep ravines that encircled the city. In some places shacks flowed down the slopes like a waterfall of buildings and there were people everywhere. Men and women walked to and fro or lounged outside little cafes and bars that were painted in garishly bright colors. Hordes of children seemed to spring up like a fertile crop from the ground itself, catching a glimpse of the two white people in the car driving by and giving them curious looks or a frantic little wave and broad grin. Eventually, after attracting a little crowd of urchins trailing behind their vehicle, Lauren threw down the directions and gave up.

"We're lost," she said. "Let's just ask some of these kids."

Mike stopped the car just as the path they were on headed for a dead-end. He wound down the window and a gaggle of young boys appeared and thrust their hands and giggling faces through the open space. Mike asked them in Spanish about finding the church but received nothing in reply apart from a burst of laughter and shouts. Then one of them who, despite his tiny size, seemed the leader of the gang, spoke more clearly.

"*Dinero!*" he said and put out a hand.

Mike pulled a few grubby Guatemalan notes from his wallet and handed them over. Then he repeated the name of the church. The boy nodded with an impish grin and gestured for him to reverse the car. Mike did so, afraid that some of the kids surrounding the vehicle laughing and running might fall under the wheels. But they skipped effortlessly out of the way, like a flock of birds, dipping and wheeling in the sky.

Mike backed out of the lane and the boy came to the window again. He rapped on it once and Mike wound it down.

"*Esta aqui!*" the boy said, and pointed to a low, dirty white brick building just twenty yards away. Mike now saw the rambling structure was a church with a squat bell tower that was almost hidden by a thicket of shacks around it. They drove right by it just two minutes earlier. The boy darted away, followed by the others as Mike and Lauren opened their doors and got out. Away from the air conditioning of the car they felt the sudden heat and warmth of the air hit them like an open oven. So did the sour stench of the area, a mix of cooking fires and rotting rubbish that gave the air an acrid tinge that they could taste. They walked side by side to the church. Its whitewashed walls were covered in cracked and faded plaster, exposing the mud bricks beneath. It looked several hundred years old at least, clearly founded as some sort of rural mission back when this whole area was open fields or thick forest. Now it was swallowed by a vast urban slum.

Mike and Lauren walked through an arched gateway and immediately it was like they stepped back in time. They were in a cobbled courtyard opposite the church building but the high walls kept out the sounds of the city. It was suddenly quiet and peaceful. Mike led the way through an open door into the church.

Inside the atmosphere was dark and lit only by a dozen or so flickering candles. It reminded Mike of the shrine of Maximón back in Santa Teresa; of stepping over a threshold into a different and much older world. The walls were festooned with golden statues and a huge figure of Christ crucified on the cross hung at one end. The figure's skin was black in color with the trails of blood from his wrists and forehead painted a bright, thick, garish red. A group of young women kneeled in front of the Christ and prayed fervently with their heads bowed. Mike and Lauren tiptoed forward and one of the women looked up, cocking her head.

"We are looking for Father Gregorio Villatoro?" Mike whispered. The woman gestured in the direction of a door at the back of the church and resumed her quiet prayers. Mike walked over and gently pushed the door open to reveal a short corridor branching off into several rooms. From one they could hear the soft sounds of a male voice speak. Mike and Lauren walked forward and slowly pushed open the door. Inside a priest in a black robe talked to a group of young women and boys who lounged at a series of desks set up like a schoolroom. The priest stopped at the interruption and looked at the unexpected visitors. He was a short man, with a graying beard and hair that made him look around 60. But there was a sense of energy about him, a physical presence that dominated the room. He waved Mike and Lauren to sit down and then resumed his talk.

Mike thought it would be a religious sermon but as he listened it became clear the subject was anything but spiritual. Father Villatoro lectured the group on the health perils of drug use and how to practice safe sex as a prostitute or a user of prostitutes. He did not refrain from using blunt language but there was no sense of judgment. It was an honest talk and he cracked rough jokes to enliven the mood. Mike looked at the assembled group. None of them was much older than about 16. But the dead look behind their eyes and the grim lacing of crude gang tattoos on their bodies spoke of life in the slums. They listened to the priest without murmuring a word of complaint. In that way, at least, it was like a Sunday sermon. At the end, Villatoro led the group in a short prayer. Each of the kids bowed their head and clasped their hands in front of them, following the priest's words and then chorusing: "Amen." Only when they had all shuffled out did the priest turn to Mike and Lauren.

"We don't get many aid workers here. Have we met before? Forgive me, usually I have such a good memory for faces," he said in English that was only lightly accented.

"We're not aid workers," Lauren said. "We've come from America. We work for Senator Hodges. He is running for president. Have you heard of him?"

The priest said nothing, but the friendly smile on his face flickered for a moment, like a TV screen getting a burst of electrical static. "I am not sure that an American senator can have much interest in our humble church," he said.

Mike decided to plunge in. He took out his picture of the shooter and showed it to the priest. "We have come from Santa Teresa. We were told that you will tell us who this woman is."

The priest looked at the picture. He reached out to take it, and then, thinking better of it, he let his hand fall to his side. He sighed and suddenly seemed years older than he looked, inhabiting fully each and every one of his six decades. He walked to one of the students' desks and sat behind it, slumped down.

"Do you know her?" Mike asked.

The priest nodded.

"Do you know her name?"

The priest regarded them for a long time. Mike felt his heart quicken. This was the moment. He thought of the woman back in the Iowa jail, so full of mystery and dark silence. Now he was about to switch on a light in that chamber of secrets. He would finally understand what was unknown.

"Her name is Natalia Robles," the priest said. "She was a member of my flock. I knew her when she was born and I was a young man…"

Suddenly there was a rap on the door to the room and the priest stopped talking. A young woman was there. She was probably in her mid-20s though she looked much older. She was rail thin with lank, dirty blonde hair that dripped over her eyes. Her wrist bore the blue ink marks of a series of gang tattoos and her skin was pimply and stretched taut over her frame.

"*Padre,*" she whispered, asking for ten minutes of his time.

Villatoro stood up and asked her to wait for him back in the church. The young girl turned around and looked confusingly at Mike and Lauren. She opened her mouth to speak but the priest hushed her and repeated his command. He then shut the door after she left. His expression had changed now. He was angry.

"Put that picture away," he said. "I have more important things to do than talk about the past. People here have needs for the present that I must attend to."

Mike folded the picture and put it back in his pocket. But he didn't move. "We've come a long way, Father," he said. "We're not going anywhere."

The priest looked at the pair of visitors. He shook his head slowly, but he seemed to soften. "Very well. Please speak to no one here," he said. "Come back tomorrow. At noon. I will tell you more then."

"Okay," Mike said. "We do not mean to cause any trouble. We are just seeking out information."

The priest opened the door and held it wide for them. There was no smile on his face. They walked silently past him and back into the church. The young blond girl waited there, kneeling at the altar of the black Christ, her head bowed and deep in prayer. She did not look up as they walked quietly by and out into the sunshine outside.

———

FEDERICO SAT in the café in the lobby of the Marriott hotel, and lurked furtively behind a newspaper. The General's man had been there all afternoon, nursing the same tiny cup of bitter espresso, casting a quick eye at the sight of anyone white walking through the air-conditioned space or at the sound of a snatch of English. He felt like a spy in one of the Hollywood movies that he watched as a boy. He felt proud to remember the newspaper ruse from some long lost adventure film, ducking his pockmarked face behind the comforting newsprint. He was half tempted to cut tiny holes in the paper to peer through them but then decided against the idea.

But Federico's stoicism in the service of his master wilted after such a prolonged wait. It was tiring in the extreme to sit for so long, especially at a place like the Marriott with its constant stream of foreign and wealthy businessman meeting their government contacts. Federico watched them laugh and joke together, shake hands and discuss deals, enjoy the riches that peace, prosperity and power brought them. He shook his head angrily and thought of the General's exile on the coast amid the accursed Garifuna and their devilish culture. Then, at last, he saw his quarry. He recognized the red-headed American immediately and ducked behind his newspaper. Then, peering over the top, he saw a woman accompany him. He admired her figure for a moment, wondering who she was, and then positioned himself so he could watch the pair cross the lobby through one of the many mirrors on the wall.

"Got you!" he thought.

He saw them talk excitedly to each other and then head for the elevators. Behind them he caught the eye of the man at reception who had given him Sweeney's room number. But he had not mentioned anything about a woman. He would pull the hotel records on her and get her name too. Maybe she was just some tourist the Yankee seduced at the bar. He watched them go, a dart of envy in his heart, and saw them get into the elevator. Federico waited a moment and walked over to reception.

"Who is that woman? Are they traveling together?" he asked.

The man shrugged and smiled expectantly.

Federico cursed to himself. "There will be something extra for you if you tell me," he said through gritted teeth. The receptionist smiled pleasantly and looked down at his computer screen.

"Lauren O'Keefe," he said, struggling with the pronunciation of Lauren's surname. "They checked in together but they are staying in different rooms. She is room 711, opposite his."

Federico grunted his thanks and took out his phone. Carillo answered gruffly.

"He is here," Federico said. "He is with a woman. I don't know where they were today but they are staying here tonight. What do you want me to do?"

Carillo paused a moment on the other end of the line. Federico heard him breathe heavily, like some animal.

"I don't like this, Federico," Carrillo said, speaking his

thoughts aloud, not looking for any response. "It looks like people are moving against me. Is my reward really so expensive that they would send people here to destroy me? Is that my fate?"

Federico imagined Carillo in his darkened living room weighing the fates of those around him. Planning, plotting, making a move. Once again his General was in command against hostile forces and Federico was his one-man army, dedicated to the mission. It felt good to get orders like this, rather than just make coffee and beat up the blacks who did not pay Carillo sufficient respect.

"I want to know who they are seeing and where they are going. Stick tight to them. Don't let them out of your sight. Call me the moment you know something else," Carillo said.

"Yes sir," Federico said and snapped the phone shut. He smiled. He would book into this hotel tonight and instruct the receptionist to call him the moment the couple got their breakfast. He would stay on them so tight that they would not know they wore him like a coat.

CHAPTER 20

DEE KNEW SHE was only a few miles from where her candidate was being made up in a TV studio, but it felt like a whole world away. She sat with Christine and a few other senior staffers in the Hodges' hotel room in downtown Columbia and nervously watched a huge flat screen TV in the corner of the room. The local Fox station broadcast its news report. The news anchor had already flagged up the network's exclusive live interview with Hodges for an hour, and the time of its airing fast approached.

Dee poured herself a thick glass of scotch and offered some to Christine, who shook her head without looking at it. Dee shrugged and gulped down half of it. She needed the warmth and the buzz to kill her nerves. The anchor, a woman with a big mane of blond hair, started the lead-in to the interview.

"Do you think she'll go for it?" Christine asked, not looking around, resting a long-nailed finger on her perfectly rouged cheek.

Dee shrugged. This was her plan and she knew the stakes

were high. Swampy had dug up a grainy piece of video recording of Stanton talking at some long forgotten town hall meeting more than a year ago. For years Swampy had someone go to every meeting anyone held down here, recording away with a cell phone for thousands of wasted hours. Most of it was useless but it all went into Swampy's files ready for a day it might be useful. That day had now come for this clip. Stanton riffed carelessly in front of a wholly white upcountry audience about the need for self-sufficiency and against benefits cheaters.

"You know," Stanton said. "It pains me that some members of our society look for a handout when they really should want a hand up."

It was a snappy line. One that Dee could easily admire in a different sort of contest. But she knew that putting that quote in a racially charged context could be explosive for them. In a good way. That was precisely what they would now do. Two days of Swampy's push-polling on Stanton's race record prepared that ground already. Beneath the surface the black community started to burn with rumors questioning Stanton's commitment to their cause. This video would ignite that powder-keg.

Dee just needed to tee up the release so it did not seem completely underhanded. So she took the news anchor out for lunch the day before and spun a web of off-the-record comments that should prompt the achorwoman to bring up the race question they wanted. That would allow them to release the video at others' behest. But who knew if it would work. It was lighting a bomb fuse in a rainstorm. All you could do was apply the fire and watch it burn down to the charge, hoping a steady pour of other events would not over-take it.

Now the cameras cut away to the candidate. He sat beside the anchor and she opened with a question on the latest run of bad news from Afghanistan. Hodges listened intently his eyes never leaving her and not a flicker of a smile on his lips. He oozed military competence.

But Dee felt a stab of disappointment. "Come on, you bitch. Ask my question," she breathed.

She need not have worried.

The interviewer shuffled slightly in her seat and glanced down at her notes. "Senator Hodges," she began. "Our news team has learned from its sources that there are a lot of racial accusations starting to float around out there about your opponent. This is the sort of dirty politics that you are supposed to be standing against. Why have you allowed this to happen?"

That was it. Dee stopped breathing for a moment. That bitch of an anchor phrased the issue more negatively than she feared, but it was out there now. It was up to Hodges to run with it like Christine promised he would.

Hodges grimaced thinly. "You're right, this is the sort of campaigning I am standing against. Innuendo and rumor have no place in my campaign," he said and looked firmly into the camera.

That's good, thought Dee, he's defused the weapon she threw at him.

"That is because we are fighting this election on the issues and the policies," Hodges now continued, never shifting his gaze. "But when it comes to affirmative action that helps some of the weakest members of our society, I am worried about my opponent's opinions. My campaign recently uncovered some disturbing evidence of Governor Stanton's real beliefs. She appears to think that we are all born with the same opportunities in this country. That we all start at the same place. But I know we do not. The sad thing is I wish she were more sensitive to the realities of life for minorities in America today."

Hodges turned back to the interviewer who could not hide a widening of her eyes.

"What are you saying, Senator?" she asked.

Hodges smiled disarmingly. "I'm saying I wish Governor Stanton could be a little more sensitive. I heard some comments she made on a video that my staff came across and they worried me. Now, if we can move onto some of the real issues pressing this campaign, I am sure we would all appreciate it."

Dee did not hear the anchor's next words. She stood in the middle of the hotel room, danced a little jig and giggled uncontrollably. She reached down and tried to grab Christine's arm but the candidate's wife flinched away. Dee pumped a fist in the air.

"He hit it out of the park!" she yelled.

Hodges' comments would have pricked the ears of every news reporter watching and they would soon start calling. Then the campaign would release their video to anyone who wanted it. Dee stared at her Blackberry. She held it up in the room and watched all the other staffers' eyes turn to it, including the media director. Dee motioned for her to get her phone out too.

"It won't be long," she said.

And it wasn't.

Less than 90 seconds passed and Dee's phone started buzzing. So did the media director's. Dee laughed and tossed the phone to another staffer.

"Everyone who calls gets a copy of the video emailed to them," she said. "Even if it's a telemarketer dialing a wrong number and trying to sell you insurance. Take down their email address and send them that tape."

Christine looked over at Dee. Her face masked whatever emotions lurked under that surface, like a mirror-smooth sea.

"Does it bother you that you just played the race card?" Christine asked. She seemed to be studying Dee's reaction, a little like a scientist looking at a specimen she was about to dissect. Dee was surprised that the sensation slightly unnerved her.

"Look," Dee said. "We haven't played anything. Stanton made those comments, we didn't. You know what sort of audience she was talking to? A bunch of white folks up in the mountains. They know what she means when she's talking about people cheating on benefits. It's code. We're just deciphering it for general consumption."

Christine seemed unimpressed.

"You really believe that, Dee?"

Now Dee got angry. "I'll tell you what I believe," she said, leaning in a little closer than she planned. She got a buzz of satisfaction when Christine flinched slightly. "I believe that this is going to knock ten points off Stanton's support with blacks in this state. That's enough to have us sliding for home plate."

Dee walked out of the room. How dare that woman take a moral high ground with her? After all Christine was instrumental in getting Hodges to play along and commit to getting the video out there. Dee stood in the corridor, suddenly aware she was alone, sealed off from the frenzy of activity in the hotel room. It was quiet, just the low buzz of the artificial lights above her. She took a series of deep breaths, getting back her center and her sense of calm. Then she smiled.

This is the final stretch, she thought. I can see the finish line and we're in the lead. No mistakes and we'll win. No mistakes and no surprises.

MIKE AND Lauren's shoes clip-clopped loudly on the marble floor of the hotel lobby as they walked out into the heat of day and toward their rental car. Behind them, a mere twenty yards or so, Federico watched their every move. He wore a hat pulled low over his eyes. A sheen of stubble now grew over his chin, giving him the hint of a beard. He walked slowly and looked for a sign that they spotted him. He was confident they did not.

They climbed into their car, laughing with each other like young lovers, and drove off. Federico quickly jumped in his car to follow them. He was lucky. A morning traffic jam snarled the road just a few hundred yards from the hotel and his target was already marooned in a sea of vehicles. He relaxed and enjoyed the sensation of the chase.

It brought back many memories of tracking and following a human target through the streets of Guatemala City. Even after so many years in that stink hole of Livingston, the pursuit was still as natural as walking. He was good at it too. The General always knew that.

A steady trickle of distant names and faces flowed through Federico's mind. There was the priest out in the suburbs. The union leader in the coffee warehouse. The teacher from the village near his own home town. All of them were problems he solved. He recalled them like looking back on his school days. A brighter period that was more full of life than his current circumstances. He had purpose then. A sense of a life fulfilled by a cause. It was the best of times.

The traffic started to clear and he wormed his way forward to just a few yards behind his target. He opened the glove box and saw the dull metallic glint of the gun. An old fashioned revolver, but reliable and well-oiled. He took it out and rested it on the passenger seat beside him like an old friend and comrade. He liked to imagine the weapon too was full of happy thoughts; of a joint purpose rediscovered back in the fight. Federico whistled a marching tune, repeating the chorus over and over as the car ahead drove in the direction of the slums.

Federico had not been in this part of the city for many years, but the pursuit was easy. The roads were so pitted and crowded that they barely went above the pace of a slow jog.

He could follow these people on foot and be able to pull off his mission. Finally the car ahead parked outside an old church, half-hidden by the slum buildings around it and his targets went inside.

Federico remained seated and reached across for his revolver. He tucked it into the back of his waistband and got out of the car. A gaggle of kids watched from a nearby corner, no doubt eyeing his potential worth as a target for begging or someone willing to pay for them to look after his car. The largest of them sauntered over.

"I'll clean your car, *señor*. It is all dusty from the *barrio*," he said.

Federico ignored his offer and pointed at the church. "What is this place?"

The child was silent. Federico toyed with the idea of grabbing him by the throat. But he did not want to create a scene. He handed over a single quetzal note and repeated his question.

"San Gabriel," the child said.

Federico frowned. Why on earth would these Yankees come to this place?

"Who is the priest?" he asked. The child was silent for a moment as he mulled over whether to ask for more money, but something in Federico's stare made him rethink his strategy.

"Father Gregorio Villatoro," he said.

Now Federico understood. He squinted through the sunshine and the dirty adobe walls of the old mission. He had not heard that name in a long time. But he knew it. He could not forget it. How could he? He shooed away the child and got back into his car, feeling the weight of the gun at his back. It felt even stronger and more comforting than before. Then he pulled out his phone and waited for the General to answer.

───────

THE HOT chocolate that Father Villatoro handed him tasted bitter and Mike forced himself to swallow it politely. Next to him Lauren had no such compunction to hide her reaction. She spluttered loudly and put the mug down like it was poison. Villatoro laughed kindly.

"It is an acquired taste for foreigners," he said.

"We have hot chocolate in America too," said Lauren. "But it does not taste like this."

She gestured at the steaming, blackish-brown liquid. Again Villatoro laughed.

"No, my dear," he said. "This is the country where chocolate comes from. This is the real thing, the natural way it was meant to be served. What you have in America is something else entirely. What you have is all sugar and fat. You took the body of the coca bean but you sucked out its soul."

Mike put down his own mug. He would not be picking it up again. He swallowed hard and tried to clean his palate of the powdery taste. The priest seemed nothing but amused.

"I give all my guests from other countries a little local taste of life here. It reminds them that we are our own country with our own way of doing things. That what you might find familiar is in fact very different."

"Yeah, that's not the first time," Mike said. "In Santa Teresa there is a statue. It smokes and drinks alcohol. They call it Maximón," he said.

The priest raised an eyebrow. "Ah, they took you to see that old idol. I was twenty years in that village and I could never break their respect for it. It did not take me too long to learn to just work with it not against it. You know the people around that lake were worshipping Maximón long before our Lord and Savior was born."

"And here?" said Lauren. "Do you have a statue of Maximón in this church?"

Villatoro chuckled.

"No. My flock here is from all over. Some Indios, some Mestizo. The things that bind them are not language or history or culture. It is poverty. That is the glue that holds us together here. But you did not come all this way to listen to the problems of an old priest. You came to ask questions about Natalia Robles."

Mike could still scarcely believe he knew her identity. Now she was no longer some mysterious force of nature; some lurking, dark spirit trapped in an Iowa jail with an unknown past. She was flesh and blood, rendered so by the knowledge of her name. Her past life was about to be born to him, revealed like an unspooling film reel. His chest tightened with anticipation and the room shrank around them, shutting out the rest of the world.

"The man we met in Santa Teresa was called Rodolfo. He

would not speak of her. As soon as I showed a picture of her he kicked us out. He was terrified of her," Mike said.

Villatoro sighed and gave a bitter laugh.

"They have their reasons, I suppose," he said. "They see her as a demon. A sort of curse from the underworld on their village. Their old ways tell them that to even talk of such a devil spirit is to risk bringing her back. Those are Maximón's rules."

Mike's mind filled with the vision of the strange, smoking, drinking statue Rodolfo revealed to them. He realized they had betrayed his acceptance by breaking their taboos over Natalia Robles. By showing Rodolfo a picture of a woman he thought a demon they risked bringing the curse of the past back to life. No wonder he chased them away.

"What are your rules, Father? Do they make you afraid to talk about her too?" he asked.

"No," he said. "They do not."

But, before he spoke again, Villatoro took a deep breath as if stealing himself to some hard labor.

"Natalia Robles was a brutal killer," he said. "The worst of the worst. I remember her when she was just a little girl in Santa Teresa. A sweet child but born to a bad father who beat her. Perhaps he did even worse things than that…"

The priest's voice faded for a moment and let the unspoken accusation hang in the air. He shrugged.

"No matter. I will not make excuses. The lovely child turned into a terrible teenager. She fled the village for Guatemala City and joined the gangs in the slums. I have lost count how many follow that path, thinking that the city will give them an easier life than the village, though it never does. Natalia was different. She found a talent for killing that came to the attention of the army. Or, more accurately, a very secretive special part of the army. An elite unit that flourished back in those times of the war. Natalia was useful to them. Not only was she an expert killer, but she was a Mayan country girl. She knew their enemy. She spoke their language. She had been one of them. The army trained her well."

"Who trained her?"

It was Lauren's question and her voice that broke a spell for Mike. He looked over at her. She eagerly craned forward.

"General Rodrigo Carillo," Villatoro said. "He headed up a unit that the army used to fight the dirtiest parts of the war. It was Carillo who took Natalia under his wing."

Lauren gasped. Mike held his head in his hands. Oh God, he thought. Carillo and the shooter were linked. And Hodges and Carillo were friends. None of this was down to chance. Natalia was not some victim. She was a perpetrator. She was not some random crazy. She was a cold-blooded deliberate killer. Mike looked over at Lauren. She glared at him and he knew she was making some of the same links, realizing the enormity now of what they discovered. Natalia was a murderer and an assassin. Carillo had been her boss. Hodges had paid Carillo money. Was it still remotely possible that Hodges was an innocent drawn into this mess? Mike felt a cold sweat break out on his forehead.

"I remember seeing her when she drove into Santa Teresa

on the day of the massacre," the priest continued, oblivious to the impact of his words on his audience. "It was the first time I saw her in the flesh for five years and she was changed. I barely recognized her. I thought that because the village had been her home that she might have some mercy. I begged her to control her men. But she laughed at me. I think she was avenging something that day."

Again the priest stopped. The corners of his eyes were moist and he wiped them with a corner of his sleeve. "Forgive me," he said. "It has been a long time."

"What did she do?" Mike asked and remembered the look in Natalia's eyes when she attacked him. The icy, cold, dead darkness that lurked there and the merciless urgency of her grip. He felt his skin tighten at the memory.

The priest shook his head. "She has blood on her hands. I saw her kill many that day. Men, women…children."

Then he fell quiet. He stood up and walked over to his desk. He brought out a battered cardboard box and rummaged in it for something. Mike and Lauren watched him transfixed. Eventually Villatoro found what he was looking for. It was a tattered Polaroid photograph. He walked over and showed it to them. Mike could scarcely believe his eyes. It was Natalia – not as a young killer, but as the middle-aged woman she now was – and she stood by the priest in front of the church of San Gabriel. They both smiled broadly at the photographer, their arms wrapped around each other's shoulders like brother and sister.

"I don't understand…" Mike began.

The priest laughed. It was a pure sound that dispelled the darkness that seeped into the room.

"You see," he said. "The Lord shows us his miracles in ways of His choosing. Not ours. This box contains all that remains here of Natalia's life. A few pictures, her army documents and her diaries. Most of them show that Natalia was simply a killer. But this photograph shows she was also my dear friend."

"How?" whispered Lauren.

"About five years after the massacre she came here. She had a child and it changed everything within her. She was given the gift of life. She found something to love and be loved by. It was profound. She came to understand what it was that she had done and what she became. She threw herself on the mercy of this church and of the Lord and we took her in as we do all sinners," the priest said.

He got up again and gestured at them to follow. They left his office and went into the main body of the church. It was empty of worshippers. Only a few candles flickered in the darkness. Villatoro walked up to the front and stood beneath the looming, black statue of Christ on the cross. "She rededicated herself to the faith and gave herself to God. The love of our Lord burned so brightly in her. Can you imagine that?" he asked.

Mike, for a moment, thought he heard Natalia's voice in his head, whispering softly of vengeance and righteousness like she had in her jail cell. He understood now why she recited the Bible at him on his visits to her in Iowa. She flung herself into religion to cope with her past and her dreadful guilt in the wake of becoming a mother.

"She quoted from the Bible when I saw her," he told the priest.

Father Villatoro nodded.

"She knew it all by heart. I think she found the answers to her questions there. At least, for a while. It was not easy. She talked of ending it all, of punishing herself with death. But I persuaded her of God's forgiveness. That was the easy part. My own forgiveness was harder. But, in time, that came too."

Villatoro kept his eyes fixed on the statue of Christ but kept addressing them.

"I counseled her as she took her journey to come to terms with what she did. It was a mother's voyage, taken to give her daughter a chance in the world. But sadly it did not work out as we had hoped."

Villatoro turned back to them and his face was full of sadness, the ends of his mouth turned down as if weighted with rocks. He walked to the front pew and sat down, again facing the statue of Christ.

"Patterns repeat themselves. Life in the *barrio* is hard. The daughter, Gabriela, fell into the same trap of the gangs. Drugs took hold of her. Gabriela became a prostitute and a drug addict. For Natalia that was a far worse punishment than any death sentence. To be given something to love and then to have it taken away from you. It was so cruel."

"Is Gabriela dead?" Mike asked.

"No. She comes to the classes I hold here. Occasionally she tries to give up her habits, but most times not. I fear for her. For someone who lives like her, most of them do not make it past 30."

At that moment a door opened at the far end of the church. A young woman walked in: the same one with the light skin and dirty blond hair they saw last time. The priest looked up and she lifted a limp hand in greeting. Mike saw her more clearly now. She looked painfully thin, her arm ragged as the flesh hung from it in translucent folds where the muscles wasted away.

He looked at the girl and, despite the ravages of her life, he could sense some of the resemblance of her mother. He knew it. This was Gabriela. She was Natalia's daughter. Mike opened his mouth to speak. But the priest shushed him before he uttered a word.

"Enough!" he said. "What you want to know is man's work. But for the rest of the day I will do God's."

There was no room to voice any opposition. Mike and Lauren shuffled out of the church and walked quietly past the young girl at the door. Mike glanced at her once but she would not return his gaze. Instead she looked down at the floor, searching for some answer in the dust of the church's hallowed ground rather than these strangers from a faraway land.

———

THE FIGURE that walked across the parking lot of the suburban Columbia mall looked like a spy from some third-rate B-movie. He wore a thick trench coat that failed to hide his portly figure and he pulled up the collars to hide his jowly face. Dee watched him come towards her car for a happy minute. She had no idea why Howard Carver wanted this private meeting with her. But she knew it must be good news. She put her palm on the horn and beeped at him until he saw her. He waddled over and looked around worriedly. Dee could not help but laugh. Jesus, she thought, this guy is in even worse shape than I thought.

Carver opened the door and squeezed his large frame into the passenger seat beside her. He wheezed slightly and grunted a hello.

"Thanks for meeting me out here, Dee," he said.

Dee shrugged. His tone was apologetic. A far cry from the previous times they talked when he was full of arrogance and bluster. She felt a surge of pride and satisfaction. This old parasite was on the losing side and he knew it, she thought.

"What do you want, Howie?" she asked.

Carver took a moment to gather himself. "I want you to stop putting this race shit out there, Dee. It's beneath you and it's beneath your candidate."

His tone was not so much angry, as aggrieved. He practically whined out the words. "It's not fair! You know Governor Stanton doesn't have a racist bone in her body. She's worked all her life to raise the chances of African-Americans."

Dee shrugged.

"Well then, maybe next time she speaks to a bunch of crackers in the mountains, she might want to defend the welfare state, not condemn it."

"She didn't say that!" Carver said, his face suddenly red and his tone angry. But the storm quickly subsided and he struggled to strike an accommodating tone.

"Look, I think we both know that after South Carolina is over we are going to have to come together. The party is going to need unity as much as anything else. We've got four days left until the election. Let's keep it civil. We're on the same side here in the end," he said.

Dee looked at him. Christ, she thought, their internal numbers must be worse than she thought. Swampy's video of Stanton's little error destroyed them. No one ever talked about uniting in the future when they thought they were going to win. That was strictly talk for the losing camp.

"We have to think about the general election," Carver continued. "The nominated candidate is going to have to combine the strengths of both campaigns. We will need to be sure that our two sides have enough respect for each other so that we can be on the same team."

Dee suddenly got it. This bastard was angling for a job. He knew they were going down and he was a rat looking for the first lifeboat off the ship. She suddenly felt light. She looked at him and rested a hand on his arm. She toyed with the idea of sticking the knife in and giving it a good, hard twist. Part of her longed for it. It was the part that was still an outsider and wanted to destroy those who always looked at her as a misfit. But she was a winner now. She was strong. It was better politics to be merciful.

"There will be a place for you," Dee said softly. 'You know that, Howie."

Carver smiled gratefully. "And my candidate? There's been a lot of talk in the press about a united ticket. That would bring both sides together pretty nicely."

Dee nodded. "I can't speak for the Senator, but that looks possible. We're very open to it."

Dee could scarcely believe it. This was virtually a capitulation. Somewhere deep within her, though, an alarm bell went off. This was no time to be too magnanimous. No one had even started voting yet.

"But, look, we've got one more debate to get through yet. We'll keep it clean if you will and then we can talk," she said.

She was offering a deal. A calm, straight road to the finish line. No upsets, no surprises, no more nastiness.

Carver nodded. "Sounds good to me, Dee," he said and he proffered a chubby hand. Dee took it gladly, surprised at his feather light grip in her own.

She had to give him something in return. "You fought a good fight, Howie," she said. "But you chose the wrong horse. My guy was clean as a whistle. That's all it was. He was spotless."

CHAPTER 21

THE HOT BREEZE from the Caribbean blew in like an unwelcome guest at General Carillo's table and sent his napkin fluttering skywards like a released seabird. He made a futile grab for it, but it was beyond his grasp, caught in the air and flying from his terrace into the streets below. Carillo cursed his luck and pushed away his plate of rice, pork and beans.

He was not hungry anyway. He slept poorly the previous night and was unable to rectify that with a long siesta this afternoon. Now, even though he was fatigued, he still felt fidgety and nervous. His mind raced ever since he heard the American was back in Guatemala in the company of some woman. A "blogger" whatever that was. Something like a journalist, he was told. It was confusing and unnerving. Just as he started to believe he was getting his just reward – that his life's efforts were not in vain and unrecognized – this happened.

Still, Federico was a good man. He was loyal as a dog and could be trusted to do his duty. Any General was only as good as the men he commanded. He knew that. With

Federico deployed out in the field, he knew he had options. Carillo stared out as the blue waters slowly darkened as the sun went down. A smattering of Garifuna fishing boats dotted the horizon, not yet choosing to come into the shelter of their homeport. Carillo sighed. He longed to get out of here and go home. Back to the mountains. Back to the green hillsides and cool fresh air of his youth. Soon he would have the money to grease the right palms and buy the return from exile that sheer politics itself would not allow.

He imagined his *finca* in his mind. One just like his grand-father had owned on the outskirts of Antigua. It would not be too big. There was no need to be greedy. It would just be a plot of good land on which the coffee beans would practically burst forth. His workers would be loyal village folk and he would be a good master to them. Perhaps he might even take a wife. It was not too late for him, even though he was past sixty. Such things were not unheard of for men of power, money and dignity. She would be a young village girl and he would fill her belly with children. He closed his eyes, sleepy at last, his mind filled with the sound of wedding chimes.

Except it was not church bells he heard. His mind snapped away from its reverie to register his phone downstairs. He hauled himself to his feet, hearing his tired bones crack in complaint, and went to answer the call.

It was Federico. "Sir, I followed *los Americanos* and they went to visit a church in the slums."

"A church?" the General said and dared himself to feel a little glow of relief. "Are they just playing at being tourists?"

"I do not think it was the church they were interested in. It was the priest. Father Gregorio Villatoro."

The General felt a stab of adrenalin at the name. It surged through his body and left him feeling like a just struck cymbal with a ringing sound in his ears. He could not find the words.

"General?" Federico asked. "What would you have me do?"

"That son of a bitch priest," Carillo spat and at last found his voice. It was like the collapse of a dam and a torrent of emotions poured through his mind. Visions of a long ago day of blood and mayhem; of fighting a righteous cause and striking a blow against the enemy. A day forgotten for many years and that should remain so.

"I thought he was dead long ago," Carillo shouted. "What is he doing in the slums? Stirring up trouble with his communist bullshit. It sickens me that he is allowed to preach Marxism still after all these years."

"It is an offense against God and the Motherland," Federico said.

An abomination, Carillo thought. But his anger was only a thin veneer for the panic he started to feel, like a slick of oil on a deep and raging ocean. Why were these Americans digging around in that part of the past? He thought they had an agreement on all that. Silence in return for money. It was simple. It was in no one's interest to excavate old history; to dig up the bodies of the long ago dead. Were they turning on him now? Was he to be betrayed yet again?

Carillo set his jaw firm. "Federico," he said. "We cannot

let the enemy move against us. We must strike back. You know what to do."

Federico said nothing. He did not have to. He had his orders now. His leader needed him. His country needed him. The phone line went dead.

———

FOR MIKE it felt like giving someone a Judas' kiss. He and Lauren spent the last hour in the bar of the Marriott talking and drinking. She was enthralled at the revelation about Natalia and her links to Carillo. She seemed to forget Mike worked for the Hodges campaign. She believed they were on an adventure together and had stumbled upon a scoop. A story she would write and post on the Internet once the South Carolina race was over. A story to make her a household name. She was almost light-headed with the excitement and flirted with Mike by resting her hand on his arm.

Mike responded in kind, laughing and joking. But inside he felt physically sick. He wanted to come to Guatemala to exonerate Hodges. To prove his payments to Carillo were innocent. Or that Natalia was some sort of traumatized victim, driven mad by what she witnessed. But it turned out to be the opposite. Carillo was a monster. Natalia was too. They killed and slaughtered scores of people in just Santa Teresa alone. It was truly a nightmare.

He knew he could not contain himself any longer if he

drank more, so he suggested they make it an early night. Lauren smiled, perhaps thinking he was suggesting something else, but he simply kissed her on the cheek at her hotel room door. He registered what he thought was a flicker of disappointment on her face, then he waited a breathless ten minutes before he sneaked out of his own room and headed downstairs.

Now he was in the car alone and trying to navigate his way back through the streets of the city to San Gabriel. He looked through the windshield at the confusing streets and lights and tried to remember the way. Slowly, after many mistakes and diversions, he headed in the right direction. He took out his phone and called the number of the church. Villatoro answered. His voice sounded sleepy.

"Father," Mike said. "I'm so sorry but there is an emergency back home and we leave early tomorrow. Can I come and see you tonight to look at Natalia's papers? It is very important for us to be able to see them."

Villatoro sighed down the line, a weary sound full of resignation.

"Please, Father," said Mike. "We have come a long way."

For a moment Mike felt a stab of shame. He lied to a priest. It came to this, this breaking of a taboo that he knew his own mother, steeped in her Catholicism, would find shocking. But there was no choice. He was desperate and feeling his way blind now.

"All right," Villatoro said eventually and without pleasure.

Mike breathed a sigh of relief. At last, he thought. A break. He could check out those papers without Lauren and search for any link back to Hodges, and hopefully, if he was lucky, discover a fuller explanation of why Natalia wanted to kill him. Then he could spin some bullshit to Lauren and get home. She would be furious, no doubt, but it was for the best. Best for him, best for the candidate, best for the campaign.

He thought about that as he drove down a rutted road he was not sure he recognized.

The campaign existed in another world now. He could scarcely remember the long months in Iowa in all that snow and cold, all those meetings with bored farmers and stumping through tiny college campus after campus to win over a few students. What did he tell those young kids, he wondered. He tried to summon up some of the slogans and talking points that filled his life back then. That gave him drive and ambition he barely felt before. But he got nothing. They were just words now: dead things devoid of meaning. He pressed down his foot on the accelerator as his mind raced. He thought of Hodges and the amazing love he felt for the man when he first heard him speak, but he had not felt that way for a long time now. He was sucked into this investigation instead, not realizing until too late that his head had sunk under water and into the murky depths. He was adrift of the campaign now and dealt only with bloody events of the past, desperate to both find them out and cover them up.

He saw that his hands gripped the steering wheel so tightly that his knuckles were white. He forced himself to relax, noticing as he did so his car drove past the dark silhouette of Villatoro's church. He pulled over, got out, and paused to look up skywards into the darkness and gather his breath. Finally, he felt calmer and he entered the church.

Villatoro waited for him, seated on a pew at the back. Mike walked up to him. To save money, Villatoro did not keep electric lights on and only a few flickering candles illuminated the darkness. The priest was like a shade or ghost, the paleness of his face melted into the dim half-light and the dancing shadows. Mike sat down next to him. The two were silent for a moment. Then, to Mike's surprise, Villatoro spoke first.

"I am glad to have called Natalia my friend," he said. "You should know that. She taught me more about the power of God's love than any priest."

His voice was low but calm.

"She helped murder all those people in Santa Teresa," Mike said.

Villatoro shook his head. "The fact is for a time Natalia knew God's forgiveness," he said. "She was truly sorry for what she did and she loved her daughter as much as any woman I ever knew."

Villatoro stared at the altar as he spoke but now he turned to look at Mike. His face was serene. "If someone with her past can do that, then we all have hope," he said. "Do you not see the wonder of God's work in such a thing?"

Mike could scarcely believe his ears. Yet he felt envy at the priest's emotions and the sheer love and forgiveness that radiated from him. But that was not all. There was something else. It was Faith. Mike envied him the surety of his beliefs. That these terrible events were not proof of God's cruelty nor his non-existence but, in fact, the opposite.

"But after that she tried to kill Jack Hodges," Mike said. "She traveled to America and hid herself with a rifle in a school in Iowa and then tried to shoot him. I've followed her trail. She tried to commit murder again."

"Yes. Not every star shines forever. But we should be glad for her period of Grace. Her choice to become angry once more was a sad one." The priest paused.

"But your candidate was saved, no? Perhaps that shows God's hand. You must trust that the universe unfolds as it should. Our Creator would have it no other way."

The priest stood up and walked in the direction of his back office. Mike stared at his broad back. The feeling of envy nearly over-powered him. How was the priest not angry? How was he so sure of things? But Mike followed obediently behind him like a twig dragged swiftly over rapids by a fast-flowing stream.

In his office Villatoro sat in his chair and reached into a desk drawer. He took out the same tattered box from which he got the photograph of Natalia. He placed it on the table reverently as if it were a Bible. Then he folded his arms across his chest. Mike tried to read his face but it was impassive as stone.

"You may have this. You can find your answers inside, I am sure. It is all of her personal things that she left behind. It is a small box yet it contains the mementoes of her life. But I ask you to think carefully about what you will do with it."

Mike peered into the box. There were identity papers, what looked like a diary, bundles of military documents and dozens of photographs. Mike saw several in which Natalia stood with a young woman, her daughter, and smiled shyly in the front room of a humble-looking shack. It was a jarring moment of familial normality. Natalia's smile was unexpected for its sheer banality. But Mike knew what history lay behind it. Villatoro closed the box.

"They are yours now. You will face a choice about what to do with them. I do not envy you that."

Mike looked up.

"Trust in God," the priest said.

It was Mike's cue to leave. He mumbled a thank you and picked up the box, which was light to the touch but somehow felt weighed down by its contents. Villatoro watched him go without another word and offered no blessing to go alongside his warning.

AN HOUR later Mike sat on his hotel bed with the contents of the box sprayed out in front of him. It looked like an explosion had scattered the contents all over the room. He painstakingly tried to build up a picture of a life from the myriad of papers and pictures all around him. It was like a vast jigsaw puzzle, but one that locked together through time as well as piece-by-piece. There were a few scattered photographs from childhood, including one of a ragtag little girl standing next to a youthful-looking Father Villatoro. She wore a dirty white dress but her smile was confident and beaming. Mike thought he recognized the wall of the church in Santa Teresa behind them. There was also a picture of a glum-looking peasant, posed in black and white like an official portrait. Mike guessed he was her father. He searched the deep lines on the man's face for some sign of the cruelty that Villatoro mentioned: the man who sowed the seeds of the monster that his daughter would become. But he saw nothing; just blank, dark eyes that stared back at the camera with a deep tiredness, not malevolence.

He sorted through the military papers and looked for order in the clutter. Induction papers showed she passed into the army in Guatemala City and a recommendation from her graduation ceremony revealed she joined the military police with an award for marksmanship. There were other citations from her police school too. Then Mike saw Carillo's name for the first time. It was on a letter written to the General which praised Natalia's skills at interrogation and suggested she be attached to Carillo's own unit. Mike followed her career easily now, rapidly putting the papers and letters in the right order and tracked her movements through the past and the war. Nothing was mentioned obliquely. Just names and dates of places scattered across the highlands. A few were clearly reports of combat. They were lists of names arranged into columns: one for dead, another for wounded and/or captured. Mike wondered at the stories behind each name. They were just a random collection but he felt his breath slow in his chest as he thought of the real people behind them:

farmers and revolutionaries, fighters and peasants all mixed in together, their lives crushed down to a list. Natalia's name appeared on addendums to some of the action reports, which were brief summaries of intelligence gained from "after action questioning sessions." All of them were from Carillo's unit, to which Natalia was now permanently attached. The language of the reports was terse and simple. Subjects were asked for information about the guerrillas and their replies were summarized and written down. They were often "pressured" or "encouraged" to answer. Mike knew what that meant; it was a euphemism that suggested little but covered everything.

He recalled the pictures and reports he saw back in Washington. He thought of the grimy interrogation chambers, the beatings, the pins slipped under fingernails, the limbs broken by clubs and the backs churned into bleeding flesh by whips and ropes. He felt sick as he read the terse prose that detailed session after session with Natalia's name by it. He envisioned her in her own prison now, caged in like a trapped wild beast, pacing between four blank walls. He remembered her expression as unreadable as a book in a foreign alphabet, some cruciform hint at a lost and terrifying past.

Why did she keep them? he wondered. Perhaps she was proud of her record and used them as medals of honor as she blazed her way through the civil war. Then, later, changed by motherhood and counseled by Villatoro, she used them as a reminder of her sins, a sort of mental scourge to beat herself with her bloodied past.

He scanned through more reports. Carillo's unit was prolific and traveled across the country from village to village and slum to slum. Sometimes they carried out an action themselves and other times arrived after the army already did its work, picking up the pieces and carting off the prisoners for interrogation sessions. Carillo was everywhere in the later reports; giving orders and taking part in some of the interrogations. He and Natalia operated as some form of team, with her rapidly rising to become his most trusted lieutenant.

Then Mike froze.

A sheaf of orders from Carillo to senior commanders in his unit bore a familiar name: Capt. Arnold Andersen. Hodges' old friend from the School of the Americas. His former comrade-in-arms. Mike remembered Andersen's grinning, friendly visage suddenly turned to cold fury at the mention of his time in Guatemala. How Andersen ended their interview and practically threw him out of his plush Washington corner office overlooking the Mall. Now he knew why. Andersen worked with Carillo, advising him and guiding him.

Mike's blood quickened as he read on. Then another familiar name snagged his eyes. It came out of a sheaf of papers like a rock ripping out the underside of a boat at sea: Santa Teresa. An interrogation Natalia led pinpointed the village as the site of major guerrilla support. A suspect cracked and revealed guerrilla groups from the surrounding hills stayed over-night in the village. Mike read the report grimly. The interrogation went on for hours and, at the end of it all, the subject was reported "deceased." Whatever horrors Natalia inflicted upon the victim broke him. Carillo had handwritten a note on the bottom: *"Is this actionable? Major operation would be needed in troubled area."*

Carillo signed it in a grand flourish, his name written in long loops and curls that expressed his ego in the midst of the ugliest of possible thoughts. But below his mark was more handwriting. It was small and neat, official and curt.

"Actionable" it read. Just one word. But below it a name.

"Lt. Col. J. Hodges."

Hodges too was an adviser to Carillo.

Hodges knew what was going on.

Hodges gave a green light to the massacre at Santa Teresa.

Mike dropped the note like it was suddenly a hot coal. He felt the skin on his fingers sizzle and let out a loud yelp. The world swayed in front of his eyes as he staggered to the hotel window and looked out at the glittery lights of Guatemala City stretching out like a starry night sky fallen to earth.

Hodges advised government death squads.

Hodges signed off on a massacre committed by Carillo and Natalia.

Hodges read intelligence reports scraped out of torture sessions in which prisoners were murdered.

Frantically, Mike tore through the rest of the papers. Each time he found Hodges signature it was like a knife wound pierced his flesh. Written on the bottom of interrogation reports and memos from Carillo, Hodges' tiny, impossibly neat handwriting screamed out from the past, loud enough to tear down the walls of Mike's world.

His heart pounded in his chest and a wave of nausea bubbled up in his stomach. He ran for the bathroom, making it just in time, as bile rose in his throat and he leaned over the toilet, throwing up with a strangled yell, his eyes streaming hot, burning tears of rage and shame.

———————

MIKE OPENED his eyes and glanced at the glowing red numbers on the clock beside his bed. It was 5:34 a.m. He supposed he must have slept for a few hours but it did not feel that way. He stared at the ceiling through a deep emotional exhaustion that was uncoupled from a physical ability to sleep. His mind kept going round in circles. What would he do with this information? What happened to the candidate he believed in like no other politician? Was that man a lie? Or had Hodges really changed since his days as a warrior who fought the Cold War in the most brutal possible ways.

He sat up and kneaded his temples with his knuckles, trying to bore his way into his skull and wrestle with his confused thoughts. But it was no use. He just felt physically sick; bleary-eyed and yet panicked. He looked at his phone. He knew he should call Dee. Perhaps she would take matters into her own hand and make some decisions for him. But how would she react now that he had information to destroy Hodges' campaign? And was that what he wanted?

Mike thought of all those long nights in Iowa and New Hampshire, the faces on the growing crowds of hopefuls, the people who believed in Hodges and what he stood for, who were looking for him to transform their lives. Nothing changed there. Hodges could still be the candidate they needed. But he could not reconcile that Hodges with the documents he saw. Hodges' face, which always seemed so calm and compassionate, now appeared cold and calculating. His blue eyes were those of a killer, not a hero.

Mike stood up and thought of the hotel pool down below. He would take a swim, he decided. He would lose himself in the cool waters and surrender to the rhythms of exercise. He dug out a pair of trunks and padded downstairs through the silence of the still-sleeping hotel.

The pool was empty when he arrived and he slipped in and let the water caress his whole body and engulf him into its depths. It felt good and a glow of relief lit in his mind. Somewhere deep within him, at that moment, he knew he would make the right decision. He knew he could do it, even though he still was not sure of what it was. He slid into the easy routine of length after length and kept his pace absolutely steady, never varied, turn after turn. It was a Zen-like motion and his mind cleared. It was like he became weightless in the water as the burden of his thoughts lifted. On and on he swam until he hauled himself out of the water and lay, panting and gasping on the edge of the pool. He heard a noise and looked up. A cleaner walked in. She was surprised to see someone swimming so early and she nodded a shy hello and then turned on the television above the cabana bar at the far end of the pool. The distant drone of an early morning news show filled the air as Mike toweled himself dry.

Suddenly he heard the cleaner give a loud, sharp shriek and drop her mop with a clatter. She stood with one hand clamped in front of her mouth and stared at the TV screen. Her shoulders shook as she began to sob. She crossed herself quietly and mumbled a prayer.

Mike walked nearer so he could see the TV pictures more clearly and understand the newscaster's breathless Spanish. He saw film of flashing police lights in a chaos of cars. He assumed it must be some awful car accident, perhaps near where this cleaner lived. He was about to offer her some words of consolation when suddenly the newscaster's words struck him and became as clear as a bell with a single name ringing out like some toll of doom.

"Father Gregorio Villatoro…" the voice said "… was found dead in his church office in the early hours of this morning. Police sources will not say how he died but friends say he was shot and killed by an assailant who broke into the San Gabriel mission. Villatoro was one of the most outspoken critics of the army during the civil war but in recent years was a beloved figure among Guatemala City's poorest residents for his charity efforts…"

Mike was transfixed. Villatoro was dead. The man he spoke to just a few hours earlier was no more, gunned down in the very building they met in. He looked at the cleaner. "Perhaps it was a robbery," he said.

The cleaner looked at him, her cheeks streaked with tears and her bottom lip quivered. "*Señor*," she said "Who would want to kill such a man? A robber would only have to ask and he would give him all that he had. Everyone knew this."

Suddenly it was as if Mike's whole world narrowed down into perfect clarity. Someone knew he was here and that he met Villatoro. They followed him to the church last night and broke in after he left and then murdered the priest. If that was true, then they also knew he stayed in this hotel. And, he realized almost in slow motion horror, they knew Lauren was here too. He looked above the pool, up seven stories to where their rooms were. The mirrored windows glinted opaquely in the first rays of the morning sun.

He started to run.

CHAPTER 22

HODGES APPEARED, AS he always did now, to a huge cheer along the rope line. Corralled at the front, that part of the crowd always first spotted the exact moment the candidate emerged from behind the stage and out into the auditorium. They screamed like teenagers welcoming the Beatles, even here among the usually sedate Myrtle Beach crowd. Hodges strode out and soon the rest of the giant convention center took their cue and the cavernous room filled to bursting with sound. A foot taller than most people anyway, Hodges seemed to grow to fill the space. He strode to the rope line and shook hands and grinned and laughed as people thrust themselves at him, palms outstretched like supplicants looking for a cure.

Dee watched from the side, like a prompter watching an actor go through his best lines. As she looked out over the 5,000 odd people crammed into the room, she itched for a cigarette but she did not want to miss any of Hodges' speeches these days.

Dee surveyed the audience and noticed that the average complexion at Hodges' rallies was a little darker in recent days. Their tactics in raising the race issue worked and under-cut Stanton's support among a lot of black voters. They had driven a wedge right through Stanton's base.

Hodges was on stage now and waved his palms up and down gently trying to calm the noise. He glanced to one side and caught Dee's eye as if to say: "What can I do?"

Let them applaud, Dee mouthed.

Hodges turned back and absorbed the cheers He sucked them in until finally the room fell quiet all by itself. Then he launched into his stump speech like a virtuoso conductor with an orchestra. He started slow, built up to the applause lines carefully, and then sprang them on his audience so they could not help but respond by rising up in their seats. As had happened in New Hampshire, many in the crowd were at their second or even third rally but they didn't care. They did not come to listen to the speech. Not really. They came to partici-pate in the experience. Like a revivalist meeting.

Dee looked at a young aide standing next to her. He was no older than twenty and decked with Hodges buttons on his smart jacket. Dee guessed this was his first campaign judging by the wide-eyed awe with which he watched the spectacle. Lucky bastard, she thought. It was not like this for her first time, she thought. Nothing had ever been like this. It took her thirty years to find it and this intern got it right off the bat. A home run at his first ball game. She felt a sudden, and rare, almost maternal urge for the young student.

"We're almost there, kid," she said. "Almost at the finish line and we'll have this nomination in the bag."

The boy did not tear his eyes away from Hodges. "You really think so?" he asked.

"Yup." Dee nodded. "We're on track to win this state. Once we've done that it is just a matter of letting Stanton draft her resignation speech."

Dee thought of her recent meeting with Carver. If only he could hear this crowd, she thought. She knew he was probably out there watching it somewhere on cable news. But what she really wanted was for Carver to *feel* this crowd in the flesh, to fully understand why he lost. He made the safe bet with Stanton; the sensible bet. But Dee went with her gut. She knew Hodges was special and she trusted her instinct, like a fisherman working a bayou he had known since boyhood. Not planning anything, not consulting a guide, just using a feeling for her home waters.

A huge roar snapped her out of her thoughts. Hodges finished his speech and walked back to the rope line to work the crush of supporters that surged forward. She knew it would take an hour. Hodges never left anyone disappointed. It was time to satisfy her nicotine craving, while she waited for him in his car.

She went outside, enjoyed the gentle warmth of the night air, and smoked cigarette after cigarette until she was surrounded by the nubs which lay on the ground around her like gun cartridges. Eventually Hodges joined her and together they got in the car to drive back to Columbia, a few hours away. Usually Hodges got a quick debrief from Dee and then grabbed a few hours precious sleep. But this time he was on a natural high, as if all the adulation he soaked up still bubbled around inside him, like a surfer riding a monster wave. Hodges talked animatedly about some of the people he met on the rope line. The young black guy who drove all the way from Spartanburg, a single mother of three from Charleston, a World War Two veteran who fought at Iwo Jima.

"You know, Dee, I've got about six hours sleep in the past three days, but I feel as fine as I've ever felt in my life," Hodges said. "It's like these folks give me their energy. I walk away from meeting them feeling like I'm on fire."

Hodges stared out of the window into the darkness of the freeway; just lights and signs hurtling by in the gloom.

"That's great," Dee replied. "One more push and South Carolina is ours. The numbers are strong enough. We just have to stay on track."

Dee thought for a moment. She had not planned on bringing up the next step until the result was in. She wanted no jinx on their heads. But her last encounter with Carver convinced her the moment was right.

"We need to have a chat about the national campaign," she said. "We're going to be taking on an incumbent president. Doesn't matter that he's a fuck up whom everyone hates, that's still no easy task."

Hodges turned to look at Dee, but remained silent at the implication of her words. Dee continued. "We need to think about what we do with Stanton and her staff. Whom to bring on board, whom to ditch, whether you want her on the ticket."

Hodges pursed his lips, nodded slowly, and then turned

back to look outside. A sign flashed by, pointing the way to Marion, a town a few miles off the Interstate. "I'm hungry, Dee," he said. "Let's grab a bite."

Dee tapped the driver on the shoulder and told him to get off the main road and head to Marion. Within a few miles they were crawling down the main drag, all but deserted except for a couple of dilapidated bars and a half-empty diner. They pulled up outside the restaurant and Dee and Hodges walked inside. There were half a dozen customers and Dee and Hodges settled themselves into a corner booth, its leather worn but spotlessly clean. A young waitress walked over with a cheerful grin and handed them menus. Dee thought she caught a look of recognition in the woman's face as she glanced at Hodges as he ordered a cheeseburger and fries. As she walked away, she looked over her shoulder, slightly puzzled.

"You know," Dee said and gestured around her. "You ain't going to be able to do this sort of thing anymore."

Hodges sipped his iced water. "I know," he said.

"The White House is going to be at stake soon," she said. "Nothing is going to be the same once we win here. Everything will change. Everything you have ever known."

Hodges nodded. "I knew that going in," he said. "Christine and I talked about what it would do to us. We knew the pressures but we figured it was worth it."

He paused a moment and held Dee with his gaze. "I mean what I say out there, Dee," he said. "That's why they respond the way they do. They know I'm different. That when I say I'll change this country and help them make their lives better, I mean it. They're not cheering for me out there. They're cheering for themselves. They're cheering because they've finally got a bit of hope that things will be better."

The waitress returned laden with two plates piled high with food. She turned to leave but then stopped herself and looked at Hodges. "Say, I hope you don't mind me asking, but aren't you running for President?"

Hodges smiled, stood up and shook her hand. "Yes, ma'am. Jack Hodges. I'd be honored to have your vote and help change this country."

The waitress squealed with delight and almost curtsied as she yelled back towards a knot of regular diners hunched over a corner of the counter. "Ya'll were right, John and Larry," she said. "It's Hodges!"

Three of the men stood up and walked over. They were followed by another waitress. Then a couple of Hispanic chefs from the kitchen. Soon a knot of a dozen people crowded around the table, talking with Hodges, shaking his hand and clapping him on the back. Dee settled back in her seat and stayed out of the action. She looked down at Hodges' burger, which was steadily going cold. He had managed to take just a single bite.

Poor son of a bitch, she thought. This win will send him to Heaven and he ain't even had a chance to finish his Last Supper.

MIKE DID not wait for the elevator to come down to the lobby. He burst through the emergency exit doors, triggering an alarm, and sprinted up the stairs. He leapt them three or four at a time and counted off the stories as he ran. He had no idea what waited for him, but he knew he must move as quickly as possible. At last, while his breath came in great ragged gasps, he reached the seventh floor and pushed open the door. He turned left, down the corridor and toward his and Lauren's rooms. He ran around a corner and stopped short.

A man stood outside Lauren's room. His back was to Mike. The man studied a bit of paper and then slowly folded it and put it in his back pocket, looking first at Mike's room and then at Lauren's, apparently weighing which to try first. Then he turned to Lauren's door and Mike saw his face for the first time. He recognized the pockmarked features immediately. It was Federico, the General's guard. Mike had a sudden flashback of sitting in the back of the man's car listening to him swear and rail against *los Indios* and praise all the hard things the General had to do during the war.

Mike was unsure of what to do. Federico was still unaware of him. He put his hand up to knock on Lauren's door and his other reached around to the back of his waist. His hand hovered over a bulge in his belt and Mike saw the dark outline of a revolver poke from underneath his shirt.

"Hey!" Mike called out, without thinking. Federico stopped with his fist just inches from rapping on Lauren's door. His mouth flinched with surprise as he turned to Mike, but his expression betrayed nothing of the calculations going on in his mind. Mike realized the insanity of his situation as Federico looked at him like a wolf regards its prey, just waiting for the moment to pounce. Mike suddenly knew what it was to be hunted by something that wanted to kill you; to coldly and mercilessly rip away your life. He knew, in that instant of fear that Federico could not be reasoned with. He could not be talked out of this act. Federico moved. He walked purposefully forward and the weight of his predatory eyes pinned Mike to the spot. Federico removed the gun from behind his back and let it hang in his hand against his thigh, holding it casually as he continued to walk. He was thirty yards away now. Then twenty. Then ten. And still Mike could not move. Luck saved him. A cleaning lady pushed a trolley piled high with fluffy white towels around the corner behind Mike and almost slammed into him.

"*Perdon, señor!*" she blurted and then looked at Federico, her eyes drawn as if by gravity to the weapon he carried. She let out a bloodcurdling scream. Federico stopped, suddenly unsure of what to do. At that moment, drawn by the sudden yell, a door burst open on Federico's left, and a fat, white man emerged, wearing a hotel dressing gown.

"Hey buddy, what's all the…" he said in a loud American accent.

The movement caught Federico by surprise but he spun around on instinct. He whipped his pistol across the man's face and struck him in the temple, sending a fine spray of blood into the air. The man went down like a collapsed building and from inside his room another scream rang out. Suddenly all was a blur of movement. The spell on Mike broke and he ran forward. A look of panic crossed Federico's face. He gazed at the fat American on the floor in front of him and leveled his gun at the man's head. Then he turned to see Mike charge towards him, yelling at the top of his voice. Any semblance of control that Federico had over the situation evaporated into thin air. With a strangled groan of frustration, he tucked the gun back into his belt and sprinted away down the corridor.

Mike ran after him, past the stricken American, and stopped at Lauren's door. He knocked on it furiously. "Lauren! Lauren! Get up!"

The door opened and Lauren's stunned and confused face greeted him.

"What the hell is all the noise?" she asked.

Mike burst past her into her room. He pulled her after him and kicked the door shut. She looked angry and yanked herself away from him.

"Mike!" she snapped.

He put a finger across her lips.

"Villatoro is dead," he said. "He was murdered last night and the guy who did it was just outside your door. We have to leave right now. It's not safe."

Laurent went pale and slumped down on the bed. "He's dead?" she whispered.

Mike nodded feverishly and tossed Lauren's empty suitcase on the bed and threw some clothes inside it. He felt himself losing his grip as panic flicked at the edges of his mind.

"Yes, he's fucking dead!" he said. "And we will be too if we don't get the hell out of here."

Lauren looked at him blankly. "But why?" she whispered.

Mike stopped and closed his eyes. He breathed in and out like a steam engine gathering strength. "Hodges and Carillo worked together during the civil war. They helped murder and torture opposition fighters, peasants, guerrillas, the whole lot. Natalia too. We've stumbled right into a war crimes cover up."

Now Lauren understood and fear and panic replaced her confusion.

"Oh my God," she said and she began to cry. Mike held her close and hugged her for a precious few seconds as he felt the world that he fought so hard for begin to collapse around them.

––––––––––

THE INCESSANT buzz of the phone on Dee's night-stand dragged her into consciousness. This would have been the first morning in weeks that she was able to sleep past 7:00 a.m. and she planned to do just that. But now she rolled over and saw Mike's number flash on her mobile.

"Oh *merde*," she said as she turned onto her back and stared at the ceiling. She knew she had to take it and flipped open the phone.

"This better be good, *ami*. You're taking away my beauty sleep."

Mike ignored her attempt at humor. "Dee," he said. "We're

fucked. We're beyond fucked."

Dee heard the panic in Mike's voice and bolted upright. "What did you just say?"

"It's over, Dee. Hodges helped Carillo run a death squad down here. Real bad stuff; torture, extra-judicial killings, massacring villages. The money Christine paid to him must be hush money."

For a minute Dee thought this was a joke, a sick prank that Mike was trying to pull.

"What are you talking about, Mike?" she said. "This is crazy."

"No, Dee. It's the truth. I've got the documents. Carillo is a psychopath. The woman who tried to kill Hodges is named Natalia Robles. She was a government assassin. Hodges worked with them both during the civil war. They ran a death squad, Dee. A fucking death squad. Now Carillo killed a priest here who knew about it. We've got to pull the plug on this campaign."

Dee took a moment to gather her thoughts. It was as if time ran slowly for her as she digested the information. "What's your evidence, Mike?" she asked.

"I knew the priest. He was killed right after he handed me the documents that proved all three of them were linked. I've got those documents with me. It's all Natalia's personal effects. She kept a record of her whole career."

Dee thought fast now. "Okay, Mike. Calm down. We've got to think about this. Stay where you are," she said.

"No," Mike snapped back. "I'm coming back to America.

I need you to meet my flight when it lands in Washington."

"Okay, Mike. Go over to my apartment there."

There was silence on the other end of the phone.

"No, Dee," Mike said. "A bar at the airport. It'll be public. In daylight."

Dee was amazed. "You're joking right?" she asked.

"No, Dee. No joke."

The phone line went dead and left Dee holding the receiver. She was stunned and sank back down onto her bed. She looked over where someone pushed a copy of the local newspaper underneath the door. She read the headline touting the latest polls that put Hodges comfortably ahead with just two days to go. She walked over, picked it up, and screamed loudly as she shredded it in her hands, tearing it up and flinging it into the air like confetti.

MIKE PUT a hand on Lauren's shoulder but she shrugged it off with great, jagged, angry sobs. A few other passengers near them on the plane looked at him with pity, and assumed they were witnessing a lovers' tiff.

If only. The drive to the airport was a panic-stricken one of fear and anger. They hurriedly packed and hailed a taxi from the street, not knowing if Federico would return or arrange some other attack. Mike stared at the back of the cab driver's head the whole way to the airport and looked for the slightest hint something was wrong. His hand gripped a thick, glass ashtray in his jacket pocket. At the first sign of betrayal by the driver he planned to ram it into the back of the man's skull.

But they made it onto the plane safely, buying tickets at the counter, with no further incident. And now, as the plane lifted up into the air, they reflected on exactly what happened. Lauren wept as the wheels left the tarmac.

"I can't believe he's dead," she said.

Mike knew she was out of her depth. "We have to go public with this," he said. "It's the only way to ensure his death means something. He died because he talked to us. Because he knew who Natalia was and that that trail led back to Carillo and Hodges."

"So what?" said Lauren. "None of this will bring him back. None of that alters the fact that if we had not poked around in this then he would still be alive."

"But Lauren, this is the biggest story of your life. You can break this story and if you do, you'll break Hodges' campaign."

Lauren looked at him horrified. "I don't care," she said. "Don't you get that, Mike. I. Don't. Care. People are getting killed for this. It's just too much. I don't want anything more to do with it."

She leaned forward and buried her head in her hands, as if the aircraft were about to crash and she was bracing herself. "I'm not brave enough. I want out," she said.

Mike could not push her to breaking point. He looked out the window as the plane climbed through thick towers of cloud surrounding Guatemala City that roiled up into the sky like fat, angry fingers. He was alone. Utterly alone and flying to a fate that he could not imagine. But somewhere, he knew, in the maelstrom of the last 24 hours he made a choice. You could not bury the past. You faced it.

He glanced down at the landscape below him, a patchwork of green fields and thick jungles that shrouded the mountainsides. It looked pristine, not a human stain upon it. He turned his eyes away and did not look out again until they were safely over the ocean, leaving the visual lie long behind.

CHAPTER 23

THE SHORT WALK through the brightly lit terminal towards the airport bar seemed like a marathon. Mike's feet felt heavy as concrete – like they dragged every single mile from Guatemala to Washington. He was alone too. The moment she was back on American soil, Lauren unleashed her pent-up emotions. She burst into loud sobs and fled from his side, hauling her luggage behind her, as soon as they cleared customs.

"I'm sorry," were her last words to Mike, mouthed over her shoulder.

Mike did not follow. He just watched her ragged figure disappear and then looked at the bar in the distance. His eyes immediately settled on Dee. She watched them both implacably with arms folded across her chest. Then Mike started to walk towards her.

Dee ordered him a double scotch. She pushed it across the table without words and Mike watched the brown liquid slosh from side to side and listened to the clink of the ice cubes. It was like time slowed down. He felt Dee's gaze weigh on him as he reached for the drink. He downed it in one gulp and winced as the fierce, cold spirit seared the back of his throat.

Dee finally spoke. "Now, calm down and talk to me, Mike," she said. "Whatever's happened is something we can get through together. Okay?"

Mike did not know where to begin. The last few days were an intense blur. The drive to Santa Teresa, the meeting with Maximón, the anger and terror of Rodolfo and the villagers and finally the revelations of Father Villatoro: Natalia's whole, damning life contained in a single box. He told her about the murders and tortures that Natalia committed. How she worked at Carillo's command in the dirtiest corners of the civil war. How Hodges was a liaison for Carillo and consulted on missions. How Hodges signed off on interrogations during which suspects were tortured and killed. How he agreed to orders that led to the massacre of Santa Teresa, carried out by Natalia. Finally, he told her of how Natalia – spurred on by motherhood – came to regret her life.

Dee listened intently without saying a word or moving a muscle. She never flinched at the descriptions of murders and killings even as Mike's voice rose and fell like an angry sea. Then, when it was over, and Mike's shoulders slumped, Dee leaned back in her chair.

She gestured at the barman who popped open a bottle of beer and placed it in front of her. She took a deep swig and wiped her mouth with a flourish.

Then she began to laugh, though there was a hysterical edge to the sound and her bravado could not disguise that fact that her hand shook. "Relax, Mike," she said. "If this gets out we can handle it. It will be okay. But first things first, where's Lauren? What's she planning to do with this?"

Mike was appalled. He stared at Dee, his mouth agape, like he no longer saw her in front of him, but some unknown devil who took her place. He struggled to speak.

"Dee... a man has been killed. Villatoro is dead. Hodges has been involved in war crimes," he said.

Dee frowned.

"Hodges is a great American, Mike," she said. "Now what about Lauren? You've handled that, right?"

Mike felt unexpectedly calm, like he emerged into the eye at the center of a hurricane. The howling winds left him battered and bruised, and they surrounded him, but his mind was quiet and still. He saw things clearly now; his thoughts blinked in the sudden sunshine in his mind. Dee did not care. She believed this was a contest to be won; a great game to be played. There were scores to be tallied and battles to be fought. But that was it.

It was not enough for him. "Dee," he said. "This is wrong."

Dee was puzzled. "What is?" she asked.

Mike shook his head. For so long the campaign dominated every waking moment that he began to feel it became his whole life, his reason for being. But no longer. He realized with a sudden start that he saw life anew; he was outside the campaign now, peering in.

The bubble had burst.

"I'm going to end this campaign," he said.

Dee understood his meaning. The air between them grew

thick and the space narrowed. She leaned forward, her voice low and menacing, like a hissing snake disturbed in the grass; a sound that should freeze the blood of anyone walking by.

"Think about this, Mike," she said. "Think about it long and hard. This is the most important decision you will ever make."

Mike shook his head. "I can't come back. Not knowing all this," he said.

Dee's eyes reduced to slits. She needed him. They both knew this. She made her pitch.

"Mike," she said. "Look around you. Not here, but out there. Think of the millions of people this campaign will help if we win this goddamn thing. We are here because we believe in our candidate. We are here because we believe in his message. We believe we can make a difference. Don't tell me you never believed, Mike."

Mike thought for a moment. Dee was right. He believed in Hodges like nothing before in his whole life. It was a drug that coursed through his veins. It was like finally having faith. Not in a God. But in a cause and a mission.

"What's changed, Mike? Nothing. Nothing has changed, Dee said.

But everything had. "I can't go back," he said. "We can't elect a man who did the things Hodges did. Who helped people like Carillo torture and kill people."

"He was a soldier, Mike. He took orders in a greater cause. He made tough decisions and sacrifices. Have you never done that, Mike? Have you not done things you never thought you would in the service of a greater good?'"

The accusation stung home. He thought about the lies he told Lauren. The lie he told Father Villatoro. At the betrayals of his duty to friends and family. To Jaynie. At the way he abandoned his principles to fight as part of a ruthless political machine, focused on victory. At the way he passed out secrets from Dee's "vault" to undermine and sabotage Stanton. He too became a loyal soldier in a dirty war.

"Be careful to cast the first stone," Dee said.

Mike shook his head. He would not go there. "That's bullshit, Dee. You know it. Hodges helped kill and torture people."

Dee threw up her arms in exasperation. "The war was twenty five years ago! Christ! You really want to throw everything away on something that happened so long ago in a country most Americans have never heard of?"

There was a hint of desperation in Dee's voice. Not exactly pleading. Mike knew Dee would rather die than beg for anything. But she needed him on her side. She needed him quiet. She needed this story killed.

"Mike," Dee said. "What do you want? You can make this work for you. Whatever you need."

Mike saw his future split in two. He saw a glorious path laid out ahead of him, rising up through the ranks under Dee's protective wing. He could end up in the White House with his own office in the West Wing. This campaign would sweep into Washington like a victorious army. They *would* change this country. Millions of people would be helped. But even as the vision passed through his mind he knew it was unreal. A mirage. You can't build such things on a foundation of lies. That was the problem. Mike would not bury the truth or the past. He owed that to himself. He owed it to Villatoro. And even Natalia too, silent in her cell.

"Dee," he said and he grasped her hand. "You have to help me. Together we can do the right thing."

Dee was stunned. Then she began to laugh. "Mike," she said. "I gotta admire your balls. You want *me* to help *you* destroy what we've built here?"

She slowly and methodically pried her hand out of his grip. "Do you really doubt my will to win this thing?" she said.

She let the question hang in the air and raised an eyebrow at him. "I'm *already* doing the right thing," she said. "The right thing is to see Hodges win. I'll do it at all costs."

Mike opened his mouth to speak. But Dee reached over and put a finger across his lips. "You've said enough, Mike. Take 24 hours. Think it over. Come back to me and I'll forget all about this. But if you decide to go public and try to take us down, you should know one thing." She looked at him, her eyes absolutely unwavering, her glare like an unbreakable promise.

"I will destroy you," she said, and with that she stood up and walked out.

———

MIKE DID not need 24 hours.

He stumbled out of the airport and took out his phone.

He punched in a number and barked a few shouted orders down the line. Then he waited for the call back. He crouched down on his haunches and shivered in the familiar cold. The sunshine and warmth of Guatemala was a memory. Here it was still winter. He looked up at the thick gray clouds, blocking out even the promise of sunshine. Then the phone rang.

Howard Carver took just five minutes to call him back.

"Mike Sweeney?" he asked.

"Listen, Howard," Mike said. "I haven't got time to explain on the phone. But I have information that I want to give you. If you use it, you can save Stanton's ass and maybe take Hodges down. You want it?"

There was the briefest silence on the other end of the line as Carver digested Mike's words. Perhaps he sensed a trap.

"Where are you?" Carver asked slowly.

"Washington."

"Rent a car. We'll pay for it. I'm on the road in South Carolina with Governor Stanton but I can break off. Let's meet in Columbia tonight. Shouldn't take you more than five or six hours."

"I'm on it," Mike said and was about to hang up but Carver stopped him.

"Mike," he said. "What do you want?"

Mike snorted in disgust.

"Nothing," he said. "Nothing at all."

THEY MET on a bench in the park at the front of the State House in Columbia. The long drive south boosted the temperatures and the sun came out. The cold, weary skies of Washington were replaced by a sparkling pristine blue, not warm, but hinting at spring.

Mike found Carver already waiting for him. The man did not get up but he spread his arms wide in greeting and gestured for Mike to sit next to him, all the while grinning like a shark. They sat beneath a flagpole on which fluttered a Confederate battle flag, a reminder of past sins.

Mike got out a sheaf of papers. They were photocopies of some of the documents that Villatoro gave him from Natalia's possessions. He handed them over and told Carver the whole story. He told him he suspected the payment to Carillo that Carver's team uncovered was hush money. That Carillo was a former war criminal and he and Hodges were involved in terrible human rights abuses. Prompted by her daughter's problems in the gangs, Natalia shot at him to atone for her own sins by inflicting the punishment that few other people even knew he deserved.

Carver could not disguise his glee as he leafed through the papers and listened to Mike talk. He fidgeted on the bench like a naughty schoolboy kept behind after class; desperate to leave as soon as possible.

"Hodges was involved in torture," Mike finally stated. "I can't stand by and let that be ignored."

Carver nodded his jowly face. He looked puzzled, as if trying to figure out what game Mike played. It unnerved him to get something so valuable for free. It broke the rules. It was unnatural.

"We knew something was up with that cash going down to Guatemala. We just couldn't figure out what," Carver said.

"That's why you slipped the money order under Lauren's door?"

Carver nodded.

"Her and about a dozen others. We hoped the press would do its job. But everyone bought Dee's spin about the college fees."

Carver shook his head, but Mike knew there was admiration, not anger there. Then Carver turned to squint at Mike and his watery eyes glistened slightly in the sun.

"If we can bring Hodges down with this, we'll have space for you," he said. 'Do you want a position?"

Mike suddenly felt tired. "No," he said. "I just want people to know the truth."

Carver shrugged. "You're very old fashioned," he said and got to his feet. He looked down at Mike and quickly stuffed the file into his brief case as if he feared Mike would make a sudden grab for it. He seemed awkward and then he stuck out a hand. Mike shook it. Carver's skin felt clammy and cold.

"Good luck, Mike," Carver said and he turned and walked away.

Mike watched him go. He stayed there for a long while and tried to feel the warmth of the struggling sun. He realized, almost as a surprise, that he had nowhere to go. He had no job. He had no purpose. It was all gone the moment he made the call to Carver. He got up. There was only one place to go. Back to Corinth Falls. Back home to wait out the coming storm.

————

THE DOOR to the conference room at Hodges' campaign headquarters burst open with a violence that saw it spring back against the wall and chip off a spray of plaster flakes. Inside, Hodges, Christine and a half dozen campaign workers jumped at the sound and the sight of a red-faced, furious Dee exploding into the room.

"Dee!" Hodges said, getting to his feet.

Dee ignored him. "Everyone get the fuck out!" she yelled and then jabbed a finger at Hodges and his wife.

"Except you and you!"

Everyone was stunned at the outburst. No one had any doubt that Hodges had not been spoken to like that for many years. No one moved. But Dee did not see her candidate anymore. She saw a red mist drawn like a veil across her vision.

"Could I make myself any fucking clearer?" Dee yelled.

Hodges looked at her and then turned to everyone else in the room. "It's okay," he said. "Give us some time."

Now the spell of immobility broke and, with a scrape of chairs being pushed back on the floor, people raced to get out, casting worried glances at each other. As soon as the door closed Hodges stood up to his full height. But Christine beat him and spoke first.

"You better have a good reason for talking to Jack like

that?" she said. "Or you're out of a job."

Dee rounded on her without hesitation. "Oh, shut the fuck up, Christine," she said. "I'll deal with you later, you goddamn bitch. But right now we've got to defuse a bomb that's about to destroy this whole campaign."

Hodges was lost for words. He and Christine exchanged glances and then he sat down again, folding up his lanky frame like a machine. He crossed his legs and looked at Dee. His expression gave away nothing.

"I know the truth about the payments to Carillo," Dee said.

Christine put her hands in the air with an exasperated sigh. "Dee! I told you already! He is an old friend. We're helping his family out with university fees."

Dee offered a fake laugh. "Christine. That is the last time either one of you lie to me. The *last* time. Do you understand?"

Christine fell silent. Hodges still did not move or say anything. Dee turned to face him. "Carillo may be your friend. But he has no family. You're paying him hush money because you two worked together during his country's civil war."

Hodges finally opened his mouth to speak but Dee shushed him. "No lies, Jack," she said.

He closed his mouth.

"Mike Sweeney found evidence that shows you signed off on some of Carillo's more dubious fun and games back in the 80s when he was a real sick puppy. Torture, death squads, village massacres. The usual Central American shit-storm."

Dee's voice was laced with venom but it was impossible to tell if it was disgust at the acts she described or the fact she felt

Hodges played her for a fool.

"The woman who tried to kill you…" she said, but then switched gears. "As I am sure you already know, she used to work for Carillo. She was a psychotic case, which he found useful when it came to shooting peasants. Mike found out all of this on a road trip I sent him on to identify that crazy bitch and your man Carillo seems to have taken a swipe at him."

"What do you mean?" Hodges asked.

"I mean your good buddy from the old days tried to kill one of your own staffers. And he *did* kill a priest who was helping Mike."

At last Hodges reacted. He groaned and his head sank to his chest. "Oh God," he muttered.

"Yeah, exactly," Dee said. "Not surprisingly Mike's kinda pissed about it. He's talking about going public with all this."

Hodges looked up. The blood drained from his face. His face was shockingly pale. The only color was in his eyes, like blue pools of shallow melt water on the surface of a glacier.

"It was war, Dee," he said. "We were fighting against the Soviets. I was serving my country to the best of my ability and I will not apologize for that."

For the first time Dee was quiet. Hodges walked over to Christine and stood behind her and rested his hands on her shoulders. She looked up at him and squeezed one of his hands in hers.

"I was a much younger man," Hodges said. "It was a different time and place. Do I have regrets that certain things happened? Of course. But someone needed to make tough decisions. I challenge anyone to put themselves in my place. I had a duty to protect my country and I did my duty to the best of my ability."

"So why pay money to Carillo?" Dee asked.

Hodges shook his head grimly. "He asked," he said. "I advised his unit during the war. I helped him and the government win. But I had not given him a thought for years. Then he rang out of the blue after he saw my picture in a newspaper. He said he needed help as he had fallen on bad times. But the implication was clear: pay up or he would start talking about our time during the war."

Hodges stopped talking for a moment. He cast a resigned look in Dee's direction.

"It seemed the easiest thing to do," he said. "To just go along with it and put it in Christine's name to give me a little distance."

He kneaded Christine's shoulders now and slowly the color came back into his cheeks. His face gradually hardened, his jaw setting along a firm line as he came to terms with what happened. "I'm sorry I did that, Dee," he said. He forced the words through clenched teeth. "But I will not apologize for being a loyal American soldier. I will never apologize for serving my country."

At the words a flash went off in Dee's brain like a firework. It reminded her of the moment she first saw the photograph of Hodges under fire from the shooter back in Iowa. Once again, she envisioned the future. She smiled grimly.

"That's it," she said and then again, louder: "That's it.

That's our line. You are a patriot. You took the hits for your country back then. Just like you'd take them now."

Hodges looked at her, slightly confused. "Is this going to sink us if Mike speaks out?" he said.

Dee thought about it long and hard. She looked at Hodges and then Christine and then back to Hodges.

"Not if I can help it," she said. "If the worst happens, we get out in front of it. Push back immediately. Get out all the facts and then control the message afterwards. You were a soldier in the line of fire. You did your duty for the stars and stripes. Repeat that until you are blue in the face. Anyone who disagrees is a goddamn coward who wasn't there."

"Ok," said Hodges. "But what about Mike?"

Dee shook her head. "That's my business. I'll deal with him."

CHAPTER 24

THE COUCH REEKED of staleness and age. The smell filled Mike's nostrils as he sat on it, dressed in shorts and a T-shirt, with his laptop open and the TV tuned to Fox News. His mother was at work which left him alone to await the impact of his actions. He knew he should feel some sense of righteousness that he had done the moral thing. But he felt only numb failure. He looked back at the months dedicated to the campaign as if they belonged to someone else; a close friend perhaps, but not him.

He understood now that he left the real campaign the moment he accepted Dee's offer of a job investigating Natalia and the shooting. As soon as he stopped working the streets and retreated inside the inner workings of the machine, he was lost. Ending up in this position was as inevitable as a rising sun. Sitting here in the home he grew up in, alone on this couch, destroying everything he worked so hard for, was always his final destination.

He wondered when it would happen. He handed over the

documents to Carver the night before and now it was mid-morning. He could imagine that Carver and his team poured over them all night, verifying and exploring, and then worked out the best strategy. The one with the maximum impact to seize the news agenda. After all it was just two days until South Carolina voted. They had little time to knock down Hodges.

But so far there was nothing on the cable news. He flicked through the channels again, stabbing at the remote control and whirring through CNN, MSNBC and Fox in a never-ending tableaux of talking heads. He guessed Carver wanted to get it out early enough in order to ensure the evening news shows could prepare for more in-depth reports. But it was also worthwhile waiting just to keep Hodges' team guessing. Carver undoubtedly, and wisely, aimed to put Dee under maximum pressure. Mike flicked through the stations yet again and then refreshed the Drudge Report on his laptop.

There it was.

"HODGES A WAR CRIMINAL – SHOCK CLAIM!"

The headline shouted the news in huge type complete with a flashing animated siren above it. Mike felt shocked even though this was the moment he waited for. Seeing it happen was still something else. He got up, his brow suddenly covered in a film of sweat, and went into the kitchen. His stomach was in knots and he leaned over the sink, wondering if he would throw up. He gripped the counter-top and then poured himself a glass of water.

By the time he returned to the living room the story had spread across the cable channels, at first citing Drudge and then slowly their own sources. It metastasized like a blossoming tumor. Within an hour the *New York Times* website spat out details no one else had. Then the *Washington Post*. The whole picture emerged. The payments to Carillo, his history of murder and massacre and the identity of Natalia as a brutal government assassin. Hodges' signature on the orders giving the go ahead to the attack on Santa Teresa quickly formed the center-piece of the story. Anchors and talking heads raced to pretend to be experts about a country and a war about which they knew next to nothing.

It took three hours for Dee to make her first TV appearance. Mike flinched at the sight of her. It was a live link-up from Hodges' campaign headquarters in Columbia to the Fox studio. Dee looked relaxed and calm and refused to respond to the details of the anchor's persistent questioning. She was on TV to deliver one message only and she kept finding ways to repeat it.

"Senator Hodges has always done his duty by his country. He is a patriotic American. He will be giving an interview tonight to answer any questions you may have fully and frankly," she said. She intoned the sentences over and over again like a mantra.

The message seemed to work and subdued some of the more hysterical fever around the story. Finally Mike could not take it anymore. He switched off the phone and rooted around in the kitchen. He knew his mother would have left a half-smoked pack of cigarettes in there somewhere. He quickly found a crumpled pack of Camels. He pulled out one. He had not smoked since he left for Florida, but now he welcomed the sudden need for nicotine like an old friend putting an arm around his shoulder.

He stepped outside and shivered against the cold but didn't bother to put on a coat. He inhaled deeply and looked out over the houses and streets that he had known all his life. He felt the smoke go into his lungs and he held it there for as long as he could, until it burned. Then he breathed out and his head became wreathed in blue gray mist. It obscured his vision for a moment, stinging his eyes, and gave him an excuse for the tears that streamed down his cheeks.

———

"SHUT UP and get away from me!" Dee snapped at the young TV runner who hovered next to her and carried a clipboard. The woman, probably no older than 25, skittered away like a fly avoiding a swat.

"Jesus!" Dee swore.

She was aware her hands were tightly clenched into fists and the rest of the people in the studio green room looked at her, including Hodges who sat in a chair having thick layers of make-up applied to his craggy face.

Dee shrugged an apology for her outburst. At least Hodges looked calm, she thought. She understood now just how ice cold his blood must be and why he was such a good soldier. He rarely revealed any hint of emotional turmoil throughout the day. He kept his head calm and clear and absorbed Dee's advice, taking it all in and then agreeing to her plan. One interview. Go with the national security line. Stick to it. Do not lose your head. No matter what the provocation.

They practiced for several hours earlier that evening. Dee fired question after question at Hodges and goaded him with insults veiled as questions.

"What do you say to those who compare your actions to My Lai in Vietnam?" she asked.

Hodges did not budge. Each time he calmly and quietly asserted his patriotism as an American soldier in the middle of the Cold War. "I never shirked from doing my military duty for my country," he said.

Dee was impressed. We can do this, she thought. We really can. But she knew that keeping calm in the face of her questions was a whole different beast from weathering the blasts from a trained news anchor on live television. It would also be an arena in which a single mistake could cost them everything. Even a stutter or a pause could destroy their whole campaign. They must get everything, absolutely everything, right. First time.

The runner reappeared nervously. "Three minutes to air," she said, avoiding Dee's gaze.

Hodges stood up, his spine as straight as a board. A US flag adorned his lapel, bigger than usual. Dee insisted on it and put it on like the medals that once were pinned there. It was a deliberate echo. She wanted him to look every inch the American hero.

Hodges strode out without a glance at her. He looked like he was going into battle. Or to face a firing squad. She was not sure which. Dee followed.

The walk to the studio was only a few yards and Christine waited there. Hodges leaned in and kissed her, putting a hand up to her cheek reassuringly. He then strode over to the interview chair.

The anchor, Katie Reynolds, was already seated, adorned in an explosion of expensively coiffed blond hair. Having Reynolds was part of the deal on granting the interview to this channel. She was good and well respected. But she was also young. Dee figured she was more likely than most to be a little susceptible to being star-struck.

Hodges sat down opposite her and nodded a hello. The countdown began. Sixty seconds to go… then fifty… then forty. Suddenly Hodges leaned forward and rested a hand lightly on Reynolds' forearm.

"Be gentle with me, Katie," he said.

It was a trick Dee told him to pull. But she was not sure he would do it. Yet he pulled it off seamlessly. Even from where Dee was standing she knew Reynolds was flustered. It might have been the physical contact, or Hodges' open flirtation, but she squirmed on her chair and glanced around nervously. Thirty… twenty… ten. Then the show began.

Reynolds gathered herself and moved right in. "Senator Hodges, these are very serious accusations that you face. People are saying that you were complicit in torture and massacres by Guatemalan death squads. Do you really believe that the American people should vote for you?"

The question was hard enough. But Reynolds tone was respectful. She smiled nervously, clearly a little intimidated with

Hodges in front of her. Hodges nodded seriously.

"Katie," he said. "I would never presume to tell the American people who they can or cannot vote for. Nor should you."

It was a good strike back. Dee felt a little visceral thrill in her gut. She loved the cut and thrust of it, even when everything they worked for was on the line. Hodges did not give Reynolds a moment to say anything but ploughed straight into his standard defense.

"When I put on the uniform of the United States army I made a decision to serve my country. That was at the height of the Cold War, Katie. It was a different world. The very existence of this country was at stake. Tough choices were made and sometimes I was the one who made them."

Reynolds opened her mouth to interject. She already felt she was losing control of this interview. But Hodges leaned into her and fixed her with his eyes. "I have never regretted a moment of wearing my country's uniform," he said.

Dee felt a wave of relief and exhilaration wash over her and she sighed. She knew now this was going to be okay. She knew it in her gut. The gut she trusted to guide her for the last thirty years. The same instincts that took her out of the godforsaken bayous of Louisiana and brought her here; at the right hand of the best political candidate she ever saw. She relaxed. Hodges was in full command of the show now. His line never wavered. Reynolds never succeeded in rattling him. He stood tall as the American soldier who kept his country safe. After all, Dee thought, would the average voter really care about the fates of a bunch of Guatemalan peasants twenty years ago? Not a chance.

Her phone buzzed in her pocket. She took it out as she walked out of earshot of the studio. It was Roger Armstrong, a conservative-leaning columnist at the *Washington Post*. Dee had known him for years and he owed her numerous favors, both professional and personal. She rang him that morning to prime him on Hodges expected line of defense and drop subtle hints that a column defending Hodges would be a great boon for the candidate. Armstrong's voice filled her ear and his rich Southern accent oozed out of the phone. Dee always bit her tongue when she spoke to him. He was born in Maryland and was about as Southern as a Maine lobster roll, but it suited his image and Dee was in no mind to nitpick.

"How's it going, Roger?" Dee asked. "What do you think?"

"I think your man has been deeply impugned," Armstrong said, lengthening the word *impugned* so that it rolled like treacle. But it was what Dee wanted to hear.

"You're damn right," she said, summoning genuine outrage. "What's happening here is a national disgrace. It's typical of the way we treat our soldiers these days."

"Too true, Dee. Too true," Armstrong said. "It's a sad reflection of our modern age. But I, for one, am determined to stand against the unpatriotic tide. I will not let a fine servant of our nation be raked over the coals by a bunch of liberals who would rather burn the flag than wave it."

"I'm glad to hear it," Dee said and fought down an urge to laugh at Armstrong's pompousness. It was not like he ever joined the military himself. Typical chicken hawk.

"So can we expect to see your thoughts expressed in print?" Dee asked.

"You can, Dee. Keep up the good fight."

Armstrong hung up and Dee smiled. There was a long road ahead of them and it would not be an easy one. But she at last could see a path. She walked back into the studio. The interview was over and Hodges and Christine stood together, their arms around each other's waists, and chatted amiably with the main producer.

Dee watched them for a moment. She was actually happy. She even enjoyed these moments of crisis. It was when she was at the peak of her game. She thought about Mike and could not believe he did this to her. That he sought to sabotage everything they worked for. For what? Some misguided idea of principle. Did he think principles were best served by destroying their best chance for the White House and letting that fool currently in the Oval Office get a second term? Well, she needed to deal with Mike now. She promised to destroy him and Dee never broke promises. Never.

———————

AS HODGES' interview ended, Mike felt physically sick. His face was pale and sweaty as if he had a fever. His mother, perched on the arm of the couch, put a comforting hand on his shoulder. He was desperate for a shot of alcohol. It was a physical ache, like a gigantic hole opened inside his chest and he needed to pour something in it to fill it up.

"Hon, it wasn't too bad. You've done the right thing. You stood up for what is right. That's all that matters," she said softly, her voice full of concern.

But Mike knew the interview went like a charm for Hodges. The talking heads were already on the television discussing the nature of patriotism and if the mainstream media was inherently anti-American. The details of the allegations against Hodges were lost in the miasma. They were too difficult to process, too obscure and too long ago. It was easier to frame the debate with domestic politics, not Guatemala's bloody past, and Hodges' interview played into that superbly. He cried out to the public to defend those who defended it and few pundits dared not follow that cry. He saw Dee's cunning behind it all.

"Their strategy is going to work," Mike said. "They're going to get away with this."

His mother shook her head. "The South Carolina election is nearly here, Michael. He'll lose it. People will never vote for a man who did those things," she said.

For a moment Mike wanted to scream that he knew better. That he worked inside this campaign and that no one ever lost an election on principles like that. He always despised the cynics before but now he knew he was one. Dee's strategy was pitch-perfect. It appealed to the voters and the media alike. Suddenly, he needed to get away from the house. His mother would never understand. She led her life keeping strong to her belief in her community. But she was able to do that because she never left this god-awful dying town. She never tried to influence things beyond her home and her friends and people she knew. He tried to change the whole system. Now he realized just what sort of madness that was. He got up and flung on a jacket.

The cold air outside slapped him in the face like a spurned lover. His cheeks stung with the force of it. But he drew his jacket close around him and trudged down the streets heading for O'Rourke's. Unlike the last time he had been there, with Sean and Jaynie, the grimy bar was virtually empty. So much had happened since that night of laughter and drunkenness that it felt like a lifetime ago. He sat in the darkness and ordered a bottle of beer and a chaser of bourbon. The only other customer was a scarecrow-like old man at the other end of the bar who stared myopically into space. His face drooped like a melted candle and the folds of his sunken cheeks hung like drapes around the windows of his eyes. A TV murmured dully in the corner and carried a debate show about Hodges' recent interview. Mike looked in vain for the barman to get him to switch it off. The old man saw Mike look at the TV and called over.

"That boy Hodges really served our country," he said with

a determined glare. "It's disgusting what they are doing to him. He was just doing his duty."

Mike tried to smile but he could not. A feeling of dark horror crept up his throat and froze the expression on his face as a grimace and turned it into a mask for his despair.

CHAPTER 25

MIKE STRUGGLED INTO consciousness from a dream in which he was tossed at sea, caught up in gigantic waves that swamped him and left him gasping for air and clawing to escape from the suffocating waters. But he opened his eyes and realized it was his mother shaking him awake with a look of concern on her face.

He only dimly remembered a scattering of details from the last few hours at the bar. He knew he sank beer after beer in the gloom. Then he argued with some faceless group of men at the bar. He did not recall whether it was over politics. It could even have been about sports. Then he was shown the door by the burly barman and stumbled out into the streets. He weaved home and paused over the railway tracks. For a moment he thought about going to Jaynie's trailer and taking the old shortcut over the rails. But then he remembered she was not there. She was in jail. Then he half-walked, half-stumbled home and collapsed into bed. He felt the remnants of the night's alcohol course through his system like poison.

He blinked his eyes and sat up and registered the look of dismay on his mother's face.

"It's okay," he said. "I just needed to let off a little steam."

But his mother's look of worry remained. Still, she offered him a steaming cup of coffee. The bitter smell filled his nostrils and he fought down an urge to gag.

"Mom…?" he said.

He noticed that in her other hand she held a copy of the *New York Post.*

"There is no easy way to show you this," she said.

He took the folded paper and spread it out in front of him. Splashed on the front page was a grainy picture. It was a police mug-shot of a man, staring into the camera with a look of blank shock. It took him several seconds to recognize the photograph.

It was him.

He was on the front page of the Post. He sat up and read the headline.

"HODGES LEAK MAN IN DRUG BUST" it blared in massive type.

Mike was not sure his heart beat anymore as he read the story. He just felt his blood freeze in his veins and his vision tunnel down to a small hole, focused on the printed words, like he read the story from the end of a long telescope.

The man who leaked details of Senator Jack Hodges' military record in Guatemala was a disgruntled former staffer recently arrested on drug charges, sources told the Post.

Mike Sweeney, 29, was picked up in a trailer park with his ex-wife, Jaynie Collins, by police acting on a tip over a suspected drug lab.

Police discovered drug-making equipment and over two pounds of meth amphetamine, a drug which causes havoc all over rural America and whose effect is likened to a heroin epidemic.

Sweeney, who worked for Hodges until recently, was kicked off the campaign once details of the drug charges were discovered, senior Hodges campaign sources claimed.

"He was always a problem. But the drugs bust was the last straw. We had to let him go. We hope Mike is able to get the help he needs," said one top Hodges aide.

Dee had done it. She promised to destroy him and now she had. She got the arrest report from the night with Jaynie and spun it to wipe him off the face of the earth. He was finished. It was finished. The world thought he was a drug dealer. No one would touch the Hodges' Guatemala story now. She had poisoned the source.

———

IT WAS a long and tense election day in South Carolina. Dee spent the morning driving around a few of the voting stations in Columbia by herself. She wanted to escape the hothouse atmosphere of the campaign headquarters for a while. It was hard to breathe in there. The last few days rocked everyone and everything. The campaign was a high flying jetliner suddenly hit by a downdraft and sent plummeting towards earth until the pilots frantically put it back on track. The experience jangled everyone's nerves. It bloodied them all, especially the first-timers and the newcomers.

So Dee drove slowly around the suburbs and just soaked up the feeling. It did her good. The brutal truth was ordinary life carried on around them, she thought. Despite all the heat and fury of the campaign, most folks still went about their daily routines. What the neighbors did behind closed doors still meant more to the average voter than what Jack Hodges did twenty years ago. She watched harried moms, lone construction workers and a few students troop into the polling booth and then troop out again. They voted. They passed the ultimate judgment on Dee's greatest lifework. And they did it while worried about a college football game or what they would cook their kids tonight for dinner.

The thought did not upset Dee. It calmed her. She remembered her own childhood and how far she came. She smiled, breathed in, and seemed to catch a waft of bayou air amid the South Carolina sunshine. Then, equilibrium restored, she got in her car and drove back downtown. Hodges stood up when she entered the campaign headquarters main meeting room. He looked tense and glanced at the sheaf of papers she clutched in her hand that an intern had foisted on her as soon as she walked in.

"How are we doing?" Hodges asked. His voice was a little hoarse as if he shouted all morning.

Dee put up a hand and scanned through the papers. Her

eyes flicked down row upon row of polling numbers and cross-referenced back and forth. She tried to pull out some headline details and look into the poll's entrails to divine the future.

She looked up. "I'm not going to lie you and say we haven't been hit by this Guatemala shit storm," she said. "We have. We got hit good and hard. But looking at this stuff I would say we're still on top. We can win here and when we do Stanton is going to be out."

Hodges lips creased into a thin smile. "How old is this data?"

"Before your TV interview. So, if anything, it shows us weaker than we are."

Dee walked over to him. There was an air of unease about him that she never sensed before. Maybe, finally, after everything that happened over the last few months, the pressure was finally starting to chip away at him.

"It's okay, Jack," she said. "There's nothing certain in this life. We have to hope the voters come through. Maybe they won't. But this poll shows us in the lead. We've just got to wait."

Hodges sat back down but she felt his nerves twitch inside him. "Goddamn that fucker Sweeney," he said. "How the hell did we let someone involved with drugs get that close to us, Dee?"

Dee shrugged. "I was as shocked as anyone," she said. "He comes from a troubled family, I guess. We shouldn't blame him entirely for his problems. He's not had it easy."

Hodges shrugged. "Loyalty, Dee. I put a high value on that. It's what we're taught in the army. If he had a problem with my record he should come to me privately. Not try and bring us down."

Dee almost replied but thought better of it. She thought of what Mike told her about Carillo's man stalking him and Lauren outside their hotel room. The dead priest in a slum church. She saw Mike's point of view. She did not blame him for the choice he made. Nor did she blame herself for destroying him. Hodges was wrong. Blind loyalty was not the ultimate virtue. Winning was. That was where Mike made a mistake. That was what she could not understand. He picked a losing strategy.

——————

THEY WATCHED the countdown to the polls closing on CNN in Hodges' hotel suite. It was just Hodges, Christine, Dee and a few other key staffers. A rally was planned in front of the Capitol just a few blocks away and they knew thousands of people were gathered there. Every so often the CNN camera switched to their reporter on the scene and they could see the throngs behind him and hear their cheers drown out the poor guy's voice. But inside the room it was like an examination hall. There was complete silence and all eyes were glued to the screen. There was just five minutes until the polls closed. If they were lucky, the pundits would immediately call the race using exit poll data. If things were narrower, they would hold off.

Dee walked to the balcony door. She slid it open and lit up a cigarette. Christ, Dee thought, it feels like waiting to have teeth pulled. She longed for the sound and pain of actual drilling.

Three minutes to go now.

Then two.

Then one.

Then… nothing.

"Too close to call," the graphic on the screen flashed, underneath smiling pictures of Hodges and Stanton opposite each other. Christine groaned and stood up, her hands clasped together. Hodges followed her and cast a glance at Dee.

"Relax," Dee said. "I told you we'd get hit a little. I never thought we'd be ahead enough to declare victory straight away."

She sounded confident. She felt confident. But still. A worm of doubt wriggled around deep her in her mind. What if… what if… it whispered.

A few minutes later the first results trickled in. A handful of counties in the Low Country reported their numbers. They were about six percent of the total and they put Hodges at 45 percent and Stanton at 46 percent. Again Hodges shot Dee a glance. Christine could not look at the screen. Dee shook her head and went back to the balcony again. She lit up and inhaled deeply on another cigarette even though she did not want one. She stared out into the night and strained her ears for the crowd she knew was just a thousand yards away. But, try as she might, she could not hear them.

Then she heard Christine yell. Dee jumped back in and saw Christine pointing at the TV screen and holding one hand over her mouth. Dee followed her gaze. Another clutch of votes was in, from all over the state: a few college towns, Charleston itself and a swathe of the mountain counties. Just over a quarter of the vote was counted. She looked at the score. Stanton was at 43 percent. Hodges was at 48.

Christine laughed and smiled a toothy, delighted grin. She danced a little jig and squealed in delight. Hodges clapped and suddenly Dee found herself swept up in his firm embrace and lifted off her feet. She wanted to resist, she wanted to urge caution. This was not over, she wanted to say. We must wait. But she could not resist him. She surrendered to the moment and five minutes later, as champagne corks popped on a dozen bottles and flowed into white plastic glasses, she heard an electronic boom come from the TV and watched the magic words explode across the screen.

"Hodges wins South Carolina."

And Dee laughed. She laughed so hard she thought her lungs might burst in her chest from the sheer, soaring, unadulterated joy of it. They weathered the storm. They took the hits and they won.

———

MIKE WATCHED the results in a dulled haze in his mother's living room. She sat by him and squeezed his hand as Hodges' victory was announced. It's okay, Michael," she said. "It's just South Carolina. Stanton is still in the fight, you know. We're just three states in. This could be a long race."

Mike knew they were just words meant to cheer him and bandage his wounds. He imagined the scenes inside Governor

Stanton's headquarters. The final, desperate hope of the last few days, as the Guatemalan scandal broke, was no doubt shattered. They knew the score. They were the frontrunner for so long but now they had only one narrow victory to their name, back in far-off Iowa, which felt like it happened in the last century. The momentum was with Hodges and it was unstoppable. Across the country the vital donors that fed money to the campaign machines would shut off the supply of cash to Stanton and open their wallets for Hodges. The two campaigns were mirror opposites: one collapsing, the other in the throes of celebrating victory. Every open door for Hodges would be a closed one to Stanton.

It was over.

Mike watched Stanton appear on the TV screen. In stark contrast to the crowds cheering at an outdoor rally for Hodges, her supporters gathered in a hotel ballroom. They waved campaign placards but nothing disguised the flat atmosphere. As Stanton drew herself up to the microphone, her face was lined and tired. Her smile looked as if the corners of her lips were tacked up with pins. She waved at them to stop and then thanked them all for coming.

"Obviously, we've all got a lot of thinking to do over the next few days as to where we go from here," she said. Her voice was drowned out by a series of boos and cries of: "Stay in! Stay in!"

She smiled her fixed grin. "We will do what's right for America. Thank you all for your work and support. God bless us all."

It was not a concession. Not yet. But it paved the way for one. Mike guessed Stanton's team figured they gained nothing from dropping out immediately. It made more sense to see what sort of negotiations they could pull off with Hodges' campaign. With Dee. Even now Mike laughed to himself when he thought of how Dee would revel in all this. She would be in her element. He did not envy anyone on Stanton's staff charged with striking a deal that did not basically amount to abject surrender.

He switched off the TV and went upstairs. It was done. What the hell would he do now? What was it all for? Perhaps he was cursed, he thought. He should never have left Corinth Falls in the first place. He should never have gone to Florida. He should never have gone to Iowa. It was not his place to try and shape the wider world. He should have stayed here and looked after those he loved; attended to their problems, not those of people he never really knew.

He thought of Jaynie in her prison cell and wondered what she was doing. Again he thought of how she tried to touch him in the back of the police car and how he shrank away from her hand. He felt a surge of guilt as crippling as the moment as when he told her he was leaving town; leaving her and their marriage behind; abandoning her to the twisted maelstrom of the drugs that controlled her. No one escapes their past, he thought. Not me. Not Jaynie. Not Father Villatoro in his freshly-dug grave. Not even that sick bastard Carillo, who was still stuck in exile, once again murdering people to try and win favor.

Out of the corner of his eye Mike saw his luggage. It was still unpacked in the corner of the room where it had lain since he came back to his mother's house. He went over and opened the case on his bed. There it was. The simple, battered box that contained all the records of Natalia's sad, murderous life. It was just a pile of random photos and papers now: the remnants that he did not give to Carver.

No, he thought, no one ever gets away from their past. Definitely not Natalia whose struggle was defeated by her daughter's descent into the gangs. Only Hodges seemed able to ignore his history. He emerged from it unscathed as if encased in a suit of armor. Nothing penetrated it.

Mike picked up some of the pieces of paper and let them fall to the bed through his hands. A photograph flew out of one notebook like an escaped butterfly. It fluttered in front of him, landing face up. Out of it three people stared, captured together on some distant parade ground. It was Natalia, Hodges and Carillo. They all stood together and grinned into a bright sun that shone from over the shoulder of whoever held the camera. It looked like a snapshot from a vacation.

Mike flipped it over. A pencil message was scrawled on the back.

"Camp Victoria, Julio, 1988" it read. Mike guessed it was taken at some sort of training camp all three attended, most likely with Hodges as a liaison to Carillo's group; briefing them, advising them, signing off on their plans for murder and mayhem in the name of freedom. He flipped it over again trying to read some sort of emotion into the distant faded faces that stared back at him. But there was nothing; just the emptiness of the past, a record of a fleeting moment.

Then he saw it.

It was a tiny detail, but now it caught his eye and made his heart skip a beat. Hodges arm looped around Natalia's waist. There was no denying it. His fingers were clearly visible, resting lightly on her hip. In a moment it changed the picture. Now he noticed how Natalia leaned into Hodges and her back rested against his side. Carillo was suddenly the odd man out.

Mike knew. He knew with every fiber of his soul that Hodges and Natalia were not just comrades-in-arms back then. They were also lovers. He fired up his laptop and Googled for Christine's campaign biography. He scanned through it. In July 1988 Christine was away from Guatemala. Her father was ill, diagnosed with terminal cancer, and she went back to help nurse him. She was away for an entire year. Hodges and Natalia had free reign for an affair. Perhaps that was why they got careless and let this photograph be taken.

Then another thought struck Mike. He could barely breathe now as he ransacked his way through the scattered papers. Finally he found it. Natalia's daughter's birth certificate. Gabriela Maria Robles. Father unknown. But that blank did not concern Mike. It was the date that mattered. March 21, 1989. More or less nine months after the photograph taken at Camp Victoria.

"Holy shit," Mike breathed.

He thought of the girl they saw in the church with her paler skin and dirty blond hair. Gabriela, Natalia's daughter who became a prostitute in the slums, was Hodges' child.

Suddenly it all fit together. That was why Natalia snapped. That was why she targeted Hodges. Gabriela's problems finally broke her and she took out that grief on the man who abandoned them both. It was not just revenge for a deadly past she regretted. It was personal: the action of a distraught mother struggling to find a place for her emotions and her pain.

Jesus Christ.

He picked up the phone and punched in a number.

Carver answered.

"Don't let her concede!" Mike blurted before he even said hello.

"Mike?" Carver said in surprise. "Is that you? What are you talking about?"

"I've found something else. I just need time to prove it. If I am right, Hodges is over. For real this time."

There was a silence on the end of the line before Carver spoke. "Governor Stanton's concession speech is already written. If we fuck Hodges' team around it will threaten her chances of being his running mate. She wants to be vice president. We can't endanger that on a wild goose chase."

"Twenty four hours," Mike said. "Wait that long. You lose nothing. Just trust me."

Mike knew trust was not a word Carver put much faith in. "You can still *win* this fucking thing," Mike said.

That was better. The dying coals of Carver's ambition glowed warmly at Mike's words; breathed back into life by the promise of victory.

"You've got 24 hours," Carver said. "I can hold things off that long. But no more."

Mike smiled for what felt like the first time in weeks. There was only one way to prove it. He started to pack.

CHAPTER 26

HE FACED HER across the bare prison table. She faced him. Natalia Robles. It felt completely different to know her name. To know her past. To know what she did. To put a history behind those dark eyes.

Mike was afraid she would not see him. Or that he would not even get the chance to ask for a visit. But the guards remembered him from his previous trips and put a phone call through to the head warden. The rough voice down the line snorted at the name of Hodges.

"He really do all that shit down in Central America?" the warden asked.

"Yes, he did, sir," Mike replied.

Another snort. "You work for him?"

Mike almost said yes. But the time for lies was over.

"Not anymore," he said.

"Good," came the response. "That son of a bitch is a disgrace after what he's done."

At last someone cared. Just when he needed it. Perhaps

Maximón looked out for him after all. So Mike was led down a familiar route deep into the bowels of the prison.

Now she sat silent, perhaps thinking of their last meeting when her hands tightened around his throat. The guards kept her handcuffed this time. But not a flicker of emotion crossed her face.

Mike's heart pounded. He had one shot, one chance to make sure that he had not sacrificed everything for nothing. That Natalia had not either. That the moment she squeezed that trigger in Iowa she did not really miss.

"Father Villatoro is dead," Mike said.

Her mouth opened slightly and her bottom lip quivered.

"He was killed by one of Carillo's men. But before Villatoro died he gave me a box of your things."

Mike reached into a bag and pulled out some of the old photographs and notebooks from the box. They looked a thin remembrance of a life, scattered across the table. Natalia cast them a glance and then her head sank down and rested on one arm. She began to weep, soft sounds etched with pain that came from deep within her like rumblings within the earth; the distant surface signs of gigantic plates shifting.

Mike shook. He wanted to reach out and put a hand on her shoulder. But he did not. He hewed to his chosen course.

"You knew Hodges," he said. "He was above you in your chain of command."

Natalia slowly raised her head. "America does not care what he helped do to my country," she said. "It does not care what I did to my country."

"Is that why you tried to kill him?"

Natalia paused a moment. "I missed my shot," she said at last. "Now I will be in jail forever. I am happy about that. It is not even half the punishment I deserve. I have no regrets at being behind these bars. But he will escape his punishment."

Mike leaned forward. "It is not over," he said.

She jerked her head up and fixed him with eyes he now saw were wet with tears. Mike pushed the papers forward. "Your daughter," he said. "There is no name for her father on her birth certificate."

Natalia flinched as if bit by a snake. "No!" she cried. "My life was a curse on my daughter since the day she was born. She is nothing to do with this. She is the reason I am silent. She will be freed from her mother at last. She never deserved to be born to me."

Her face collapsed into despair. Her eyes welled with fat tears that streaked down her cheeks. Mike was astonished to see such emotions in her, to glimpse the depths that raged beneath.

"Who is her father?" he asked quietly but firmly.

She shook her head. "I never told. Not her. Not anyone."

Mike pushed forward the birth certificate and then a book of papers from her time at Camp Victoria.

"She was born nine months after you went to this training camp. Hodges was there too. His wife was back in the United States."

She did not look down at the papers. She just sat wordlessly opposite Mike. Her chest rose and fell with deep, panicked breaths as she sought desperately to keep self-control. It felt like sitting opposite a gigantic glacier that was slowly beginning to crumble into deep ocean waters, shedding a creaking facade of ice.

Mike knew there was no turning back.

He pushed forward the photograph of Natalia, Carillo and Hodges together and all the while he held her gaze. She returned his stare for what seemed an eternity. But Mike did not flinch, instead he mentally willed her to look down.

She did.

"He was your lover," Mike said. "Your child is his child."

Natalia reached out to the photograph and ran a finger along its edge as if she was touching a body.

"If you say this publicly, it will destroy him," Mike said. "You don't need a gun. Not anymore."

He took her hand and curled his fingers around her palm to feel her muscles tense and as hard as iron.

"Make a statement to me. Then I'll tell the world. You will get your wish."

"And Gabriela?"

"I will make sure she is fine. Once the world knows the truth, no one will harm her. I'll see to it personally. You have my word."

It was a rash promise. But he felt a rush of will inside him, a sense of certainty and purpose that he had not felt for many, long months. Perhaps not since the first time he saw Hodges speak and decided to join his campaign.

For the last time they stared at each other across the prison table. Then Mike felt her hand relax in his grasp, like a sudden melting of ice. Stone became flesh. Her eyes softened. They understood each other.

THE VIDEO was short. Mike held the tiny camera in front of him and Natalia spoke directly into its tiny, unflinching electronic eye. She gazed into the machine and via its lens outside into the whole world.

"Senator Jack Hodges was my lover," she said. "We had a child, my daughter, Gabriela. He has never seen her. He pretended she never existed. He forgot her just as he forgot our country. He forgot me just as he forgot what he did there. Gabriela is a good girl. I love her and tried to care for her. But the gangs took her. She is now a prostitute in Guatemala City. She has trouble with drugs. But she is his flesh and blood, just as much as she is mine. That is her curse. But it has never been her fault."

She pronounced the words slowly. When it was over her head sank back down to the table and suddenly Mike saw her afresh. She was a petite middle-aged woman, utterly exhausted now. Utterly alone. She did not seem a killer or a threat. Or a mystery. He noticed that a streak of gray shaded her jet black hair and deep crow's feet gouged the edges of her eyes. Her hands that held a gun so expertly, and tried to squeeze the life out of him, were tiny, the fingers delicate and the nails bitten down to the quick. He touched her arm. It felt frail now in his grip. She lifted her head.

"Michael," she said. It was the first and only time she would ever use his name.

"Save my daughter."

He squeezed her hand, trying to pass some warmth through their skin together.

"I will," he said.

Then he stood up and walked out. He never looked back. Never turned his head until he was outside once more and freed from the boundaries of the prison, the weight of the camera in his pocket as heavy as the past.

He had one phone call to make. He dialed the number and waited for Lauren's voice. She sounded hesitant and afraid, but Mike was calm, soothing, his voice simple and in control.

"I have something for you," he said. "I'm going to attach it on a file as an email. You'll understand when you get it."

He waited for her to say something. But just the sound of short, sharp panicky breaths came down the other end of the line.

"You'll know what to do with it," Mike said and then added: "This time it is the right thing to do." Then he hung up.

It was done.

———

MIKE UPLOADED the video onto his laptop and emailed it to Lauren who posted it on the *Horse Race* twenty minutes later. The footage spread over the web like a virus. Within three hours it was on the cable news shows and the front page of the *New York Times*.

Mike sat in a dingy motel room and watched it all unfold. He took no pleasure in the squawking commentators and talking heads who shouted at each other over the faux protestations of the news anchors. He gained nothing from the now endlessly updated blog posts and news stories. Eventually, and with no ceremony, he switched off the TV and closed his laptop. A sense of peace invaded the room and he lay back on the bed. He stared at the ceiling with his hands folded behind his head. His phone was by his side. He waited for the call. He knew it was coming. But to his surprise she did not sound angry.

"*Feet pue tan*, Mike. You did it," Dee said.

She actually sounded impressed. A little stunned, but calm. "You've killed the campaign. You've brought down the candidate. You know that, right?"

"I know, Dee. I'm sorry. But you told me once this was the only way that I could end it."

"What?" Dee said.

"A sex scandal, Dee," Mike said. "You said it was always sex scandals that brought down people. You can kill the innocent for your country. You can torture someone and call it your patriotic duty. But when you father a daughter out of wedlock, that's when we've had enough."

Dee gave a sharp laugh. Then another longer one. There was genuine mirth there.

"Jesus, Mike. I taught you too well."

"Where are you, Dee?"

"I'm in my car, driving over to Stanton's headquarters. Things exploded with Hodges. It's all over. Christine has gone bat shit crazy. She's the reason they can't have kids and she sure didn't take kindly to her husband fathering one elsewhere. I thought she was going to kill Jack for a moment. Maybe chop his balls off. She's talking divorce now and Hodges completely lost it. He knows this kills us. We can't run a presidential campaign with an illegitimate daughter in the wings. Jesus, even the rumor of one killed McCain in 2000."

"Hodges didn't even try and deny it?"

"No. He'll give a speech in a few hours bowing out of the race. Congratulations, Mike. You've triggered our campaign apocalypse. Hodges is going down in history as the biggest campaign flame out in American politics."

"Are you all right, Dee?" Mike was amazed to find he genuinely cared. Even though she used the dirtiest tricks to destroy his reputation he was not angry at her. He only felt concern. There was no sense of revenge or satisfaction.

"I'll be fine," she said, the twang in her accent suddenly loud and strong. "That son-of-a-bitch Carver is playing coy about giving me a place in Stanton's campaign. But I expected as much. I'm going to have to persuade him to make space for me, but he knows I won't beg."

Her voice faded a little but then perked up. "I'll be fine," she insisted. "Something will come up once time has healed a few of the wounds I gave them."

Mike was glad. She was, after everything they did to each

other, still his friend. He cared for her. "I'm pleased you're going to be okay, Dee," he said.

Dee laughed again. She seemed surprised at the idea that he would doubt it. "Mike," she said. "Folks like me and Carver are always going to be okay. We're not like Hodges. Or Stanton. We're not the players in this sport. We run it. It's *our* game."

EPILOGUE

A YEAR LATER

THE MESSAGE LIGHT flickered on the phone in the gloom of the back office room. It glowed dull orange, off and on, off and on, like a little lighthouse. Mike felt tired as he flopped down in the chair with his face covered in the grime of Guatemala City, the product of an uncountable number of cooking fires that left a brown smoke hovering over the city like a frown. His brow was covered with sweat and he wiped it off with a sleeve.

He sighed exhaustedly. It was a happy sound though. Tired was good on days like this. Days spent out in the community around San Gabriel. Days of labor and toil, of battering away at corruption and vice and all that plagued the slums. But days that seemed to matter even if the few victories were small. He spent the morning at a local clinic run by nuns that fed and treated the orphans and the homeless. He used the opportunity as a kind of outreach to gang members. There was a vicious turf war going on and he needed to know the details so he could try and calm down things. He did not have much influence. But after nine months here in Guatemala, he had some. He did what he could.

He pressed play.

He recognized the familiar lilting accent immediately.

"Miiike," the voice crooned. "You are a hard man to find these days. I guess I should have known you would be down there. But somehow it never occurred to me until now."

Mike froze like a statue and his finger hovered over the button. He did not move a muscle. Suddenly he felt a cold chill on his skin, the frost of a thousand miles driven on frozen Iowa roads or among New Hampshire's snowy forests. He thought, just for a second, that he heard the roar of a crowd; the magical moment when a candidate made that elusive connection; when, for a fleeting time, a room filled with such electricity that you believed it might set the whole world on fire.

"You're wasted down there," Dee's message went on. "I'd like you to come back and help me out with something. Somehow working out of President Stanton's office ain't all it's cooked up to be. Turns out I hate being behind a desk even if it *is* in the West Wing. Who would have believed it? I actually just love the fight, not the reward."

He laughed at the image of Dee in an office. She would be like a caged tiger, pacing up and down in a zoo, longing for freedom, not wanting to be safe and well-fed. She could not fight her instinctual desire to hunt and catch her own food.

"I got my eye on a nice little governor's race down in

Arkansas," she went on. "This time the candidate's a real special one. Reminds me a lot of Hodges when he was at his peak. I could do with someone who…"

Mike jabbed a finger down and pressed erase. The spell was broken. It was not real to him anymore. That world of the campaign. It was a ghost world. He got up and walked out of the office. He passed through the church where the glowering black Christ looked down from his high cross and then Mike paused in the open doorway that led outside.

In the courtyard vegetable garden a figure crouched and planted an upturned furrow of earth with seeds. She moved slowly and deliberately down the rows seeming to take exaggerated care as she placed each seed in a carefully dug hole. It was Mayan corn. In a few months, nourished by the frequent rains, even in this slum earth, it would grow tall and strong. The young woman looked up, her face shielded by the flat hat she wore to help shade skin that was paler than that of her countrymen.

Gabriela smiled at Mike. He waved back. She was doing well, he thought. It had been a long struggle to help, but she was clean of drugs for three months now and off the streets for twice that. Perhaps she would yet fall back into the gangs. But perhaps she would not. It was impossible to tell. You just did what you could to help. To try and fulfill a promise made far away.

This world was the real one, he said to himself. Right here. Right now. He watched Gabriela from the shadows of the church doorway. He was suddenly full of hope that she would make it. He stepped forward out of the darkness and the thought warmed him even more than the sudden light of the bright, shining sun.

ACKNOWLEDGEMENTS

I WOULD like to thank my agent, Laney Becker at Markson Thoma, for working so hard to make sure The Candidate made it. I owe you one, Laney. I also want to express my deep and heartfelt gratitude to my editor Joseph Pittman at Vantage Point Books, both for taking a chance with the book and for his careful work in making it as good as it can be. Mike Luongo brilliantly copy-edited the final manuscript and made sure my British English prose was thoroughly and correctly Americanized. I would also like to thank the many people who have helped me write about the bewildering but fascinating and inspiring world of American politics. They include Julian Coman, Paul Webster, John Mulholland, Matt Seaton, Shaun Bowler, Larry Haas, Tracy McVeigh, Janine Gibson, Stuart Millar and many others. Thanks also to my parents, Sandra and David Harris, for all their love and support and my brother, Mark. A final word of gratitude to many friends over the years who have engaged in endless political debates with me that have still, somehow, failed to solve the world's problems. They include but are far from limited to Simon English, Lee Bailey, Burhan Wazir, Vicky Graham, Helen Jones, David Teather, Imogen Wall, Dave Stoller, Lawrence Siegel, Adi Leshko, Andrew Clark, Peter Alexander, Robin McKie, Mark Townsend, Peter Beaumont, Glen Owen, Francesca Gessner, Mike Green, Gary Shannon, Ian King, Hugh Chow, Tom Campbell, Tim, Sheila and Ellen Herbst and all of the Friday night poker guys in New York.

CPSIA information can be obtained at www.ICGtesting.com
Printed in the USA
BVOW080908180712

295556BV00001B/3/P